Cat Fight

www.penguin.co.uk

Cat Fight

Kit Conway

bantam

TRANSWORLD PUBLISHERS
Penguin Random House, One Embassy Gardens,
8 Viaduct Gardens, London SW11 7BW
www.penguin.co.uk

Transworld is part of the Penguin Random House group of companies
whose addresses can be found at global.penguinrandomhouse.com

First published in Great Britain in 2025 by Bantam
an imprint of Transworld Publishers

A CIP catalogue record for this book
is available from the British Library.

ISBNs
9780857506597 (cased)
9780857506603 (tpb)

Typeset in 11.25/15.25 pt Sabon by Falcon Oast Graphic Art Ltd
Printed and bound in Great Britain by Clays Ltd, Elcograf S.p.A.

The authorized representative in the EEA is Penguin Random House Ireland,
Morrison Chambers, 32 Nassau Street, Dublin D02 YH68.

Penguin Random House is committed to a sustainable
future for our business, our readers and our planet. This book is
made from Forest Stewardship Council® certified paper.

dedication to come

Panther noun *[pan·ther]*; plural noun: panthers

1. a black leopard, *Panthera pardus,* or jaguar, *Panthera onca* (= large wild cat)
2. a very fierce person

Example sentence:

The *panther's* retractable claws enable it to creep up, and incapacitate, its prey.

MAY

1

Emma

The air crackled as the first hot day of the year began to fold in on itself, cobalt eclipsing pale blue sky. The wasp juddered at right angles over the table, like a hitchhiker unable to reach their desired destination.

'Bit early for wasps,' Matt muttered, spearing an olive with a flourish. Beside him, Emma, his wife, resisted rolling her eyes. A small bead of oil had slicked over the olive's smooth surface and landed on Matt's 'wacky floral shirt', as he liked to call it.

'Bit early for that shirt,' Adam quipped, raising his head and meeting Emma's eyes playfully. She couldn't help but notice that Adam's form-fitting, relaxed grey tee was much easier on the eye than Matt's shirt. She bit back a smile as Matt brandished his napkin, thrust it into the water jug and daubed ineffectively at the oil stain, somehow making it worse.

'Says the man wearing the eye-watering aftershave,' Matt retorted, abandoning the napkin. He rolled the olive pip into the side of his mouth as he spoke. Emma shouldn't observe him at such close range. It made her queasy. Her husband had been handsome when they met, but age was rendering him piggish; his skin pink and tough-looking, his remaining tufts of tawny hair flecked with white. Adam, on the other hand . . . he was looking better every day.

'Hey,' Coralie gently admonished him, 'I bought him that aftershave.' She put her hands on Adam's shoulders and leaned in, kissing him on the cheek. 'Don't listen to him, darling, you smell divine.' A burgundy flush rose from Adam's neck to his cheeks. Emma noted the way he gently tilted his phone away from Coralie's eyeline. *Interesting.*

'Coralie's supper party always opens the summer season, so I had to wear this shirt,' Matt continued, all bonhomie, tipping his head towards their hostess deferentially: his 'benevolent leader head tilt', which he frequently employed on his Cub Scouts troop. Emma found it soothing to label his mannerisms; it created a distance between her and them, as though she were reading about his irritating quirks in a book rather than witnessing them first hand.

'It's hardly a party.' Coralie smiled, modest as ever. 'It's a light supper between friends.'

Coralie was right, a get-together between a few neighbours wasn't really a party. There was Coralie and Adam; Twig and Blake with their kids Elwood and Skylar; and her and Matt with Henry and Daisy. But Coralie had that effortless way about her where everything she did felt elevated somehow: festive, ambient, *fun.* As though with every wave of her arms candlelight would appear, or a fizzing tray of gin and tonics, the ice cracking in the glass. Partly it was money and her posh upbringing; it was unclear where the Kings' wealth came from (*Her family? Her divorce?*) but it certainly wasn't possible to live the way the Kings did, in a house as magnificent as theirs (the crown jewel of Briar Close), on Adam's tree surgeon wages.

There was little evidence Adam himself did much work, his output seeming to wane the more comfortable his life with Coralie became. On the one hand, Emma found that unattractive, but on the other, it was refreshing. He was unthreatened by society's perception of him as a wastrel and carried with him a sense that he had nothing to prove. Which, obviously, made all the other Sevenoaks husbands hate him. He was younger, better-looking, agile enough to shimmy up a tree and married to the gorgeous Coralie King.

'It's global warming,' Elwood inserted keenly, his fair eyebrows raised, his blue eyes bright and wide above his slim nose. The wasp dived at his sister Skylar's plate, and she shot back in her seat.

'Everything's global warming with you,' Twig said fondly, pulling Skylar's chair further away from the table.

'He's quite right,' Coralie said with a small, worried frown, as though the future of the planet rested on her shoulders. Elwood looked up at her adoringly, as he so often did, and Emma wondered, not for the first time, if it bothered his mothers – particularly Twig, since she stayed at home while Blake frequently travelled for her work as a music producer – that Elwood looked at Coralie that way. Mind you, most people did. She was a modern angel, gliding around the suburbs with her halo of wavy blonde hair and her devoted husband, collecting for the local food bank, a governor at Puddleford School (an independent *volunteer*, since her daughters didn't attend Puddleford), organizing community litter-picking weekends. People would literally gather trash off the street for her.

Emma had always had the sense that, underneath it all, Coralie needed to keep busy. Everyone felt so sorry that her daughters were still living in London with their dad, a brutish-sounding man who had bought them off with screens and excessive pocket-money, eschewing the kind of fairy-tale countryside childhood the girls could have had with Coralie here in Kent. Coralie said she was determined not to unsettle them with a protracted court process, though Emma expected she would certainly win her case. No one, not even a judge, would deny Coralie King.

Maybe Elwood's closeness to Coralie didn't bother Twig and Blake, Emma mused. Maybe they were grateful to have him occupied while they tried to raise the money for Skylar's cancer vaccine. They were desperate for her to have it, she knew; you'd have to be, to move back in with your father and into your childhood bedroom.

'Where did you two meet again?' Blake asked Coralie, her American accent heightened and a lop-sided smile on her face, alcohol invoking more interest in her neighbours than usual.

'On Battersea Bridge.' Coralie swooned wistfully. 'I asked Adam for directions and he insisted on taking me right to the door.'

Emma was familiar with the Kings' meet-cute and hoped Blake didn't turn her attention to theirs. How could she follow that with, 'well, we admired each other's mugs – hers Disney, his *Star Wars* – in the kitchen at work?'

'It was love at first sight.' Coralie's eyes dropped before lifting in Adam's direction, but Adam didn't seem to register, preoccupied as he was with his phone. Emma felt a stab of curiosity. *What secret world was enticing Adam away as he sat surrounded by his wife and friends on a beautiful early-summer evening?*

'Mummy . . . Mummy . . .' Skylar was as agitated as the wasp ambushing the strawberries and raspberries liberally scattered over her meringue.

Emma's lips twitched as she watched the battle being wrought on her husband's face. Matt couldn't stand people getting het up over wasps. He became furious with Henry and Daisy if they so much as moved a muscle in consternation at a bug: *just sit still*, he would intone. *If you don't bother it, it will fly away.*

Henry and Daisy had abandoned their plates and left the table, standing back and staring as the wasp's siren grew louder, its dive-bombing more intent, each time Twig – and now Blake – tried to swat it away from Skylar's plate. *Poor little Skylar*, as she was commonly known, was wedged so far back in her seat, angled towards Twig's side, it was hard to see where the chair ended and the child – thin and pale with only a smattering of downy fair hair – began.

'It's getting angry!' Daisy shrieked, and Matt snapped his head in her direction, shooting her a look, as if to say: *you should know better, girl.*

'That's not why wasps buzz,' Elwood was saying, the only child still sitting calmly at the table, opposite an equally serene Coralie.

'Yes.' She was nodding at him encouragingly, master to apprentice, an open palm extended to indicate he should continue.

'Social wasps do it when they're building their nest!' Elwood shot back. 'Or! Or!' He wiggled his fingers as though summoning his thoughts. 'Some wasps fan their nest to keep it cool!'

Coralie clapped her hands together delightedly, as though they were in a private conversation.

'Gah!' Skylar yelped as the wasp rebounded on her plate and flew directly towards the shiny *Wakanda Forever* motif in the centre of her shirt. The force of her convulsion sent her chair rocking on to its back legs.

'For goodness' sake,' Matt muttered as Blake and Twig each reflexively reached out and gripped either side of the chair to stop it from falling. Matt leaned his bulk over the table and with calm precision squashed the wasp with a click of his fingers. At the abrupt extinguishing of the wasp's buzzing the whole table fell still, catching even Adam's attention.

'Woah! What the— You coulda got stung, mate!' he exclaimed, hand to his stubbled jaw.

Matt shrugged, his broad chest puffed with bravado. 'It's hardly going to hurt, is it? Look at the size of me compared to the wasp.'

Elwood was regarding Matt in horror as the rest of the table contemplated him with looks of shock or withering stares.

'What?' Matt was unrepentant. 'Now we can get along with our evening. Can't believe this is vegan!' he exclaimed over-zealously, spearing more meringue on his plate. 'Tastes just like the real stuff!' And Emma knew then he was really grafting because chickpea water was a poor replacement for an egg. All the Dorsetts had become vegan after Skylar's diagnosis, and Emma could imagine Coralie having spent the whole day trying to come up with a suitable pudding to satisfy all her guests.

'Murderer!' Elwood shouted, and Matt straightened, ready to chastise one of his troops. Sometimes he forgot he was a Cub Scout leader for ninety minutes a week, and not every second of every day.

'That was unnecessary,' Twig said, reprimanding Matt as though he were *her* husband, rather than Emma's, causing Emma to raise an eyebrow in her direction. Twig didn't notice, continuing to rub Skylar's arms, checking she was okay.

'It was just a wasp!' Matt retorted shrugging and rolling his eyes. 'Nothing even eats wasps.'

'Everything eats something,' Coralie said mildly, lifting her gaze to stare at Matt directly.

'Wasps are pollinators!' Elwood supplied. 'And they do cool things like capture their prey, chop them up and feed them to their babies! They're *apex predators*.'

'Yes, thank you, Elwood, that's quite enough,' Matt interrupted.

'That means they're top of the food chain,' Elwood explained.

Coralie smiled at her protégé indulgently and ruffled his hair as the other children squealed and pulled faces.

The vegan meringue wasn't enough to entice the kids back to the table. Henry tapped his sister on the arm, shouting 'It!', and soon they were both running and jerking around the end of the garden, towards the dark recesses of the Parkland beyond.

The Parkland was partly what made the Briar Heart Estate so exclusive. It was the outer eastern section of the larger Jutland Estate, over 2,500 acres of Kent countryside, with the Briar Heart Estate nestled just within its boundaries. The residential roads formed a loose heart shape, Briar Close cutting through the middle like an artery, its end – where all the supper-party guests lived – puncturing the perimeter. It lent the estate, and especially their part of Briar Close, a secluded, countryside feel, even though they were a ten-minute walk from the train station in one direction, and ten to Puddleford School in the other.

Puddleford School was the highest-rated state primary school in the area. It was universally agreed (by the local middle-class parents) that it was the next best thing to paying private-school fees. And in some ways, thanks to its sense of community, it was better.

Emma longed to be at the centre of it, like Coralie. Hosting garden parties, and mulled wine and mince pie soirées, the best-dressed house at Halloween. It was impossible to compete until her crumbling eyesore of a house was renovated. She couldn't wait; already had builders lined up to begin as soon as their plans were approved.

Elwood shot up to join the others, quickly being tagged by Henry as Daisy tore off ahead. He never had been very strong at sports, Elwood. With his wiry frame and choppy fair hair, he reminded Emma of a gangly magician.

'Can I go too?' Skylar asked, looking up at Twig and Blake, but Twig frowned and before Blake could finish saying 'Sure,' Twig was shaking her head. 'It's getting too dark out there, little one.'

Matt shot Emma a look as if to say 'See'. *'She wasn't like that when we were younger,'* he frequently told Emma, blind to her annoyance.

When Twig and Blake had moved in with Twig's father, Bob, Emma had been excited – there weren't many former famous musicians in Sevenoaks – but Matt hadn't mentioned his history with Twig. When she'd learned – *via Bob, of all people* – that Twig had grown up with Matt, that they had been each other's first proper boyfriend and girlfriend in fact, she'd been wary. She didn't enjoy the pally way they'd chat at school events or Coralie's parties. But things had soured between them since Elwood had joined Cubs. Twig found Matt overbearing and muttered about 'toxic masculinity' whenever he was within earshot. Emma found the hostility between them a much more welcome atmosphere, like an ambient temperature. Like underfloor heating.

'But Elwood's playing,' Skylar said plaintively. 'And Daisy!' Skylar was a year older than Daisy, but they were in the same class as Skylar's illness meant she was repeating a year.

The closeness in the children's ages and their homes had forged the three women's friendship. Their lives had become so entwined that Emma could no longer tell whether they would have been friends if they'd met elsewhere. She found Twig too nervy, and Coralie too do-goody, although she had grown fond of them both, and she sometimes wondered, was this always the way when women spent time together at close range? A societal impulse to pit themselves against each other? Was she destined to view herself by comparison, good or bad, to others?

'Look, you've not finished the meringue Coralie made for you,' Twig coaxed. *And for which they were all suffering*, thought Emma.

Emma's heart tugged at Skylar's downcast expression, but she also felt for Twig. She couldn't reconcile the Twig Matt described from their teenage years with the one she knew, but she guessed that was what happened when your kid got sick and you needed to raise zillions of pounds for the best treatment in America: you lost your edge.

Later she would find herself wondering if the opposite was in fact true: that Twig would do whatever it took to keep Skylar safe. Her edge never faltering, sharp as a blade.

2

Twig

'Lady T,' Adam addressed her with a smirk. She'd spotted him leave the dinner table and had ducked round the side of Coralie's house to join him.

'Adam.' She raised her eyebrows in mock indignation as he lit up, drinking in the heady scent.

Adam had once teased her about her accent, the slight estuary lilt of her vowels. 'You're one of those posh types who want to sound common.' If anyone else had said this, she'd have been fuming, but with Adam, of course, it was different.

He exhaled and they locked eyes, the air between them charged. Her breath hitched in her throat. It had been such a long time since they'd been alone together.

Adam wasn't well liked around Puddleford. He was handsome – square-jawed, dark-haired, with the sort of beardy stubble a lot of women probably wanted to run their fingers over, and lean and muscular from running and working outdoors. He wasn't a parent, so the things that might have bonded him with the local dads – rugby or cricket coaching or sending misogynistic memes to the fathers-only messaging group – weren't available. He was different, an anomaly in their suburban landscape. Maybe that was why Twig had been drawn to him. She had always felt the same way.

Beyond Coralie and Emma, he was pretty much her only friend in Sevenoaks, the time since she'd moved back not having been conducive to coffee mornings or Prosecco-fuelled nights out. That was the easy explanation. For Twig, female friendship had always felt like a game she was meant to be participating in but didn't know the rules. So she avoided it. Carved out her own spaces. At school she played football with the boys, climbed trees rather than plaited hair. As a teenager she hung out with Matt, which turned into her first relationship. At university she hung out with Blake, which turned into her second. And then in Sevenoaks came Adam, which didn't turn into anything she could define at all.

'Smoke?' he offered. She shook her head, though she ached with longing, shifting her shoulders from side to side, letting the music emanating from discreet speakers – chilled Ibiza house – move within her instead.

She also appreciated how, unlike many other Sevenoaks residents, Adam didn't bore on about how much he earned. Perhaps because the Kings were the sort of rich that meant Adam rarely needed to think about money; there'd been plenty of times they'd met up and Adam hadn't even thought to bring his wallet out with him and then never remembered to repay her. It wasn't a lot, the odd coffee or off-peak pint back when she was still drinking, but Twig had to be ultra-cautious with money. She felt so out of step with the other Sevenoaks residents.

Adam exhaled, the earthy smell of weed still alighting something within her, taking her back to last summer. His eyebrows were raised, the upwards pull conspiring with his small half-smile; they were often in cahoots, his eyebrows and that half-smile, disarming the women of Sevenoaks. His eyes searched her face, intense and dark, the soft glow from a subtle light at their centre.

'I'm sorry about before . . .' His voice was low, gravel-edged, a flinty spark of something dangerous wavering beneath its surface which suggested he wasn't sorry at all.

She traced back over the evening, to identify what he was referring to. The atmosphere had taken on a reckless quality. Not just Adam, here, smoking drugs in secret, but at the table too. Everyone was pissed, apart from her. Even Blake had let loose, knocking back icy-cold beers, her pale cheeks flushed.

'Under the table.' He spoke in a slow, steady drawl which sent goosebumps prickling all over her skin.

'What?' she asked, her attention caught.

Adam's forehead pinched together, before he looked away to exhale.

'Adam?' Her arms were folded against her chest, but she felt her body shifting, leaning towards him. Like reaching from the swing of a flying trapeze, arms outstretched, trying to make a catch.

His lips parted, about to reveal more, just as Matt rounded the corner. She rubbed at her arms, which had chilled with irritation, despite her cardigan. *What happened under the table?*

'I was hoping to catch you,' Matt said jovially. Instantly the electric atmosphere between the two of them morphed into one of frustration. She glanced at Adam. Saw the annoyance on his face too. She and Adam didn't verbalize their dislike of Matt; it was something unspoken, yet understood. The occasional eye roll or *here-we-go* expression exchanged when no one else was looking.

Twig didn't *dislike* Matt as such. She was even faintly ashamed at how she'd behaved when they were younger, getting caught up in Matt's idea that they both stay in Sevenoaks and go to uni in London. Alongside the shame was a tinge of embarrassment, like how you might feel if a parent kept producing your baby photos; Matt was a walking embodiment of her cringey teenage years, living right next door.

Twig was expecting Matt to bring up the planning proposals for their home, which had the whole of Briar Heart Estate up in arms, and so she was surprised when he opened with, 'Still waiting on a deposit from you for Cub camp, Twig.'

'Oh yeah,' she replied, non-committal.

'Cub camp is . . .' Matt continued in the same genial tone.

'Yes, I know, "*the most fun you can have at Cubs,*" but I'm not sure Elwood would like being away from home. You know, things have been difficult for him lately.' 'Lately' meaning the last few years. Usually, this reference was enough to make someone back down from whatever community-minded shit-show they were trying to rope Twig into, but Matt was undeterred.

'It would be good for him.'

Twig hated what that implied; like there was something lacking in Elwood that needed fixing. With a strong male influence. Matt had asked a lot of questions about Kev, their good friend and sperm donor, continuing to pry until Twig had politely asked him to *just shut up, would you?* The history between them meant they both occasionally overstepped, and usually back-pedalled, but today Matt kept ploughing on.

'Skylar's old enough now; she should come too.'

Twig physically shuddered. 'Oh, no way. Once Skylar's better I'm not letting her out of my sight,' she joked, but even as she said it, she heard the truth in her voice.

'I'll be there. I can keep a close watch,' Matt said gently, and although the past lay untidily between them, she did trust him; she didn't doubt her children would be safe in his care. Perhaps it *would* be good for Elwood, to foster some independence, but in his own way he was the most independent of all the children. He liked his own company, was often lost in his own world and imaginings, much as Twig had been as a child.

'The kids love it. The campfire, the ghost stories, making their own breakfast in the morning. It's brilliant fun!' Matt concluded, as though the matter was settled. She hated it when he did that. She glanced at her watch. She should be getting Skylar to bed soon.

'And one other thing. Wondered if I could ask you both a favour, actually?' Matt stood stoutly, hands clasped behind his back.

Here we go . . . Twig and Adam wordlessly exchanged.

'We were hoping we could count on you . . .'

Twig wondered when Matt had begun speaking with the delivery of a politician. 'We' this and 'we' that. He was one of those people who carried a sense of ownership about him, of entitlement.

To his work, to his wife, to his children, to his castle – quite literally, a castle, if he got his way. 'A letter of support from our neighbours would go a long way in persuading the planning officer to not pay too much notice to the . . .'

Twig knew Matt wouldn't say 'objections'; it would go against the ethos of the many leadership manuals he carefully studied. She listened keenly to how Matt would frame the fifty-plus complaints received within a single week in relation to their planning application for the redevelopment of their home.

'. . . other comments,' Matt concluded diplomatically.

'I dunno, mate,' Adam said, turning his head to one side as he exhaled. He flicked his spliff; such a familiar movement. Twig had to glance away.

Her gaze landed on Matt's puzzled look as he mentally deduced what Adam was smoking, the effort he made to unfurl his brows and not appear judgemental.

'I'll talk to Coralie, but I think we'd rather not get involved,' he said.

Twig knew that wasn't true; Coralie was *furious* about the proposals and any potential environmental impacts (*'digging out the basement!'* she'd exclaimed to Twig. *'Who does Matt Brooks think he is?'*). She wondered for how long she'd keep her views private. Coralie was mild-mannered to a fault, until it came to nature or her beloved daughters.

'Why not?' Matt asked irritably, hands pushed into the pockets of his chino shorts.

Twig, unlike the other residents of the estate, wasn't invested in the Brooks' plans either way. *The Disney House*, they were calling it, and that wasn't a compliment. Twig had bigger problems, but she could see things getting nasty.

'The thing is—' she began, but a sudden violent twitch from Adam stopped her. He sounded like he was gasping for breath and, for a second, she thought he was choking, or having an allergic reaction.

'Adam?' she asked.

'Fu—' He reached a hand out to the wall to steady himself.

'Are you okay?'

Adam's eyes, the only part of him which seemed able to move, grew wide as he stared behind her into his front garden. She snapped her head round in fear but saw nothing, heard nothing beyond the rustle of leaves.

'What's going on?' Matt looked behind him too as Adam babbled: 'Was that? What the— No.'

Twig felt beads of sweat sliding down her skin. It didn't take much these days to activate the darkest parts of her. She lived on high alert: fight or flight?

'Did you see it? Its tail! Like a fucking baseball bat!' Adam stumbled closer to the wall for support, his spliff still gripped between his fingers. 'Did you see that?' He eyeballed Matt, his breath coming in ragged gasps as he pulled at the neckline of his T-shirt. 'What the— mate? *Mate!* Did you see it?'

Matt moved his head between Adam and the dark hedgerow behind him, looking bewildered. Suddenly it was dark, the front garden layered with shadows, and Adam was moving backwards, groping with his hands, eyeballs flared. He grabbed Twig's wrist, and she saw her skin pale against his, fine hairs on end. 'Come with me.' He spoke quietly, his tone almost menacing.

'Adam, you're scaring me.' Her eyes darted to Matt, fearful he might glimpse the intimacy between them.

'Shhhhh!' Adam hushed her. 'Shhhhhhhh!' There was a beat before he backed away, staring at the wide darkness behind her as they moved. He murmured to himself, his sentences colliding: *'Get the kids out of the garden. Why don't I have a gun? Could I get a gun? Don't be stupid, you're in Sevenoaks. You don't need a gun. Get inside and lock all the doors.'*

And then, she couldn't be sure, but just before they rounded the corner, back to the apparent safety of his garden, where he started shouting, she thought she heard him say to himself: *'you weren't imagining it.'*

3

Coralie

Coralie was sharing an amusing anecdote about the badgers in the Parkland when Adam appeared from around the side of the house, eyes wild, face ashen, a peculiar look playing over his features. There was a jerkiness to his movement, as though he were hustling, or even pushing, Twig and Matt over to the pergola, beneath which Coralie was still sitting with Blake and Emma at their outdoor dining table. It was enough to make her pretend she couldn't see the joint still burning in his hand; he knew she hated him smoking. Fear gripped her: was he about to announce his affair at the table in front of their guests? She had an unnerving sense of history repeating itself. She looked on in horror, willing him not to do it, not right now.

'Everyone!' he shouted shakily. 'Out of the garden!'

Instantly the convivial atmosphere she had worked so hard to cultivate, despite the Brooks' being here (she had invited them before their monstrous plans were submitted), dissipated.

'Adam?' she called, imploring Twig and Matt with a silent look and knotted brows: *what's going on?*

'We just saw a . . . a . . . I dunno.' He was white as alabaster, sweat bubbling on his skin as though he might vomit at any moment.

Adam drew back from her as she approached. She stopped

short, not wanting to draw attention to their fractious dynamic. 'Adam? Are you okay? You don't look—'

He tried to speak but he swallowed his words, making a strange coughing sound as Emma awkwardly proffered a glass of water. He waved her away.

'A tiger! Or something! It was dark, I couldn't make out its colour. A big cat! A wild cat! On the bonnet of my car.' His voice was twisting like a schoolboy's and the table grew uneasy, exchanging lowered glances.

Coralie was grateful when Emma spoke first, so that she didn't have to. She didn't want to undermine her husband, but he sounded bonkers. Totally bonkers.

'A wild cat? In Sevenoaks?'

'I know,' he was saying, his voice shaky, 'I know how it sounds. But it was there. On my car! It just stood up, stretched out and slunk off!' His throat strangled his words again and he put a hand to his chest.

'Socks was here, just a moment ago—' As the words flew from her lips Coralie knew instinctively that she'd said the wrong thing. She wanted to push them back inside her mouth.

Adam openly glared at her. 'It wasn't Socks,' he spat. 'It was big. Four foot, or more.'

Coralie threw a pointed look at his joint, the distinctive smell wafting over the garden. He dropped it on the grass and stamped on it, defiant. She willed someone else to speak. She couldn't question him; she didn't want to provoke him.

'Did you see it?' Twig asked, her chin towards Matt. She had already returned to her seat and scooped Skylar from her chair, lifting her on to her lap protectively.

Elwood, Henry and Daisy had emerged and were standing on the lawn, slack-jawed. Adam was ushering them nearer the table, as though there was safety in numbers.

'Did you?' asked Emma.

'I was facing away,' Twig replied, visibly rattled.

Matt was standing behind Adam, lips pursed. He folded his arms and frowned.

'Well?' Twig's voice rose an octave higher, her arms grasped tight around Skylar's middle. The air seemed crisper, the garden so dark the outline of the lawn was disappearing from under their feet and merging with the trees and bushes surrounding them, swallowing them up. The gently shifting candlelight rendered their table a spotlight. A target.

'I didn't,' Matt said carefully. 'But clearly' – he glanced apologetically at Adam, as if to say *sorry you're in such a state* – 'he did see . . . something.'

Coralie exhaled with relief and, she realized with surprise, a tiny peppering of disappointment. *A wild cat. In Sevenoaks.* The power of those words. The fear, the awe, the incredulity. It was all there, writ over Adam's face in the garden. The power of nature. She couldn't deny the buzz of interest, a spark ignited.

'Do you have a video doorbell? It might have picked something up?' Matt asked.

'A what?' Coralie asked, distracted, her index finger tracing over her upper arm. 'Oh, no, nothing like that.' She couldn't think of anything worse than being under constant surveillance; she detested the scourge of modern technology.

'I definitely rate ours, for peace of mind.'

Coralie found it unsurprising that Matt would like to keep an eye on the comings and goings at his house at all times.

'Are there wild cats around here?' Twig asked urgently, turning her head towards Coralie. Coralie could see the beach-battered leather sandals Twig favoured drumming against the floor.

Coralie shot her a quizzical look and smiled, trying to slow the hectic atmosphere Adam and Twig were creating. 'Well,' she began congenially. She felt a dart of warmth despite the rapidly chilling air. She used to be an authority on things. Not in a big way, but in her own little realm of zoology. She had had papers published. Research students had interviewed her for their projects. But that was in the past, before she had children and slipped off the academic radar. She was so rarely asked her opinion on anything these days she'd almost forgotten what it felt like. A tiny throb of utility thrummed in her chest.

'You know about animals and things,' Twig cut in, referencing the project Coralie had started in the Parkland – litter-picking had evolved into building hedgehog shelters and tracking badger sets. The tiny throb grew and flared.

'I have a zoology degree,' Coralie said mildly. 'But I'm not an expert on wild cats. It's something you hear about from time to time, but not a wild cat on your doorstep.' In actual fact, Coralie *was* a bit of an expert on cats, but it didn't feel like the right time to get into it now.

'Or the bonnet of your car,' said Elwood, aping her tone, the tiniest hint of condescension. Twig shot him a warning glance before returning her focus to Coralie, awaiting her response.

'I can tell you about wallabies. I did a project on them once, as part of my degree. There are definitely wild wallabies in the UK and Ireland.' She directed her response at Elwood, to assuage his mother's concern. *Poor Twig. She'd had such a tough time.*

'Wallabies!' Elwood exclaimed. He began jumping on the spot.

Coralie looked down at him and smiled, an attempt to redirect the evening back on course. 'It started with a wasp . . .' she mused amiably, preparing to ask if anyone fancied a post-supper espresso martini. She could feel Adam's eyes boring into her with disbelief.

'. . . And it ended with a tiger,' Elwood finished. He looked up at her reverently, raising his bony fingers into claws.

'A tiger,' she repeated, ruffling his hair. Still, she felt the cold beam of Adam's stare and couldn't help but think, *oh, finally I have your attention.* She knew that, to many, the Kings had a perfect marriage. Sometimes she longed to confide in someone that her husband was not only emotionally absent but increasingly agitated, bordering on hysterical at times. That her marriage felt like a sham, that she suspected he'd had an affair last summer and ever since had been waiting for him to leave her.

But she hadn't been raised to share confidences. She'd been raised to just get on with things. The classic stiff upper lip. Her index finger found the fleshy seam that ran beneath the thin material of her sleeves. She inclined her head towards the children to show Adam she wasn't ignoring him – something had obviously spooked him – but it wouldn't do to terrify them all.

'Right.' Elwood smirked. 'As if a tiger would be here in Sevenoaks. They live in Asia . . . in rainforests . . . and grasslands . . . and . . .'

Adam snapped, 'Fine! Not a tiger. A leopard. A jaguar. *Something.*' The light of little Elwood's pale face dimmed as Adam spat his words out, breath harried. 'It was dark. Its . . . fur, or whatever. Almost black.'

Elwood's eyes blinked rapidly and he looked to Coralie for reassurance as they filled. She gave him a gentle nod to show he wasn't in any trouble.

'There *are* occasional sightings of wild cats, across England, and especially in the south-east,' she conceded. Sevenoaks itself was a veritable *feast* for a big cat, given the vast numbers of deer, its supper of choice, in Knole Park. There were even some wild herds in the Parkland. It was rumoured that the gamekeepers at Knole chose to turn a blind eye to the odd carcass stripped bare. 'Even so,' she reasoned, 'one is hardly going to stride into our front garden. They're elusive, secretive creatures. *Terrified* of humans. They don't come around for tea.' Her tone was light but tinged with aggravation. She thought of how amusing her zoology course mates would find this situation and wished briefly she hadn't lost touch with them.

'We need to go inside,' Adam said, as though she hadn't spoken. His arms jerked towards the house, sharp-edged and uncoordinated.

Coralie could feel Twig's gaze scooting between her and Adam, performing a danger assessment. 'Yes,' she agreed, rising quickly. 'Yes. Kids—'

Coralie sighed. How much longer could she pretend this wasn't happening? That her perfect marriage didn't exist? Their world was becoming smaller, their time together more fraught. Sometimes she wished Adam would get it over with. Come clean and leave her already. At least then she could start over. But the next moment she was gripped with fear and panic. She suspected a psychologist would say it was her old abandonment wounds being ripped open. Would that explain the molten jealousy she felt course through her veins at the thought of Adam with another woman?

She closed her eyes and breathed deeply, fingering the silk fabric of her dress. She had a brief recollection of her mother, standing with a cocktail glass in one hand while Coralie tugged at her skirt for attention. She'd been so determined to break the cycle. So *convinced* it was possible.

'Adam's right,' Twig continued. 'Everyone in.'

'Fine. Let's just not make a big deal out of this.' Coralie exhaled wearily, beginning to stack the plates. 'We don't want people panicking needlessly. No posting big cat theories online.' She directed her words at Emma, who, as Admin of the local Puddleford Mums Facebook Group, was far too nimble a keyboard warrior at the best of times.

'There could be a tiger on our street and you don't want to make a big deal out of it?' Twig shouted, with an air of exasperation at the group's lack of urgency.

Coralie and Emma exchanged a look: unsurprisingly, Twig's tolerance for agitation was fragile and the glass had just smashed, as it did every now and then.

Adam appeared beside her, and she felt his hands on her elbows, his body pressed close as he whispered in her ear: 'Seriously, Coralie, I know what I saw—'

It was briefly intoxicating, the smell of him so close, the *fear* radiating from him. He was more of a man to her then – wild, alive, blood pumping right at the surface level of his skin – than he had ever been. *So, it takes him thinking he's seen a wild animal to arouse him, does it?*

She spun round. 'This is why I don't like you smoking,' she hissed. 'Go inside if you're worried. I'll be in soon.'

'Fine.' He stalked off, and she shared a conspiratorial look with

Matt and Emma: they clearly agreed Adam was overreacting, had probably seen nothing, and Matt had actually been next to him, thank God.

'What about Fwuffy?' Skylar called anxiously, referring to Coralie's pet rabbit. Coralie sighed. She wished she'd never agreed to get one. A pathetic attempt to encourage her daughters to visit. 'And where's Socks?'

'Good point!' Adam reappeared and hoisted a startled Fwuffy from her hutch, marching self-righteously over the lawn with the big ball of white fur under his arm. *For goodness' sake.*

'It was probably a fox,' she muttered, loud enough for everyone to hear except Adam. She didn't want a big fight about it later. She had too much on her mind after tonight. Gears turning. Questions forming.

Daisy had disappeared under the table and emerged clutching a wriggling Socks. Socks was technically the Brooks' cat, in as much as you can ever own a cat, but really the whole neighbourhood looked after him.

As her guests dispersed, she could sense them dividing into two camps, like fabric ripped through the middle: those who thought Adam had totally lost the plot and those who believed a wild cat had just casually disembarked from the bonnet of his car.

Later, she wouldn't think of fabric being split. She would think of much worse. She would think that's where it all began, the destruction of the Briar Heart Estate. This small exchange, which shivered through them all, destroying the comfortable lives they had known.

It started with a wasp, and it ended with a tiger. But there was so much more to come.

The Mystery of the Sevenoaks Panther

Freja, chair of Puddleford PTA: Emma was slightly skittish. One of those all-over-the-place mums. She could've been smashing it, doing loads of stuff, vanquishing her to-do list, or she could've been teetering on the edge of a nervous breakdown. It was impossible to tell. And she was always so . . . *perky*. All the Disney stuff. [Shrugs.] I just assumed she was on antidepressants.

Megan, Number 16: Emma was, like, this *insane* Disney-mom. She had a fancy-looking handbag – tan and camel, like, *designer-looking* – but it had Donald Duck on it. Donald Duck! That's a *weird* look for a grown woman, right?

Chloe, Number 16: *Right?* Twig and Blake though, they were cool. For mums.

Megan: Their hair! Blake's was long and dark and glossy, with this amazing fringe that was never out of place. Sometimes she wore it in side-buns. Like Princess Leia. I tried so hard to do that with mine. Never could get it right. Twig had this wavy, pinky-blonde bob. You're going to include that I'm a fashion influencer, right? @BriarHeartsMegan

4

Twig

A few days after the supper party, Twig thundered down the stairs in her gym clothes.

'Hey, did you remember Elwood's PE bag this morning?' Blake asked, a black coffee in hand.

'What?' Twig replied, distracted. She had an hour. A small, perfect pocket of time.

'Elwood's PE kit,' Blake repeated, opening the garage door, the portal to her makeshift studio. She was working with a US-based artist, meaning she would often work late, sleep in and then be scurrying to catch up on anything from her UK collaborators.

'Yes, I remembered.' Twig felt a prickle of irritation that all the household chores fell to her. She scoured the floor for her small gym towel. She'd left it hooked over the bottom of the bannister.

'Then why are his trainers still by the back door?' Blake pressed.

Twig's hands flew to her hips. 'Why didn't *you* put them in his PE bag?' Now she'd have to drop them at school.

'I was asleep. After working all night,' Blake shot back.

They stared at each other, eyes blazing. Sometimes Twig couldn't remember the people they were, before all this. They'd met in university at RockSoc, the alternative music society. Blake had been unlike anyone Twig had met before: so comfortable in her own skin, not riddled with insecurities the way Twig, and Matt, were.

Being with her emboldened Twig to explore a side of herself she'd worked hard to ignore. Soon they were hanging out daily, writing music. They formed Pineapple Punk and were such a hit at university that they began playing in London pubs. Her parents had been supportive – attending every gig, her mother in pineapple earrings she'd made herself, bearing home-made sausage rolls, her father tapping his foot not quite in time to the music and nursing a warm half=pint of ale – but quickly changed their tune when Pineapple Punk took off and Twig announced she was dropping out of university and moving to Berlin with Blake. Imagine that? To just take off! After Berlin came another stint in London, before they'd embarked on another adventure, to Bali. They had been so *young*. So carefree. And now they were grounded in Sevenoaks.

'Are you okay?' Blake sighed, snapping her back to the present. She placed her coffee on the wooden console table in the hall and reached for Twig, ending their stand-off. Of course, Blake's confidence and ease had been all smoke and mirrors, concealing the buried trauma from her parents' refusal to accept she was gay, her struggle to see where she fit with her part-American, part-Japanese, part-Finnish background. She had been in therapy for years.

Twig jammed her fingertips into her eye sockets. She wasn't sure if she was crying with frustration or overcome with hay fever, but she didn't have time for either.

'Gym?' Blake asked. She knew Twig needed to let off steam. Would return less knotty and aggravated.

Twig nodded, trying to compose herself. 'Yes. If I can find my stuff. God knows where Dad's tidied it all away to.'

Blake glanced at her watch. Someone else needed her. But Blake always seemed to know when Twig needed her too. 'Lemme help you. What do you need?'

Gratitude made her voice small. 'Water bottle. Towel. My car keys.'

The back door slammed as Bob stomped in from the garden. 'Look at this! Imagine if Skylar had touched it, or accidentally ingested it!' Twig arched back as he passed, waving the contents of his dustpan animatedly. '*Bloody Cupid.*'

Bob inspected the lawn for cat poo every morning. Had done ever since they'd moved in, ostensibly to protect his granddaughter's delicate immune system, but Twig suspected he'd long been pissed off about the local cats using his lawn as a litter tray and was glad to have his disgust with his neighbours' beloved pets seem more reasonable. The garden had been her mother's pride and joy; Bob had never been all that interested in it before she got sick. His preservation of it now was a homage to her.

'Remember: *cat rage is his emotional outlet*,' Blake counselled in a whisper, appearing by Twig's side with everything she needed for the gym.

'I know it's nice he checks the lawn, but does he have to go on about it so much?' Twig's voice was low and clipped, and for a second she basked in their connection, the relative ease with which they understood each other.

'Most men do the same with football,' Blake pointed out, draping Twig's small gym towel over her shoulder. She said it in such a calm, empathetic tone it made Twig suspect Blake had been discussing it with her therapist, and instantly her irritable mood returned. If anyone should be moaning about her father and his obsession with cat shit in therapy, that privilege should fall to her, surely?

'Now go.' Blake thrust Twig her keys and water. Twig couldn't resist placing the cool bottle against her forehead.

'Iced coconut water,' Blake said. 'It's too hot for just water.'

At her act of care Twig felt guilty. And Blake did have a point. The cat vitriol had started shortly after Twig's mother was diagnosed with early-onset dementia. Brutal in its speed and efficiency, stripping her mother of all that was dear to her. She couldn't even remember how to garden by the end. How to plant a bulb in the soil.

Blake was retrieving her coffee as Twig leaned in and kissed her. 'Thank you.'

'Any time.'

Twig had still been grieving her mother when Skylar started

complaining of tiredness, even falling asleep sometimes in the shady playground at the little school in Bali. But she was in her reception year, and it was a big adjustment and, honestly, Twig had been so focused on Elwood at that point, her little spaceman drifting, untethered, since his grandmother died. He had a hard time comprehending what had happened to her, was afraid, struggling to sleep. And Skylar, too young to have formed the same bond with her grandmother, had barely seemed to notice.

Twig's eye was off the ball when the fatigue turned to stomach aches, turned to barely eating anything and a mouth filled with ulcers, all while Twig wasn't looking. Could they have caught it sooner? Before Stage Four? Could they have avoided at least some of the chemotherapy that had been pumped into their beautiful little girl, leaving her unable to even *walk* for a time, crawling over the lawn, to treat her high-risk neuroblastoma?

Her heart was palpitating in that low-level way she had grown used to since Skylar's diagnosis and treatment. Her thoughts followed her outside to the car. She wouldn't be caught out the next time. She wouldn't let Skylar down again. She couldn't.

'Hey!' a voice called. She had to stop her eyes rolling back in her head as she slammed her car door shut, pretending she hadn't heard.

Don't be a bitch. Don't be a bitch. Don't be a bitch. She smiled as best she could manage as Emma bounced over, head-to-camel-toe – *don't be a bitch!* – in a sickly, salmon-pink tracksuit. Embroidered outlines of Mickey Mouse materialized as she came closer. Twig wound down her window in defeat.

'I don't suppose you fed Socks anything earlier, did you? I've been cleaning up cat sick all morning.' Emma snapped off her pink rubber gloves.

'God, no. Dad would throw a fit if I started feeding the local cats.' She flashed a grin to complete their exchange and put her hand on the gear stick. She hated driving a manual – her dad's old Volvo – but there was no way they could afford their own car.

'I keep telling people he's gluten free, but no one listens.' Emma

28

ran the back of her hand over her forehead, dislodging frizzy fair strands of her shoulder-length hair.

Twig suspected it was more that Socks was a glutton rather than an issue with gluten, but said nothing. A cluster of ladybirds had gathered on her wing mirror, and they took off in flight as she turned the key and the engine thrummed.

Emma placed a hand on the wound-down glass, oblivious. '*How weird* was the other night?' Her tone bore the whiff of excited anticipation at a dissection of the supper party. 'Do you think Coralie and Adam had a big row after we left? He looked mad.'

'I dunno.' Twig glanced at her watch, hoping Emma might read her cue and leave her alone. Twig liked Emma. She didn't take herself too seriously, like some of the other mums at school, and Twig appreciated the way she eye-rolled and side-eyed Matt when she thought no one was looking. But she felt it more appropriate, given her history with Matt, to hold herself apart slightly from Emma. They could never be real friends, could they, confiding in the darkest parts of themselves? And besides all that, she just wanted to be alone and in the gym. Powerlifting, that was *her* therapy.

She wasn't sure if Emma would understand. Emma was one of those women taken for granted by her children. A devoted housewife, talked down to, almost, by Henry, and bossed around by Daisy, even though, pre-children, she'd worked in the City, where she'd met Matt. Emma had told her once that every morning Daisy insisted on dressing her; selecting her outfit and even insisting on doing up her bra, choosing which colour lip gloss she should wear.

'Do you think Adam really *did* see something?' Emma pressed. On the lawn behind her, buttercups were scattered like freckles, the sunny disposition they conjured at odds with Briar Heart House looming in the background.

When Twig had woken the day after the supper party in her old bedroom, Blake by her side, a wave of giddiness had rushed over her. 'Can you believe last night?' she'd laughed. In the soft morning light, the whole thing seemed so ridiculous. She'd barely given it another thought since. But today she felt restless, fear needling her skin. It was the unpredictable dangers, the ones you could never expect, which wreaked the most damage.

'I doubt it.' Twig answered Emma, shaking the look on Adam's face from her mind. 'Here in Sevenoaks? It doesn't make sense.' She put the car in reverse.

'I googled it afterwards. There've been a lot of sightings. Dating back to the fifties. And some photographs, too.'

'Really?'

'Hm, but they're always a bit grainy or inconclusive . . . weird perspectives, you know?'

Twig didn't; she thought you would either be able to see a wild cat in a photograph or not, but she gave a non-committal murmur. She needed the calm lines of thought which greeted her in a deep squat, not the frenetic energy radiating from Emma.

'And if you look at Sevenoaks on a map, we're surrounded by countryside. Plenty of places for a big cat to hide.'

Emma continued to talk, addressing Twig as she adjusted her mirrors, her patience evaporating. In her rear-view mirror Socks skipped daintily over the road, an ellipse of shadow beneath his soft belly. For a second, she envied him his freedom; she envied *a cat*. She rubbed the heels of her hands into her eyes as they itched and watered.

'Just *weird* though, isn't it, to be on the bonnet of Adam's car? I can't shake the image. What if one of the children had been in the front garden?' Her hand was still resting upon Twig's open window.

'It was probably a fox,' Twig said, echoing Coralie, eyes blinking as she tried to clear them. This was her time, her meagre window to find the calm zone in her mind and briefly crawl into it. She wasn't about to let Emma steal that from her.

'Maybe I should post about it? Do you think I have a moral duty to? As Admin. Now that I know more? Coralie said not to, but she probably doesn't realize *how many* sightings there've been in the area – and all over the UK!'

God, would she ever stop talking?

'If there's been loads of sightings over the years, what's the difference this time?'

'Well, it's a *bit* different, isn't it? A big cat hanging out on Adam's car? Although they have been spotted in residential areas before. There was the Beast of Broomfield in Essex. The Suffolk Panther! Do you remember? It was in all the papers? Seriously, if you google it, there's so much information. Podcasts, books! Sightings *all over*!'

Stories had been circulating ever since Twig was a child, the rumours – myth – of the Sevenoaks Panther. Resurfacing every now and then, often at sleepovers or round a campfire, ghostly shadows playing over the storyteller's features from an upturned torch. It's partly why she'd felt an initial rush of panic at Coralie's before realizing the next morning how ridiculous the whole thing was. 'There you go then . . .'

'But late at night, not at dusk, when there's still children around and . . .'

'Em.' She sighed. 'Just do what you think's best. I'll see you later.' She began to back out of her drive.

'Really? Because Coralie did say—'

'Fuck Coralie!' It ripped from her before she could stop it. She slammed on the brakes. Angry tears pricked at her eyes. 'I'm sorry.'

Emma nodded as though she understood. As though a question were being answered. It was easier though, wasn't it, being a great mum like Coralie when you had two quiet girls, always polite and well behaved and in full health, who you saw on alternate weekends? Twig could bake fucking cookies and answer questions about wild animals if she had fewer responsibilities. Fuck, she'd still be in Bali, writing music and spending weekends on the beach. She looked down, curving the pad of her index finger over her thumbnail, and felt instantly guilty. She shouldn't take her stress out on Coralie, or Emma for that matter. She rubbed at her face, garrotting her eye sockets with her fingertips.

'Don't worry.' Emma finally, mercifully, had removed her hand from the window and was fanning her fingers in Twig's direction, as though she'd overheated and needed to cool down. 'It's fine.'

Of course Emma would feel sorry for her; everyone felt sorry for her. It was a far cry from her twenties, when Pineapple Punk was at the height of their fame. She and Blake had always prided themselves on getting out when they did, when their last album failed to chart, when their singles stopped doing anything at all. They'd bought a flat in London, rented it out and went to live in Bali. Basked – literally – in their contentment that they were living life *right*. Not festering in the suburbs back in the UK as Twig's parents had done when she was growing up.

They ate papaya from the tree, they sang on the beach and, after Twig had spent a cold and dreary week back in Sevenoaks, when her mother was diagnosed, they resolved to escalate their plans to have a baby. Their good friend Kev had *assisted*, let's say, and the following Christmas they were all on the beach: Twig, Blake, Kev, baby Elwood. Skylar followed a year later. And for a few years, when it appeared her mum still had plenty of life left in her and Bob was learning to manage, they were all, truly, living in the moment. Everything was beautiful; their lives were beautiful.

Emma was looking at her helplessly, the way everyone did. The whole world knew Twig's woes by this point: her mother dying, her daughter getting cancer, the move back to London for her treatment, and then having to rent their flat out again and live at her dad's to fund a £250k vaccine treatment in New York to stop the cancer returning. The problem was, even with knowing all this, they only knew the half of it.

Twig finally extracted herself and pulled away. As she glanced at Emma, still planted on the kerb, in her rear-view mirror her features arranged in pity, Twig couldn't help but imagine Emma's reaction were she to discover the rest.

5

Emma

'Oh, you're home. Thank God!" Emma said, flustered, entering the kitchen in flipflops, shorts and a bralette, clutching a bowl. It was a hot, sticky evening, the heatwave they'd been warned about transpiring.

Matt turned from the cupboard, an eyebrow raised hawkishly. Emma didn't usually wander around in a state of half-undress. 'Are you okay?'

She crumpled into a chair. 'The carpets are infested, Matt. Infested! I've been up there for hours, tweezering maggots into a bowl.' She proffered Matt said bowl. White, wriggly things were emerging from delicate papery cases. 'What are we going to do?'

Matt took the bowl, squinting. 'These are carpet-moth larvae,' he said conversationally, as though his skin wasn't crawling, as though the sight didn't make him want to itch all over.

'Urgh. Get rid of them, would you?' Her voice rose as Matt walked over to the bin.

'Not the bin! They might crawl out! Outside. Down the end of the garden. Right down the end where I can't see—'

'Emma, I think you're slightly overreact—'

'I've hoovered them, I've sprayed them with bleach—'

'Bleach?' He baulked. 'Those carpets are real wool.'

'And they'll be really out of here as soon as we start on the

33

reno,' she retorted. 'I don't know if I can sleep in there tonight.'
She shuddered.

'Emma,' Matt said carefully, 'where's the hoover?'

She twisted to look at him, eyes narrowed. 'Why?'

Matt looked as though he were choosing his words. 'Nothing. Only . . .' His voice was a masterpiece in measured calm. '. . . I have encountered carpet moths before and, um, well. They can crawl out of hoovers.'

She let out a little scream. 'Are you kidding me?' she cried.

'Let me sort it out.' He sighed, opening the back door with the bowl in his hand. 'You stay there.'

She would be grateful for his intervention were she not maddeningly angry with him for their being stuck here in the first place.

Emma had been totally opposed to buying Jutland House, as it was then (she'd had it officially renamed Briar Heart House as soon as they moved in). It had originally been the developer's house when the estate was built in the thirties, and their great-great-great-great-something-or-other had fought in the Battle of Jutland, hence the name. The connection had clearly gone to his head: the house was very square, blockish, almost like a fortress. It was larger than the neighbouring houses, as though surveying them. The brickwork was in keeping with the rest of the estate, but the style was different, the windows smaller. It was imposing and dark inside too, fitted throughout with mahogany and walnut.

Worst of all was the neglect. It had sat empty for years while the previous owner's family had a more modern battle – that of an inheritance dispute – until it was finally settled and sold. In the meantime, this once-grand house had all but gone to rot. The family had done the bare minimum to keep it secure (and sellable), but that hadn't been enough to stop the condensation and accompanying mould around the leaky lead-latticed windows, or the carpets being eaten, or huge spiders taking up residency.

She scanned her decrepit kitchen: the clunky old Aga she couldn't work, the incongruous glitter ball – the first thing she put up when they moved in – wondering for the hundredth time whether they'd made a mistake. What if the plans didn't go through? If they were forced to live in this creepy old house, in its current state? It was unthinkable.

The plans were beautiful. The ugly, imposing red-bricked facade of Jutland House literally split down the middle – the old making way for the new – and filled with glass, floor to roof, letting in masses of light, a wide central staircase ascending, her dream castle.

She remembered their first viewing of the house. Matt had been staring out of the window in the direction of Bob's house – you could see right into the garden from the first floor – and she was surprised to see a look of near rapture on his face. 'Imagine the kids growing up here,' he'd said, his arm gesturing to the long expanse of the garden, the Parkland beyond. 'Houses so rarely come up,' he'd wheedled. 'This is our chance to live on the Briar Heart Estate.' She knew what it meant to live here and she knew what it would mean to Matt.

'Fine!' She'd acquiesced, her face cracking into a smile. 'Yes!' And he had scooped her up and spun her around, and she had felt, briefly, like a princess.

'I saw Twig earlier,' she said when Matt returned from his business with the hoover. Her eyes studied his face, as they often did when she mentioned his childhood sweetheart, but he appeared unmoved and instead joined her at the table with his latest business tome: *Disarm the Competition with Kindness!* 'She didn't seem too good.'

'No?'

Emma stretched her calf out on a dining chair. After a long hiatus, since she'd had her children, Emma had recently returned to running. She'd needed to do something to burn off her agitation, the nervous energy zipping in her bones, which was buzzing more forcefully than ever since their plans had been submitted.

'In a bit of a state, really. I'm sure it's the pressure of funding this vaccine. I don't know why they don't sell their flat in London.'

'They can't.' He turned his page.

Now she was the one with her attention caught. 'Why not?'

'It's got that dodgy cladding. They can't do anything with it except rent it unless they spend money on repairs.'

Emma's eyes narrowed. 'How do you know all this?'

Matt looked up from his book and his glass of red wine. 'I'm sure I told you this before.'

'No, you didn't.' Emma's hand found her hip. 'I'd have remembered.'

Matt's expression remained bullish. 'It was ages ago, Emma, you've forgotten. Don't you remember? I heard them arguing about it over the fence.'

'I think I'd remember my husband eavesdropping . . . on our neighbours.' She stopped herself from saying *on his ex-girlfriend*.

'I was not *eavesdropping*! I couldn't miss it. They were having a right old barney.' He lifted his book from his lap and shrugged. 'That's why they can't sell the flat, anyway.'

It was annoying that Twig and Matt had a history, because Emma's natural inclination was to like Twig. She could be a bit prickly, and Emma had witnessed how it translated into aloofness with the other mums at school, not helped by Twig's brief flirtation with fame. It led others to assume she was 'up herself', as she'd heard someone say, but Emma was certain it was awkwardness, rather than arrogance, that made her shy away on the school playground and in the class messaging groups.

She looked at her phone, her post poised: *Hey, lovelies, I don't want to alarm anyone, but one of my neighbours thinks he saw a large wild cat on the bonnet of his car a few nights ago. Briar Heart Estate. Nothing to worry about but just so everyone can keep a look out. Thnx. Admin x*

She was torn between posting it and keeping quiet, as Coralie had instructed. On the one hand, Twig had given her the go-ahead to post. On the other, she might be deemed to be as crackers as Adam had seemed the other night. *A wild cat.* But there was a chance it could take the wind out of the sails of the WhatsApp group Agatha had told her about, established to protest their planning application. Although, would the other residents see her post for what it was: a distraction?

Emma didn't get why everyone was so het up about their proposals. There'd been a few grumbles when they'd renamed Jutland House to Briar Heart House. Who'd want a reminder of war and bloodshed every time they inputted their address? Was this revenge for that? It was so childish.

She cringed as she posted the update. *There, it was done now.* She exhaled breezily. 'I thought I'd better post about what Adam saw in the mums' group? You know, as Admin. Let people know to be vigilant.'

Matt looked up and gave her a withering stare. 'Really, Emma?' Sometimes she wondered why she was married to him, but in moments like this she remembered that Matt could see right through her. It gave her a tiny thrill, to be recognized.

'What? It can't do any harm to shift the focus a little.'

'It's fine. The architect said—'

'The architect hasn't seen what the local WhatsApp group has been posting . . .'

She began to read:

'*It's a monster!*

'*Everyone else has respected the estate's planning conventions. Why can't they?*

'*I'd have liked a whole top floor to myself with walk-in wardrobes, too, but we stuck to two storeys. LIKE EVERYONE ELSE.*

'*Matt Brooks should know better. He's lived here all his life.*'

'What?' Finally Matt put his book down, spread-eagling the pages. 'Who said *that*?'

'Anjit at Number 20.' She should have gone straight in with the criticism of Matt, she realized.

It was one of the bonds that united them, coming from ordinary backgrounds, unlike a lot of their Sevenoaks contemporaries, who, like Coralie and Twig, had grown up in comfortable, cossetted bubbles. Matt had been the first in his family to go to university; Emma hoped that, on her side, it would be Henry.

'Where are you reading all this from?'

She moved round to his side of the table. 'Aggie sent them to me. Tim set up a WhatsApp group, you know what he's like – busybody – and he's a property solicitor, isn't he? And part of Sevenoaks Friends.'

Sevenoaks Friends was the suburban mafia. A group of men and women, many in the autumn of their life, who, in between enjoying their semi-retirement with rounds of tennis and long boozy lunches, had secured plum roles on various committees and enjoyed nothing more than to scupper the plans of anyone who they felt *wasn't in keeping* with the local area.

'I bet he's loving throwing his weight around.'

Matt, not accustomed to being criticized, straightened and frowned.

'Look at this, from Coralie: *"I'd like to check the environmental impact on digging out the basement and refashioning the current turrets. Anyone noticed any bats?"'*.

Emma glanced warily towards the roof. 'Do bats have special protections?'

Matt ignored her, craning his head to read more of the posts.

'I *knew* she was pissed off about the plans. Okay for her, isn't it, in her *enormous* pad next door?' railed Emma. 'You know, I'm *sure* I saw a rat scuttling down the side of her house that night as we were leaving the supper party.' The forgotten detail returned, the blink of movement from the corner of her eye, bringing with it a sensory reminder. She wriggled her nose. 'There was a peculiar smell, too, do you remember? Just as we were leaving? God knows what vermin she's attracting over there with her injured hedgehogs and whatnot.' Last winter Coralie hadn't stopped banging on about hedgehogs. Emma threw her phone on to their white wood table, which had coordinated so perfectly in their old house but looked so incongruous here. 'If it doesn't go through, we're selling up. We'll move elsewhere,' she said, chin in the air. Who did these sniffy Sevenoaks people think they were?

'Don't be too hasty. We won't get a better location than this.'

'I don't care. I'm not living here while the place falls apart, surrounded by people who don't like us. Why would you want to?'

'Look.' He flicked through the screenshots, bringing her back
to the present. 'They're not annoyed about the plans full stop, it's
the extras. The third floor, the glass running all the way down the
front. The pink door and window frames. There's lots we can do
to improve the house without upsetting the neighbours.'

'It doesn't need a few tweaks. It needs a total renovation!' she
said as he reached his arms around her and drew her down on to
his lap. Her vision was crumbling before her eyes. She felt trapped.
Like Rapunzel.

'But we're happy here, darling. Aren't we?' He nuzzled his nose
into her neck, and she felt the usual push and pull, between comforting familiarity and revulsion.

'I'm going out for a quick run now that it's cooler.'

As she ran, she pictured the moth larvae wriggling under their bed
and her stomach turned. She forced herself to picture pink encaus-
tic tiles and brushed-brass rainforest showers instead. Parties on
the lawn and mulled wine by the fire.

She thought of Adam secretly touching her and her stomach
fizzed at the memory. Emma had been so preoccupied with the
planning situation she hadn't had time to dwell on Adam touching her under her blanket at Coralie's supper party, but the last
few days, with the objections flooding in, she'd been able to think
of little else.

It had happened just before the cat incident. Emma was feeling
a bit tipsy by then, so her recollection was somewhat hazy, but
she remembered a deep feeling of contentment and the ease of an
early-summer night. And then suddenly, it had happened. *Two fingers? Three?* travelled up the side of her leg, shifting the material
of her skirt. Skin meeting skin. Slowly. Purposefully. The barest of
touches, and yet it was definitely there. Her face had flamed as
her skin fizzled.

She'd glanced to her left, perplexed, expecting to see Matt, although he'd never done anything so risqué, but confusion had turned to incredulity and she'd had to stop herself from gasping aloud. It was Adam. Adam, who, like her, was tucked right into the table, his eyes on his phone atop its ceramic surface.

Adam King.

Adam King was touching her under the table.

She'd risked another tiny glance in his direction, but he'd angled his head steadfastly to his left, away from her, his gaze calm but for a muscle throbbing in his clenched jaw.

It had been so long since anyone else had touched her besides Matt. It had felt alien and strange, but also intoxicating. She'd felt something wild and feral shift within her.

Shortly after that he had abruptly stopped and, without so much as looking in her direction, stood up from the table and walked to the side of his house, disappearing from view. *Should she follow him?* she'd wondered. 'Excuse me,' she'd said to Blake, her voice high and fluttery as she rose, but as she was dithering she saw Twig appear from the depths of the garden in pursuit of Adam, disappearing into the shadows too, and then Matt, and it wasn't much longer after that Adam came stumbling around the corner shouting about the cat, his whole countenance and *being* altered.

What had the touch meant? Was it possible that the Kings, the golden couple, had a coffin marriage, the type that litters the suburbs? An empty facade, nailed down with broken dreams and resentments, affairs and disappointments? Sometimes, in unsatisfying moments – when they were having perfunctory sex, or Matt was walking around in his shorts and long socks obsequiously greeting higher-ranking Scout leaders – Emma feared she had a coffin marriage of her own and longed to break free of its confines. But never, in her wildest dreams, would she have imagined doing so with *Adam King.*

Yesterday, on a whim, she'd texted him: *Just checking in after the supper party.* She hated calling it a 'supper party', but that was how Coralie had referred to it. She was so posh. *Hope you're feeling better?* she'd written, as if Adam had had a headache rather than a moment of abject terror. She'd never texted him privately before – he was always curt but funny in their group chat – and she'd felt a frisson of excitement, waiting for him to respond.

There was a feeling in the weighted summer air of wildness unfurling, and she felt the same stirring within her; a feeling of coming loose, the promise of change with their plans submitted and this potential *dalliance* with Adam, too.

No, they wouldn't move. She would make her downtrodden house a castle, whatever it took.

6

Coralie

Next door, Coralie raised her eyes from her phone as outside something caught her eye: Socks emerging from a bush. He cocked his leg, shook out his torso and flicked his tail, like a suited killer straightening his tie. She smiled. She loved that cat. She slid open the doors which framed the back of the house and moments later he strolled in, tail proud, no doubt wondering what was for dinner.

'There's no food for you here,' she said, closing the door to keep out the heat. Socks flicked his tail again, as though shrugging. He had the most beautiful markings, gold and fawn stripes fanning out like a tiger and four delicate white 'socked' paws. *Whoever heard of a gluten-free cat?* Coralie bit down on her irritation: *the Disney princess*, as she privately thought of Emma, a twee little housewife, living in her insular pink bubble.

'I suppose you've come to hear all the gossip, have you?' She smiled over the top of her phone.

The thread she'd been following in the local mums' Facebook group remained at the top of her newsfeed. Coralie wasn't a fan of technology, but had joined this platform to keep people up to date with her projects in the Parkland. She'd been checking it periodically since the supper party. She'd just had a feeling that Emma, or maybe even Twig, would panic and post something. And she'd been right.

She scrolled down with a knot of anxiety in her stomach.

OMG! I'd have been terrified. Are they okay?

The Sevenoaks Panther is back!

We saw one in Knole Park about five years ago! It ran away, but it was definitely a big cat.

She startled at a cacophony of crashes and bangs from the side of the house that was gathering pace and volume. She stood quickly, her heart pounding, but in seconds Adam materialized in a flash of orange and, rather than stretching outside as was usual, careered straight for the door, yanking it open, rushing inside and slamming it closed. He whirled round and grabbed for the lock, only to find it empty.

'Where's the key? Coralie? Coralie, where's the key?' His words were broken by jagged inhales of shallow breath, his body twitching with fear. She rushed over to him, eyes wide.

'Adam, what's happened?' Her eyes raked over his face.

'The key, Coralie! Where's the key!'

'Here.' She felt behind the radio and produced it. Put a hand to his arm. 'Are you okay?'

He locked the door, before shuddering out an exhale.

'I was chased. It was chasing me.'

'Oh my God, Adam.' He was wet with sweat but freezing cold from fear, despite the balmy air outside. 'Muggers in *Sevenoaks*?' She shook her head. 'Did they take your phone?'

He eyeballed her incredulously. 'The fucking cat, Coralie! I was chased by the fucking cat! First it's on my fucking car bonnet and the next it's stalking me in the woods! I'm being followed by a fucking big cat!'

'What?' She baulked, leading him through to the kitchen, her forehead lined with consternation. *Had he been smoking again today?* She looked around the kitchen for drug paraphernalia. 'Tell me exactly what happened,' she said.

Adam sunk down on to a chair, his head in his hands.

'I was running through the Parkland. I'd been going maybe fifteen minutes? Way past the paths, and the skate ramps and, I don't know how to describe it, I just *knew* I was being followed. My muscles immediately felt tight, like they were gripping to my bones in fright. Like they *knew*.'

'Knew what?' Her tone was precise, focused only on separating fact from fiction.

'That the wild cat was there! That I was being stalked!'

'Did you *see* a cat?' Coralie splashed whiskey into a squat crystal tumbler and placed it before him. His eyes were still free-wheeling, roaming over the table and back to the door.

'I didn't need to see it, Coralie. I could *feel* it. It was chasing me!'

'What did you do?' She had a strange and desperate urge to laugh. The whole scenario was so ridiculous.

'I didn't know what to do! I wondered about climbing a tree—'

'Well, that wouldn't help,' she said drily. 'They can climb trees.'

He hadn't touched his whiskey. She pushed it nearer towards him.

'Really?' His face was a perfect picture of shock as his hands cupped the glass.

She nodded slowly, wondering how far she should entertain this. 'It's often where they stash their prey.'

He shuddered with revulsion, his face stripped of colour. 'I kept running. I crossed over the Parkland and under the bypass. All the way until I got to Ide Hill village. And then I ran back through Weald, sticking to the main roads and up through town. It took ages. And the whole time I had this horrible feeling, like I couldn't breathe.'

'You shouldn't run. That's the worst thing you can do.' Her tone was conversational, an attempt to lighten the mood, but Adam's body sank, his forehead suspended over the glass of whiskey. 'Adam' – she gently squeezed his shoulders – 'you wouldn't have been able to outrun a wild cat. You *can't* have been chased by one.'

'Maybe it just wanted to scare me! Or was, you know, checking me out?' he mumbled.

Could he hear himself, she wondered?

'And I heard a *growl*!' He raised his head. 'Like a low roar

44

behind me as I was running.' In the telling of his own story, he was sounding less and less convinced.

'Could it have been traffic noise? It's not too far from the M25. Or someone from the skate ramps? Thinking you were from the council and trying to scare you off?'

'In my running gear?' he questioned, exasperated, his head popping up.

Socks, whom Coralie suspected trusted her husband about as much as she did, sauntered to the back door with casual looks in Adam's direction. Adam, who was (kind of amusingly if you thought about it) allergic to cats, watched him warily.

Coralie unlocked the door, releasing him. 'It's fine,' she said, to the look of horror on Adam's face as a sliver of warm air entered the air-conditioned kitchen. She locked it again, walked purposefully back to Adam and stood in front of him, gesturing at his top.

'Take it off,' she said softly.

'No.' He shook his head, a flash of irritation passing over his face.

'I said, take it off.' Her words were laced with intent. 'You're a mess.' She took the whiskey, still untouched, from his hands. She leaned forward and tugged at the hemline of his sweat-soaked top, starting to raise it.

'*I said, no.*' He was more insistent this time and it shot a spark of fear through her. He never used to say no. That is, until he had the affair last summer. She pushed the thought from her mind. Wouldn't allow it to cloud her thoughts the way it did sometimes, dragging her down, making her feel discarded and unwanted.

She knelt before him, gently pushing apart his knees. She worked her hand up the inside of his thighs, which were damp with sweat as she teased her fingers over the Lycra layer beneath his shorts that cushioned his cock. Instead of the electric feeling she craved, she felt a wave of humiliation. She was trying so hard, and it used to be so *easy*. She longed to go back to the times when he would return from a run and she would lick the sweat off him, still fresh and almost sweet-smelling. He'd always had lovely clean skin. It was one of the things she liked most about him. He took care of himself.

She tried to ignore the flat, dull feeling of rejection settling in her stomach. She reminded herself of the way other men looked at her, but it was Adam she wanted. Adam she craved. *Why did he still have such a hold over her?*

She bent her head down and began licking and kissing him through the stretchy fabric, waiting for the moment, the shift. She could do this. She could have sex with her husband. They used to be good at it, for heaven's sakes! She reached her hands up to the top of his shorts, preparing to ease them down and away, but he slammed his hands over hers with a jolt, as though he were being attacked.

'I don't want to.' There was a weariness there, a resignation. She masked her disappointment, shrugging and smiling an *okay, whatever* grin to indicate she didn't care, all while feeling like she was being disembowelled as she quietly rose and left the kitchen. Adam's relief was audible as she gently closed the door.

She stood in her large entrance hall, her laptop against her chest. Readying herself for a call with her girls later that evening, where she'd have to pretend, as she always did, that her heart wasn't breaking from being apart from them. And now Adam; the distance between *them* widening too. And all because of a cat.

She'd had to downplay her interest in cats at the supper party. It was a reflex she'd honed since childhood: *Weird*, the other girls had called her at school when she arrived, immediately pinning a photo of her with Cleopatra and Duchess up next to her bed. The truth was Coralie King had been searching for wild cats her whole life.

Ever since the unfortunate incident at Cresswell Place, her family home. Her parents had had to give away all their cats after that. They never forgave her. Her punishment? Familial estrangement. It had been such a shock at the time, devastating to be wrenched from them and shipped off to boarding school. Although, the older she got, the more she realized it was little loss. Every time she saw her scar in the mirror, she remembered she was better off without them. But you don't see it that way when you're a child.

She'd spent her life trying to atone, researching wild cats in the hope that she could protect them. Even her final project at university, the wallabies, was really about cats. Her course tutor had told her she needed to widen her focus. She did, but every bit of data she evaluated, or call-out she investigated, she couldn't help but look for evidence of a big cat. She would have dedicated her entire life to it, had she not had the girls.

The prospect of Adam having seen a cat sent shivers up and down her spine. These creatures were wild. They didn't wander into front gardens or climb on to cars. The idea of having one so close. It felt exhilarating. It felt like . . . redemption.

She strode back into the kitchen. Adam was where she had left him. Staring out at the Parkland, his fingers again gripping the whiskey glass.

'I'm sorry I didn't take you seriously before,' she said, a well of magnanimity opening in her chest. 'It is possible you've seen a big cat,' she admitted. '*Unlikely*, but possible.' His eyes sprung to her face, alert. 'But cats don't hurt people. They avoid them.'

'It doesn't feel like that when one's chasing you,' he snapped as she circled him, pulling out a chair and sitting beside him.

'I'll investigate it. I'll track it, if it's out there. Like I did with the wallabies. I'll find out, once and for all. There are things you can look for, if you know. I just need to remind myself. Use the correct methodology.'

'And then what?' He cut her off. 'Can you catch it? What will you do?'

'If I find proof, we'll contact the big-cat sanctuary. There's one in Kent. See if they can help us, have it relocated there.' She looked away. Big cats belonged in the wild. But she needn't worry about that now; it was almost impossible to trap one, wherever you were in the world.

Cats are clever. You'd have to weather the trap in, camouflage it, scent it. You'd need live bait. A goat. A bleating kid. Illegal here, of course, quite rightly. Permission from a government agency. Who knew what the cat sanctuary would be able to do, but already she could see the effects of her reassurances. Adam was staring at her intently, but with hope in his eyes, rather than disinterest or menace.

She was by his side now, wondering, *will you stay if I do this for you, Adam? Will you be mine? Wholly mine? Will you return to being the man I fell in love with?*

She put her hands over his, held them in communion between them. 'I promise, Adam. I'll figure this out. I'll get to the bottom of whatever's going on. You can trust me.'

The Mystery of the
Sevenoaks Panther

Agatha, Puddleford parent: We specifically moved to the Briar Heart Estate so we could get our kids into Puddleford and walk them to school through the Parkland. We had to rent for two years before the right property was available. But it was worth it. It's the kind of set-up you dream of for your children. We feel extremely fortunate.

Tim, Number 16: It sounds idyllic, doesn't it? But the Parkland had problems of its own.

Bob, Number 8: I never had a problem with the skate ramps. If the local teenagers wanted to take it upon themselves to dig out ramps, erect that swing and build the campfire area, then fair play to them. You've got to admire their tenacity? To keep rebuilding it over and over again.

Tim: [Primly.] I think the council would've been more inclined to turn a blind eye if they hadn't been taking drugs.

Mei, teaching assistant at Puddleford School: My eldest was there most days after school. He said he never once saw anyone taking drugs. *Not once.*

Tim: Of course he did. [Smirks.] Someone had to have their stomach pumped, for goodness' sakes.

7

Twig

There was a buzz through the Parkland the next morning, mums asking Twig if she'd seen Emma's post on social media and keen to know who it was on Briar Close that had seen the wild cat. Elwood and Skylar were running ahead, kicking dandelion clocks, their seeds scattering and floating in clouds of golden dust.

Oh, Adam, they would say in surprise, drawing out the 'm', and there'd be a slight shift in their excitement because laconic, laid-back, sexy Adam wasn't the sort of person who would go around making wild accusations.

Twig's nose itched, her hay-fever medication providing less respite as the temperature climbed. Twig didn't mind the heat itself, she was used to it from Bali, but the streaming nose and eyes which accompanied it were cumbersome.

'I heard it was a leopard,' one mum said.

'You don't really believe all that, do you?' Twig said to Emma as she drew level with her.

'Believe all what?' said Coralie breathlessly, catching them up. Her thick, wavy blonde hair fanned out below the silk headwrap she often wore in the summer (in the winter it was replaced with a wool beanie), with trousers which could be mistaken for pyjama bottoms, her hiking boots and a long-sleeved white linen top, an orange fleece tied around her waist. As a school governor, Coralie was often going to and from Puddleford School and timed it to walk with them. The only mum without her children. *Her ghost run. Ghost-run mum.*

'Morning,' Twig said. 'The wild cat. The comments on Emma's post. About local sightings? Did you see them? There were loads of people saying they'd seen strange things too. Around Knole, Otford. A few up by Kipstead Lake.'

Coralie shrugged in a jaded manner, her eyes cloudy and tired-looking. 'Well, it's possible.'

Twig frowned. 'So, what, there *could be* wild cats around here? Maybe Adam saw one on his car after all?'

'They do like diesel, apparently,' Coralie said in a jocular fashion, as though rallying herself. There was something slightly off key about her this morning, on edge. 'I'm joking.' She nudged Twig gently with her elbow. 'A professor mentioned it once. I'd forgotten, but it popped into my head the other day.'

She drifted off for a moment then held her palms to the sky. 'They could be anywhere, right? Isn't that the wonderful thing about nature? Its ability to surprise us?' Her zeal was almost evangelical. Twig could imagine, in a doomsday scenario, Coralie leading all the animals to her ark.

Emma pulled a crumpled tissue from her bubble-gum-pink cardigan sleeve and wiped Daisy's streaming nose.

Twig was grateful Skylar had insisted on wearing her Black Panther mask that morning, but nonetheless, she gently guided her to her left, further away from Daisy's germs. 'Where do they come from then, these cats?'

Daisy sneezed and Twig saw the droplets fly, dissipating into the air. Her shoulders tensed and she rolled them back, hearing her joints crunch. She waved a hand in front of Skylar's mask in an attempt to divert anything airborne.

'There's a few different theories,' Coralie continued as they slowed; they'd reached the steep section of the path, flanked by a huge tree trunk, carved to elicit eagles and owls and mice and voles from its surface. 'There used to be a lot of exotic pets in England. They were a status symbol. Some people did see them as lovable pets.' A weary expression crossed over her face.

'There was a pub near us – in the eighties – that had a bear in the garden,' said Emma. 'In a cage. I was telling Henry about it just the other day. It seemed normal at the time!'

Coralie nodded. 'They'd have had a licence. That's the thing: you can keep wild and exotic pets even now, if you have a licence. But that costs money. When the Dangerous Wild Animals Act came into effect in '76, a lot of people just released their pets into the wild. Leopards, alligators, venomous snakes and spiders . . . But Britain has a long history with big cats. The Romans had them, circuses, travelling menageries . . . Are they *naturalizing* in Britain? Now that's a bigger question . . .'

They were crossing through a part of the Parkland covered with trees, where a carpet of bluebells still lingered. Twig felt a cool chill ripple along the back of her neck and scalp.

'The theory is, however they got here, wild cats bred. They're *very* elusive. And of course fantastic hunters.' Her eyes sparkled. She was clearly enthused by the topic and Twig noticed that Elwood had slowed to listen. His eyes were striking: wide with adoration as Coralie spoke. Twig had written a song about them once. *A boy made of stars.* Her little spaceman. So alert to the world and his place in it. She hadn't thought of the song for a while, but the riff returned to her now.

'Sure, I buy that, on moors maybe, like "the Beast of Exmoor". But surely not around here?' Emma's words were round with scepticism. 'It's too suburban.'

Coralie tipped her palms upwards. 'There's woodland shelter, abundant prey, a water source. All the things they need.'

Twig frowned in alarm, her eyes drawn to the woods surrounding them.

'I'm not saying there's thousands of them, but I believe there *are* wild cats in the UK in small numbers. But they're far more afraid of us than we need be of them. I, for one, would love to see one! Wouldn't that be cool?' Coralie's eyes met Elwood's, and he nodded his head up and down vigorously.

Twig should've expected this. She'd witnessed how much Coralie delighted in creatures that made others squirm: like spiders and grass snakes and slow worms. She'd returned home from a hospital appointment with Skylar last winter to find Elwood and Coralie at the kitchen table, bent over his microscope in fascination: Coralie had collected him from school, noticed his excessive head-scratching, de-loused him with a natural remedy and together they were inspecting a head louse, marvelling at its antennae.

'Wouldn't you have seen something?' she asked Coralie. 'On the night cameras you put up in the Parkland? When you were tracking the badgers? I know you had to take them down, but they were up for months before that.' Skylar was walking up ahead with some other girls from her class; Twig fought the desire to pull her close and not let go.

'What's this about cameras?' Emma asked curiously.

'I installed them for the project I did for the preschool,' Coralie explained. 'But I had to get permission from the council and mark on a map where they'd be. Every time I did, they'd last a week or two – one even managed a month – until they were stolen. I replaced them initially – I didn't want to let the kids down; *they were so sweet* – but eventually I gave up.'

'Fancy stealing something like that.' Emma frowned.

'Terrible,' Twig agreed.

Emma shook her head. 'You wouldn't think you'd get that round here.'

Coralie shrugged. 'The cameras aren't cheap. I expect they get sold on. You really shouldn't have posted about the cat though, Emma. You know what people are like. We don't want everyone getting hysterical over it. Even if there *is* a wild cat, it wouldn't go near anyone.'

'How come there's sightings then?' Emma said, neutrally but with a tiny flick of defensiveness in the lift of her chin.

'They get disturbed,' Coralie said amiably, Attenborough-esque in her delivery. The path widened, the canopy of trees giving way to blue sky and sunlight. Some other mums had heard their conversation and fallen into step with them, while another group walked close behind, and they began asking more questions.

'Has a wild cat ever attacked a human?'

'Have you ever seen one?'

'What should we do if we come across one?'

Coralie's laugh tinkled through the Parkland in tune with the morning light:

'Really, ladies, it's a beautiful day. Let's talk about something else. Twig and I are planning a benefit for little Skylar in my garden in July. Who's in?' Coralie's eyes sparkled as she spoke and Twig couldn't help but smile at how twee the event sounded when, knowing Coralie and her legendary parties, there would be a huge marquee on her lawn, a band, caterers . . . Coralie had it all booked already.

Anything to avoid the dark in her heart; ghost-run mum . . .

A new song was biting at the edges of Twig's subconscious, but she knew that's where it would stay. She wouldn't have time to tease it out, to create something new. And what would be the point anyway? Anything she released would sink into an online abyss, like 'A Boy Made of Stars'. *It wasn't like she had a music producer for a wife, was it?* she thought glumly. It had been a long time since she and Blake had collaborated musically. She couldn't hold it against Blake. They were each doing what they could to survive.

'I don't suppose you know anything about carpet moths?' Emma was asking Coralie, her face a picture of revulsion. 'I thought I'd got rid of them, but I found a whole host of them between the wicker slats of our laundry basket this morning!'

As the conversation moved on, Twig couldn't help but scour the Parkland, dense with trees and bushes, and wonder what might be lurking within.

8

Emma

Emma ran downstairs and received the parcel with delight: a box of heavy-duty moth killer. That's what she needed. The more skulls and crossbones the better. Not the home-made concoction of baking soda and lavender which Coralie had insisted on using as she wittered on about toxins and chemicals and eco-balance or whatever.

She ran back up to Henry's bedroom, almost tripping over his drone. She put it on his desk and resumed her watch from the window. All the local women knew Adam ran on Tuesdays, Thursdays and Saturdays. They'd joked about it in the pub after someone had noticed it on Strava. Emma had often glanced him leaving from the back of her house, through his garden and into the Parkland, always on those days. She knew she was becoming a little too preoccupied with her handsome neighbour, but he *had* touched her that night in their garden. Maybe nothing would happen, maybe it was a brief moment of intoxicated madness on his part, and maybe she just needed a distraction from being trapped here, feeling like everyone hated her. The thing was, she'd moved here to make Matt happy, but he didn't care that *she* was unhappy. Didn't seem to notice the toll it was taking on her. So, she reasoned, it couldn't do any harm to put herself in Adam's path . . . to find out what he'd been thinking.

She had to be subtle about it though. Imagine if Coralie realized that Emma fancied her husband. She wouldn't have thought twice about pursuing Adam, if you could even call it that, if she still felt like she and Coralie were friends.

It had all happened innocently enough. When she still hadn't had a response from Adam to her text days later, Emma had checked their smart doorbell, remembering Matt's mention of it. Their footage didn't extend to the Kings' front garden, but, she'd recalled from when they'd had it installed, it was *possible* to see, and hear, further.

She'd changed the settings to maximum range. A mere two hours later she'd noticed Coralie and Valerie through the window, on the Kings' front lawn, their eyes darting like daggers towards her house. She'd immediately listened in on her livestream, and heard them, word for word: 'You know what I call her, Valerie? Between you and me . . . *the Disney princess.*' Both women had chuckled. Emma's face flushed red at the memory.

Loyalty ran deep in Emma. But she felt betrayed, knowing how Coralie truly felt about her. In the scheme of things, because Coralie's husband had made the first move, it felt like fair game. It felt like . . . payback.

She craned to see herself in Henry's mirror and assessed her new running clothes: a pink vest with floral leggings. Both were extremely tight-fitting and she wished she'd ordered them in black, like her old set. Emma wasn't big, but she wasn't small either. She'd been called, variously, chubby (her mother), stocky (a well-meaning work-friend – and that was *before* she'd had children) and curvy (Matt), but the stress of the last few weeks and the neighbourhood uproar was taking its toll, and she was reaching for wine and chocolate more often. She needed to up her running programme.

'*Find a partner to motivate you and help you commit!*', the 'Get Back to Running' article she'd read had proclaimed. Watching Adam run was basically the same thing, if he would just leave the house. She pinned a foot against her bum, stretching out a calf in anticipation. It was almost noon and, if he didn't leave soon, she wouldn't be back in time for school pick-up. Not if he took that circuitous route he had the other night, down to Ide Hill and through Weald. She could barely keep up. It was frustrating; she used to run long distances. Surely she had some muscle memory, or something, which might help?

Finally, from her vantage point in Henry's bedroom, she saw him emerge. She charged down the stairs and out the back door. Flattened herself against the fence and scuttled behind their shed and the children's playhouse so she wouldn't be seen by any nosy neighbours. But by the time she'd got there, Adam had disappeared. Her heart was pounding in her chest. It was exciting! The subterfuge! She could see why people had affairs.

As she was wondering what to do next, she lurched directly into Adam, causing a startled 'WOAH!' from him and an 'ARGH!' from her, where he'd trod on her foot.

'God, sorry, Emma.' His arms were outstretched to steady himself, his concern for her visible. 'I skidded on something.' He looked down and shook out his shoe, as though something was stuck beneath it.

'It's fine,' she said, trying not to wince. Her face flushed. 'Hi,' she said breathlessly. 'Are you okay? I haven't seen you since the supper party.' That wasn't strictly true, but she could hardly tell him she'd been following him on his runs.

He startled, looking back to the house. Emma followed his gaze. Coralie was in her 'greenhouse' at the back of their garden, her hand extending up to a shelf to reach a green-tinted bottle. Coralie called it a greenhouse, but Emma would call it an orangery, or something more grand. It was a small brick building with a high ceiling and tall, rectangular windows, the tops partly obscured by ornately stained glass. Wooden shelves were visible, cluttered with books and gardening tools and jars stuffed with random objects, presumably from her zoological research.

Oh, she thought, catching Coralie's eye as she retracted her arm and stepped down, waving. Emma waved too, with a strained smile she couldn't seem to relax. *Had Adam been giving her a signal with his pointed look to Coralie? To let her know they could be seen?*

'Off out for a run, are you?' She turned back to him.

He was still frowning at his trainer, rubbing the side of it against dry leaves on the floor in the manner of a bashful teenager, and Emma flushed again. It crossed her mind to mention her un-answered text message, but wasn't it cooler to have not noticed? To remain aloof? He seemed strange and jumpy around her, but she pretended not to see. Didn't want to draw Coralie's attention to it if she was, as Emma suspected, watching.

'I'll be off then,' he said awkwardly, indicating the road ahead but not moving. *Did he . . . not want to leave her?* Her face glowed in the morning sun, blooming like a sunflower. She pushed out her chest, as much she could in her sports bra, and sucked in her stomach.

'Okay,' she said cheerily, noticing the way his lips seemed to be moving of their own accord, his eyes roaming the shaded path. He was short of breath, as though he'd already been for a run, not about to set off.

'Adam, are you really okay?'

'Sure!' he said, too quickly. Too exaggerated. 'I'm good. Everything's good.' And with a nod in her direction he jogged away. She stared after him, her brow furrowed.

The Kings' back gate creaked open, and Coralie appeared with a small frown. 'I'm worried about him.'

Emma eyed her evenly, determined not to betray her disappoint-ment in Coralie's duplicity.

'Is everything okay?' Emma asked, curious. Coralie King wasn't the sort of person to invite sympathy, but she appeared exposed somehow, adrift.

She instinctively reached out a hand to touch Coralie's fore-arm, but Coralie jerked away reflexively before Emma reached the linen fabric.

'Sorry,' Coralie said with a gasp, her fingers flicking up defen-sively, but offering no explanation.

How could she bear to wear long sleeves in this weather? But then, thought Emma, she always did. She realized she'd never seen Coralie's arms exposed, but her style was so in keeping with her eccentric demeanour, ethereally gliding around the Parkland, it hadn't occurred to her as odd before now.

'It's fine,' Emma said. Acting normally around Coralie was one thing; pretending to be her best friend was another. She began to turn away.

'He had a difficult childhood . . .' Coralie trailed off.

Emma remembered that Adam had been adopted, but knew little else about him. She'd asked him once where his tanned skin had come from – she'd been admiring it in comparison to her own pinkie-pale hue – and she'd pondered it herself before: was he of Mediterranean, or even Middle Eastern, heritage? But he'd explained he'd been adopted and didn't know.

'He can be very anxious. Sometimes, I feel like I can't do anything to please him.' The words tumbled from Coralie, who immediately winced, as though chastising herself. 'Sorry, I shouldn't have said that. I don't want to put you in an awkward position, as our neighbour.'

She shook her head, her thick hair rustling like taffeta silk. Coralie was beautiful, but up close there were small signs of neglect: her teeth were slightly stained and wonky – not terrible, but not the mega-watt smile you'd expect from someone who'd clearly grown up around money. Her hair was long, but in an untamed, uncared-for way, not the glossy manes of some of the other Sevenoaks women: the ends were split; she was too busy saving the world to schedule regular trims, Emma guessed.

'I didn't know you ran?' Coralie's tone was peculiar. She was slim and lean-muscled, but from carrying wood through the Parkland, building shelters and the like. You couldn't imagine *her* in a gym, like Twig, or out running. The idea was ridiculous.

'I've recently started.' Her face was aflame beneath Coralie's inquisitive look. She felt for a second as though Coralie could peel away her skin and read her thoughts, discern her childish schoolgirl crush on Adam, before realizing that Coralie was distracted by her own preoccupations.

'Did he say anything to you, about a cat?'

Emma's eyes widened.

'No. Why? He's not . . .?'

'Maybe I'm worrying about it too much. I have a habit of doing that.' She smiled at Emma; the eclipse had passed, she was restored to her usual assured self. 'Oh, I made you something!' Coralie ducked back to her greenhouse, returning with some small, netted bags.

'What are they?' Emma held them up to her nose, suspiciously. She knew Coralie didn't like her, so why was she behaving like a friend?

'Just something I put together: lavender, bay leaves, cloves, rosemary and thyme. To deter the moths!' Now it made sense; more natural deterrents to avoid Emma spraying anything toxic. *Well, too late, Coralie!*

She returned home and dotted the fragrant bags from Coralie about her bedroom: under her bed, beneath her pillow, at the bottom of her laundry basket. A churning energy zipped around her body: she still needed to run.

She sprung through the residential streets, darting and side-stepping into pockets of shade as snatches of music pumped out of hot cars. Girthy plant stalks, not noticeable last week, had clawed up through the soil and arched towards the sky, tightly clenched buds seeking sunlight.

The Sevenoaks Panther, she mused as she ran, breathing deeply, her muscles working beneath a burning sun. She had been on to something when she'd posted about it. It had the power, she realized, to change everything.

9

Coralie

Coralie sat perched on her grandmother's chair, binoculars pressed to her face, as she had been since she sent Emma away with the lavender bags. A baby bird was in the middle of her lawn. Still alive, just. She scanned the grass and the trees, looking for its mother, or a predator. *Come on*, she entreated, the baby bird's wing flickering in the gentle wind. *Come on . . .*

She should check the cameras; she'd been meaning to all morning, but instead she found herself here, transfixed, the hard rim of the binoculars pressing against her eye sockets, willing the minutes to pass until Adam returned from his run.

Was he still meeting *her*? Somehow, with the business of the last few weeks, her tracking and investigating, she'd been able to forget Adam's affair. His plans to leave her. But now she cast the binoculars aside and drummed her fingers on the arm of her grandmother's chair. She checked her watch. He'd been gone for over an hour. She checked his fitness app: nothing. No dot to follow. No route to check. When had he last turned the live tracker on?

She'd spent the last week trying to focus on gathering as much information about cats as she could: if local hysteria built, as she feared it would, she wanted to be ready to quell it. Her greenhouse bore the evidence: books and notes littered the floor.

She moved and sat at her desk, her feet planted firmly as she sat forward eagerly, opening her laptop. The excitement – the hope of spotting something on the cams – never dissipated, but today she felt distracted, skittish. The fine hairs on her neck prickled as though she were being watched.

She turned in her chair, her eyes finding only the framed pictures on the wall behind her. Her gaze was drawn to the most familiar one – *iconic*, *Vogue* had called it – a beehived woman walking a leopard along Knightsbridge. She turned back, the unsettled feeling following her, trying to focus again on the blurry recorded footage. Only Adam knew she still had the cameras up. She'd told everyone else she'd given up after they kept being stolen, but really, she'd moved them to secret locations. Camouflaged them well. She didn't like to keep secrets, but sometimes it was necessary.

She used to spend hours down here watching the cameras alone while Adam was out at work. Now he knew what she was doing, attentively asking her for updates when she emerged from her greenhouse. It was bringing them closer together. Would it be enough to save their marriage?

Suddenly he appeared. Her wildflower patch – sunshine-yellow celandine, purple ragged robins and blush wild roses – a blooming backdrop to his stretches. His face was red, etched with ill temper, and she experienced the usual unsettling turbulence: her wish for Adam to return home meeting with the reality of his presence. The charge in the air, the pressure change. *Would it be so bad if he left?* a tiny voice asked as she rose to greet him. *Yes*, she thought. *Yes.* She'd given up so much for him.

'Can you stop feeding that fucking cat?' Adam panted as soon as she walked outside.

'What?' She startled, watchful. Was this the beginning of one of his moods?

'Socks! I almost fell over earlier, skidding on some slimy cat food. It's gross. You shouldn't be encouraging him. You know I'm allergic!' His voice was piercing, eyes narrowed as he spat out the words. His face wasn't handsome, it was monstrous.

'Not to cat food.' She glanced around, hoping Emma or another neighbour passing along the Parkland pathway might see him like this as he glared at her. No one would ever believe her otherwise.

'No, of course I'm not allergic to cat food, but you know what I mean. I felt so awkward around Emma. That's who I skidded into, for fuck's sake.' He moved closer, his low voice sibilant, sweat curdling on his skin, sour in the warm air.

What was happening here? What narrative was he constructing? She dug her nails into her palm. Emma, Emma. No, it couldn't be Emma. She wasn't his type. She was too frumpy. Too Disney. Too . . . Emma. He's meeting someone else. Emma's his cover. Her brain was working overtime.

'I never feed him in the house. Only out here by the greenhouse.' Her voice had a pleading edge to it which she despised, but it worked. Adam's body language altered. He stepped back, shook out his legs and arms, as though shrugging off the moment.

'Don't feed him at all. He's not your cat.' His tone was normal now. Hyde returning to Jekyll.

'I'll stop,' she promised, slowly moving back towards her greenhouse, but without looking away from Adam.

Never turn your back on an ambush predator, she thought, and then glanced at the spot where the baby bird had been. It was gone.

The Mystery of the Sevenoaks Panther

Agatha, Puddleford parent: [Huffs.] Come on! Are we still doing this? [Kisses teeth.] Twig and Blake had money! They had a flat in London! Blake was a music producer, for God's sake, jetting round all over the place. You never saw her at school.

Freja, chair of Puddleford PTA: Don't believe what you hear about the Dorsetts. Blake might have been a hotshot at one point, but her work was drying up. And they had Skylar to think about; her treatment wasn't cheap. The Dorsetts were getting desperate.

Agatha: Working late. That's what Twig always said if you asked her about Blake. But if you ask me, she was up to a lot more than that. [Crosses legs and clasps hands in her lap.] Drugs? I couldn't possibly comment.

DI Mackintosh: Why was the Dorsetts' situation at that time relevant? It was the same with the Kings and the Brooks. Someone was lying. And we needed to work out why. Who had the biggest motive?

10

Twig

'How was Cubs?' Twig asked, stirring a bowl of overnight oats (organic, gluten free, with added probiotics and ground seeds). Her mother had always been obsessed with them having a proper breakfast, and it was the one tradition Twig routinely kept up with her kids that made her feel like she was being a good parent. 'How was Matt? Sorry, Akela?'

There were so many different names she could ascribe to Matt Brooks, and yet, in some ways, Akela, the name of all Cub Scout leaders, felt the strangest. Twig had been a Cub herself (unusual then, her friends opting for Brownies, but Twig wanted to light fires and build dens, not bake and craft), and her own Akela had seemed so *old*.

'He was okay. A bit grumpy,' Elwood answered, eyes fixed on the book he was reading: *Stig of the Dump*. A birthday gift from Coralie last year. He'd re-read it a hundred times since.

'Just with you, or with everyone?' She coughed, something tickling the back of her throat. She'd spent the walk home from school feeling like she was choking as peachy clouds of blossomdisseminated in the sky.

'Hmmm, everyone, I think. Maybe with me a bit more. I couldn't get the Square Knot right.'

Twig frowned. She could raise it with Matt again, why he was so hard on Elwood, his insistence on, 'toughening him up'. And they could do their usual dance: her skirting around whether it was because Elwood's parents were both women; and Matt's usual sermon on the importance of male role models for young boys and the vital work of the Scouts.

'Coralie's investigating the wild cat.' Elwood lowered his book.

'Is she now?' Twig asked, only half listening, her mind still on Matt Brooks.

'Yeah. Henry said that the wild cat had eaten Rafe's kittens, so I wondered if that's why she had so many books and notes on them. But she told *me* she isn't sure. She said wild cats are very rare and pets die all the time, probably of *boredom*.'

Twig looked up at him sharply. It had been the talk of the playground yesterday, that the Butterfields' kittens had been unceremoniously skinned by a fox.

'I think that bit was a joke.' He shrugged. 'But she said she thinks it's interesting so she wants to find out more about them. Wild cats.'

'What?' Twig said, tuning in. 'Henry said what, about the kittens?'

'That the Sevenoaks Panther ate them! But Coralie said . . .'

Twig's eyebrows knotted as he repeated himself. Not at Elwood's story – every now and then a fox did get at a cat, or another pet, unfortunately; that sort of thing had happened when she was a kid, that's why they'd stopped keeping chickens – but in trying to recall when Elwood would have seen Coralie this week.

Blake popped out from the garage and Twig smiled warily. Things had been tense between them this week. She didn't know why, but it seemed like every time she mentioned Skylar's vaccine the temperature between them dropped, Blake's lips pursed, her demeanour closed.

'Mummy, do you think *aliens* could have done it? Not in a mean way – because you shouldn't automatically assume that people who don't look like you are mean, like you and Mummy always say – but as a sort of sign, or sacrifice, like the Greek gods used to do?'

Hearing Elwood's hypothesis, Blake met Twig's eyes with an indulgent smile, before ducking back into the garage with a bag of mixed nuts. Twig was relieved by their warm, albeit brief, interaction.

'No, sweetheart. I don't.' She was grateful to Coralie for sparking his imagination, but she wished she wouldn't fill his head with these crazy ideas. She didn't seem to understand that it would preoccupy him for hours, although Twig had told her as much. 'When did you speak to Coralie, anyway?' she asked.

'Yesterday, after school. She saw me in my treehouse with my binoculars when she was coming home from the Parkland. I was trying to spot the panther! She said I could come over and we went into her greenhouse, and she had books and folders about wild cats spread all over the floor, and—'

'Did you?' Twig interrupted, alarmed, not because he was with Coralie but because he had been somewhere outside of the house and she hadn't known. 'I thought you were playing with your solar system in your room last night?' Was it possible that while Twig had been glued to her computer, exhausted from travelling to the hospital each day, and while Skylar was watching TV and Blake was in the garage working, that Elwood was outside, navigating the world alone?

'Yeah,' he said nonchalantly, hands in his pockets as he slumped back in his chair. 'Like I always do.'

'*You do?*' Behind Elwood the evening sky was violent: strips of vivid purple and magenta, stacked in layers, fading to a blue-grey bruise.

'Yeah.'

Twig felt wrongfooted, although it shouldn't really be a surprise. Elwood had slipped into Coralie's garden many times before, especially when Blake was away working and Twig had to take Skylar to the hospital. Spending time with Coralie was more enriching than leaving him with Bob, which she tried to avoid since the pellet-shooting incident. And he *loved* Coralie: loved how she could spot different birds in their garden or identify them by their call alone; and build a proper bug hotel without getting squeamish or bored.

'Because, Mummy, I had lots of questions and I didn't want to ask them all at once because it makes you cross, but Coralie doesn't mind my questions and she always knows the answers.'

A cold, wriggling sensation crawled into her stomach and settled there. *She was a bad mother.*

She knew her son adored Coralie, and it didn't hurt her usually, not really. It was like outsourcing parenthood. A temporary, short-term thing. She had to focus on Skylar, on her treatment. Some days, it felt as though Skylar's illness might kill them all. And Coralie was always there, sweet and gentle, offering and helping and nurturing, and Elwood was content in her company. Twig was happy if he was happy. It was still the best she could do, encouraging their closeness, facilitating it, if need be. Something a good parent would do. And it was only until Skylar had her vaccine and things could return to normal.

'Am I in trouble?' he asked, a confused look hooding his pale blue eyes.

'No, no, of course not. I don't mind you going over to Coralie's . . .' She felt lost for a moment, like she wasn't sure what to say. She often drifted off like that, forgetting, these days. 'I didn't realize you were still doing it, that's all.'

What she should say is *I'm sorry that I haven't noticed. I'm sorry that you still do that, and I didn't know.* But it was easier to push the thought aside, to reach for a mug and tap the coffee machine to life, to jolt herself awake because it was 8 p.m. and she still had so much to do: comments to reply to, a GoFundMe page to update – anything to get more traction online, a bit more cash in the pot. It was nearing the end of May and they were only halfway to their £250,000 target.

Skylar had ended up in their bed again last night—her anxiety an illness running parallel to her cancer since her diagnosis—tapping her every hour throughout the night, saying in the smallest voice: 'Mummy, are you still there?'

She was still here, just. She needed that money. She'd do any-thing to get it.

'You don't go anywhere else, do you? You'd never just wander off into the Parkland at night?' Whereas other children were afraid of the dark, Elwood loved it. Welcomed the change in seasons and the early nights. Eyes fixed to the sky in the middle of the garden or to his telescope when it was time to come in. The upside of returning to Sevenoaks, to the suburban bubble she'd been desper-ate to leave as a kid, was that she felt safe here. She realized now the danger inherent in it. She'd become too relaxed. 'It's okay, as long as it's just to Coralie's.'

She pictured a wild cat prowling beneath the streetlights outside and felt an involuntary shudder of fear. He reached over and put his small hand in hers.

'I like Coralie's greenhouse because I can look over and see our house and know that you're here. I don't want to go anywhere else.' He looked alarmed at the suggestion.

She pulled him towards her, her hand on his head as he snug-gled into her.

'Me neither.'

She slept fitfully that night, feeling as though she had never gone to sleep, but she must have done because, all the next day, a dream-like image recurred in her mind: a shadow stalking the street outside their house, its coat catching in the amber glow of the streetlamps, waiting for them to emerge, to rip her family to shreds; but it wasn't a wild cat, rabid, crawling, eyes piercing, teeth bared, on its haunches primed to leap. It was Matt Brooks.

11

Emma

Arriving home from school drop-off the following week, Emma shoved her key into the lock and made the mistake of looking upwards. Blossom was trapped in the huge cobwebs which had gathered in the porch's corners, highlighting its hidden crevices.

In her ear she was listening to Coralie and Tim via the live feed from her smart doorbell. They were on the far side of Coralie's lawn, nearer Tim's house, so the sound wasn't great, but she got the gist. Something about Emma's plans and the parish council. She sucked a breath in through her teeth, straining to hear. When she had widened the reach of her smart doorbell she'd felt an initial surge of power, but already she felt its limits; restricted by the small radius of its range. All it took was a strong, gusty breeze for a sentence to be wiped out entirely. Still, it was serving its purpose, for now.

Last week, Blake, in conversation with Twig by Bob's car, had referred to her as 'Admin'. It was so derogatory. It made her blood boil. *Admin!* At least Emma engaged with her local community! But she couldn't confront Blake without revealing her new neighbourhood hobby.

She'd brooded on it until the following afternoon, when Socks came in with a little gift: a mouse. Emma had shooed Socks away, picked the mouse up by its tail and dropped it into a shoebox.

Hers and Twig's garages were a mirror image of each other. She knew Blake was always locked away in theirs, doing something pretentious or other. Outside she pretended to stumble, the shoe-box angled away from her as it flew, landing at Bob's garage. She clapped her hands to her cheeks in fake shock (lest anyone be watching on their own smart doorbell) as the mouse scuttled immediately into Bob's garage. She cackled to herself back in her kitchen as she listened to Blake's reaction via her audio feed: 'What the . . .! Twig! *TWIG?* I've spilt fucking kombucha all over my MacBook Pro!'

The smile died on Emma's lips as she heard a noise upstairs. A rumble somewhere in the bowels of the house. Blood drummed in her ears. There was always a perfectly logical explanation for whatever sound had made her jump, but lately it was taking longer to locate the answer, for her nerves to be soothed. She felt like she was constantly looking over her shoulder. She knew eavesdropping on her neighbours wasn't helping her anxieties, but she couldn't stop herself. Emma had switched something on. She'd tapped into a network: lines of hostility streaming in her and Matt's direction. And now she *needed* to know. She couldn't turn the tap off. But in the back of her mind, there was a note of warning: what if she ended up hearing something really bad?

It was silent as she entered the kitchen, Socks sunbathing on the warm tiles as the heat of the day pressed in. The floor was flecked with mustard smudges, leading from Socks' front paws out of the room. She followed the trail: to the gardener's room, then the piano room, through the utility, leading to the boot room, which housed Socks' cat-flap. There she found it, just inside the door: a stinking yellow puddle of cat sick.

Socks appeared beside her mewling sadly as she stroked his head.

Who is feeding you? She snapped on her rubber gloves, the familiar restlessness trickling through her limbs. She scraped the vomit on to a thin chopping mat with a knife, trying not to gag.

She couldn't stagnate here in this decrepit old house, trying to keep it clean and insect-free.

What if she could extend her reach and *hear* someone feeding Socks? Discover the culprit? Her money was on Bob. He hated cats. But did he hate them enough to make one sick? Emma narrowed her eyes, peeling off her gloves. She was determined to find out.

She found additional smart doorbell cameras online. Her dad was a sparky and always said how easy they were to install. Emma used to love helping him with jobs when she was younger. She had her own toolbox, which was gathering dust in the garage. Matt always insisted on 'getting someone in to do the job properly' when a light fitting, or the original smart doorbell, needed installing, even though Emma was perfectly capable.

She would put the new cameras round the outside of the house and down by the shed. Maybe she could affix one to a tree? When she clicked to check out, the website recommended some other, smaller, listening devices too. Maybe she could have some fun with those. *Thank you very much*, she thought, adding them to her basket.

It might not be malevolent. It could be someone nearby who didn't know Socks was gluten intolerant. She'd posted about it in the neighbourhood WhatsApp group, but not everyone was on there. That group was largely silent now anyway, the breakaway group to rail against her project far busier, according to Agatha, although, gratifyingly, it was sometimes drowned out by the Sevenoaks Panther. She looked again at Socks, at his tired collar, and another idea came to her. Looking online, she found the perfect item and included a customized engraving: DO NOT FEED ME. And below that: *Gluten free*. Now no one could claim they hadn't been warned. *Ha!*

She sat back on her knees and slapped her rubber gloves against the floor with a satisfying *thwack!* She was taking action.

12

Coralie

Her daughters arrived after school on Friday, emerging from Fraser's air-conditioned car into the stifling heat. They trawled their way reluctantly over her front lawn. She welcomed them garrulously, arms extended wide. She avoided Fraser's stare, his short auburn curls and intense blue eyes vivid from the passenger seat of his new electric car. He'd always reminded her of a fox: a handsome, regal, dastardly scavenger.

He was the same age as Coralie – they were both older than Adam – and ageing frustratingly well. Elvira, whose age fell between them all, was straight-backed and glossy-haired with her hands on the steering wheel beside him. She and Elvira used to be on friendly terms, but who knows what lies Fraser had fed her since.

'It's so good to see you,' Coralie beamed, squeezing the girls in for a group hug. 'And what's this?' she asked Iris in a chummy tone, as if they were best friends out shopping together, lifting the small, delicate bag from her younger daughter's shoulder. Her head whooshed and for a moment she thought she might faint. She held the bag closer, flustered, struggling to identify what was bothering her, a scent she couldn't place invading her nostrils. 'A new handbag?' Her smile died on her lips as she fingered the intricate beading and the recollection finally reached her.

'You saw Grandma?' Her head whipped up to glare at Fraser.

The girls shrunk away. She felt a stab of frustration at Fraser's actions causing tension between them. Beside her, Adam stiffened as he looked between Coralie and Fraser.

'Did you know about this?' she asked quietly.

He refused to meet her eyes, giving Fraser a look and an open-palm hand gesture which clearly indicated: *what the fuck, mate? Why did you turn up with the bag?* Fraser returned the look with a haughty eyebrow raise, and humiliation burned within her as she realized the two men had spoken about this, colluded in her girls visiting Cresswell Place, the scene of her childhood trauma. She hated to think of the girls there, upright in the formal lounge or playing in the nursery. In her mind's eye, the fittings and furnishings – the thick carpets, the woven lampshades, the heavy brocade drapes – were imbued with tiny gasps of horror.

She swallowed away the lump in her throat and brightened, waving Fraser and Elvira off with a tight smile. Seeing her upset is what Fraser wanted. Perhaps Adam too. Why else would he permit her daughters to see the very people who had caused her so much pain? She felt a spasm in her chest. The four of them turned towards the house. She forced herself to focus: her girls were here, that was all that mattered.

Adam had prepared pizza dough earlier that day, and they rolled it out on the marble kitchen island. She stole glances at him as she stretched out her dough, snapping her gaze away whenever they locked eyes and beaming at the girls instead.

'What the fuck?' she mouthed angrily as the girls washed their sticky fingers in the butler sink, unable to contain her anguish any longer. 'Following Fraser's lead now, are you?' A clear reference to his affair, since Adam wasn't the first husband to have cheated on her.

'I only speak to Fraser so you don't have to.'

Fucking gaslighter! she wanted to scream, but it thundered through her head instead, her hands trembling. She wouldn't cause a scene in front of the girls. 'What's the plan? Upset me enough that I lose my cool?'

This was Fraser's playbook: cause her abject pain, like the affair with Elvira, and when she responded – she was only human – accuse *her* of being in the wrong.

Adam's face wore a look of exasperation that she knew well. She laughed to herself bitterly. How well Adam had played this. How she should have seen it coming. *She wouldn't be drawn in, she couldn't be, she had to think of the girls*, but at the same time she was wondering how much more of this she could take.

'What possible reason could Fraser have given as to why it would be a good idea for them to see my parents?'

Adam ran a hand over his stubble. 'I know they're not good people.' He raised a hand when she rushed to interject. 'They're terrible people. But they're the girls' grandparents, and Fraser promised he would stay with them and, well. They do control the trust, Coralie.' He gestured to indicate their beautiful home.

'They owed me that money,' she hissed.

'Yes. But none of that has to do with the girls. And your dad's older now, he's frail.' He sighed. 'At the end of the day, they're family.' She hated that excuse for all ills, all sins: *they're family*. Family wouldn't have treated her the way they had. Family wouldn't have blamed her to cover up their own crimes. But the look in Adam's eyes, Adam, who had been abandoned as a baby and had longed to know his own family, gave her pause. She was stymied, felt herself the recalcitrant child her parents had always deemed her to be, were she to argue the point. This was how a lot of their arguments concluded.

'I'm on your side, Coralie.' Adam gave her a pleading look, and she wished she could believe him.

She turned her attention back to her daughters, and together they lavished their individual wonky circles of pale dough with tomato sauce and toppings, cooking them in the pizza oven outside. They sat beneath the pagoda with its ceiling of aromatic lilac wisteria.

'Look, Mummy! The spiders are playing!' Iris pointed at the pale grey patio stones where tiny red dots were circling and climbing over one another.

'Actually' – Coralie grasped Iris under the arms – 'those are clover mites!' She tickled her until she heard a giggle from her youngest, sweetest, girl, her velvet skin and red curls brightened by a peach sky.

'Did your mum tell you—' Adam began, at the exact moment she remembered she hadn't told him not to mention the wild cat.

'Anyone for pudding?' she cut him off, signalling to Adam not to say anything with a sharp jerk of her head. He didn't read her cue.

He sat forward eagerly, a slice of pizza dripping with mozzarella in one hand. It was the most animated he'd been in months. It thrilled him when the girls came to stay; it was one of the reasons she still loved him, despite the way he treated her. It wasn't easy to find a partner who cares for your children as you do. 'Did she say I saw a big cat on my car?'

It had been an anniversary gift from Coralie, the sleek black Range Rover on the drive. She couldn't bear it herself, but she'd seen him appreciatively eye the Jeffersons' Range Rover. At the time, she'd have done anything to appease him, and she had to concede it was more comfortable as a passenger than his Treescapes truck. Her own car, a duck-egg-blue vintage Fiat 500, lived in the double garage at the front of the house. She wasn't a huge fan of driving, but she used to love pootling along the King's Road in her little bubble car. Even breaking down was part of the experience, passers-by smiling at her as she laboured over the intricate engine, her long, golden mane flipped to one side.

'Adam . . .'

'What? I did.' His tone was sharp with warning, as though she'd displeased him enough already this evening and he had his limit. He turned to the girls, his voice suddenly terse, any lightness evaporated. 'And I think one chased me when I went running. I'm just telling you so you know to be careful while you're here.'

'Adam,' Coralie repeated, more forcefully. These were her children. It wasn't right to terrify them. And what would Fraser think if they repeated this back to him? He was unscrupulous. He'd use any excuse to stop the girls from seeing her.

'For real?' Bea, her elder daughter said, eyes wide and alert.

'For real.' He nodded.

Her usually reserved girls both began asking Adam questions at once, talking over each other. Their enthusiasm stunned her into silence as Adam genially answered their questions. Why did she suddenly feel as though she were in competition with him, her daughters the prize?

'What do you think, Mummy?' Iris finally asked, and even Bea deigned to look interested in her response.

'It's . . . possible,' she said. 'They have been spotted in Kent before.' In spite of her disquiet, her heart fluttered in her chest. Could this be the thing to interest her daughters in nature, rather than lip gloss and synthetically manufactured fruit-smelling pens? When Bea was younger she'd loved sounding out the Latin names for flowers and plants, the families and sub-families of insects. Coralie could remember clapping in delight at her recall. But that sunny little child had gone, morphed into a sullen twelve-year-old who pretended she was bored by just about everything.

'Wow,' Bea breathed.

'Have you checked the cams, Mummy?' Iris asked enthusiastically. 'Maybe we could look with you tomorrow?'

'Remember I told you they had to be removed—' she began, but Adam spoke over her: 'What a great idea! We could all look in the morning!'

'Sure,' she said instead, wrongfooted. How many times had she tried to show them a playful family of foxes, replete with a skulk of cute fur babies, and they'd curled their lips with disinterest? But she recognized this look, knew it was the way she used to gaze at her own grandmother. With rapture. She fingered the delicate chain around her neck.

'Have you seen anything? Have you seen the cat?' Iris pressed.

'No, I haven't,' she faltered. She had the girls' attention. In that moment she'd have done anything to retain it. 'But—'

'What have you seen?' Bea's voice jumped with excitement.

Coralie glanced at Adam, who was looking at her curiously. She couldn't remember the last time Bea had looked at her this way. It was arresting. Wasn't this what she'd always wanted? To replicate the bond she'd felt with her grandmother with her daughters?

It wasn't a coincidence that when Adam had wanted to move somewhere more leafy to develop his tree-surgeon skills Coralie had convinced him it had to be Sevenoaks. She'd told him she'd spent summers here as a child, at her grandmother's cottage, and that much was true. But they hadn't been spent picnicking in long grass or swimming in streams, as she'd implied. Her grandmother had been like her. She hadn't wanted to see big cats locked up in cages. Had never forgiven Coralie's parents for keeping them at home. She had believed, even then, that big cats were naturalizing in England. She had been drawn, like Coralie, to finding them.

They had spent their summers watching deer silently from afar, or eyes to the ground, searching for scat and paw prints. Just instinct and attention to detail. The first time Coralie had seen a big cat in the wild, rather than in her living room, was with her grandmother, in the woods bridging St Michael's Club with Knole Park. They had heard stories on the grapevine: a local farmer had lost two sheep and there had been two sightings in the same spot.

They had kept going back, night after night, until finally, they had seen it. It was still light, only dusk, and Coralie, at nine, the same age as Elwood, had spent that whole summer feeling on the cusp of something. She could still remember the moment, the weight of her binoculars resting on her chest, her shoulders bare in her lemon sundress, pressed against the cool cotton of her grandmother's, all her senses on high alert. The cat had stared at her, their eyes locked in a moment of connection, before elegantly slipping away. She couldn't help but think of Cleopatra. It had felt like a message, a sign, from a higher power. And just like that, she was hooked.

'I— she faltered again. 'I saw a hare being chased. By something *fast*. It's difficult with the cams. The area is huge – you're lucky if you catch even a small snippet of—'

'Yes, yes, Mummy,' Bea urged impatiently. 'But what did you *see*?'

'Well . . . nothing,' she admitted. 'But I heard a strangled cry off camera, as whatever it was caught up with its prey.' Her fingers flared, witch-like, as she became caught up in her story, thrilled to be holding their attention.

'Did it eat it?' Iris shrieked.

'I'm afraid so,' Coralie said, snuggling her on to her lap.

'And do you think that was a wild cat?' Bea asked, more measured now, scientific. An echo of Coralie.

She felt the heat of Adam's attention back on her, felt herself caught, the ubiquitous rabbit in headlights. She readied herself to look at him.

'Could be.' Her eyes met his, her palms open like a storyteller, but what she said was true.

'Imagine if we see one,' Bea said, in as excited a tone as Coralie suspected it was possible for a tweenager to generate.

She scratched the side of her head as Bea and Iris babbled excitedly about finding footage of 'Adam's cat' *(for goodness' sake)*, asking whether she'd be able to download it so they could show their friends. *'Imagine how many likes you'd get!'* one was saying, and she made a note to remonstrate with Fraser. She'd been very clear she didn't want either girl on social media yet.

The girls went inside with Adam to watch a reality show she'd never heard of. She tidied the table as slowly and as quietly as she could, listening in the gaps between the clink of cutlery and glassware. Her breath held, every twig snap sending a jolt through her, every gentle lift of the breeze stirring something untamed within her. She felt *alive*.

The earlier peachy sky had evolved to streaks of blue-grey and lilac which darkened, fraction by fraction, as she watched. Her eyes couldn't help but be drawn to the dark expanse of the Parkland beyond their garden, its soil, its very soul, rich with dangers and secrets.

The Mystery of the Sevenoaks Panther

Jimmy Sands, member of Puddleford Angling Society: I was night-fishing, with my dad. We did it once a month. Never had any bother before. But that night, it was different. We'd set up as usual, and we were staring out at the lake. The bigger one, in Puddleford Parkland. Suddenly, I heard breathing. Coming from behind us. Raspy breathing, like an old man . . .

James Sands, member of Puddleford Angling Society: Oi!

Jimmy: [Smirks at his father] All right, like a zombie. I said after, didn't I? That sounded like a zombie. [Looks back to the camera.] Seriously, though, we were shitting it. Just eyeballing each other in the dark.

James: Never heard a sound like it. Like Jim said, we were too scared to move! Frozen, like. And we're both big lads.

Jimmy: The sound got closer and closer and closer . . . [Pause.] But then? [Pause.] It went dead silent.

James: And that was worse than the breathing! We must've stayed another, what? Ten minutes? Felt like ten hours.

Jimmy: And then Dad just looked at me and said: 'Son, I think we'd better leg it.' So we did. Look, we're laughing about it now, but believe me, we weren't laughing then!

13

Twig

It was around 9 p.m., the children tucked up in bed when Bob staggered into the kitchen, his face wan and pale. Twig was engaged in her nightly routine, responding to comments on her blog. She didn't notice her dad at first, preoccupied as she was with the analytics from her website.

Dad?' She realized Bob was still standing motionless by the back door.

'It's Cupid,' he croaked, referencing the grey-and-white cat from Number 16. 'I think. I was just out doing my final check of the lawn . . .'

His arms were raised, bearing a tea towel. With his eyes locked on hers, he raised one half of the checked fabric. It revealed a big, fluffy tail.

'What the—' Curiosity won over revulsion and, in fact, Twig was rarely squeamish. She sprung up to inspect it, her eyes flicking to the tail and back to her father. It had Cupid's distinctive grey-and-white stripes.

'I found it.' He swallowed. 'In the garden. While I was out checking for cat business.'

'Yikes.' Twig frowned. She didn't need to articulate what no doubt Bob was thinking. It was unfortunate that it was Bob, vociferous in his dislike of cats, and Cupid especially, who had found its tail. 'What are you going to do?'

'I don't know, love.' He kept his hands raised. His voice was a curious mix of calm with a wobbly intonation, like he could cross over into hysteria at any moment.

'Maybe it isn't Cupid.' She put her arm around him. 'Do you want me to come with you to Tim and Martina's and they can take a look?'

'What can I say?' The hysteria was gaining an advantage. 'I found this in my garden? I mean . . . where's the rest of it?'

They turned their heads towards the kitchen sink. The garden, and the Parkland beyond, were a deep blue in the seconds before darkness fell, framed in the window between pine cabinets that hadn't been updated since the eighties.

Twig had a sudden, jarring image of her parents' old-fashioned kitchen as the scene of a slasher flick, a blood-red rip torn down the middle of a cinema poster. *It's just a fox*, she reminded herself. *A fox on a crime spree.* But she felt her pulse quicken with anxiety.

Every now and then – despite the penances of the vegan and alcohol-free diet, and the weightlifting – she could feel panic building, a low, rumbling roar. She knew, if it got too loud, it had the power to engulf her. She didn't have time to think about all that now. She had to focus on Skylar and raising the money for the vaccine. Worrying about the Sevenoaks Panther would have to wait.

14

Emma

Emma had an ear bud in, eating breakfast in the garden, when the ringtone of her phone interrupted her, cutting off one of Coralie's monologues to Adam from a few days earlier. Her new listening devices had arrived and were all in situ, keeping her busy. She considered declining Agatha's call to finish listening. Poor Adam didn't say a thing as Coralie wittered on about her conservation work. God, it was boring, but she couldn't help feeling that eventually it would yield something. *Say it to my face*, Emma thought crossly as she daydreamed about shagging Coralie's husband. Nonetheless, she accepted the call.

'Emma,' Agatha said urgently, 'something's going on.'

No shit, she thought. The more you paid attention to this neighbourhood, the more you realized there was *all sorts* going on. 'What do you mean?'

'Kofi's *freaking out*. He went out early for a cycle—'

'*Again?*' Emma was exasperated for her. Kofi's lengthy cycles had been a sore point in the Jeffersons' household for some time. He'd got so obsessed at one point that he had a minor heart attack after a particularly long ride. That had put him off for a while, that and the recovery time, but he'd been slowly building his activity levels up since. She didn't know how Agatha could stand it.

'No, it's fine. We agreed he could go out super early, so he went at five.' She spoke quickly, as if keen to get back to the main point. 'But that's the thing. Just as he was about to set off, he saw something *dead* by our back gate!'

Agatha and Kofi lived further around the curve of the Briar Heart Estate, the top-left ventricle, if you like, and, as with their end of Briar Close, their house also backed on to the Parkland.

'What do you mean, "something dead"?'

'Like a dead body!'

'A dead *body*?'

'Not a *human* body. A deer. A carcass, or whatever you call it. He said its throat was all bloody and just spilled all over the path and—'

'Aggie! I'm eating my breakfast!' Emma pushed her sausage sandwich away. An upside to her running regularly was eating sausages guilt-free.

'Sorry, sorry. Anyway, he was super grossed out, but he went for his ride and then, when he got back – it was gone! There was nothing there, just *blood* seeped into the soil like something from a—'

Emma frowned at her plate. 'Did he take a photo?'

'No, he hadn't taken his phone, just his watch, and he was going to take one when he got back,' Agatha said in a frustrated, *seriously, could you keep up* tone.

'Okay.'

'Okay? He must have narrowly avoided the panther! It must've been *mid-kill* when he set off, *hiding*, and then came back to get the rest of its breakfast.' She shuddered. 'What if it had fancied *Kofi* for breakfast?'

Emma couldn't help but laugh at the idea of big, muscular, six-foot-something Kofi served up on a plate for the Sevenoaks Panther.

'It's not funny, Emma! This is serious! I think Adam was right. I think he did see one on his car! And the Butterfields' kittens being eaten. More people are talking about it now. It's a thing, Emma! I don't care what Coralie King says: there's a panther on the loose, and it's only a matter of time until it attacks someone!'

Come on, Emma wanted to say. It was too fantastical. Something Elwood would have read in one of his science-fiction books. Still, if that's what it took to distract them all from her planning proposals, a made-up campfire story, who was she to complain?

'What are we going to do?' Agatha's voice was still panicked. 'Are you walking Henry up to cricket?' In the summer term, cricket dominated Saturday mornings.

'Of course I am. What, do you think we're going to be hunted in the Parkland?' She was joking, but saying those words aloud still made her shiver involuntarily. She glanced at her watch and stood.

'Maybe!' Agatha shrieked. She lowered her voice. 'People are saying Adam King is too afraid to go out. No one's seen him in ages. He's not turning up for jobs. And he's married to a zoologist! He would know if we were in danger. Don't you think it's all a bit suss?'

Emma raised her laptop from the lawn, balancing it on her knees. The bookmarked webpage loaded. Her theory was right; there'd been a slump in complaints on the planning portal. Only two this morning, compared to thirteen by this time yesterday. The Sevenoaks Panther to the rescue! She struggled to swallow a bark of laughter. Punched the air silently instead.

'You're right,' she agreed, 'that is strange. Let me know what I can do to help.'

15

Coralie

She'd slept in the greenhouse. She often did if she had trouble sleeping or if Adam was in one of his moods. She felt safer out here. Adam used to complain but grew sick of her tossing and turning beside him and now seemed relieved when she did. Sometimes she felt there was no greater place to slumber, no better start to the day than coming round in her grandmother's chair as a new day dawned, a fresh start.

She mused on the girls' excitement last night, her promise to show them the cam footage this morning. She hoped they'd forget; she'd feel terrible having to dash their hopes, but what if, small as the chance might be, there *was* something interesting to see in the footage? Bea would have it on social media in seconds. There wasn't time for her to check it all now. She'd have to tell them she'd forgotten to turn them on. Perhaps she could distract them with something else? A walk around the nature reserve with a picnic? Although she had a sinking feeling that wouldn't cut it.

She strode up towards the house, sun already warming the pale brick, all the people she loved inside.

'Morning, Socks,' she sang, seeing him up ahead. The lawn was covered in something – snow? but no, it couldn't be snow; it was May – and Socks was in the middle of it all, bent over.

Her approach might have scared another cat away, but Socks

was always confident of his position in the street, and certainly in Coralie's back garden, and besides, he was too actively engaged, licking and nibbling at . . . a dead bird?

She gasped, her stomach elevating to her throat. '*Socks!*' she cried out as she ran. 'What are you doing?' The sad wet mass wasn't feathers, or a bird at all, but Fwuffy, the girls' pet rabbit. Her eyes flicked up to their bedrooms, where the curtains were still drawn. *Oh my God!* She'd have to hide it somehow! But the white fur was everywhere. She felt tears of panic spring into her eyes.

What the— She must have escaped from her cage, but Coralie had checked it herself last night on the way to her greenhouse.

As she got closer to Fwuffy's delicate white bones, flesh cleanly torn, she was engulfed with unease. All that remained of their beloved pet was a rib and a fibula and a pillowcase-worth of fluff. Socks hadn't done this. She wasn't sure even a fox could have done this. They lacked the clean precision. But she knew what could . . .

She turned towards the house and saw Adam and the girls, not in their rooms but watching her from inside, their pale faces ascending like stairs, their mouths perfect 'O's of shock.

The house and the garden and the Parkland beyond began to swim, encircling her.

'*Now* do you believe me?' Adam was saying when she stumbled towards him. '*Now* are you going to take me seriously?' She couldn't answer, her brain struggling to catch up with the reality before her.

'We need to do something about this,' Adam was saying. 'Investigating it' – his fingers made air quotes, his tone implying that this was her fault – 'isn't enough!'

'Girls,' she said weakly. 'Upstairs.' And when they didn't move: '*Upstairs. Now.*'

'Has Socks eaten Fwuffy?' Iris sobbed.

'A fox,' Coralie stated, not wanting to alarm, her thoughts racing. 'Fwuffy must have got out of her cage – you know how she escapes sometimes – and a fox got her.'

'A fox!' Iris repeated, her sobs turning to a wail.

'Did any of you take Fwuffy out last night?' She struggled to dampen her accusatory tone. Adam and the girls all shook their heads.

'Was it the Sevenoaks Panther?' Bea whispered in a scared, quiet voice.

'Maybe we should call the police,' Adam muttered beside her.

'To tell them our pet rabbit died?' she sniped in a low voice.

He glared at her, eyes liquid with hate. She held it for a beat.

'What do you want to happen?' she whispered. 'Let them loose on the Parkland with guns?' She flung out her arm.

'If that's what it takes!' he hissed.

'Fwuffy!' Iris had her face pressed to the glass, staring at the unmoving pile of fluff. Her cries escalated something within Coralie. A long-buried loss. She put her hands to her ears as she tried to think, but Iris's wails penetrated her flesh and bone.

'Bea, Take your sister upstairs,' she said sharply. 'She's *traumatizing* herself.' Then she muttered: 'This is why I never wanted to get a pet.' She didn't mean it, she was lashing out in the moment, but she couldn't help herself.

Adam gave her a look as if to say, *that's a bit unfair*, but she silenced him with a steely stare. It was novel, having the upper hand. She needed to think.

'But—' Bea said.

'*Now*, Bea.'

'Fine.' Bea stomped sulkily over to her sister, prising her fingers away from the glass. Her voice dropped unusually softly as she tried to tug her sister away. 'Come on, Irie.'

'You said you were looking into this. You said there was nothing to worry about.' Adam's mouth was inches from her face. She swallowed, sweat prickling along her hairline.

'There isn't!' she cried. 'Cats don't hurt people.' She bent over, her hands on the table. That much was true. 'And they don't hunt . . . pets.' On that, she wasn't so sure. This was Bea's fault. She was sure of it.

He strode away and slammed a hand on the kitchen island with an anguished roar, as though to stop himself lashing out at her. 'Didn't you learn about this sort of thing when you were at uni? There must be ways to deter them? To protect ourselves.'

She closed her eyes. Even if a cat had done this, she couldn't let Adam hurt it. She couldn't allow him to involve the police, to have it *hunted*.

'But Adam, I have been looking into it. I told you. It's all conjecture, bored suburban housewives gossiping, wild theories spiralling out of control. I don't know what else I can tell you.' Her voice had taken on the pleading, wobbly tone that usually appeased him.

She pictured the news getting out. Police, or trophy-hunters, flooding the Parkland. Her heart hammered in her chest, her mind drifting to the photograph on her greenhouse wall. The fur-coated woman walking a leopard along Knightsbridge. Humans have been close to wild cats in the past. Where was that wild cat, or its cubs, now?

She turned back to the garden, where Fwuffy's remains lay scattered. She gripped the back of a chair, the world gently spinning. 'Cats don't hurt people,' she repeated, comforting herself with facts and science. *Unless they're provoked.* She batted the thought away.

'Please, Coralie. There must be something we can do? I don't feel safe going outside any more, let alone the girls. I think we should get a gun!'

'A gun? Jesus Christ, Adam, this is modern suburbia, not the Wild West.'

Just then the doorbell sounded. Emma stood on the step outside, an apologetic look on her face. 'Sorry to bother you so early, Coralie, but I promised Agatha I'd pop over . . .' She trailed off as Coralie pondered the least rude way to get rid of her.

Emma lowered her voice. 'Kofi saw something early this morning in the Parkland. A deer *carcass*. And then it disappeared, but there was no one else about.' Her speech became slow and drawn out as she overenunciated: 'They think he disturbed the Sevenoaks Panther *mid-kill-*'

Coralie nodded her head. 'Leave it with me,' she said – *did she say it, or did she just think it as she closed the door on Emma?* She wasn't sure. She didn't care. She leaned back against the thick oak, knowing the girls and Adam were all waiting for a solution from her. An answer. A way to fix this, because that's what she did, and if she couldn't fix things, what use would she be to them? What use would she be to anyone? Sweat dripped from her temples.

Deep breaths, Coralie, deep breaths.

In her hand, her phone lit up: the messaging group was buzzing with concern about the big cat.

I heard the Channings' cat is missing too. Do you know them? They live near the duck pond, apparently.

Yes, and did you hear what happened to Tim and Martina's cat, Cupid? Just its tail left! It's quite frightening, isn't it?

Valerie's old cocker spaniel's been had. Crawled under a hedgerow and disappeared! I mean, that's not a small dog.

No, no, he's been found. Turned up back at home. Poor Valerie. Can you imagine how scared she was?

This isn't funny now.

Someone needs to do something.

Who's up for joining a patrol, or something, in the Parkland?

Moments later: *Please follow this link to indicate your availability: Parkland Patrol.*

She walked as if in a trance into their lounge, to the vintage globe, removed a bottle of whiskey and swigged straight from the bottle. She had a flashback. Her father doing the same. Revulsion shot through her.

She took another swig, and a deep breath. She thought of Cleopatra. The policeman with the gun. This was her chance at redemption. She couldn't blow it.

JUNE

The Mystery of the Sevenoaks Panther

Dax: Look, I don't wanna talk bad about the bloke. [Rubs fingers along his jawline.] He was a mate.

Tommy: [Interjects:] Be fair though, Daxy. He messed you around a bit, mate.

Dax: Well. [Falters.] Yeah. But. I dunno. I felt like there was more to it.

Tommy: [To camera.] It was like this. Housey – Adam – had just moved to Sevenoaks from London and was looking for a job. He got in touch with Sol, our boss, and started working at Oaks Tree Surgeons. So far so good. Don't get me wrong, I liked the bloke; he was funny, he liked a smoke, we had a laugh. But he was unreliable. His bird would turn up and just stand there watching, and he'd get all flustered – I suppose it was quite sweet, really – but then he wouldn't turn up for the next few days. Didn't finish the job. Never known someone have so many stomach aches. He was forever in bed. With his bird. [Laughs again.]

Dax: It wasn't like that. He told me he felt awkward with some of the clients. [Shoots a knowing glance at Tommy.]

Tommy: Oh, yeah. Housewives' Favourite. That must've been awful for him. [Rolls his eyes.] That's why we called him Housey. Sol told us his word-of-mouth recommendations went through the roof after Housey joined. [Grins.]

Dax: Anyway. He decided to start up his own business. TreeScapes. So he'd have more control over the clients, who he worked for, like. Persuaded me to come and work for him. He'd bought all the gear, got a new truck.

Tommy: [Interjects:] His bird bought him all that.

Dax: [Dismisses Tommy with a wave.] I thought, why not? Sol was raging, but he hadn't given us a payrise in three years. What did he expect? [Shrugs.] Anyway, for the first few months it was great. Loads of work, more money. But then it just sort of petered out. He'd say we weren't getting any enquiries, but my mum heard people complaining that Oaks Tree Surgeons was too short-staffed and Treescapes was too busy to take on more work. It didn't add up.

Tommy: Tell 'em about that last job.

Dax: [Shoots Tommy a look. Shakes his head.]

Tommy: Go on. It might have something to do with what happened.

Dax: [Looks off camera, as though weighing something up.] Fine. [Sighs.] It was back in early June. The job was for an old bloke on the Briar Heart Estate. He had a big oak tree with Ganoderma. It needed felling. Such a shame. Beautiful old thing, but they hollow out from the inside. You don't know when they'll come down. Nothing to be done. Anyway, we're there at the bottom, harnessed up, chainsaws ready. You have to start with the highest branches.

Work your way down. We had a couple of other lads helping as it was big job. And Housey just stood there at the bottom of the tree, shaking, like. He couldn't go up it. Never seen anything like it on a job. I had to go back to Sol and ask for my job back. I was pissed off.

Tommy: You ever heard of it? A gaffer scared of trees! [Laughs.]

Dax: It wasn't funny. He was terrified, like. And I only heard after that it was him who first saw the Sevenoaks Panther. On his truck. I think he was . . . he was really losing it. I wish now I'd said something. Checked he was all right.

Tommy: [Sobers.] It wasn't your fault, mate. You weren't to know what would happen. [Squeezes Dax on the shoulder.]

[Dax nods. Both men exhale loudly and look down.]

16

Coralie

Restlessness suffused the packed church hall more effectively than the thin breeze from the high windows and wedged-open door. The whispers travelled from those standing at the back to Coralie centre stage at the front: *Did you hear about the sighting at the lake? The pizza delivery guy saw it too! Have you joined the patrol?*

The clawing heat didn't help the rumours. She pictured sweat dripping down red-hot skin as her neighbours clustered before fans, fingers pounding disgruntled messages into the neighbourhood chat. The majority were enforcing a 'pet curfew', locking their beloved pets in for hot, sticky nights when they should be outside, air cooling against their fur. She had to do *something*.

She began to speak, sensing the change in atmosphere, the charge in the air peaking and falling, like a star. 'Thank you for inviting me to join you here today. As some of you know, I have a degree in zoology and know a little about big cats.' She wore a long white dress with flared sleeves cuffed at the wrist and muddy boots, as though she'd traversed a moor like an Austen heroine, set on saving them. 'I'm at your disposal.' She gave a little bow.

The hall had originally been booked by the Jutland Residents' Association, to discuss the Brooks' planning application, but so many of the neighbours had begged Coralie to provide an information session on the Sevenoaks Panther instead that she couldn't say no. Tim sat sulkily to her left in tennis whites, hoping for a chance to speak.

'Thank you, Coralie, love,' a watery voice called from the front: Valerie, with her cocker spaniel in its pram.

Coralie opened her arms to her congregation. 'Where would you like to begin?'

'Do you think there's a wild cat in the Parkland?' a man in a linen shirt with a fedora on his lap asked.

She had a role to play here, a remit: to reduce local hysteria. Stop this thing in its tracks before it got any more out of control: 'I don't think there's one *living* in the Parkland, but I do believe they occasionally pass through.'

'One's taken a liking to Sevenoaks, have they? Decided to stick around.'

'He must like cricket!' a big-bearded man in a pink-and-blue-checked suit joked, and Coralie tipped her head to one side and raised her eyebrows: *don't waste my time.*

'Cats are more likely to utilize train lines. They're lazy. They'll take an easier path rather than pushing through bush and undergrowth like in the Parkland. But the Parkland's not a million miles from the track.' She shrugged.

'So it's the fast line he likes!' the checked-suited man joked.

She smiled benignly.

'They've been spotted at Bluewater Shopping Centre. Ever since it opened,' a woman in high-end athleisure, sunglasses perched on her head, called eagerly.

'Yes. I've heard that too,' Coralie agreed. 'But this is different. There's no real evidence of a big cat operating here. A sighting at dusk with poor visibility . . .' She was referring to Adam's infamous sighting, grateful he was at home. 'And the loss of a small number of pets, does not—'

'What should we do if we see one?' a teenager with huge headphones slung round his neck called out, cutting her off.

'That's *extremely* unlikely.'

'But what if we do?' a lady in a marigold silk dress and a string of pearls urged, and the crowd pressed too, a sea of mumbled affirmations.

She sighed. She pictured her mother, smoothing her golden hair behind her ear, a pearl earring gleaming: *Give them what they want.*

'Very well.' She drew herself up, squaring her shoulders, and moved to the aisle, a clear path dividing the rows of chairs into two sections to her left and right. Strips of sunlight cascaded through the windows, illuminating dust motes as they fell. 'Let's pretend there's a big cat over there.' She gestured to the middle of the aisle. The crowd's heads turned collectively to the shimmering space, balletic. She twirled her hand, conjuring a beast made of sunlight and dust. She could see it so clearly.

'First thing – enjoy the moment.' She gave the teen, and the phone on his lap, a pointed look. 'You are two wild creatures, on this wild earth, in a unique moment of connection. Don't rush to grab your phone. Give this majestic being the respect it deserves.'

The room was silent for a beat. In truth, she was beginning to enjoy herself, holding court.

'Oh, come on!' a man in a rugby top heckled. 'What if it chases us?'

A hubbub of chatter rose like a wave, but she raised her left palm, stilling its swell.

'In the – again – *extremely unlikely* event that you feel threatened, remember: if a cat is demonstrating aggressive behaviour, it is afraid of *you*. Especially if you have gone wandering into its territory.' She adjusted her tone to sound teacherly, an anticipatory telling-off, hoping to inject a sufficient note of fear. 'Think for a moment, how would you feel if an intruder wandered into your home unannounced?' She pointed a finger at the check-suited man. He crossed and uncrossed his legs under the beam of her gaze, pulled on his lapels.

Her speech took on a musical quality, almost like a drum beat

100

as she paced at the front of the room. She wanted her audience to learn by rote.

'Don't aggravate the cat.

'Don't run. That could trigger a predatory response.

'Stand tall. Keep your composure.' She extended her arms outwards by way of example and walked down the aisle, her magical cat evaporating in the golden light as she passed through. 'Walk calmly away, keeping your eyes on the cat. *Always* remember the golden rule . . .' She reached the end of the aisle and spun back around, her long blonde hair glowing as it caught the early-evening light, every eye in the room fixed upon her. *Never turn your back on a cat.*'

A young man in a 'herbivore' T-shirt gulped as she clipped briskly to the front of the room. Across the sea of faces she noticed one or two phones pointed in her direction. She felt a prickle of unease.

'Cats don't like loud noises.'

'So should we all be carrying a horn?'

'Maybe. They prefer to hunt at dawn and dusk.'

'So should we avoid going out at those times?'

'If you like.' She shrugged, secretly thinking: *imbeciles.*

A neat-looking woman in the middle of the room with straight dark hair and glasses raised a hand, and Coralie nodded, trying to place her.

'If it's true, like you said, if they're out there, not hurting any-body, why isn't anything being done to protect them?' Oh yes, she was a teaching assistant at Puddleford School.

'I don't know,' Coralie answered truthfully, surprised by the question. 'It would require an enormous amount of research. They'd need to become a recognized species in Britain, granted protected status. My hunch is the authorities fear insurance claims, from farmers and the like. Effectively, if they were recognized, they'd become the government's problem.'

'And they've got enough of those themselves!' a young woman with a baby on her lap shouted.

'Quite. It could also spark vigilante behaviour.' She prayed this wasn't a prediction of what was to come.

There was a clamour of voices and, again, the neat-looking woman calmly raised her hand. 'But isn't there a counterargument, that it could encourage tourism to certain areas? Isn't that what happened with the Beast of Bodmin?'

'Perhaps. But that's very risky. There's a high chance you could encourage the wrong sort of people.' She paled at the thought. She couldn't allow that to happen. She wouldn't.

17

Twig

Twig opened the fridge, enjoying the waves of cool air, as she stared at her dad's icy beers longingly. Blake materialized, and, as if reading her thoughts, reached into the fridge for a beer herself, popping the bottle cap on the side of the kitchen counter.

'You don't mind, do you?' she said apologetically, pulling herself up to sit on the worktop. 'It's so hot today.'

Twig chewed on the inside of her cheek, gazing past Blake to her mother's roses outside. The once tight-lipped buds had turned blowsy and indecent, swaying sultrily in the warm air. 'I know. I've been stuck in the car on the motorway with no A/C.'

'Sucks,' Blake said companionably, missing Twig's pointed tone and taking a long swig of her beer. 'Can you believe this meeting Coralie held? I heard your dad talking about it. Why is everyone going so nuts?'

Twig felt a wave of irritation. Later she would wonder if she had been trying to start an argument with what she said next. 'I've had an idea.' She looked Blake square in the eye. 'I'm going to update my GoFundMe page. Tell people who we really are.'

Blake spluttered on her beer. 'I'm sorry? Who really are we?' she asked sardonically.

Blake had never explicitly told Twig she didn't like her bringing Pineapple Punk up, because, despite her many hours of therapy,

Blake rarely explicitly said there was anything she didn't like. It was in the trace of disdain as she pouted, or flicked her eyes away, her unwillingness to engage. Twig just knew it would press her buttons and, fuck me, did Twig want to press her buttons. Did she want to make Blake feel an ounce of the irritation she was feeling, watching her swig at her icy-cold beer in the unbearably hot kitchen?

Twig began rooting around in the fridge. 'You know, mention that we used to be in a band. Maybe put some links to our old music. *Galvanize* people.' She began pulling salad ingredients out of the fridge with gusto – spinach, peppers, tomatoes. 'I want to make some noise. Really ramp things up. Bring this home.'

'Woah there, Nelly,' Blake was saying, both hands clutching her bottle, leaning back on the counter as though rearing up. 'What's the point?'

'So more people see it, obviously.' Twig pulled some quinoa and chickpeas from the cupboard. Filled the kettle. 'Maybe some of your colleagues in the music industry will notice. Generate some buzz.'

Blake had gone quiet. When Twig glanced over she was silently sipping at her beer. 'I've told you I don't want to tap up my clients. It's inappropriate.'

'*Inappropriate?* How?' Twig had a large knife in one hand and a chopping board in the other.

'They'll feel obliged to—'

'Well, good,' Twig cut in. 'That's the whole point!' She pulled a bag of sweet potatoes from a cupboard and tore at the plastic. They spilled out, rolling over the countertop. 'How is it any different to when we sponsored Laird to run the marathon?'

'*Totally* different. That was for, like, a generic charity.'

'Right. A generic charity. That's far more important than our daughter.' She seized a sweet potato and chopped at it viciously.

As though sensing they had gone off course, again, Blake said in a placatory tone: 'It's still months away. We have time.'

'The procedure, yes, but we need the cash in our account to book everything. To be ready to go. Why are you being so obtuse?

Now isn't the time to be all laid back about it.' Twig was all clipped tones and business now, covering the potato cubes in olive oil and rosemary and switching on the oven. She was doing everything backwards, because she could barely think straight, she was so angry.

'I don't want to put us – *our family* – on show,' Blake said, disembarking from the counter and landing gently on her feet. There was a quality in how she said it, as if that's what Twig was proposing, putting them on show as some sort of selfish attention-seeking, rather than because she was getting desperate. And Blake should be desperate too. Why wasn't she?

Blake placed the empty bottle in the sink and headed back to the sanctuary of the garage, no doubt to download their argument to her therapist.

Twig stayed in the kitchen, silently preparing dinner, tears streaming down her face.

Later, after the plates had been cleared away, the children were in bed and Blake was back in the garage, Twig crept outside. She walked to the end of the garden and climbed the rickety steps of her old treehouse. Like everything else at her parents' house, it was dilapidated, and her foot slipped on a rotten rung. She still felt a sense of calm when she crawled inside. It was just light enough to see. It felt like a bunker, her own sanctuary, once everyone had had a piece of her for the day.

She flopped on to a beanbag and leaned back, looking out of the window. She could see the tops of the trees, the outline of a crescent moon waiting for its chance to shine. She reached into her pocket and pulled out Adam's half-smoked spliff from the dinner party a month ago. In the fuss, no one had noticed her pick it up, squirrel it away into her pocket. She sniffed its aromatic scent and placed it on her lap.

Ahead of her, the dark Parkland brooded in the close summer air. Elwood's binoculars hung on a nail beside the window. She smiled; her own binoculars had hung there when she was a child,

105

though she had been seeking stars and planets, not a mythical panther. Increasingly, Adam's 'sighting' felt unreal, Cupid's fluffy tail an unfortunate fox-related incident, and the panic since, as Coralie had predicted, people overreacting. They would know, wouldn't they, if there were a huge carnivore living just beyond their back gardens? Twig would know.

Another memory popped into her head, unbidden. She removed the lighter from her pocket. Flicked the dial, watching the flame, but she couldn't stop the recollection. If anything, it burned brighter. A crackling fire, a cosy pub, an arm, heavy, weighing her down when she felt in danger of floating away, her hand warm on his leg beneath the table as if they were eighteen again. She flicked the lighter off.

The flashbacks had started with her dream: Matt outside, prowling the streets. She'd kept a lid on what they'd done, just after her mother had been diagnosed, for almost a decade. Twig back from Bali to see her mum. Matt visiting his dad, Frank, who was also unwell. She'd bumped into Matt at the pharmacy, collecting prescriptions. It was instinctive. Seeking out any comfort they could find, any connection to their past when they were young and life was easier and their parents were vibrant and still themselves. But they'd gone too far. They both knew it, the second they awoke in Twig's childhood bedroom, her father, mercifully, having stayed overnight at the hospital with her mother.

She hadn't known then that Emma was going through IVF. Hadn't met her at all. She hoped it would have changed things if she'd known Emma then, but she couldn't be sure. All she remembered was the relief as warm red wine tipped down her throat and the evening blurred. She'd returned to Bali. Returned to her life. Convinced Blake it was time to start a family. Accepted Kev's previous offer of help. It had been easy to forget. But being back here, living so close to Matt and Emma, it felt like the secret was rattling in its box, readying itself for escape.

She raised the spliff to her lips, flicked the lighter a final time and took a long, blissful drag.

18

Coralie

Coralie eyed the two notebooks on her desk. One notebook contained what she actually knew about the local wild cat (*the Sevenoaks Panther*, if you will) and the other what she'd like Adam, and everyone else, to know. She was working with a fervour she hadn't experienced since university. It was enthralling. Exhilarating. She didn't want it to stop.

She'd been shaken up when she'd found Fwuffy in the garden, briefly engulfed by fear, but then she'd reminded herself of the facts: cats didn't hurt people. They avoided them. All the evidence pointed to an active wild cat nearby, but she couldn't share the whole picture, what was really going on, with anyone else, except perhaps Socks, just to get it off her chest.

It made her feel whole and full, as she had when she was pregnant, harbouring this secret. Whisper it: *a wild cat living in Puddleford Parkland*. A girlish giggle escaped her, light and full of air. *The wonder of it. A majestic creature unsettling the balance of the bland suburbs*. It sent a delicious thrill through her body. She could never divulge it. It would alarm people. Terrify them. That's why she had to keep downplaying it. No one else would recognize the beauty of it. Their misplaced fear would turn it into something else. Something ugly. Big cats didn't go near humans unless they were forced to, like in a zoo, or if they were starving, she supposed, but that wouldn't happen *here*; the countryside was their larder. Hares and badgers and pheasants. Foxes, ducks and geese. As well as the deer in Knole Park, there were plenty of farms . . .

Of course! Pulling up Google Earth, she located the nearest farms to Puddleford Parkland. Then she narrowed her search to those which had livestock. Duggan's Farm was the nearest, on the very outer perimeters, close to where the Parkland met the A21, the dual carriageway linking the M25 to the coast. She slipped both her notebooks into her large crochet tote and laced up her boots, a long-sleeved but loose-fitting dress her concession to the warmth.

She calculated how long it would take to walk: too long, especially on a hot day. Had Adam left the house this week? Maybe a drive out would do him good? She considered the risk of him insisting he accompany her during her interview: low. He'd stay in the car as he did a week or so ago when she needed to make a delivery to the food bank: air conditioning on, doors locked. She called up the stairs: 'Adam, could you give me a lift, please?'

'Mr Duggan?' she called a short time later as she crossed his yard. The air was still and close, the stench of the farm – excrement, ripped hides, the beginnings of life and the claw of death – rising in curving clouds of steam. She heard the crunch and scrape of metal clashing with earth. A beautiful golden ground beetle scuttled over the uneven stones, disappearing into a scattering of wild chives resplendent with their lilac crowns.

She walked through a stable, stroking the neck of a lone tan horse as she passed. *Poor creature.* Just beyond she found the source of the noise: a hot-looking man with red cheeks, a squashed nose and an incongruous curtain of hair swept to one side (her mother's voice purred in her ear delightedly: *a gentleman farmer*). 'Mr Duggan?' she called again. He was digging a trench, a half-drunk cup of tea on the wall beside him.

'Hello?' There was an uplift in his tone as though he were surprised, but pleased, to have a visitor.

She stuck out her hand, her grip as firm as his own as they shook hello. 'Coralie King. I'm investigating local sightings of the Sevenoaks Panther.' She kept her tone purposefully light to avoid an ugly scene: if he was a non-believer, as many were, she could gently laugh along with any mockery or scorn he might hurl her way. 'Have you seen anything?'

His face closed, immediately shutting down. 'From the paper, are you?' His voice arched with suspicion as he resumed digging.

'No,' she reassured him. 'I live locally, on the Briar Heart Estate. I have two daughters. I'm a governor at Puddleford School. And I'm a zoologist. I'm not here to cause any trouble.'

He struck his spade deep into the earth and rested his right foot on it.

'Who's the headteacher there these days?' he asked, appraising her properly now, visibly softening as she told him it was the amenable Mr Ambrose. Once she provided enough convincing commentary – Duggan's children had gone to Puddleford – and showed him her phone wasn't 'recording anything for the internet' he stepped away from his shovel and faced her completely.

'I've seen it.' He lowered his voice, his brown eyes penetrating hers. 'I went right past it on my quad bike last week. Thought I'd left out some black baler plastic. *I'll come back for it later*, I thought. But then when I reached the next field I remembered: *there wouldn't be baler plastic out there in June!* I turned back, curious, and it had gone. It was later I found the sheep. Throat ripped out. Blood still warm.'

'Did you tell anyone?' Coralie's heart juddered in her chest.

He turned back to his shovel, gripping it with his hands, shook his head. 'I told someone last time it happened. Laughed me out the pub. I won't make that mistake again.'

'It's happened before?' She felt the sun beating down on them both.

'A few years ago.'

Her breath swam out in relief. *A few years. Not last week.* It was like she'd said at the meeting. Like she *knew*. Wild cats had been around here for years, and might periodically take some livestock, but there were no reports of humans being hurt. *There was no danger.* The beads of sweat which had been holding along her temples began to drip down her cheeks. She wiped them away with a long cheesecloth sleeve as she offered her own reassurances: *I absolutely do believe you and, yes, I agree, it's best to keep it to ourselves.*

She heard the click of Adam releasing the central locking as she approached the car. It had been difficult to coax him out of the house. Through the windshield he looked defeated, his skin pallid, his very essence faded, as though he wasn't really there: a hologram. She had to hold her line: *wild cats don't hurt humans.* She plastered on a bright smile.

'Good news!' She climbed in and slammed the door. 'He's not seen *anything* untoward, nor heard anything from his contemporaries. And farmers love to gossip!' She tried to sound as upbeat and knowledgeable as she could.

Adam said nothing. His knuckles white as he clutched the steering wheel.

'Honestly, Adam, if there were an active wild cat in the area, the farmers would know about it.' She squeezed his leg. He stared resolutely ahead. It was easier, in some ways, him being like this. 'Come on, let's get back. I said I'd help out at the school this afternoon.'

The Mystery of the Sevenoaks Panther

Anton, Puddleford's milkman: Yes. I saw the Sevenoaks Panther. It followed my van early one morning. Tailed me through the quiet streets. Of course I was terrified! There's only so fast those vans can go, you know.

Why didn't I tell anyone at the time? [Scoffs.] Because who would've believed me then? [Laughs softly.]

19

Emma

Emma waved at Blake as she reversed off her drive, but her smile was forced. Blake had always held herself apart from her neighbours, with an air of 'just passing through'. This was all a stopgap for the Dorsetts, until Skylar's treatment finished and their financial constraints were over. Emma had never thought too much of it, but the more she got to know Twig, the more lonely Twig seemed. And the more she overheard them together, Twig trying to vent some of the stress of her day, Blake responding dismissively, Emma wondered whether, when it came to Twig, Blake was just passing through too.

She drove along a section of the thick stone wall that lined the outer perimeter of the Parkland, a relic from the days when this was a large private estate, passing purple and blue sprays of forget-me-nots, and parked down a narrow lane. Today she wasn't out hoping to catch a glimpse of Adam in his running vest, the fabric clinging to his tanned, muscular frame. Today she had bigger ambitions in mind.

A few days ago she'd overheard Coralie instructing an excitable Elwood on other possible evidence to look out for which would point to a big cat, and that had given her an idea. *Was she bored? Was she going mad?* She glanced at herself in her rear-view mirror: her cheekbones were taut, brushed with bronze from the warm weather, her skin clear. If she was bored and mad, it suited her.

Rather than letting the humiliation of the comments in the planning portal and her neighbours' sniping overcome her, on the contrary, their vitriol had invoked in her a sense of purpose, like the quickening flash of road rage. When she ran, formulating plans and ideas, she often pictured herself holding a flag aloft as she crossed an imaginary finishing line before a recalibrated Briar Heart House, its pink window frames and door glinting in the sun, her neighbours cowering in their dreary neutral homes, afraid to go out lest they encounter the Sevenoaks Panther. Emma Brooks triumphing over the small-minded snobs of Sevenoaks.

Leaving the car, she stretched and removed the small running backpack hidden below the shelf in the boot. Vines choked the fence posts which marked the lesser-known entrance to the Parkland. She gingerly side-stepped tangled patches of cow parsley and nettles that had sprung to knee height overnight. Then she ran.

The benefits of consistent running were starting to show, her breathing becoming more regular, the stitches – sharp little knives in her abdomen – coming later, or not at all. She didn't even follow Adam any more. In fact, she couldn't remember the last time she'd seen him go out for a run.

She stopped at a place she'd noticed last week: a tree the frequent Parkland walker, and certainly someone with a trained eye, would notice. She dug around in her bag, producing Matt's beloved penknife. Carefully removing the safety sheath, she began cutting scores into the tree, slowly working the wood as she smiled to herself: *claws out, Emma.* She turned the blade this way and that, shredding the bark until it mimicked the marks she'd seen in a photo. 'Cats like to keep their claws sharp and clean,' she said quietly, in a parody of Coralie's voice, her speech punctuated with exertion, sweat breaking over her skin. 'Look higher up,' she repeated as she stretched. 'Imagine a cat on its hind legs stretching. How tall would it reach?' She was on her tiptoes now, her vest riding up, the bark pressed against the bare skin of her torso. Finally satisfied, she stood back and grinned.

Next, she searched the ground until she found stones of a suitable size. She pressed them into the earth. It was close to clay, soft and malleable. If the local teenagers could fashion a pump track from it, she could manage a few paw prints. 'Look for the leading claw,' she intoned, waggling a finger like a schoolteacher as she leaned back on her heels to survey her handywork. She worked as quickly as she could, all her senses on fire. Moisture from the soil seeped into her knees despite the warm weather. Finally, her *pièce de résistance* (an oft-used Coralie phrase): small bones scattered in loose piles.

She ran a little further and repeated the process; ran further still, knees kissing the earth over and over. Traffic through the Parkland had already significantly reduced, especially outside of the school-run-patrol hours, but she still had to do it quickly in case anyone chanced upon her and asked what she was doing (*foraging for wild garlic*, she would say, or *she'd fallen over*, and gingerly indicate her ankle).

Someone would stumble across one of these scenes, surely? She imagined panic escalating swiftly enough that her renovation plans, and the steady stream of objections to them, would be long forgotten.

Her concentration was broken by a rapid crunch of twigs and leaves as though someone was crashing through the forest. For a second, she panicked: the cat! She gave herself an internal shake: *don't be daft, Emma*. Nonetheless, she was surprised how close to the surface her fear was, but it wasn't fear of a big cat, was it? It was fear of being found out. Her nerves were still alight when she heard a child's shout. She exhaled in relief, but that quickly turned to trepidation as the noise came closer. Suddenly her reasons sounded feeble, her intentions ridiculous.

How would she explain the tools in her hands, the small bones scattered nearby? Her heartbeat rose to join her brain in alarm. She began to crawl further into the woodland, away from the shouts, cursing and drawing in breath, her bare skin scraped by sharp shoots and spiky weeds.

She paused, panting, horror coiling around her limbs as a low, breathy growl curled in her ear. She turned her head, her arms quivering, and came face to face with a set of pale green eyes. She shrieked. Her knee rolled over a stick. Pain shot through her leg. She jerked, her shoulder twisting at an awkward angle, only then realizing it was a child. *Hadn't the child's parents heard there was a wild cat roaming the Parkland?* She exhaled shakily, and the child grinned, patting her on the head like a dog and running back the way she had come. Emma held her breath, nervous she would be discovered, but she heard a deep voice reunite with the child's bubbling giggles then fade as they moved away back to the main path. Relief drained into glee and she shook her head, laughing at her own behaviour. *Feral enough to be confused with a dog!*

Mindful of how easily she could be discovered, Emma crawled on, deeper into the Parkland, away from the carefully delineated pathway, reaching a small copse of trees. Behind it she was hidden. Free to inspect her knee. She flinched as she flexed it behind her, still on all fours, until the pain dulled and disappeared.

That was close, she breathed, flipping on to her back, hand on her chest as it rose and fell. Despite the heat, her brain felt sharp, purposeful. She drank some water and an energy gel, something she'd only recently learned existed, and felt pleased with herself. She could have spent this unsettling period moping, but instead she was evolving into a better self.

Reaching into her bag, she removed the skull she'd purchased online (literally anything could be bought online). She rubbed the surface with her thumb. It felt softer than she'd expected, and slightly porous. It had obviously been cleaned, prior to sale. Perhaps it was too clean? A sudden thought came to her and she slapped a hand to her forehead. *Yes!* She'd been needing a wee for ages.

The relief was acute as she pissed over the fox skull. She stared up at the film of blue sky and sighed with pleasure, wiped herself with a tissue (*she wasn't entirely undomesticated*) and afterwards rolled the skull around in the dry dirt. The resulting smears of mud and leaves gave it a more authentic look and she congratulated herself on her resourcefulness. *Her overgrown Boy Scout husband would be impressed.* Not that she could ever tell him about this.

There against a tree, her running shorts pulled down and fresh June air circumventing between her thighs, she felt a ripple of pleasure. Endorphins flooded her body. She felt *wild*, as she had that night when Adam touched her under the blanket. She listened carefully, heard only birdsong, rustling leaves and the distant rumble of the motorway. She was alone in the Parkland. She touched herself tentatively. Sunk her head back. She thought of Adam coming to her, in the woods, his mouth between her legs as she pressed herself up towards him. Towards the tree canopy and the fragments of blue sky above. She came quickly, sunlight scattering over her eyelids. When her heart rate stilled, she pulled her shorts back up and panted, head resting against the tree.

She stayed like that a while; she'd entirely lost track of time and was glad Henry and Daisy both had clubs after school. She wondered if she *was* going mad – she'd never, in her life, done anything like that before, outside, exposed – but concluded that she felt free. Wild and free.

Knees stained with mud, eyes bright and cheeks flushed, she rose, swinging her backpack in place. She moved quickly, sprinkling the remaining collections of small bones as she went. A smile blazed on her face as she made her way back to the car, breathing in the woodsmoke-scented summer air, woozy as though drunk.

20

Coralie

Coralie, not accustomed to playground jostling at school pick-up, flinched as someone brushed against her.

'Oh, hi, Coralie!' the woman said brightly. Coralie struggled to place her. 'Bit of a bun-fight, isn't it?'

'Hm,' she offered non-committally as she squinted past the gates, where Elwood was surrounded by Henry and his little gang. She saw Henry roll his eyes and wave his hands around either side of his head goofily, a mean look in his eyes. The rest of the boys laughed, except for Elwood, whose shoulders were high, his slender fingers clenched into fists, an indignant look on his face. She excused herself, striding forwards, small clusters of adults and children expanding and contracting to allow her through.

'*Tell us more, Ellie,*' Henry was crooning as she approached. Her heart contorted.

'What's going on?' she demanded, a hand on Elwood's shoulder as though he were her own child (there were moments when she wished he were). Elwood turned, his little face lighting up when he saw her.

'Coralie!' he breathed. 'Thank goodness. I asked Mummy this morning if I could come over to see you! I saw the Sevenoaks Panther, Coralie! I saw it myself!'

Behind him, Henry was smirking, and the other boys, all in

their PE kits, were barely suppressing giggles at Elwood's expense. 'Don't you have Athletics Club to get to?' Coralie snapped.

She spun on her heels, her long skirt lifting. 'Come, Elwood. Tell me about it on the way home.'

'So yesterday—' he began, and she glanced around. They were still packed in tight with other people. She didn't want to expose him to further ridicule.

'Not here.' She passed him an apple.

He looked jittery, jerking on the spot, desperate to download his tale.

'Eat up.' Her voice was more imperious than she intended. 'Explorers need to keep their strength up,' she modified.

He nodded and sank his teeth into the apple's sweet flesh hungrily as she directed him out of the throng.

They strode to the Parkland, side-stepping dawdlers. The pavements were crammed, adults and children and pushchairs and dogs all spilling into the road, car horns beeping, since most people now avoided the Parkland and other cut-throughs which had previously been popular. A sewery stench rose, the air thick with it, no breeze to stir it.

Her mind raced. Was Elwood being bullied? Should she mention it to Twig? But she had Skylar to focus on. Or even Emma, maybe, as the mother of the bully? But she questioned the Brooks' judgement since they'd submitted their plans. They were deluded. Imperceptive. Too wrapped up in themselves to think beyond their own Disney bubble. What would be the point in telling them? She reassured herself that she was doing all she could: providing a safe space for Elwood to come and be himself, to listen to him. She wasn't sure anyone else ever really listened to him.

The Parkland was almost deserted as they entered. 'Isn't it lovely to have it all to ourselves?' she said. It was cooler here, tranquil and fragrant with jasmine.

'I'm so glad you came to get me, Coralie.' He beamed. 'I asked Mummy to send you. And she did. I couldn't wait to tell you.'

Her eyes prickled with moisture. It was Coralie who had insisted on collecting him today. Twig was with Skylar at the hospital, and she couldn't bear to think of the poor boy languishing in after-school club again. 'Tell me, Elwood. Tell me everything.'

'It was last night. I was in my treehouse and I was looking out at the Parkland through my binoculars, and I saw it, Coralie! I saw it! It crossed the path and went into the trees.'

'My goodness,' she said, a hand on the back of his neck. 'What did you do?'

'I took a photo!' he said. 'On my iPad.'

'Clever boy.' Her words were inflected with stark admiration. His face shone.

She wished her girls could witness this scene, see the sort of mother she could be, given half the chance. It might be good for them to realize that Coralie wasn't universally scorned by all children. The last time she'd seen them, after the Fwuffy debacle, they'd been desperate to leave. She'd had to downplay the whole thing to Fraser and, obviously, his natural response wasn't to assume it could be connected to a wild cat on the prowl.

'And what did your mother say?' *If she listened at all*, she resisted adding.

'She said it must've been a shadow. From a fox or a big dog or something. She was busy so I haven't had a chance to show her my photo yet.'

Coralie nodded. 'A common response. May I see it?'

'Of course!' he breathed. 'I knew you'd believe me.' He slipped his bony fingers into hers and her heart swelled.

The back door was unlocked when they arrived at Bob's. Coralie stayed outside while Elwood ran in for his iPad. Music wafted through the garage door, where Blake must be working, although a peel of laughter suggested she wasn't exactly hard at it. *That's showbusiness*, she supposed, and an image of her own parents slid into her head. Her mother walking along the King's Road, flashbulbs popping.

Back in her greenhouse, they pored over Elwood's photo. Zooming in and examining it. Comparing shapes and shoulders and the smudge where a tail might be with photos from her books. He consumed facts like snacks, his little brain processing at rapid speed.

Her gaze snagged on the familiar photograph behind her. Her mother, the famous socialite, as she took Jasper, her black leopard, out for a walk, in a fur coat and chequered tights, her hair in a beehive.

'Why do you have that picture up?' Elwood asked, guilelessly.

'What do you mean?'

'When you look at it you look sad.'

A long beat passed between them. Elwood stood and moved nearer to the photo, his eyes raking over it. Through the glass he traced his finger over the curve of Jasper's muscles.

'I used to know that lady,' she said eventually. 'A long time ago.'

Everyone always commented on how glamorous her mother was, what a different time it was then. No one ever comments on the small, plain child lagging behind her. Elwood returned to sit cross-legged on the floor beside her, retrieving his image of 'the cat'.

'It's inconclusive, isn't it?' he said sagely, replicating the language used in the books. 'But I know what I saw,' he added urgently. 'I saw a big cat. Like that one.' He pointed back at the photograph on the wall. 'You believe me, don't you?'

She couldn't bear to break his heart; to have others break it for him. 'I do,' she said. 'But what did I tell you before?' She tapped the side of her nose, like her grandmother used to. 'Real cat people . . .'

'. . . don't talk,' they finished together. He grinned and waggled his eyebrows, sitting up taller. A real cat person now.

They basked in the moment until delicate paws treading the floorboards broke the spell.

'Socks!' Elwood cried as the cat sauntered in.

'My two best friends,' Coralie said, and Elwood beamed, scooping Socks into his arms.

She walked to the small worktop at the back of the room and filled the kettle to make Elwood an apple tea. His favourite.

'Anything interesting in there?' she asked as she waited for it to boil.

'I'm reading about the Gippsland phantom cat! Did you know, American World War Two fighters brought cougars with them, as mascots, and then released them in the Australian bush! Do you think that could have happened here?'

Coralie smiled. She adored his imagination. Sometimes when she was with Elwood, she imagined herself as a teacher. Or adopting. Taking a child under her wing who wanted to be nurtured and doing all she could to make their lives better. The impact she could have. She pictured herself at a long dining table at Christmas, the people she'd helped all around her. Lives improved. She could have had more children with Adam – at one point he had been keen – but how would it look? If she not only moved, but started a new family? She couldn't do it to her girls. And in any event, she was through the baby years, out the other side of stretch marks and reflux. She didn't want to go back.

'How's Mummy doing, Elwood?' She poured steaming water into their mugs.

He didn't seem to hear, absorbed in his book.

'Lots on her mind, I imagine,' she said idly. She'd been meaning to catch up with Twig about the benefit for Skylar next month. A final fundraising push. How could Coralie say no? She'd do anything to help, and holding it in Twig's back garden, with Bob fussing about his lawn, wasn't an option. Besides, Coralie loved a party. Especially these days: no longer the small child tugging at her mother's skirt for attention but at the centre of it all, the genial hostess. 'Maybe . . .' She paused. 'Maybe don't show her your photo. We don't want to worry her too much about the cat.'

'Sure,' Elwood agreed, his eyes still on the page. 'But I don't think she'd mind. She said the panther's helping to raise money.' He raised his voice to be heard over the noisy jackdaws and cawing magpies outside.

'Really, how so?' She placed their drinks on the galvanized metal table and sat back in her big, squishy, rose-covered chair. She'd inherited it from her grandmother when she passed away, the only thing, other than the necklace she'd gifted Coralie when she'd grown too old to track. She knew it was the neglect she'd felt from her parents growing up that connected her to Elwood, that had forged this bond between them. Elwood didn't see it that way of course, because he, like everyone else around here – including Adam – didn't know how she'd grown up.

Adam knew about the scar, she'd told him about her father, his quickly flaring temper . . . She'd had to explain why she no longer saw her parents even though she had access to her trust fund. Guilt money. That's why she never felt bad spending it. She could still remember the agony at being uprooted and shipped off to boarding school as though she were perpetrator rather than victim. She hadn't liked school, but she was safe there at least. She ran her right hand up her left arm reflexively, finding the grooves of her scar beneath the thin material of her sleeves. It was irrelevant now. She had escaped her past.

'She adjusted her esseo,' Elwood said authoritatively, eyes still on his book. Outside, a low rumble of thunder sounded.

'Did she?' Coralie didn't want to ask what 'esseo' meant. Elwood was mocked enough at school. She didn't want him to feel patronized.

'Yes, and she said now she's getting more hits on her website. Since her last post. And people are playing Pineapple Punk songs again. We danced to one in the kitchen the other day.'

Coralie had been so busy lately she hadn't caught up with Twig's blog for a while; she didn't need updates, living next door. She clicked on it now, seeing her latest post: 'Living in the Shadow of the Sevenoaks Panther'. She scanned it quickly: it covered rumours Twig had heard as a child about the panther right up to the recent ones, including Cupid being found in her back garden. How she'd struggled to sleep since. Neatly rounded off with links to streamers which – Coralie clicked through – landed on her artist pages.

How . . . exploitative. And out of step with her usual posts, which were sparse, but emotionally resonant, like her music.

'Esseo,' Coralie mused. 'Oh. SEO.'

'Search Engine Optimization,' Elwood confirmed, and Coralie laughed – how could she ever think for a moment she could patronize Elwood? He'd rule the world one day.

'SEO,' she repeated.

'Yep. She's used "key words".' He enunciated 'key words' as though he was still testing it out. 'Every time someone googles "wild cat Sevenoaks" or "the Sevenoaks Panther", one of the first things they see is the link to Skylar's fundraising page. Isn't that clever?'

'Yes,' said Coralie, putting her feet up on the tasselled leather pouffe, a relic from Cresswell Place, and resting back with her hot drink, her scar and the past forgotten. Outside, heavy summer rain began to lash down. Inside, they were insulated, like the bulb of anger which flared in her chest. 'That is very clever indeed. But all the more reason not to show her your photo.' Imagine, opening the boy up to ridicule on that scale! She wouldn't put it past Twig. She was desperate, after all, and Coralie knew what lengths desperation could drive a person to.

Elwood tapped a slender finger on the side of his nose in agreement. 'Cat people.' He smiled.

21

Emma

'You're in a good mood,' Matt commented, joining Emma on the wooden bench in their garden. The once-ornate plot was overgrown, the flowerbeds wild, Matt's weekly battle with the lawnmower doing little to tame the combative foliage. Emma sank back against him with a glass of wine, resting her head on his chest, in a thin vest and knickers. It was clawingly hot. 'I thought you'd be licking your wounds.'

The comments on the portal had been particularly vitriolic that day. Agatha had told her that Tim had been active in the WhatsApp group, quoting legislation they were apparently breaching, and sending guidance on what language to include in their objections.

'I won't be beaten by their bullying,' she said, an upbeat inflection to her tone, picturing her carefully curated Parkland scenes.

Just then the sky split above them, the heat which had been building all day finally cracking the dense clouds open, fat droplets of summer rain falling on them and bouncing on the crumbling patio slabs at their feet. As they shrieked and ran inside a low rumble of thunder followed them. She thought of her painstaking work, the claw prints filling with rainwater, the bones slowly slipping away, covered with mud and silt. Lost for ever. Worse still, her good mood had put Matt in a good mood. She could see his bulging erection as he surveyed her damp skin and vest.

'I've got a headache,' she said flatly, and marched herself off to bed.

Upstairs, the heat was worse. She opened the windows, soft rain splashing on to the sills. What did it matter? They were already half rotten.

She peeled off her wet clothes and got into bed, a book – her usual prop – open on her knees, her phone tucked inside. Ear buds in, she caught up on the day's comings and goings. It was her nightly ritual now. She'd seen Bob and Tim talking outside earlier and had been meaning to listen in. She pressed play. Saw Twig leaving for the hospital. Bob opening the door for a parcel. Blake, complaining about the heat inside the garage and sitting beneath the canopy of the weeping willow out the front of their house, phone snug between her neck and shoulder as she set up her laptop.

Emma was about to fast-forward, still seeking the interaction between Bob and Tim, when she noticed the change in tone in Blake's voice. Her words were generic – *yes, no, totally, I get it* – but her usual timbre (relaxed yet professional) was rendered soft and velvet. It changed again as the call neared its climax, her voice raw and intense as she whispered: 'I love you.' Emma fast-forwarded, checking Twig hadn't returned home. No. Twig wasn't there. Blake was talking to someone else.

22

Coralie

Coralie, who had been busy finalizing plans for the new outdoor play area at Puddleford Primary, quickened her pace to catch up with Twig and Emma, who were walking up ahead in the Parkland. Lustrous violet balls of California lilac – *ceanothus* – hung over back-garden fences as they passed, as though trying to eavesdrop. She smiled thinly at the men in red T-shirts with the black lettering *Puddleford Parkland Patrol* flanking the route as she stomped past. She'd thought it was a joke when someone suggested having them produced 'to ensure patrol members are easily recognizable'.

Her mood hadn't recovered since reading Twig's blog post. For days, she'd stewed on it: Twig manipulating people, driving hysteria, for her own gain. To raise money for Skylar, she could understand; to link it to her outdated music, she could not. Hadn't Emma said it was Twig's idea to post about the wild cat in the local mums' network? It really was *very* clever. Calculated. She clearly didn't give a second's thought to the poor animal she might be endangering unnecessarily. Or the panic that could be wrought as she did.

It explained the renewed interest in Pineapple Punk. She'd heard a few of the mums talking about it when she was setting up for the cake sale at school last week. Exclaiming how they

hadn't realized who Twig was, that it was *her, her from that band.*
Pineapple Punk. You remember, they were all gothic and grungy
and cool-looking when the Spice Girls were jumping around in
leopard print and sequins? (Coralie had noticed then they were all
wearing a leopard-print item of some description: bag, trainers,
T-shirt. She couldn't abide leopard print and would rather walk
naked through Puddleford than wear it herself.)

She shot short, sly glances at the back of Twig's head as she
approached them. Twig would claim it was to help Skylar, but
the way her music was rocketing into the nation's subconscious
wasn't exactly an unexpected side-effect. She'd literally linked the
two online.

'Hey! How's the fundraising going?' she asked, reaching them,
unable to resist saying *something*, as the children ran ahead and
the three women slipped in line together.

Small, hard apples, not given a chance to ripen, peppered the
ground. Henry and Skylar were kicking them like stones as they
walked, while Elwood reverently gathered as many as he could
in his hands for his budding 'nature collection'. Coralie imagined
scooping one up. Firing it at Twig at short range. *How would*
Twig like to be hunted?

'Better,' Twig said, relief in her voice. 'It was flatlining for a
while, but this wild cat thing has helped. People are more interested in Sevenoaks and are finding the fundraiser that way.'

At least she was acknowledging her opportunism, even if it was
in oblique terms.

'Not interested enough to distract people from complaining
about our plans,' Emma said glumly. 'We've had another dozen
objections come through this week. And they're so *personal*.
Everyone's ganging up on us.'

Coralie grimaced at Twig, indicating her views on the proposals, but Twig simply shrugged.

'What will you do,' Coralie asked, 'if it doesn't go through?'

She used to like her neighbours, she thought bitterly. Now
she longed to be rid of them. Instead she felt entangled in their

lives: helping Twig with the benefit, trying to avoid Emma's monstrous plans being passed, mitigating the effect of her son's bullying on Elwood and looking after Elwood, giving the poor mite some attention.

'I don't know.' Emma shrugged. 'Matt's adamant we stay. He can't see past the Briar Heart Estate. Says it's the place he always wished he lived growing up – probably when he was busy hanging out with you, Twig,' she said drily, and Coralie arched an eyebrow in surprise. It was a rare admission that Twig and Matt's history might bother her. 'And it's perfect for the children and blah blah blah. At this point, I want to move even if the plans are passed. Why would I stay when everyone seems to hate me?' She walked with her sandals slapping the ground, like a teenager having a strop.

Coralie glanced at her quickly, amazed. Emma was one of those women who never acknowledged anything was wrong, who acted like it was normal to be controlled by a five-year-old girl, who didn't seem to notice her son was turning into a bully.

Twig caught Coralie's eye and raised an eyebrow too. Coralie couldn't help but notice a frostiness emanating from Emma towards her. The atmosphere was strained. Coralie had been quite disparaging about Emma's plans, but only privately. There was no way Emma could have heard her. There was the messaging group, but Coralie took care to be measured on that, as much as she could manage anyway, and had often dialled back on a message before posting it, conscious that Agatha or one of Emma's other PTA cronies could be feeding information back to her.

Emma flicked her pearly-pink fingernails. 'How's Adam?' she asked in a tone Coralie couldn't place.

'Fine, just busy with work,' she replied breezily, purple foxgloves standing sentry like ghosts as they passed. She wished she hadn't hinted at her concerns about Adam to Emma. She had the subtlety of a brick.

Twig hadn't seemed to notice, distracted as she was, glancing around furtively as though they were about to be ambushed. *Honestly.*

'MUMMY! MUMMY! MUMMY!' The shout came from up ahead, in the direction of the stream which cut through the bottom of the gulley, and they all noted the edge of terror. They ran, school bags and their own bags pinned under their arms.

'Skylar!' Twig called, racing ahead in her ripped denim shorts and sandals.

When Coralie caught up, Skylar and a couple of other girls from the estate were off the main path, by a small copse of trees. They were crowded around Twig, pressing themselves against her legs as though she could offer them protection. Henry and Daisy were on the path, waiting for Emma, wide-eyed and nervous. Elwood was crouched on the floor, peering at something.

'What's going on?' Coralie reached Elwood at the same time as Anjit, a tall, wiry man she recognized from the neighbourhood. He was wearing cargo shorts and the ubiquitous red patrol T-shirt with a whistle round his neck. He fanned both his arms by his side, one gripping a large horn, bellowing, 'Back to the main path, everyone!' Both she and Elwood ignored him.

'Henry dropped his ball and it rolled all the way over here and he was too scared to get it—'

'Was not!' Henry shouted crossly, sounding so much like Matt it was disturbing.

'Well done.' Emma patted Henry on the head and he jerked away, embarrassed.

Elwood's eyelids fluttered with excitement. 'Anyway, I found this!'

'*Please keep to the main walkways!*' Anjit commanded, but his voice was wobbling, as though he were questioning his own jurisdiction.

Coralie offered up her most dazzling smile as she crouched beside Elwood. 'It's fine, Anjit. They're with me.'

He softened at his name on her lips. 'I know, Coralie, but still—'

'Oh.' Coralie cut him off. She sensed the small group contracting towards her. '*Oh.*' Her forehead pinched as she surveyed the alabastrine skull Elwood was presenting. 'How . . . curious.' It was large, bulbous with a prominent sagittal crest and an elongated snout with sharp, well-preserved teeth.

'What on earth?' Emma yelped.

Coralie pulled out a pencil case from her crochet bag, removing a small brush, gloves and plastic bags.

'Do you always carry those with you?' Twig asked.

'You never know when these might come in handy.' She smiled. She'd had these tools since she was a student. It was so satisfying to be using them again. To be *of use* herself.

She pulled on her little white gloves and almost sighed with pleasure. Taking the skull from Elwood she rose and held it aloft on her fingertips. A small crowd had gathered as other Puddleford parents traversing the Parkland reached them, and they all fell silent. Anjit had his hands on his head in despair.

'A fox,' she proclaimed to the hushed crowd. She wished her girls could be here to see it.

She brought the skull closer to her and sniffed it, holding and releasing her breath dramatically.

'Interesting. Very interesting . . . urine. If we had access to a lab, we might be able to pinpoint what urinated here . . .' She noticed Emma and Twig with their mouths agape.

'Do – do you have access to a lab?' Emma croaked, but Coralie barely heard her, distracted. 'Look!' She gestured with her arms, inviting them to survey the area, and of course Elwood was first to spot a cluster of pale bones nearby. Coralie moved swiftly around the scene, trying to make sense of it all. There were other bones too, small, disjointed trails of them, as though they'd been placed there and then swept away. She remembered the vivid summer storm a few nights ago, which had dead-headed her roses. She frowned. This was all so odd. She knew this Parkland. How would she not have seen anything like this before?

She used tweezers to pick up the bones Elwood had seen, studying them carefully before placing them in a small plastic container.

'*Fascinating*,' she drawled. She couldn't wait to tell the girls about this tonight.

Twig had her arms wrapped around Skylar's shoulders, pressing her in close, almost vibrating on the spot. 'Elwood,' she called. 'Let's go.'

Elwood's shoulders slumped, but he acquiesced, moving slowly back towards Twig and the main path.

'Mother fungus!' he suddenly exclaimed, pointing up at a tree. All heads swivelled to the oak, which looked as though it had been scratched, or attacked in some way, around six feet up. Coralie squinted as the crowd parted to allow her through.

'Goodness.' She placed her index finger along the exposed grooves, small shards of wood splintering her skin. Her eyes were already scouring for scat or sheaths of hair trapped in the bark. That's what you'd expect – well, hope – to see. But none of the markings were what she would expect had a panther, or any other type of wild cat, scaled this tree. She looked around her again. It was a curious scene. It looked . . . *staged*. Like something set up for a kids' Junior Ranger party. But how could it be? Who would do that?

Unintentionally, she glanced at Twig, who was buried in her phone. Stressed-out, desperate Twig. Who'd do anything to draw attention to her daughter's cause. Anything to raise the money for Skylar's vaccine. Anything for her own pursuit of fame. She looked from the fox skull to Twig's retreating back. So eager to pull Elwood away. What was she really afraid of?

The Mystery of the Sevenoaks Panther

Susan, Number 7: I'm sure Twig tipped off the press. She always was fame-hungry. Right back, like, when she was a teenager. She broke Matt Brooks' heart, you know.

Tim, Number 16: That would be more believable if he had a heart to break.

Megan, Number 16: Emma tipped them off. I have a friend who works on the news desk at the *Sevenoaks Herd* and it was definitely Emma.

Tim: Either way, once the press got hold of the story, that was it. It started in the local Kent rag, and it must've been a slow news week because suddenly it was everywhere.

Susan: Look what happened next. As if anyone would have remembered Pineapple Punk otherwise.

23

Twig

It was Twig's least favourite day of term: the Summer Fayre. She'd thought one upside to the local hysteria around the Sevenoaks Panther would be that the fayre would be cancelled, but, after various entreaties from Coralie, Mr Ambrose had agreed to let it go ahead. So here she was, surrounded by hundreds of kids high on candy-floss repeatedly asking for pound coins to buy back all the toys parents had discreetly donated. On top of that, Coralie (who conveniently was unable to attend the fayre herself owing to some conservation obligation at the nature reserve) had added Twig's name to the BBQ rota. At least she'd paired her up with Adam.

'Jeez.' She wafted her hand over her face. 'Are you bathing in aftershave?'

Adam pulled at his jumper and sniffed it. 'I didn't even put any on. I swear Coralie is dousing my clothes in it or something.'

'Very primal,' Twig observed drily, but Adam shot her a look as if to say, *don't even go there*, not that Twig would. One thing she wouldn't want to discuss with Adam was his and Coralie's sex life. 'What's going on with you anyway? I hardly see you these days.'

'The usual. Just busy with work,' he replied, shoulders hunched as he flipped the burgers.

Twig frowned. Recently, Adam's Treescapes truck never seemed to move from his drive.

A flurry of orders prevented her from pressing him on it. The benefit of the BBQ stall was that at least it wasn't parent- (or child-) facing. The negative was the hot wafts of meaty steam on an already scorching day. Twig was wearing a loose vest top with frayed denim shorts, both barely covered by a stained Puddleford PTA apron. Every now and then a small globule of fat would leap from the hotplate, landing on her arm or thigh, making her yelp.

'It's good to be out, actually.' Adam stared off into the middle distance, uneasy, uptight.

Twig had seen him like this with other people, but not usually with her. A sudden thought nudged at her subconscious: Adam in the garden just before the cat – the *alleged* cat – asking her about something that happened at the table. Or *under* the table? She'd forgotten. What was that about?

'How about you? Coralie said the fundraising's going well? When do you go to America?'

Twig shook her head from side to side as she arranged a tray of burger buns, separating the tops and bottoms. 'August.' Her tone was downbeat. 'If I can get the money in time . . .' They were still short of what they needed. 'It's difficult. Blake . . .' She paused. How could she possibly explain what was going on with Blake when she didn't know herself? Was their marriage failing? Or was it normal to be the way they were with each other, snappy and guarded, when they were going through something so intense? 'I dunno. Things are weird between us.' She lowered her voice. 'She's pissed off. My solo song is doing well, picking up traction. People are playing Pineapple Punk songs again. She thinks it's embarrassing. Not in keeping with the "cool vibe" she's cultivated since as a producer.'

Adam's lip twitched. 'Did she use those words?'

In spite of herself, the corner of Twig's mouth curved too as she nodded. 'Yep.'

Their eyes met, shining with mirth. It was still there, whatever it was – connection, attraction – an undiluted electrical charge flowing between them.

'It's *crass*, apparently, that I added my music links to my blog, and maybe it is, but it's all helping to drive interest.' She desperately wanted Adam to agree. He nodded vaguely.

'And the vaccine. She goes all weird when I mention it. And she's done nothing to help me raise the money.' Twig dragged a hand over her face as she shook her head. She was struggling to concentrate. The smell of the burgers was making her salivate; she would love to sink her teeth into one.

'I mean, I agreed to become vegan, even though there's no solid proof it prevents cancer? *Vegans get cancer too.* That's what Skylar's doctor said when we asked her. But I did it anyway, because Blake was adamant it would help. Can't she do the same for me regarding the vaccine? Back me on it? Is that so unreasonable? She won't even talk about it. She just goes silent when I bring it up.' As she ranted, she realized how much she needed this: to vent to a friend. To somebody who understood her. Unfortunately, Adam looked entirely out of his depth. Like he'd gone for a pint but accidentally wandered into a therapy session.

She looked back down at the buns, biting back tears. She would leave Blake. If it was a choice between the vaccine for Skylar or their marriage, she would choose Skylar every time. She glanced at Adam. She just wanted someone to put their arm around her and tell her she was doing the right thing. She imagined melting into him, breathing deeply for the first time that day.

'Hey!' Adam snapped her out of her reverie.

Blake had appeared, a bemused look on her face as she took in Twig and Adam in their aprons flipping burgers, Elwood and Skylar glumly trailing her.

'What's up?' Twig sniffed away her tears and waved a ketchup bottle cheerfully, trying not to think about all the chemical shit in it if Skylar requested a veggie burger.

'Mummy said you said we can't get our faces painted,' Skylar said.

Twig glared at Blake; she'd told her not to make a big deal out of the face paint. If they asked about it, just distract them. It wasn't difficult. God knows what was in that stuff.

Blake put both her hands up in a *what?* gesture.

'Or the bouncy castle,' said Elwood.

'Why do you want all those other germy kids falling on top of you?' She pulled a ghoulish face as she said it, miming a mustard-clutching zombie, but they just stared at her, deadpan.

'Do you even want to go on the bouncy castle?' she asked Elwood sceptically. They all turned to where Henry had gathered on its steps with his group of minions.

'Maybe,' he said, but he looked anxious, and she wished she wasn't covered in her fat-splattered apron and gloved hands so she could reach over and cuddle him. She shot Blake a meaningful glance in his direction.

Blake placed a hand on his shoulder. 'Come on, buddy. Shall we splat the rat again? Third time lucky? Or look, there's some kids from Cubs over there. You wanna go hang?'

It was easy for Blake to be relaxed when she was often away travelling and had never had to rush Skylar to hospital in the middle of the night when her temperature had risen, leaving Elwood behind with Bob, or spent the night there, the whirr and beeps of machines jerking her awake whenever she was lulled into sleep in the chair beside Skylar's bed. In some ways, Twig wished she could just live in the hospital. A place where Skylar was safe, protected from the viruses and bugs and dangers lurking in the air, and the school hall, and the swimming pool. Most days the kids begged her to take them swimming at St Michael's Club, which had an outdoor pool, anything for some respite from the cloying heat, and every time she flatly refused: waterborne viruses as well as airborne? No thank you.

'Hey.' She dropped her voice as Blake moved out of earshot and Adam instinctively leaned in closer to her. 'Can you get me some weed?'

Adam frowned. 'Sure, but . . .'

'But what?'

He blinked away whatever had passed over his face – judgement? – and she chose not to pursue it. 'Yeah. Sure. I mean, I don't have any at the moment, but next time I see Dax. . .'

'You can smoke it with me, if you like?' She was grinning, but her breath was bated, every instinct hoping he would say yes. She remembered the charged moments between them at the supper party, the wild, reckless energy in the air before Matt joined them. But this Adam was different to the Adam of that night. Depleted.

He looked at the rows of patties, the top side still pink and raw, their undersides sizzling in oil. 'I'm trying to cut back,' he said.

'Of course. I was just joking around.' She bustled around her workstation, flustered.

'Can't be easy,' Adam said quietly beside her.

'No.' She gestured at the mums waiting for their burgers talking about having to hide the horns they'd bought to scare off the wild cat because their kids were running round the house with them blaring. *Cat, cat, cat.* Everything these days was about the cat. Meanwhile Twig was single-handedly trying to stop her daughter from dying. The weight of her mission lay heavy on her shoulders. The cat hysteria felt ridiculous in contrast.

'Is that . . . You're not . . .' Adam's voice had turned staccato, juddery, any trace of his usual ease with Twig evaporated.

'What?' She narrowed her eyes.

Adam's voice dropped to a whisper: 'Coralie thinks there might be someone setting it all up. Scaring people on purpose. And I don't know if she's saying it to make me feel better, or . . . or . . .'

'Wait. What? And you thought it might be *me*?'

'No, no, not me. I know you'd never—' He froze. The words stuck in his mouth.

'So *Coralie then*? Coralie thinks I'm pretending there's a wild cat! For what? To raise money? How does that even work?' *What the actual.* Fury pumped in her veins. The accusation felt too close to her own prickling disquiet at her actions. 'Or for attention? Yes! Yes! That must be it.' She was pointing a finger in the air now, her voice gnarled with sarcasm. '*Twig loves attention.*' It wasn't even Adam or Coralie she was angry at now. It was Blake, it was cancer, it was the whole fucking world. *It was so unfair. Everything was so fucking unfair.*

'No!' he said quickly. He raked his hand over his dark hair and sighed as if trying to figure out how better to explain himself. The burgers began to burn. '*Shit.*' He flipped them over.

'It wasn't like that.' He was more measured now, as if trying to regain the narrative, and for a brief moment Twig felt as though she was being manipulated. She panted, the heat, and the aftermath of her outburst, radiating from her.

'Why would she be trying to make *you* feel better?' Her tone was abrupt, suspicious, not the tone she would ordinarily use talking to Adam.

She recalled some gossip which she hadn't paid attention to at the time: that Adam King was afraid to leave his house. She'd disregarded it: people had always had things to say about Adam King. Calling him unfriendly and surly when she knew he was shy, uncomfortable at the evident fangirling he received from some of the local women. She'd heard them joking about hiring Treescapes just to see him shimmy up a tree in a harness.

Adam's account of the cat was now a point of ridicule in the local community. Not so much among the mums, who remained quietly on guard, but she'd heard some of the dads, including Matt, joking about it outside Cubs. There was a zealous energy to them, a sense of taking Adam down a peg or two.

'It wasn't just that night,' he said, leaning into her. She closed her eyes, feeling his breath on her cheek. 'I've had this weird feeling, for a while. Like I'm being watched. Or stalked. I can't explain it.'

A memory wriggled up. Adam in the garden that night saying *you weren't imagining it*, to himself.

'And—' He hesitated. 'Something chased me in the Parkland, just after, when I was running. I'm *sure* of it.'

Twig froze. He couldn't possibly believe he was being regularly followed, nigh on stalked, *by a big cat*?

'Have you seen anything since?' She rolled her shoulders, felt the crunch in her ears.

He shook his head.

'Are you . . .' She trailed off. Tact had never been Twig's strong suit and now, especially since Skylar had been ill, she was blunt and to the point. She didn't have time to tiptoe around things. 'I heard you're not going out much?'

He didn't say anything, but she saw his jaw tense in profile, a vein in his eyelid flickering.

She tried a different approach. 'So Coralie doesn't think there's a cat? She thinks it's someone hyping things up?'

He nodded, flipping burgers, his jaw still working.

Huh, Twig thought. *There really was something going on with Adam.* Twig could imagine Coralie putting an optimistic spin on things, being supportive, hoping Adam's preoccupation would pass. Grappling with any remote scenario – such as Twig setting things up – to make him feel better. Meanwhile, Adam was spiralling, coming up with all sorts of fanciful scenarios. Reading into things. Catastrophizing.

'Have you thought about seeing someone?'

Adam flinched, shaking his head. 'You sound like Coralie.' His shoulders and chest visibly slumped, the energy he'd had a moment ago vanished. She touched his shoulder tentatively, wanting to comfort him, but Adam barely seemed to notice. Last summer he had had the air of a man with nothing to lose. This summer he was a man who'd lost it all.

Another batch of burgers was ready. Adam carefully lifted each one on to the waiting buns. Twig wrapped them in napkins, moving them to a different tray and passing them to the woman – a mum she recognized from Elwood's class – who was taking the cash at the front. When she returned, Adam had laid out a fresh batch of patties, and something purposeful in his movement suggested he'd straightened himself out in the seconds she'd been gone.

'It could all be nothing, like Coralie says, couldn't it? Not someone planting them there, but there could have been things like that in the Parkland the whole time we've lived here but we've not been looking before?' Twig said.

Emma had posted photos of the fox skull Elwood had found, and Valerie had commented, *I dug one of those up years ago gardening!* A stream of older women had jumped on the comments, deriding 'the young ones' for 'getting their knickers in a twist' over the slightest thing.

Twig ignored the snaps of jaws and bones splitting, and flesh tearing, that bobbed in the peripheries of her thoughts whenever she had time to consider the Sevenoaks Panther. Flashes of white and red and folds of purple entrails contrasted against the black dark of the Parkland which surrounded their homes at night.

'Right? It's just nature. *Everything eats something*. Like Coralie said.'

24

Emma

Emma craned to watch Adam and Twig, curiosity, or jealousy, tensing her shoulders, her skin already tightening in the sun. It hadn't been a good morning. As Tim had predicted to Coralie, Puddleford parish council was objecting to their plans. She pictured a group of silver-haired mafioso, cackling over their wrist supports and tennis rackets.

'Hi.' She smiled tightly as people crossed her path, her eyes firmly fixed ahead.

The weight of it all, the heaviness of her neighbours' and supposed friends' *meanness*, pressed down upon her, an anaconda round her neck. She was finding it hard to rally her optimism. Especially here, at the Summer Fayre, forced into socializing with all the people who had been so unkind. She envisaged their comments floating above their heads like cartoon speech bubbles:

The Disney House! (As if there was anything wrong with that!) *Emma Brooks has no taste!*

She glanced down at her tan Donald Duck bag, a treasured accessory picked out by the kids on their very first trip to Euro Disney, and then, appraisingly, back to Twig, who, like Emma, was wearing denim shorts and a vest top, but differently, somehow: just *cooler*. Emma had always felt that her taste – the bag, for example – was a little quirky, perhaps, but that it was offset by a classic base, say twinsets and matching tracksuit tops and bottoms, but there'd been a comment about the plans mirroring her 'frumpy mum style' and now everything she wore felt wrong. She supposed it was her own fault: she'd wanted to know what people were saying about her – and what people were saying about her wasn't good.

She looked back at Twig, who seemed to flinch as Adam said something to her. She frowned. She had hoped to speak to Twig, to tell her what she'd heard Blake say, because Twig deserved to know, didn't she? But would she *want* to know? Would it be one more thing for her to deal with? Emma didn't know what to do. Her heart felt like it was skipping beats as it raced. She couldn't help feeling now that her surveillance was tipping her closer to a danger line; to a point of no return, if she heard something she couldn't come back from. And yet, she couldn't stop.

Beside her, Matt was talking to a couple of Cubs, as often happened at these community events, engaging with them genially, knowing their parents would be within earshot. It wasn't, she thought, because he was an arsehole (although he could sometimes be an arsehole). It was because he wanted people to think well of him. He loved this idea of being a pillar of the community. His benevolent-leader-head-tilt, which he was employing now, along with his interested-eyes, was because he really wanted to *be* a benevolent leader. The problem was, being a benevolent leader required patience and kindness and putting others before oneself. All things Matt struggled with on a daily, practical basis. He, too, was stealing glances at the BBQ stall, where Twig and Adam appeared locked in a heated exchange.

'Guys, guys, guys!' Elwood had juddered to a stop in front of them. Emma felt Matt's mood shift, felt his prickle of annoyance as if it were her own. Benevolent-leader-cum-dictator.

'Elwood.' Matt greeted him with a closed smile.

'Hi, Akela,' Matt said distractedly. 'Hey, did you hear that Tim, on our street, found a dead badger in his garden?' he said excitedly to the other Cubs. One, a little girl with errant blonde curls, looked instantly as though she would burst into tears.

'*News travels fast,*' Agatha said, arriving alongside them in a tight red dress, her twin boys dangling off each arm, pulling her along like a kite in the wind. 'I'm glad you're approving the new members, Em. I can just about keep up with the posts. That group's getting insane!'

Emma shrugged, her gaze snagged on Twig and Adam. How closely they were standing together. Like magnets. She felt another ripple of jealousy.

'And it had been half eaten!'

'Elwood,' Matt said sharply.

'Hm?' Elwood looked up at him with his enormous saucer eyes.

'That can't be true.'

'Matt—' Emma tried to interject. Matt wasn't in the online group – it was primarily for mums – and therefore hadn't seen that morning's post by Tim's wife.

'It is,' Elwood insisted, chest popped in an imitation of Matt's own. 'Henry told me.'

Matt's eyes bulged, his hands flying to his hips as he looked around for Henry.

The twins resumed tugging at Agatha's arms. She politely excused herself, drifting off in the direction of the chocolate tombola.

Matt and Elwood continued to posture before each other, Matt indignant, Elwood refusing to back down. Emma sighed, searching around for Blake. She'd appear soon, surely? She was unlikely to leave Elwood roaming the fayre on his own at the moment; even the more lackadaisical parents were being ultra cautious. Although Blake didn't tend to helicopter as much as Twig, who was still engaged with Adam on the BBQ stall, his hand on the small of her back. *What was going on over there?*

As she watched, a speech bubble appeared above Twig: *Admin.*

That was Blake, she reminded herself, *not Twig.* But Twig hadn't corrected her, as though it were accepted parlance between them. In a lot of ways, that slight hurt the most, because of all her neighbours, only Twig had seemed supportive. No objections, no snipy comments to the other neighbours out on her lawn. In fact, she'd even heard her admonish Bob for his part in it: *live and let live*, she'd said, *at least it's a change, everything round here looks the same*, and Emma's cheeks had warmed. Now she wasn't sure where she stood with Twig. But then, she supposed, she never had.

Matt raised his voice, jolting her thoughts. 'It's coincidence, Elwood. All the *adults* agree.' His tone was so patronizing it made Emma's skin crawl. His head was also flicking over towards the BBQ stall. Had he witnessed the strange body language between Adam and Twig? Did it have anything to do with his evident frustration building as he was talking to Elwood?

'Not all the adults—' Elwood began, but Matt cut him off.

'All the sensible ones.' Most of the Cubs, like this small group, would immediately cease to speak when Matt – or any of the other leaders – began talking. But perhaps because they lived next door, Elwood wasn't intimidated by Matt the way the others were. It was the same with Henry. They frequently returned from Cubs with Matt admonishing him: 'Can't you respect me, Henry, and listen to me, like the other children do?'

Elwood spotted a group of children from his class and darted off; the Cubs he'd abandoned trailed after him curiously, ears cocked for more grisly details. It was like watching a scary movie, she mused. You knew you shouldn't, and you wouldn't be able to sleep later, but somehow you couldn't resist. That was why she stuck with Disney. Real life was too grim, too depressing. When something upset Emma, she flicked on her glitterball and cranked up the tunes.

'For God's sake,' Matt muttered. 'Where's Blake?'

'Can't you give Elwood a break?' Emma's words spilled out, laced with an unintentional spike of poison. 'He's a kid. Excited about something.'

She could see the tension on his face as he resisted rolling his eyes. He shook his head, his countenance saying: *I am above this.*

'What?' she asked, her voice snipped.

He leaned down and spoke in a low voice: 'Why are you blaming me, Emma? You've been on edge all day. I can't control blinkin' Puddleford parish council! None of this is my fault.'

'I'm not blaming you.'

'It feels like you are. I didn't even want the third storey. I just agreed to make you happy,' he whispered, as if to say: *and you can't even so much as give me a blow job.*

He wanted her to bite so she bit: 'You *love* the third storey. You kept going on about how much space you'd have for all your Scouting equipment.' She could hear the sneer in her voice.

They were side-whispering to each other now, smiling as people they knew circled around them like sharks. Most of the kids were in facepaint; tigers the overriding choice. Heat and sugar conspired together, some of the children –who were used to being able to roam the fayre freely – screeching at parents who in turn gripped wrists, glared and made threats about ice-cream and screen privileges being withdrawn *if you try to run off one more time!*

Emma and Matt had agreed their children could navigate the fayre by themselves as usual so long as they let them know whereabouts they'd be and they promised not to wander into the woodland. Daisy had been at the bookstall, but Emma could no longer see her rainbow flippy skirt. She scanned the crowd for her, but, with more and more people arriving, it was impossible. Tension radiated between her and Matt. The neighbours would love this, them having an all-out row in public. She could feel her jaw shaking as she struggled to hold it together. She refused to let it happen.

'I'm going to find Daisy,' she said instead, and stalked off into the throng.

The Mystery of the Sevenoaks Panther

Oren, university friend of Coralie King: Yeah, I studied with Coralie at Trinity College in Dublin. We even dated for a while. Did I ever go to her family house? No. Definitely not. I was never invited.

Diana, university friend of Coralie King: I visited her once in London. She had a studio flat in Chelsea. One day we were walking along the King's Road and we passed this lady. All the blood drained from Coralie's face. *What's wrong?* I said. She replied: *that woman was my mother.* Imagine that, to walk past your own child as though she didn't exist.

Molly, university friend of Coralie King: I could never tell if she was lonely or if she genuinely preferred animals to people. She didn't have many friends, like. But she didn't help herself.

Diana: Do you remember the gloves? [Giggles.]

Molly: [Smiling.] Zoologists never wear gloves to handle specimens. It's almost like a point of principle: *look how unsqueamish I am!* Like, Bennett, one of our tutors, would always turn up to classes with bulging pockets, whatever barely dead thing she'd spotted on her 'morning constitutional' protruding out of them, and then we'd all take a look and have a little poke around, you know? But Coralie insisted on wearing these neat little white gloves. Like a doctor, or a forensic pathologist or something. [Smiles fondly.] Always took herself very seriously, did Coralie King.

Diana: Ah, Bennett. I'd forgotten all about her. God, she was gas, wasn't she? [Looks at the camera, shaking her head and smiling.] She had an orangutan in her freezer! Just kept it there, like.

Molly: [Smiling.] Well, you know what they say . . . never look in a zoologist's freezer! [Both women laugh.]

Oren: We hadn't been in touch for getting on to *twenty years* when Coralie emailed me at work. She must've seen the paper I had published in *The Journal of Zoology*. She asked if I could test something for her in the lab. But this was way before the Sevenoaks Panther. A good year or two earlier. [Pause.] It was a whisker: 99.9 per cent *Panthera pardus*. [Nods.] A leopard. We get them from time to time, we just don't shout about it. God love 'em.

25

Coralie

'Do you have time for tea?' Coralie asked Elwood the following week. 'I don't want your mummy telling me off if you're late for Cubs.' The truth was, as much as she loved Elwood's company, he came every day now after school, often armed with a map or slips of paper. Twig, busier than ever, didn't seem to notice, or if she did, wasn't bothered by this, but Coralie herself had a lot to be getting on with. There were her regular obligations: the governor project she was overseeing to update Puddleford's outdoor play areas (almost finished, thank goodness), the food-bank deliveries, her conservation work. But on top of that, she was being bombarded daily with questions about cats and foxes and whether the faeces someone had found on their lawn might be 'scat'? Spoiler alert: they were not.

'No, she won't mind. She's busy because a song she wrote about me is trending.' Pride rounded out the edges of his words. 'She wrote it when I was little. It's about me,' he repeated.

'Well, that's good news,' Coralie said, patting him on the head. 'I should like to hear a song about you.' She began to hum 'A Boy Made of Stars'. Elwood looked up from the book he had open on the floor, *A History of Wild Cats in Kent*, and grinned. 'You have heard it!'

'I've been listening to it every day.' She went to make their apple tea, filling the kettle, still humming, as he poked his tongue out contentedly, returning to his book and map, where he was diligently plotting previous wild-cat sightings.

'Mummy recorded a podcast episode today. It's for old people who like listening to old music to make themselves feel younger.'

Coralie watched him belly down on her floor while he worked and smiled at him sadly. These last few years had been so tough for him.

The sensor light outside flicked on automatically in the dusk. Socks pawed elegantly in.

'Hello, my sweet boy.' She moved her arm to her side and clicked her finger. Socks trotted over obediently, and Coralie gave him a cat treat – *not gluten free, oops* – and stroked his head.

Elwood observed this with his eyes agog.

'I didn't think you could train a cat,' he said in wonderment.

'I think you can train anything if you set your mind to it.' She looked outside, to the darkening Parkland beyond. 'The Forgotten Child' should be the name of Twig's next track, she sighed to herself. 'I got you something,' she said, in a flare of emotion. She wanted to nurture this lost little boy so much. 'Here.'

She removed one of her leather-bound notebooks from her desk, in the same racing green as her own. 'These are for *real* zoologists, Elwood, like you and me. I've used notebooks like this since I was at university.'

His eyes were round, infused with golden summer light. 'Mother fungus!' he breathed, turning it over in his hands and stroking the cover. He scrambled up to sitting and hugged it to his chest. 'Now I won't keep dropping my pieces of paper!'

'That's the idea.' She beamed, ruffling his hair.

She sat on the floor beside him, placing both their teas on the peeled white boards. She hugged her knees up to her chest, the full skirt of her dress like a tent. She bathed in his contentment as he wrote his name on the inside cover. This is how she had imagined parenthood to be.

She thought of her own parents. She'd followed her family's

149

fortunes via the financial and high-society press for the last three decades. Her father's name had changed. He was no longer Frederick Campbell. He was 'disgraced financier Frederick Campbell':

Disgraced financier Frederick Campbell has stepped down as chairman of Campbell Enterprises.

Disgraced financier Frederick Campbell addressed the Commons today.

Disgraced financier Frederick Campbell agreed to plug a £2 billion gap in Campbell Enterprises's pension pot.

Just last week she'd seen them in the news: *Disgraced financier Frederick Campbell attended the Cleopatra Legacy Ball (formerly the Campbell Charity Ball) to raise much-needed funds for endangered animals.* Coralie had scowled and rolled her eyes.

She was fortunate to have married twice, she supposed. She was twice removed from their orbit. Coralie Campbell, to Coralie Prendergast, to Coralie King.

She remembered the week her father finally got his comeuppance, in one respect at least, with fondness. She couldn't help but smile each evening as she flopped on the sofa in her little London flat, back from a day of tracking, a bowl of cereal in hand, and flicked on the news. Images of her father, dressed as dandily as ever in a checked mustard-and-black cravat and a dark green waistcoat, were lit with a thousand flashbulbs. *Ah, justice*, she'd thought. Fortunately, her trust, and the rest of the family's money, had been protected.

She didn't miss them. She missed the idea of them. The family she could have had.

The light outside dimmed further, casting Elwood's elven features aglow. He glanced up, caught her looking at him, grinned as though they were sharing a secret.

'No one else believed me when I said I'd seen a cat . . . But I knew you would. Do you think it's still out there? Do you think it lives in the Parkland?' he asked without a trace of guile. Just a young curious boy, asking an honest question of his mentor, which deserved an honest response.

She set down her teacup. 'Can I tell you the truth, Elwood? Can I trust you?'

His big blue eyes, spiked with molten silver, nodded at her solemnly. Coralie's papers and Elwood's PowerPoint slides, marked up and annotated as he uncovered more facts, were spread around them.

'I do,' she said. 'I can't lie to you. You're the only person helping me. I do believe there's a wild cat out there, and I do believe you saw it. But – and this is a big but, Elwood – I think it's really important to protect it. To keep it safe. Because I think wild cats have been living here for as long as anyone can remember, and I think they have a right to be left alone. To live in peace. Does that make sense?'

Elwood nodded. 'Do you think it's a black panther, like people are saying?'

'I think it's a melanistic leopard,' she said matter-of-factly, and smiled at her own joke.

'Wait.' His forehead crinkled, his clever brain ticking over, his eyes travelling over the stacks of books. 'That's the same thing, isn't it? Black leopards don't exist.'

She cupped his cheek. 'You're getting too clever for me, Elwood Dorsett.'

Yes, there was a leopard out there. She had no doubt about it.

Elwood tapped his pencil on his bony knee as he mulled this over. 'But what if it hurts someone?'

She leaned over and gently took the pencil, placing it behind his ear. 'It won't. All these years, and all these wild-cat sightings' – she gestured at his PowerPoint slides – 'and no one's ever been hurt by one. They keep to themselves.'

'Like you,' he said automatically, and she went to correct him, to point out how much she helped others in the community, but stopped abruptly as tears sprung to her eyes. He saw her. Little Elwood saw her. Glimpsed at her loneliness. A shadow of pain crossed over her heart, like an eclipse. 'And like me.'

Eyes glistening, she gripped his delicate, bird-like hands with her own. 'Like us.'

151

26

Twig

Twig swung open her front door to an angry-looking Matt, and a trippy, other-worldly feeling washed over her, the scene so close to her recurring nightmare of Matt, nostrils flaring, stalking around outside her home. For a second, she couldn't place whether she was awake or asleep.

'Hi?' she said uncertainly, gripping the doorframe for support.

At first he said nothing. Just stared at her with a searching look on his face, as though he were asking a question she could not possibly answer.

'Elwood's scaring the other Cubs,' he said eventually, his voice terse. 'Riling them up about this wild cat. And it won't do, Twig. Okay? It just won't do. Not on my watch.'

Twig had a sudden urge to laugh, her nightmare of a furious Matt rendered preposterous: here he was on her doorstep sounding like someone from *The Line of Duty*.

'All right, mate,' she said. 'Calm down.' She attempted a wry smile. 'He's just a kid. He's . . .' She groped for the right word. 'Enthused.'

Matt continued to stare at her, panting, his eyes boring into hers, and fear flashed through her. She glanced behind her reflexively; she knew Blake was in her studio in the garage. Looking back at Matt, she swallowed. She saw it pass over his face again. The question he wanted, but was unable, to ask.

'Okay then,' she said weakly, her hand on the door to close it.

His eyes skittered over her face beseechingly. Beneath his bluster was the teenage boy she knew, chest puffed out and proud, hopeful that you might not notice the crawling insecurity that lay beneath. He hadn't changed that much after all. She could see the words forming in his mind. Was he going to utter them?

A pressure against her calves made her jump. 'Socks!' she said in relief as the cat weaved itself around her legs in a figure of eight. 'You can't come in here.'

She could feel Matt's penetrating stare as she avoided eye contact. She thought of Skylar in the lounge watching TV under a blanket, she thought of Elwood upstairs, who was meant to be changing out of his Cubs uniform into his pyjamas but would almost definitely be in the dark in his room, eye pressed to his telescope, looking up to the sky, or, as had been happening recently, trained on the Parkland through his binoculars. She thought of Bob pottering around outside in his shed, his nightly check of the lawn imminent. Her life, which so often felt like a disaster, suddenly felt like something precious to be protected. She needed Matt to leave.

'Anyway,' she said, closing the door, keeping Socks, and Matt, out. She held her hand up in a half-wave. 'I'll have a word with him.'

Matt's foot jammed against the threshold.

'Elwood's dad. Tell me about him,' he said in a low, urgent whisper. 'Is he into wild cats and airy-fairy stuff' – he waved his arms around – 'or is that all from you?'

She locked eyes with him and shook her head, as though saying *not now, Matt. Not now.* She felt he understood as he slid his foot away resignedly, though he didn't move from the door. She closed it quickly, pushing Socks outside with him, and turned, her back against it, eyes closed, and she was sure she heard him say through the aged wood, 'I just need to know.' But she forgot the second she opened her eyes and saw Blake standing before her, hands on her hips and eyes squinting inquisitively. 'What the hell was that about?'

153

'Nothing,' Twig answered. 'Nothing at all.' She turned to the stairs, ostensibly to check on Elwood.

Blake followed her up. 'It must be about *something*.'

Twig paused, bending her head and speaking in a whisper. 'It was Elwood. Talking about the wild cat at Cubs. Apparently, it scared some of the others.' She shrugged, hoping this would shut down the conversation, but she was out of luck.

Blake reached for her arm. A beat passed. A moment when Twig wondered if Blake had known all along too, since Twig had returned home to Bali and was adamant that now was the time, the right time, to start the family they'd been talking about. Asking Kev if he was still keen to help them. Straight away! There was no time to lose!

'Maybe he's got a point,' Blake said quietly, jolting her thoughts. 'Maybe it's time to let this wild cat thing *go*.' And the way she said it made Twig feel like it was a comment directed at Twig herself rather than Elwood.

She turned on the stairs, defensiveness rising. 'What do you mean?'

'Just what I said. Maybe we should discourage him. Remind him *it doesn't exist*. Distance ourselves from it, rather than using it for our own ends?'

Twig felt the air leave her body at Blake's look of disdain.

'Perhaps he should spend more time at home and less time with Coralie.' It was a pointed dig at the time Twig was spending online, and she felt it like a slap round her face. Couldn't she see that the resurgence of Pineapple Punk was giving Twig life again? And not only that, it was generating donations to their fund. If it continued at the same pace, they'd have all the money they needed for the vaccine and their flights and accommodation by the time of the benefit. Okay, maybe it *was* 'a bit crass', adding the music links to her blog about Skylar's treatment, but Twig couldn't help but suspect that something else underlined Blake's agitation: the success of 'A Boy Made of Stars'. Twig's solo track. Written and performed, and shoddily produced, alone.

'Perhaps you should spend less time on the phone with your therapist or your mum?' Twig said, feeling restless, argumentative. 'When did you last spend quality time with the kids?'

'What?' Blake's face contorted. 'Fuck off,' she said softly.

'It's easy for you to criticize, isn't it, when you spend most of your time in the garage?' Twig said, riled. Not just by Matt turning up, although that hadn't helped; it had started the drum of trepidation in her chest which was now sounding louder than ever. It was Blake's insinuation that she'd brought about this situation, Elwood's fascination, somehow, by what? Her anxiety? By not shutting him down when he spoke about it? 'I need Coralie's help with Elwood since I'm putting all my energy into getting Skylar on to a vaccine trial to save her life.'

'A vaccine we don't even know she *needs*,' Blake seethed pointedly.

'Are you fucking kidding me?' Twig spat, thinking, *I knew it. I fucking knew it.* 'This again?' she yelled. 'This, now? We've been through this. Everyone else can see she needs it. Every doctor we speak to thinks it's a good idea, but oh no, Blake knows better.' She rolled the words around her mouth, like candy-floss in a drum, coating them with sarcasm.

'She's in remission.'

'And what if it comes back. Huh?' Neither of them said anything at this because they both knew the horrifying stat: 5 per cent. Skylar would have a 5 per cent chance of survival if her cancer returned.

'I want her to get better as much as you do, but it's *untested*. It's a trial. You're pinning all your hopes on something and we don't even know if it will work! There hasn't been enough research! What if she suffers from side-effects? What if she gets *worse* rather than better?'

'We'll never know! We have to put our faith in the doctors. *We have to try everything.*'

'But what if it's not the right thing?' Blake's words hung suspended between them, the impasse visible.

Twig glared at her. She'd fallen in love with Blake for her independence, for the way she didn't follow conventions or care about what other people thought, never expecting it to be at odds with the health of her child.

'What if . . .' Blake spoke so quietly Twig had to strain to hear her. 'What if the whole thing is just part of the Twig show?'

Twig stared back at her, disbelieving. Too stunned to speak. Blood roared in her ears.

'We could be living quiet lives. Getting on with things. Enjoying time together as a family. Not having to listen to those old fucking songs on the radio all the time, or answer people's questions.' She spoke slower, and slower, as though her voice were thickening like tar.

'But you love the show, right? You've always loved the show.' Blake's arms were extended in a grand gesture, her contempt for Twig filling the space. 'You've always loved being the fucking show.'

Twig spun around, afraid of what she might say next, afraid it might be something she couldn't come back from, and stormed upstairs. She tried to compose herself outside Elwood's room, biting her lip and staring at the old, patterned carpet.

'Come on, buddy, it's nearly bed—' she began when she finally pushed herself inside, but she stopped with a gasp as she surveyed Elwood's room.

She took it all in. The 'viewing station' by the window, identified with a handmade sign, his trusty binoculars and the dark green notebook Coralie had given him which never left his side. The huge display which had begun as a deconstructed PowerPoint slide but was now taking over most of his bedroom wall, obscuring the space-themed laminated wall stickers she'd carefully put up when they'd moved in. He'd used one of her dad's local area maps from the eighties, stuck it to his wall with Blu-tack, and it was now populated with stickers where potential big-cat evidence had been found.

Red wool was strung taut between pins radiating beyond the

map to photos and newspaper articles and, in some cases, carefully typed eyewitness accounts. It looked like a crime scene investigation. There were various strands of wool emanating from their street. She followed one to a grainy image, a photograph he'd printed out, with the words: 'Elwood Dorsett (7 June), from his treehouse' scrawled along the bottom. As well as other printed pictures, his own drawings of cats scowled from the walls, blood dripping from their fangs. When had he done all this? She remembered last week when she'd got up to wee in the middle of the night and a thin strip of light was coming from Elwood's room. When she'd gone in, he was reading. He said he'd only just opened the book and would go straight back to sleep. Maybe it wasn't a one-off.

'What happened at Cubs today?' She moved some papers to make space on his bed: Saturn and Jupiter and Mars against a star-flecked navy sky. The last remnants of his fascination with space. She smiled at his handwriting, reams of notes neatly transcribed. 'Where are these notes from?'

The sentences were formal, as if he'd read them in a textbook and then copied them out: 'A cat can fit into any space which is bigger than its head.' Twig shivered involuntarily.

Elwood didn't move, eyes still on his binoculars as he surveyed the Parkland, a pencil tucked behind his ear, like Coralie. She sighed.

'Elwood?' She waved the pages at him to get his attention.

'Hm?' He half turned his head to her, one eye refusing to yield its spot. 'Oh, they're from Coralie's books. Things I didn't want to forget. Mummy, did you know cats are a liquid? They assume the shape of the container they're in and—'

'Elwood. I was asking about Cubs?'

'It was good.' He drew out the words, the way Blake did when Twig ventured into her studio and asked her a question and she made it clear she was too busy and important to answer.

'Matt – Akela – stopped by. He said you upset some of the other kids.'

He adjusted his binoculars, continued to stare.

She shifted back on his bed, tilting her head from side to side, the bones in her neck cricking and cracking.

'Elwood?' She propped some of his soft toys behind her head. It was too light yet for the stars on his ceiling to glow; they sat yellow against the white ceiling. 'You have to be careful what you say to other children sometimes. Especially younger ones.'

He nodded, although she wasn't sure he was listening.

'Hey, let's organize a playdate. Have one of your friends over?'

'A playdate?' He turned his head fully towards her, suspiciously.

She tried to feign brightness. To pretend guilt wasn't swashing in her stomach, making her nauseous. She'd never organized a playdate for Elwood before. She'd thought, since they walked to school with their neighbours through the Parkland, and often stopped to climb trees or play in the shallow part of the stream, that it was enough. 'Yeah! You can, um, play in the garden.' She pictured the abandoned, empty swimming pool, her old, rickety treehouse, her father's pristine lawn and flowerbeds. 'Or build something with Lego. Or watch a movie?'

'Okay.' He nodded, excited. 'Can Coralie come over? We can build a bug hotel, or, or, set a trap for the cat! But a humane one, obviously. Then we could look after it. Or give it to a zoo! All we'd need is a live goat!'

Her heart sank. She resisted the sigh that threatened to rattle her whole body. 'I'm sorry, buddy. I meant a friend from school?'

He frowned, turned back to his binoculars. 'Oh. No thanks, then.'

'There must be someone you want to invite?' Twig racked her brains for a child Elwood might have mentioned playing with before. He mixed easily, moving from group to group, chatting, but was it odd, she wondered now, not to have a best friend, or a little group of mates, at nine years old?

Coralie's his best friend. She tried to bat away the tears threatening to spill. *How had she made such a mess of everything?*

'It's out there, Mummy. The leopard is out there.'

'I thought it was a black panther.' She sighed wearily and rose, joined him at the window. But it wasn't the Parkland that drew her in, it was the ghostly shadows falling over the Brooks' lawn next door, where the real threat to her family lay. She had to find a way to fix things. She wouldn't be caught out again.

27

Emma

There were two things that Emma Brooks had always known:

The first: her husband had loved Twig Dorsett. Loved her deeply, and she had broken his heart. They had made plans to study in London and stay in Sevenoaks together – even though he'd got into Oxford (*Oxford! After clawing himself into a Kent grammar*) – and then she had callously ditched him for Blake and Berlin. He'd blamed any career, or other disappointment since, on his decision to turn down his offer at Oxford. (He'd even pondered once, half cut, whether it had contributed to his father's early demise, but Emma had gently reminded him of the coroner's report, which cited Frank's prolonged exposure to asbestos as a more likely candidate.) Worse still, Twig had profited from his heartbreak. Pineapple Punk's break-out single, 'Fleeting Heart', was inspired by Twig's *guilt* (ha!) over what happened.

The second: in their twelve years living together (eleven of those married), Matt had failed to return home just once. One night. About ten years ago. After he'd been to visit Frank in Sevenoaks. Frank was pretty unwell by then, and Matt was visiting him regularly after work, taking the train out to Sevenoaks and back to their flat in Greenwich. It wasn't strange that he'd stayed over. It was strange that he didn't call or message to let her know. His phone went unanswered all evening, eventually going straight to voicemail, until he was back on the train in the morning, having charged it, he said. And she'd believed him. She knew now that night had occurred around the time Twig's mother was diagnosed too and Twig had returned from Bali to see her.

She did not know if those two facts were connected. She did not know if there was a separate truth to link them. And now this: *What did Matt need to know?* She'd heard him speaking to Twig next door, clear as day.

It preoccupied her the whole night as she lay awake listening to Matt snoring and farting. It preoccupied her as she went through her morning routine with Daisy. There'd been another fundraiser for Skylar – an own-clothes day, with students encouraged to 'wear something that brings you joy'. Daisy had insisted that both she and Emma dress as Disney princesses, in the costumes Emma had bought for Daisy's last birthday party, but she had then grown increasingly angry with Emma as they neared school, eventually commanding her not to drop her off at her classroom, where her friends would see her, even though parents *had* to escort their children right to the classroom door in Year Two. It was mortifying to be standing in the playground dressed as Belle, being screamed at by a mini-Jasmine.

It preoccupied her all the way home from school-drop off, still in her stupid dress as she traipsed through the Parkland, which was silent, parents scurrying quietly through during the patrol hour. She needed to know more. She would find a way to know more.

Emma was putting her key in the lock when her inbox blinked: an email from their architect. *What now?* She needed a cup of tea before she could contemplate opening it. She tore off her uncomfortable polyester princess dress and froze. Her heart began to skip as a foreign noise filled the air, distinct from the house's usual moans. The burglar alarm hadn't sprung into action as she opened the door. *Was that—?* No, no. What were the chances that the one day she forgot to set the alarm an intruder broke in?

She was reassuring herself when she heard the sound again: a sinister tinkling, like the jangle of keys, the clank of windchimes on a blustery day. With a start she realized: someone was playing the piano. She was back to the front door, her hand on the door handle, ready to run outside and cry for help in her underwear, but at the same time she was thinking, *why would a burglar play the piano? A ghost then, a ghost!* She stopped, hand frozen. Emma didn't believe in ghosts. If she did, she wouldn't still be living here.

She blinked quickly, hand on her chest as she tried to exhale, a counterbalance to the sharp, jagged inhales she couldn't stop.

The noise again. A soft tinkle, tinkle, delicate and teasing this time. A horror movie's lullaby. Ignoring all her instincts, she crept into the kitchen. The door to the piano room was half closed, buttercup-yellow light filling the void. She soundlessly took the largest knife from the butcher's block and crept towards the room.

There was a loud crash, and she raised the knife, her left fist clutching in symmetry with her right, as the door opened another crack. And Socks sauntered out.

'Socks!' she breathed.

He gave her an insouciant look, like *yeah? So what?*

She pushed open the door. The piano stood empty. A washing rack to its left. She groaned, returned to the kitchen and dropped the knife on to the counter.

She ran the tap until the water was cool, splashed it on her face. It was too hot for tea and too early for wine (although she was tempted) so she opened the email from the architect, and swore.

'*The Planning Officer has advised . . . it be referred to the Planning Applications Committee . . . It considers applications which are likely to be controversial, receive major objections . . .*' Blah, blah, blah.

'*Members of the public can attend and speak at meetings if they have already sent a written comment about the application.*' For fuck's sake. That included most of the neighbourhood! No doubt they'd all be receiving a version of this letter too.

'*Alternatively, in view of the number of complaints, I think it's time we consider withdrawing the current application and make some changes before resubmitting your plans. The Planning*

Officer feels this is a prudent course of action.' I.e. your plans won't be approved.

The raw emotion she'd felt since the night before snowballed fluidly: fury tore through her veins. She would tear down this house, this fortress, *herself* if she had to, and rebuild it herself, too. She would create her own castle. There was *no way* she was withdrawing the application. *Let it go to the Planning Applications Committee! Fill the meeting with her detractors! Make them look her in the eye! She would fight her corner.*

She shoved stacks of interiors magazines off the table, kicked at the bin, punched the cushions on the low chair in the corner. In the midst of her rage, the very darkest, unreachable part, her eyes alighted on Socks, sniffing at the gluten-free cat food she'd left out, an air of distaste about him. She scooped him up, holding his back to her chest, her hand on his warm, soft belly. Her left hand reached for the discarded knife. She gripped it without thinking. She could do this. She could sacrifice this sniffy, ungrateful cat for the good of her family. Who could dispute there was horror afoot if the cat next door to the Kings' met the same fate as Cupid? Who could deny her sympathy if Socks, the darling of the neighbourhood, who always stopped for a stroke or a pat, was killed by the Sevenoaks Panther?

Socks began to mewl loudly, trying to wriggle from her grasp as though he knew what was coming, but that only strengthened her resolve. *Stupid cat.* How many times had she cleaned up his vomit, small, stinking, retched parcels left like droppings on her floor, and for what? He spent most of his time sniffing around Coralie's greenhouse.

Her right hand gripped him tighter. Her knuckles felt tight and cold, the handle shaking. In one move she had him on the floor, his spine emerging like small mountains through his fur as she pinned him at the neck. The rage was building, louder in her ears. *Too loud.* She couldn't think. It needed a release, some place to go. She had been so close to having everything she dreamed of: a family she loved, a home she could grow old in. To be her family's success story: The sister who transcended her humble beginnings, a childhood spent overlooked and in the shadows, and blossomed into a princess despite it all.

A tear rolled down her cheek, splashed on Socks' pink ear. His head twisted with violent jerks as he tried to escape. His jaw whipped open on instinct, his sharp incisors catching the light, and she willed him to clamp it shut, to rip her skin. *Bite me*, she thought. *Claw me. You stupid cat.*

She raised the knife in her hand.

She could do this. She could do this. Do it, do it, do it.

The blade clattered against the tiles as she released it. Her fingers loosened around Socks' neck and he instantly extracted himself, bolting from the kitchen. It was her own vomit, rather than Socks', which splashed on to the tiles.

The Mystery of the Sevenoaks Panther

Sofia Olsen, reporter: The first thing I did when I heard the reports emerging from Sevenoaks was google Coralie King. And what did I find? Nothing, same with all the Campbells, but for a handful of photos. It was clear someone had paid a lot of money to remove anything disparaging, or worse, from the internet about Frederick Campbell and his family.

28

Coralie

'Coralie! Coralie! Oh my God! Thank God you're here.' Adam fell against her, sobbing, his words jumbled and nonsensical.

His stink was getting worse. She covered her nose and mouth with her hand and shot him a contemptuous look. 'Adam, you need to shower.'

She opened the window, picturing his stench-trail unfurling like a skunk's, out on to their suburban street, like thick drops of blood in water, alerting a hunter to its prey.

'I saw it, Coralie! I saw it! I saw the eyes first. Two bright green eyes, and it's big – *huge!* – body, down by your greenhouse!' He gripped her shoulders and forcibly shook them. The thought zipped into her head – *enough to leave a mark?* – before vanishing as she took in his distress. 'The Sevenoaks Panther! It's here!' Red, jagged blood vessels snaked over his eyeballs. Her husband was unravelling before her. She felt herself detach, like a balloon slipped from the grasp of a small fist, drifting away. An act of self-preservation. To stop herself from falling into his abyss. She felt a scrape of misery, gutting her inside, to be in this moment.

'Okay,' she said. It was as if, the more deranged he was behaving, the calmer she became in response.

Adam hadn't left the house since the Summer Fayre. He hadn't spoken to anyone else, besides work colleagues, in over a fortnight. He hadn't showered in a week. It was like he was ceasing to exist.

'We need to call the police. This whole thing is out of control. What are you doing?' he shrieked as she put a hand on the sleek matt-black door handle.

'Come,' she said calmly, a hand on his elbow. 'I'll show you there's nothing there. And then, after that, you're going to take a shower and eat something.'

What reason did she have for fear? She wasn't even worried about him reporting it to the police. Who could believe Adam in this state?

'You can't!' he shouted. 'It could be out there. Waiting!'

She threw a glance of disdain his way. She couldn't help it. And yanked him outside.

'You have to see your GP,' she said later as they sat at the kitchen table, a cheese-and-pickle sandwich between them. He reminded her of the girls when they were sick, the only times they'd allow her to tend to them. She reached over the table and placed the back of her hand on his forehead out of habit.

He nodded dully.

'Shall I call them?' She gestured to her phone. Adam never carried his phone any more, she noticed. He'd left it by his desk all week.

'They won't believe me. They'll think I'm mad.' He stared sullenly at the table. 'Do you believe me?'

She ignored him, fetched them both an icy-cold water from the door of the American-style fridge-freezer. *Pathetic*, he'd called her once, when she'd asked him about his affair. *Pathetic*. It was such a sad, empty word. She couldn't help but remember, her lips curled inwards as she thought: *Who's pathetic now, Adam?*

She'd stopped asking him about his affair. It no longer seemed relevant. He was always at home. He was all hers. And that should've been enough. She wanted to shake herself: *make it be enough*. Stop, here, and live your life together. Start again. But

167

she couldn't shake off her irritation at not having all the facts. It was the not knowing that drove people – often women – mad. She *needed* to hear him say the words. She needed him to confess.

His affair had happened in such an ordinary, depressingly predictable way: him withdrawing from her, her trying hard to hold him closer the more he pulled away. She began to watch him carefully, noticed how long he was gone on his 'runs', how dishevelled, and yet less sweaty, he was, on his return. She had known instinctively: something wasn't right. And he had form. He'd cheated on her shortly after they met, but she'd forgiven him. *Foolish, foolish girl.*

She'd started analysing his fitness app data: noticed the gaps where he'd paused his activity, or kept it on and his heartrate was peaking but he wasn't moving. When she confronted him, he denied everything. Accused *her* of trying to control him. Worse, he stopped using the app. So, she started checking his pockets; his phone when he left it lying around; his computer when he left it unlocked mid-invoice preparation. Mostly he was clever, careful not to be caught out, until the day she found his second phone.

They were at the scout hut for Bonfire Night. Matt had organized it and the whole of Briar Close had gone in support. Adam had his arm proprietorially around her, and she'd wrapped her own arm round his waist, before slipping it into his pocket. She'd felt the phone with her own hand, smoothed her fingers over its contours. It was old-fashioned, cheap, not sleek and smooth like his smartphone. He'd suddenly flinched, pressing his elbows against his jacket, finding her fingers there. They both knew neither of them would cause a scene. He excused himself to go to the loo and Coralie knew, as she watched his retreating back, that he'd return with empty pockets.

He denied it as they walked home, whispering furiously to each other. He claimed she was imagining it. She was mad. And he was so convincing she half believed it. Until the following week, when Dax called at the house unexpectedly to pick up a tool he needed for a job and Adam had abandoned his laptop. It had taken her seconds to click on his history from that morning: pages and pages of one-bed flats and studios to rent. Again, vanished by the time she confronted him later. Again, Adam trying to convince her that she was going mad. Trying to control her.

When it came to science, Coralie was clear-headed: precise and accurate. But the chemistry of love, hormones, sex and longing couldn't be simplified into equations or quantifiable reactions. It was beyond her. She always seemed to get it wrong. Could their relationship recover from his affair? Could she pretend she'd never known about it at all? Could she learn to trust him again?

Who had he had the affair with? That's what she wanted to know.

She hated to be like this, always wondering, but he'd driven her to it. Lying to her right from when they'd met. She pictured a halo of flame-red hair. She should never have forgiven him that first time. It was a vicious cycle. Her father, Fraser, Adam. *Foolish, foolish girl. Stupid girl.*

He'd spent *hours* on Rightmove looking at one-bed flats. Places way out of his budget. What was his plan? Was he hoping to force her to sell this place? *Never.* She'd never do it. She was tied to this house, to this small parcel of land and the Parkland beyond. It had brought her back to life when her babies had been taken from her. She couldn't leave.

'Eat up,' she said, nudging his sandwich across the table.

She waited until dusk fell, after she'd spoken to the girls and Adam was sedately tucked up in the snug in front of the television. 'I'm popping over to see Twig about the benefit,' she called, ducking her head into the lounge. A white lie; she'd already seen Twig earlier that day. She'd popped over to tell Coralie she was worried about Elwood. Thinks he's becoming too invested in the wild cat. Coralie obviously told her he seemed fine to her, just enthusiastic, but inside she was thinking, *why don't you look after your own child, Twig? I've got enough on my plate over here.*

Adam nodded torpidly, his face trained on the screen, the barest flick of his head to indicate he'd heard her.

Drifts of honeysuckle lined the path: blushes of apricot and mandarin, lemon and custard. She drunk in its heady scent, needing oxygen. The aircon was a godsend in this weather, but nonetheless she craved fresh air. The shift and thrust of life beyond her constricted bubble. Noiselessly she crept into her greenhouse. She kept the lights off. She hunted around for the bits she needed, occasionally bumping her knee.

Opening their garden gate, she slipped into the Parkland and to the left, so Adam wouldn't see her silhouette in the unlikely event he left the sofa while she gathered her courage. It was after nine, almost ten, and the sky was still white, casting the turrets of Briar Heart House grey.

Coralie had grown used to having the Parkland to herself these days, particularly outside patrol hours. This section of the Parkland had always been quieter, the only access through the residents' back gardens. Nowadays, with everyone fearful of the Sevenoaks Panther, it was deserted.

The helicopter roar of a cockchafer flying millimetres from her head made her jump. Her nerves were jangling, threatening to consume her.

You must be brave.

She straightened her back. Bucket in one hand, her crochet bag slung across her body, pencil behind her ear, she marched into the darkness.

The Mystery of the Sevenoaks Panther

Valerie, Number 14: Do you remember that morning? The poor boy was hysterical. Running from house to house! No one could get any sense from him. Ranting and wailing about a leopard.

Anjit, Number 20: And the women were all going for each other by then. That was the real cat fight.

Joy, Number 20: Oh, Anjit. [Rolls eyes.] You do exaggerate.

29

Coralie

Coralie woke with a start in her grandmother's chair, a pair of electric-blue eyes floating over her. She shot back in fright, even as her head said: *it's okay, it's only Elwood.* She put her fingers to her temples as her vision swam.

'Elwood!' What was he doing here first thing in the morning?

'Coralie! Coralie! I've figured it out!' he was shouting excitedly, hands on his head and then shooting up into the air, and just for a moment, she wanted to tell him to go away. She needed to be alone with her thoughts.

'It's you, Coralie! It's you! The cat is trying to get in touch with you. It's seeking you out. You're like . . . like a cat whisperer,' he said reverently, hands back on his head.

'Good grief.' She laughed, scratching her neck and sitting up in her chair. 'Whatever makes you think that?'

'I went back to my map. After I read your book about the signs to look for and things that aren't really scat. Red herrings.'

She marvelled at how quickly he had picked up the correct language, assimilated the facts in her books.

'And then I crossed out all the things that aren't real. Like those bones we found in the Parkland, and the skull. There's no way they're connected to a wild cat . . . The sightings around Kipstead Lake, with the prints: *definitely not* from a cat . . . *no leading claw, not symmetrical* . . . The eyewitness accounts that mentioned smell. Big cats aren't known to have a particular smell. Hm, except maybe nutty, but no one said nutty . . . And the carcass in Tim's back garden, I looked again at my photos and that was *roadkill*!' He laughed incredulously.

He was rattling on, and one thing became clear: she had underestimated him.

'And then, while I was waiting for you to wake up, I read your notebook.'

Her head snapped up at this and she groped around the folds of her skirt. She'd fallen asleep with it open, rather than locking it away as usual.

'And you knew it, too, about the roadkill. I can't believe you didn't tell me.' His tone was conspiratorial, like they were buddies in a cop movie. Team-mates. 'What does this mean, though, 'e.b.'? Is it another Latin abbreviation?' He'd retrieved the notebook from the chair behind him and was flipping through the pages. His hair was scruffy, his cheeks were pink, his eyes alight. He looked like a little boy. An excited, happy little boy. She closed her eyes.

'And all the facts make sense! All your theories! It's true, isn't it? There really is a wild cat in the Puddleford Parkland. And I saw it! And it's targeting our street! Your house and our garden and the Jeffersons'!'

She tried to deflect him from his conclusion: 'I don't think it's *that* conclusive.' She reached for her notebook from his hands, but he dismissed her with a wave, the apprentice overruling his master. A blast of cold rippled over her skin despite the roiling heat in the greenhouse. It was 8 a.m., but already beads of perspiration were peppered over both their foreheads. Elwood swatted his away, flicking up his white-blond hair in the process, not breaking his stride.

'*Adam* saw a cat on the bonnet of his car, *Fwuffy* was *predated* in your garden, *rasped of flesh* – not a fox! *Kofi* saw the dead animal out the back of his garden, *Cupid* had his tail bitten off in *my* garden.' He emphasized the 'my garden' proudly, as though pleased to be placed in the centre of the action, not on its outskirts. 'And you put my sighting in.' He beamed. 'And did Adam see it too? *In your garden?*' Coralie imagined how many people he would share this with today – on the way to school, in the playground, walking home, and all of it linked back to the contents of her notebook. 'Only the sightings or signs on our road are the real ones! And the stuff you've found, here . . .' His fingers were poised to flick through the incriminating pages, but she wrenched the notebook from his grasp and slipped it into her crochet bag on the floor beside her. He looked at her, startled.

She stared at him uneasily. 'But what about all the other things?' Her throat was dry. She needed water.

'It's like you always said. If you go looking for evidence, you'll find evidence.' He knelt on the floor before her, a hand on each armrest as she shrank backwards. 'But what if the cat is looking for *you?*'

On cue, a gentle scratching at the greenhouse door startled them both.

'Socks!' Elwood cried as the cat entered, his silver DO NOT FEED ME disc catching the light like the sun.

'He's here for his breakfast. Don't tell Henry or Daisy, will you?' She attempted a weak smile, but felt her face pull into a grimace.

Elwood shook his head vigorously, not so easily distracted from his pursuit. 'The thing is, maybe the cat needs our help? Maybe it's trying to communicate with you? Maybe it's a *sign* something is going to happen.'

She noticed how red his eyes looked, his skin pale and sallow. 'Elwood, have you had any sleep?' she asked.

'Not much,' he admitted. 'I was up late with my map and then I couldn't wait to come over to tell you. I stayed up, waiting for the morning.'

What was going on at that house? Where the hell was Twig? And Blake?

'You don't look well.' She frowned. 'You look tired.'

How could he go to school like this? She put a thumb to his cheek, looking into his eyes, two pale pools of water.

Socks raised his front paws to her knees and mewled at her beseechingly.

'Hello, my sweet boy,' she said, stroking his head. 'Someone is encouraging the cat . . .' She paused, thoughtfully, holding a cat biscuit aloft. 'What do you think, Socks?'

Socks jumped for the biscuit, swallowing it in one, and then sat obediently beside her. She stood to get his bowl.

'Not encouraging it, exactly,' Elwood said, scrambling to his feet to follow her. 'But the cat's being drawn to them. To you. I've plotted it all on my map, and—' He stared at her, beguiling. 'You're the epicentre.' He breathed the word out, as if he were calling her his *universe*. and perhaps, for a short time, she had been. She sighed, swallowed away a tear. It was sweet, humbling, *beauty* in its purest form, two lonely souls drawn together by their wonderment at nature, but she had to put a stop to this.

'Elwood. My love.' She put a hand on his soft, messy hair. 'I'm sorry, but – I don't think that's possible.'

His eyes instantly dulled, as though she were just another grown-up letting him down. He flicked his gaze downwards, a perplexed look playing over his features.

'Why would a cat come looking for *me*?'

'Because you're special,' he said simply, as if it were the most obvious thing in the world.

She was always straight with children. She didn't believe in sug-arcoating things. It was important to be honest. 'I'm not special, Elwood. And, I'm sorry, but you're not either.'

He blinked rapidly, tears springing in his eyes at a rapid pace, cascading down his cheeks.

'I don't mean – you're special to me. And to your mums. But we're not—' She sighed. 'We're ordinary people on an ordinary street in an ordinary town. Me as a cat whisperer – it's not pos-sible. Nature can't be controlled in that way. We like to think it

175

can, we like to think we're superior, and in charge of everything, but we're not. That's what I love about nature. Its *wildness*. Its ability to overrule us. I understand it. I thought you did too.' She touched his arm gently.

He didn't move. He stared at her, layers of emotion peeling across his face. Shock, pain, betrayal. 'But you said—'

She closed her eyes. She was too tired for this. 'Forget what I said. I thought I was doing the right thing, in letting you "investigate"' – she drew quotation marks in the air – 'this with me. But it's gone too—'

He blinked in confusion. 'No. That doesn't make sense. You weren't doing this for me. You were doing it before I started coming over.' His arms were windmilling, gesturing wildly. 'You. You. You already had your books out. You already had your notes.'

He saw too much. He understood too much. She couldn't feed him a load of rubbish. He could see through her. 'I made it look that way.' Her arrows were delivered softly, like a spider scaling unbroken skin before delivering its bite. 'I wanted you to feel special. Like Skylar.'

Elwood's whole face fell, the last beams of light extinguished. 'You're lying!' he shouted. 'I don't believe you! You're just saying that because you know I'm right. You want to be the one to save the wild cat. By yourself!'

She put her head in her hands, her patience this early in the morning wearing thin. She'd only been trying to do the right thing.

'Elwood, when you're older, you'll understand.' She was patronizing him, as so many others did. She'd always promised herself she wouldn't. But he needed to understand. None of this could be true.

'You're lying,' he kept repeating, disbelief biting at his words. He pulled a wad of paper from the pocket of his striped pyjama bottoms and unfolded it. It was a map of the Briar Heart Estate edged with the Parkland. He'd marked his 'evidence' and placed a silver star at the back of Coralie's garden, where they were standing now, inside the greenhouse. He stared at it, tears tripping over themselves. His thin frame jerked as he struggled to process what she was saying.

'I'm sorry.' She shrugged, in a way which didn't imply she was sorry at all.

The map was shaking in his hands, his tears blurring the ink. She glanced at the clock. Adam was so fragile at the moment she didn't want him to know she'd left him alone and slept outside. The sedatives from the doctor would wear off soon.

'You need to get ready for school,' she said softly. 'Does your mummy even know you're here?'

He shook his head and she put a hand on his shoulder.

'It's time for all this to stop. Okay? You'll need to stay at home and play there after school.'

The heels of his hands swiped over his face to dry his tears as he stared up at her in bewilderment, as if to say, *what did I do wrong?* She couldn't bear to look at his sweet face.

'Come on then, time to go,' she said chipperly, as though the last twenty minutes had never happened. She ushered him out, walked him over to the gate and along the path to his own back garden. 'Bye,' she said brightly. 'Have a good day at school.'

She watched him trudge down the path, head dipped and shoulders slumped, his slippers passing over silver swirls of slug trails, map protruding from his pyjama pocket. Dried slivers of daffodil leaves greeted him at the back door, brown and wizened, falling over the edge of plant pots, or curled on the ground like shed snake skins. Just before he went inside, he turned to look at her, with piercing eyes. For a second, she matched it, chin tipped upwards, giving in to a crueller instinct, before she blinked and shook herself, replacing the challenge with a jolly wave. He just stared, visibly sighed, and went inside.

Still staring at the back door, Coralie took out her phone.

I think you were right. Elwood's getting too obsessed with the wild cat. Staying up late to research and putting two and two together and coming up with five. It would be a good idea to take away his iPad and map, etc. I really was just trying to help. I'm so sorry. Cx

She sent the text and looked up to Bob's house, hoping that would be the end of things. But in a lot of ways, it was just the beginning.

30

Twig

Twig saw Coralie's text after she emerged from the shower. She grabbed at a baggy black T-shirt dress that lay scrunched on the floor and slipped it over her head, her skin still wet.

'Elwood?' she said sharply. 'What's going on?'

She didn't know what to make of the message. What did she mean, 'too obsessed'? Twig had told her about the presentation, and the posters, and Coralie had seemed to laugh it off, saying, *wasn't it wonderful he was so inspired?* What had made Coralie change her mind?

Elwood was staring at the collage on his wall, his crime scene investigation, and back to another, smaller map, he held in his hands. He'd promised her he'd stop putting all his efforts into 'investigating' the wild cat with Coralie, but it seemed like overnight his project had grown, taking over the whole wall. 'Elwood, when did you do all this?'

She waited.

'Elwood?' She called his name again.

Eventually he turned, his big eyes shining, like flashes of rain on tarmac.

'We're in danger, Mummy,' he whispered. 'The wild cat is stalking Briar Close. Our road, Mummy, our road!' He gripped both her arms.

'It's not, honey.' She tried to calm him, but even as she was talking to him she could see a disconnect. He wasn't listening, his brain galloping ten paces ahead. Coralie's text was becoming clearer. Elwood was a mess. He looked exhausted. She drew him in for a hug, could feel his small heart thundering in his chest.

'You're safe, here,' she tried, but he wriggled from her grasp.

'No, Mummy. It's coming. It wants something. It's trying to *communicate* with us. With Coralie! She knows all about cats, and that's why it's come to find her. And it won't stop! What if . . . what if . . . to get her attention, it hurts someone?' He paced around his room, arms whipping at each pronouncement. 'She wants to be the one to save it, all by herself, but she's not listening.' Slivers of spittle escaped his lips, chapped from the sun.

The colour drained from Twig's face. *Oh shit.*

'You've got to listen to me, Mummy! No one is listening to me!' He was shrieking now, his screams carrying out into the street, louder than the early-morning birdsong. She closed his window and saw her father glance up from the lawn with a frown, evidently having heard Elwood's hysteria. As it snapped shut, the air thickened.

'Mummy?' Skylar emerged from Twig's bedroom, eyes gluey with sleep.

'For God's sake!' Twig's temper flared. 'You've woken your sister. She's been up half the night. As have I.'

Elwood didn't seem to hear, continued to point theatrically at his wall, the tip of his finger following the red lines of wool, a sergeant major preparing for battle. 'Elwood. Are you listening to me?' she pushed. 'This has got to stop!'

The atmosphere in the room felt charged, an electrical storm, heat and pressure increasing.

'It's over, Elwood! Don't you think I've got enough on my plate? Without *this*—'

Elwood flinched as though scalded. His face morphed, an angry rebuke playing over his delicate features.

'You don't care! You've never cared!' He poked his finger

away from the wall and in Twig's direction. Something about the pointed finger unearthed something within her. The stress she'd been carrying attracted to it like a lightning rod.

'*I* don't care?' she thundered. '*I* don't care! All I do is care!'

She began to tear at his wall, ripping his photocopies and pieces of paper, pulling out the small red pins he'd so carefully inserted and dropping them angrily into an empty cup on his desk, lined with the residue of chocolate oat milk. She could hear Skylar crying behind her, but it only served as fuel to her fire. She took the PowerPoint presentation he'd laboured over and ripped it clean in two. When she was done and the wall was bare she yanked his iPad out from under his bed. 'This is confiscated!' she yelled. 'Indefinitely.'

Elwood was pulsing like an athlete on a starting line. It was radiating from him, anger and frustration that had no place to go.

'What's going on?' Bob appeared at the door, Blake behind him, baulking at the look of fury on Twig's face and the mess littering the floor.

Elwood tore past them both, a sob, or a hiccup, escaping as he went.

'No one listens to me. No one ever listens to me!' he roared as he ran down the stairs and began grabbing at the lock.

'Elwood! Get back here!' Twig called, her anger already abating. *What had she done?* But he was too fast. She reached the front lawn in time to see him hammering on Matt's front door. Fear clenched at her heart. Fear, and something else too – embarrassment. Shame. Elwood was alternately ringing the bell and banging his tight little fist against the heavy wood. Her heart felt leaden in her chest as she approached, Blake, Bob and Skylar on her tail. She reached him as Emma opened the door, with the chain on.

'Oh, Elwood,' she breathed, evidently relieved, releasing the chain. 'Hakuna Matata' filtered through from the kitchen. 'Are you okay?'

She looked up and her gaze met Twig's. An unspoken *what's going on?*

181

Twig gave a small shake of the head.

'Come on, Elwood, let's go home.' Twig placed a hand on his shoulder, but he shrugged her off.

'It's the cat!' he shouted. 'It's targeting our street! No one is safe! Someone has to listen to me! We're all in danger!'

Matt and Henry appeared at the door. Matt dubious, Henry smirking. Neighbours peered from behind their front doors, or through twitching curtains. Windows were opened to get a better listen. Twig looked helplessly to Blake: *What do we do?* But Blake wouldn't catch her eye, approaching Elwood herself with a stern look. Her demeanour said: *isn't it enough I have to work all the time, and now I have to deal with this shit too?*

Matt manoeuvred himself around Emma, stepping outside. Twig was grateful he seemed to instinctively sense that something was very wrong. He crouched down and put a hand on Elwood's back. He spoke slowly and calmly, Twig and Blake flanking Elwood, forming a guard from the nosy neighbours.

'It's okay, Elwood. Everything's going to be okay. Take some deep breaths, that's it. Deep breaths until you feel better, and then we can talk about whatever's troubling you. Okay?'

Elwood nodded, and Twig's heart pinched. Blood pumped in her ears at the proximity of them all together: Twig, Elwood, Matt, Blake, Emma.

'I just want everybody to be safe.' Elwood's voice shook as he inhaled sharp, stabbing breaths. Twig thought of the number of times he had asked her if Skylar would be okay in the same plaintive tone.

'I'm sorry I didn't listen better.' She crouched down to his eye level. 'Shall we go home and talk there?'

Elwood's eyes darted around, as though weighing up who to trust. A few beats passed, the street momentarily silent. On the lawn a glossy black crow stood sentry while two magpies crossed its path, chattering and japing, their fanned wings colliding, like a bouncer escorting two drunks off the premises.

Another front door opened. Coralie emerged, frowning, on her lawn, a kimono wrapped around wide-legged printed trousers in the same thin silk, a crochet bag slung over her right shoulder. Her left arm was crossed over her chest protectively, her fingers resting on the straps.

You had to come outside, Twig thought tempestuously. *You've caused this and you can't resist being part of the action.*

Elwood turned and all Twig and Matt's work calming him came undone. 'She knows! She knows!' he shouted, pointing at Coralie. 'Tell them!' But Twig saw Coralie close her heart to Elwood and turn away, an embarrassed look on her face.

Twig straightened and noticed that Emma was also eyeing Coralie warily, her eyes flicking from Coralie and back to her house. Violently coloured roses, enormous and full-bodied, hung over Coralie's garden wall, like children being dangled by their feet. Twig caught a flash of movement from an upstairs window. *Adam?* She hadn't seen him in weeks. A tiny niggling doubt began to sing: was Elwood right? Was Coralie behind the wild cat? Not being sought out by it, but encouraging the rumours in some way? Hadn't she accused Twig of the very same?

'What's all this about?' Twig called out, moving towards her.

'I'm sorry, Twig,' Coralie said, crossing her lawn to meet her halfway on the pavement. At her feet a line of poppies lay horizontal, slayed by the heat. 'I don't know. A case of his imagination running out of control?' She looked pale and apprehensive.

'But you told me you believed me!' Elwood shouted. 'You know I saw it! You. You.' His voice shook as he panted, struggling for his brain and breath to synchronize, to get his words out quick enough. 'You said it was living in the Parkland. You said it!'

A worried frown passed over Coralie's face. 'I said there *could* be, Elwood.' She addressed the small, assembled crowd: 'Everyone heard me say that, right?'

'It's her! The cat's trying to give her a message! She's a cat whisperer! It's true!'

Twig took a step closer. 'What else have you said to him? Why have you riled him up like this?'

'Me?' Coralie declared. 'If you spent more time with him, Twig, you might appreciate what an active imagination he has!'

They faced each other, chest and shoulders squared. Twig's face burned at the insinuation that she had been neglecting Elwood.

'She talks to Socks!' Elwood shouted, undeterred, and then, as if sensing an opportunity to sway the crowd, turned to Emma: 'And she feeds him!'

Twig saw an *I knew it* look pass over Emma's face as she glared at Coralie. 'Is that true?'

'There's no such thing as a gluten-free cat, Emma,' Coralie snapped.

'You can come over and clean up all the vomit then!' Emma's face flashed with anger as Henry, holding his phone and still smirking, came closer to get a better look.

'Why don't you invest your time more wisely and sort out that bully son of yours?' Coralie snarled, waving an elegant hand in Henry's direction.

Henry stopped short as Matt straightened. 'Hang on a minute—' he started, but Emma was already streaming forward to Coralie and Twig, the three women a triumvirate of rage.

'Bully?' she spat. 'You're one to talk about being a bully! You've been picking on me ever since I put our plans in. Stirring things up and causing trouble.'

Coralie laughed haughtily. 'You don't need any help with that, Emma. You're not exactly flavour of the month around here, are you?' She opened her arms to the gathered neighbours. Some smiled, but many looked down at their feet as Emma struggled to compose herself.

'I've always tried to be a good neighbour and member of the community,' Emma said, her voice jumpy and breathless. 'But it's impossible living next door to people who are constantly making snippy little comments and—'

'Snippy little comments like what?' Coralie peered at her as though she were a specimen in a lab.

'Like *Disney princess*.' Emma enunciated every syllable. 'Or

184

Admin.' She glared at Blake, who looked momentarily stunned before opening her mouth as if to defend herself, but Emma cut across her, flinging an arm towards Coralie. 'You're not even subtle about it! I've heard you from over my fence! *And Disney princess my arse!*' Emma shouted, to ecstatic looks from Henry. 'My house is a dump! And you're doing your level best to keep it that way.' She had her hands on her hips as she glared at Coralie. 'I was so pleased to live next door to you. And to Twig and Blake.' Her eyes filled as her voice wobbled. 'But it's been a nightmare.'

'I'm sorry we haven't lived up to your Disney movie expectations, Emma,' Coralie responded caustically. 'Heaven knows you've not done anything to ingratiate yourself with the rest of us. Trying to build that absolute monstrosity.'

Twig looked between them both, finding her voice. 'Has Henry been bullying Elwood?'

'Of course he hasn't!' Emma threw her hands up. 'He hardly sees him. He's always holed up with Coralie. He doesn't hang out with the other boys!'

Twig flinched, another criticism going right to her core.

Elwood ran to Emma, sensing a comrade-in-arms. 'She has a notebook! A notebook she writes everything in.' He spun back to Coralie. 'Show them! Show them what's in it!'

'That sounds like a very good idea,' Emma said, clearly in a bid to wind up Coralie.

'I'll bet,' said Coralie eagerly, eyes narrowed. 'Not worked out too badly for you, has it, Emma, the Sevenoaks Panther? A nice little distraction from your plans.'

'I could say the same to you, *cat whisperer.*' Emma shot back.

'Oh, for God's sake.' Twig rolled her eyes.

'Don't you go getting all high and mighty.' Coralie's voice dripped with scorn. 'Using a cat to drag your career out of the mud!'

Twig recoiled. 'With respect, Coralie, I don't think I'm the one who is – *constantly* – all high and mighty. And for the record, I like Emma's plans.'

Emma blinked in surprise. 'Thanks.'

Seizing the distraction, Elwood grabbed at Coralie's crochet bag, trying to upend it on to the floor.

'Elwood!' Blake barked. 'Stop that right now!' But too late. Elwood wrenched it from Coralie's shoulder, scattering her things all over the lawn: pencils, ice-lolly sticks, a lip balm and a black stick with a red tip which looked like a loose part to something. There was no notebook.

'Where is it?' Elwood shrieked. 'Where's the notebook?'

'You've seen my notebook.' Coralie smiled at the assembled crowd. 'You know I've been keeping a record of the local *concerns*.'

'Not that one! There's another one! She's got two! She keeps it locked in her desk! She must have put it back. She thinks no one notices! But I do!' His voice was rising higher and higher in distress. 'The chain she wears around her neck. It has a little key and a whistle on it!'

A tiny flicker of surprise passed over Coralie's face and then was gone. Twig only just caught it. 'I do have a chain I wear sometimes. It used to be my grandmother's,' Coralie said, her face clouded with sadness as she opened the folds of the kimono round her neck, pulled at the neckline of the white silk top beneath: no chain. But Twig could remember seeing it before, a tiny sliver of silver, its pendant always hidden by Coralie's elegant, modest attire.

Elwood's face dropped. Twig could feel his heart breaking as though it were her own. She glanced at Emma, who was still glaring at Coralie and shaking her head. She met Twig's gaze with a sympathetic smile.

'Come on, Elwood,' Twig urged him gently, her fingertips feeling the tension emanating from his bony shoulders. 'You can stay home with me today.'

31

Emma

Emma stepped inside the house and flicked off her Disney playlist. The upbeat happy tunes were at odds with the jangling sense of unease growing in her stomach. She'd been playing them all week, trying to push down the memory of Matt at Twig's door saying he *needed to know*, trying to stop her brain zipping around in circles, like a dog chasing its tail. And now it had: finally her thoughts had quietened, overtaken by something new.

She knew Coralie had been feeding Socks. The range on her listening devices was excellent: if there was no intrusive background noise, or bad weather, she could hear all the way to Coralie's greenhouse. Had heard her offering Socks 'a little snack' as cat treats were audibly tipped into a bowl a few days prior. Finally, thanks to Elwood's outburst, she had evidence she could call her out on, but it was a hollow victory. She pictured Elwood's guileless face as she paced up and down the kitchen. Emma had a confession to make. The thing was, where to begin?

Daisy, who had missed the action, was in her room sulking. Henry had scampered immediately upstairs with his phone. She glanced at her watch; they still had time before they needed to leave for school. She found Matt sitting at the bottom of the stairs, staring absent-mindedly.

'I need to tell you something.'

'Go on.' He looked relieved to have a distraction from his own thoughts.

'It's about Elwood.'

She saw the flicker, the tiny slip of his mask. She pushed it to one side. *Stop reading into things, Emma.*

'Okay.'

'Well, not Elwood, exactly. The cat. The – well. Some of the things he was saying . . .'

Matt frowned, his disappointment evident. 'Oh, good God. Not you too.' He put his hands on his knees, rose from the stairs and walked to the kitchen. 'Does it really matter if she's been feeding Socks?' he said wearily.

'No, not that,' she tutted. 'Hear me out. Please.' She followed him from room to room, the sun pressing against the windows, baking the back of the house. In winter it had been freezing, but summer was like one of those hot yoga sessions Agatha liked to do. Emma was already uncomfortably warm. She puffed out a quick shot of air, psyching herself up. 'Um, okay. So, this is embarrassing.'

Perhaps it was the squirm in her voice, but he stopped at that and turned to her, his attention caught.

Just say it, Emma, just say it.

She took a deep breath. 'I noticed that when the rumours were flying about the wild cat, the number of objections to our plans, and the number of comments in the messaging group opposing it, went down.'

'Right.' He gave her a *please don't say what I think you're about to say look* as he turned a coffee capsule over in his hands.

'So I . . . *planted* some things.'

'Okay . . .' His brows knotted quizically as the coffee machine frothed and spluttered on the wizened two-tone wood counter-top. 'What things?'

'Like *bones* and things.' She was acutely embarrassed, and yet a tiny sprinkle of amusement was threatening to spill out. She glanced at Matt and saw the same wrestle on his own features. His

188

mouth twitched even as his eyes stared at her in bewilderment. He looked like he wasn't sure if he was being pranked or not. 'And started some rumours . . .' Her voice took on a wheedling tone.

'You did what?'

'I planted bones in the Parkland. To make it look like a wild cat had been there. And I scratched a tree, to look like one I'd seen on YouTube. And made paw prints. In the mud. They were quite authentic. Honestly . . .' Her face and facade crumbled, the jittery nervous energy leaking out of her. She sunk down on to the kitchen table, using it as a chair.

'I've been home alone too much, and everything with the house . . . I felt paranoid about what everyone's been saying about us, *helpless*. It made me feel a bit more back in control, I suppose.' She glanced up at him, trying to read his response, but his face was closed.

She continued, tentatively: 'Plus, it was a bit of a laugh. An up-yours to all those fusty Sevenoaks people slagging us off. Like bloody Tim, and the parish council.' She cringed. 'I, um, I dropped some bones over his back wall one day, when I was on a run. He never mentioned them, although I'm sure he was rattled.' Emma knew he was rattled because she'd overheard him talking to his wife. 'And then the next week, I came across some roadkill, a dead badger. It was just a random, stroke of luck! I couldn't believe it! I used the bags-for-life in the boot to cover my hands and spread out the black sacks you keep in there for your Scouting stuff when it's muddy. Then I dragged the badger to the boot, scooped it up and tipped it in. God, it was rank. Must've been fresh though, no maggots or anything like that. And *heavy*. My arms and shoulders were killing the next day.' She looked up gingerly. 'That's what Elwood was talking about at the Summer Fayre.'

Matt blinked. She had an urge to fill the silence. She could tell him about how she was listening in on their neighbours, but she wasn't ready to confront him over his conversation with Twig. Maybe it all meant nothing? She clung to the hope that it might still be nothing. That the fear she'd had since the beginning of

189

all this, that she'd overhear something insurmountable, wasn't being realized.

He moved his mouth to speak. Stopped. Tried again. She'd expected him to be angry, embarrassed by her, frustrated, incredulous. Instead, he closed his eyes and did the last thing Emma had expected: he began laughing. Emma smiled awkwardly, hesitant at first, but then, seeing an image of herself on hands and knees in the Parkland, arranging the fox's skull – *weeing on it!* – and scattering the bones, she began to chuckle too. Matt's mirth was contagious. Tears began clotting in her eyes.

'Talk me through it,' Matt gasped. 'Tell me again.'

So she did, adding more context this time, telling him about the child in the Parkland finding her and having to hide. Why were they both laughing? An edge of mania to them both? None of this made sense. It felt like the only option after the tension with Elwood outside. And what she was saying was ridiculous, right? Absolutely, totally, ridiculous.

For a moment they were frozen like that, laughing together in a trap of sunlight in the kitchen. Sadness enveloped her briefly into its folds. She curved her fingers against her lips and closed her eyes. *Why couldn't she be happy? Did it matter if Coralie fed Socks, or Twig said unfathomable things on her doorstep, or all their neighbours hated them and said they had no taste?*

'And the other rumours?' Matt asked.

'Oh. Yeah. Well. After Cupid . . . Obviously, I thought that was just a fox, but it reminded me of a story I'd heard a while back. A cat killer. Doing a similar sort of thing.' She grimaced. 'I thought that would really get people talking. I set up some fake profiles online, applied to join the local group and accepted them myself.' She winced in the retell. It sounded much worse than it was. It had only taken five minutes. 'A perk of being an admin. And then I posted on their behalf, with wild stories about missing pets. I am Mrs Channing from the duck pond. I didn't need to do much for the whole panther thing to take off . . . but now, after Elwood, I feel terrible.'

Matt was shaking his head and biting on his lower lip. Emma could feel her whole body softening, and relaxing, at Matt's response. *Forwards, not backwards.* That was something they'd always said to each other. After the failed rounds of IVF. After a missed promotion, or a lower than expected bonus: *forwards, not backwards.* Could they still be a team?

'Anyway' – she circled one hand like a composer – 'that's why I don't trust Coralie. Anyone that checked it out would have realized it was rubbish. But Aggie said she reassured people she'd looked into it. Said she'd spoken to the owners of the cats and they'd all met natural, non-suspicious, ends. All this "I've got a big degree and I know about wild cats", I think she's full of hot air.'

'She must've just realized from the off it was nonsense.' Matt slipped his arms around her waist. Her head was level with his broad chest. She dipped her forehead against it, breathing in his familiar scent as he held her with one hand and smoothed the other over her hair. She had a flashback to the early years of their relationship, when Matt folding her into his body had made her feel safe. Not suffocated, or irritated. 'You really do want these plans to go through, don't you?'

In that moment she really did love him, really did feel as though he got her. Without judgement or reservation. Like he was her person. And she really hoped that the two facts she knew – about him loving Twig and him not coming home – weren't connected. Maybe Matt, and not Adam, was her person after all. Had Adam even meant to touch her that night? It felt like a dream now. Like it couldn't really have happened.

'I feel awful for upsetting Elwood. He really believes there's a panther out there.' Something about Elwood, usually so curious and full of beans, on her doorstep crying and shaking, had triggered a wave of tenderness towards him. A rush of distrust towards Coralie. And not just because she'd been barefaced lying about feeding Socks. 'Don't you think it's weird how Coralie is usually so nice and friendly to him and she just turned her back on him? And he was so upset.'

There was a coldness in Coralie's movements which didn't sit right with her. In the turn of her shoulder, the moue of distaste on her lips. Like she'd discarded a pet she no longer wanted. She wouldn't tell Matt about her surveillance efforts. She would stop posting about the cat and stop planting cat 'evidence', would try to bring some calm to her life during the interminable wait until the Planning Applications Committee met in August and the fate of Briar Heart House would be decided. But she would keep her eye on Coralie King.

The Mystery of the Sevenoaks Panther

Valerie, Number 14: Everyone said the trouble started after the Brooks' planning application went in, but they were still friendly after that. Still having parties in the garden or waving and calling out to each other. No, it was later. That terrible scene in the street! [Shakes head.]

And by the time of the benefit for little Skylar . . . [Holds her fingers to her temples.] Poor Coralie, she'd made such an effort. But that was Coralie all over. She dropped dinner round every day for a fortnight after my last operation. Nothing was ever too much bother.

I'll never forget seeing her that night, outside on the lawn greeting guests. [Voice wobbles.] She looked aglow. Like something from a movie. She was so beautiful. [Sigh.] Such a shame what happened. And those two little girls. [Sob.] Now without a mother. *The injustice of it!* [Scrunches her tissue in her hand angrily.] I'm sorry.

DI Mackintosh: Do we wish we'd taken early reports of the Sevenoaks Panther more seriously? With what we know now, yes. [Nods solemnly.]

Valerie: [Sadly.] None of us will ever forget that summer.

32

Twig

Twig squinted at Elwood's notes. He had been bent over his green notebook since they'd returned home, eschewing all offers of peanut-butter bagels or ice lollies.

Puddleford Parkland

27 June 23: Scat found. Large oak to the right of Cam 7.

18 July 23: Goose. Decapitated. 1 wing and 1 fibular remaining.

19 July 23: Cam 3. Sudden movement and acceleration at approx. 2.41 a.m. Strangled sound off camera. Believe rabbit.

'Is this all true?'
He nodded.
'And this is from what you read in Coralie's notebook this morning?'
He nodded again.
'And you just remembered it?'
'Most of it. I can't remember everything. There was lots.' He rubbed his ink-smudged fingers over his eyes, red from tiredness and crying. 'If I tell you something, Mummy, will you promise not to be cross?' His usual opener.

Her usual response: 'I can't promise, but I'll try my best.'

As usual, it was enough.

'I've looked at her notebook before. Sometimes when she makes my tea, or if she pops inside her house and leaves me in the greenhouse.' He hung his head in shame. 'I know I shouldn't have. I'm sorry, Mummy.'

She breathed out in relief. 'That's okay. Thank you for telling me.'

She flipped to another page of his notebook:

1 Aug 22: Large footprint in mud. Not dog. Multiple deer prints surrounding.

2 Sept 22: Badger carcass. Neatly eviscerated.

15 Sept 22: One strong lamb gutted overnight. Tooth pit impacts on mandibles.

There were so many notes. From when the cameras were first installed in the Parkland to much fanfare, but further back than that, even. And the dates of the recordings were consistent; there were no big gaps. Hadn't Coralie said she'd had the cameras removed? Why had she lied? If this was all true, Coralie had known all along there was a wild cat nearby. Why hadn't she said anything?

'She didn't want anyone to hurt it,' Elwood replied, and Twig realized she'd been speaking aloud. 'She says a wild cat has never hurt a human in Britain, so there's no risk. And she didn't want *trophy hunters* to come.'

Twig didn't know what to believe. She slipped the notebook back on his desk and watched as he resumed his quiet industry before placing a gentle hand between his hunched shoulders. 'Is Henry bullying you?'

'Not really,' Elwood responded airily, his pencil dancing over the page.

Her stomach knotted. 'What does that mean?'

He said nothing. She saw his pulse flickering beneath the thin, pale skin of his neck.

'Elwood?'

He finally looked up. 'He didn't believe me when I said I saw a cat, but then . . .' He chewed on his lip, looking out towards Coralie's greenhouse '. . . I guess nobody did.' He returned to his notebook.

Twig let out a long, slow breath as she chewed on a fingernail. She vaguely remembered Elwood's excitement when he thought he'd seen a cat, how quick she'd been to assume it was a shadow or a trick of the light. Maybe if she had validated his belief, even if she didn't believe it, he wouldn't have been so vulnerable to Coralie's flattery, or to Henry's ridicule at school.

She put both hands on his shoulders now, squeezed them gently, finding them locked with anxiety to match her own. He was too little to be so weighed down by life. 'I love you, buddy,' she said, with a final squeeze. He bobbed his head, his focus still fixed on his page.

She began to pick up the notes she'd pulled from Elwood's display on the wall, neatening them into a pile, her stomach full of remorse: for tearing them down, for allowing him to spend so much time with Coralie in the first place.

Her attention was drawn to a page in her hand with Elwood's handwriting – 'CONFIRMED SIGHTING' – detailing Adam seeing a cat on his car bonnet back in May. Who had confirmed it? Elwood, wrongly? Coralie, *correctly*? She stared through Elwood's window, framed with his celestial curtains, to the brooding Parkland beyond. *Was there* a big cat out there? And if there was, what was Coralie's plan? Fudging the evidence to persuade everyone there was no big cat, because she truly believed there was no danger to anyone else, while monitoring it? What would Adam, clearly terrified of something, make of it if his wife had known about it all along? Discredited him, even, when she could have spoken up for him. Was her ardent environmentalist neighbour protecting the cat over her husband and friends? And if she was . . . what if she was wrong?

The Mystery of the
Sevenoaks Panther

Lady Violet Campbell, Coralie's mother: We paid for the flat in Chelsea and we gave her full access to her trust fund. That's how she bought the house in Kent. Credit to *us*, I should think, after what she'd done. But the truth is, we wanted rid of her. And that was the best way to secure it.

Leonora Bonetti, the Campbells' nanny: She used to say her parents weren't interested in her. That she wasn't exotic, or engaging, enough. Too plain, too ordinary. I used to tell her that she was beautiful, but it wasn't enough. She craved her mother's love, her father's attention. She would say, 'If I had the grace and beauty of Cleopatra, they might love me more.' But [shrugs] I was never sure about that.

Lady Violet: She was always looking for attention. Always something the matter. Fainting or pretending she was dead. She was *jealous* of the animals, even. Any attention we ever gave Cleopatra she resented. Can you imagine such a thing?

Leonora: Every night I had to read her the same story. Over and over again. I was so bored! I said, 'My child, please, let us read a different story.' But she would howl and cry until I picked the book up again. [Nods.] She was difficult. But in that family they all were.

Lady Violet: It was jealousy that led to all the trouble. She couldn't *bear* not to be the centre of attention. She was resorting to more and more desperate tactics. But I wouldn't give in. I thought, *she needs to learn.* Do I regret it? Hmmm. In a sense, yes. But it was all Coralie's fault. I could never have predicted what was going to happen.

33

Coralie

Coralie had been sitting in her usual spot for over an hour, the bucket a short distance away. The lid of the sky was still day-time-blue, but the horizon glowed orange and gold, ablaze. Coralie loved this time of year, midsummer, when green had entirely vanquished grey, weeds and wild grass climbing up to meet ivy, abundantly festooned over walls like curtains. Trees forming arches over roads, a verdant ceiling. If light escaped, it was through small gaps, decorating the floor in mosaics. The world felt *alive*. Nature returned in all its power, all its glory.

She knew already she'd always equate the smell of sardines to this summer. In the warm air, still sticky and close from another scorching day, the slippery fish stank. The stench rose like steam, fanning through the cool, dim woodland. She heard a woodpecker's thrum, as she often did, deep in the Parkland. Most people knew only the sanitized version of the Parkland, the metre either side of the path to and from school, but Coralie knew its dark, wild heart.

In an instant it happened, as it always did. The chattering of magpies halted. The susurration of leaves ceased. The woodland was silent. *Nature always knew first*. She could feel herself being watched. She knew, from the way the hairs on her arm stood on end, she was close. She felt calm, reassured. She was okay.

It had taken months to get here. Years. Slowly building trust. It was like a marriage. It needed solid foundations.

A crunch of dry leaves alerted her. Slow and deliberate.

A low, chuffing sound.

A growl, to the ignorant. A welcome, to the wise.

The sound repeated. She was deep in the Parkland, a long way from the track. Alone, until now.

She kept her eyes trained on the wall of shadow ahead, where the wan light of the clearing could not latch, failing to illuminate the dense foliage.

A flicker and two emerald eyes popped in the darkness.

The shadow shimmered before settling, an outline of contradictions forming: of curves and peaks, of elegance and strength. Finally, Monroe emerged, night rippling from her glossy fur. Her movement was fluid, her muscles undulating like black sand dunes rolling on a windy day.

'Hello, my sweet girl.' Every atom of the air felt charged, every particle of forest dust electric.

Monroe tilted her head upwards as if in greeting, displaying her regal neck, atop a body packed with power. Her whiskers flashed silver in the dusk; her eyes glowed like a shallow pool of moss-green water as they remained fixed on Coralie. Coralie glimpsed tiny flashes of ivory: Monroe's retractable claws, puncturing the still evening air; her saliva-slicked canines. With one bite she could gouge out a throat. Coralie raised a hand to her own neck as she smiled in wonder, pressed bone and gristle beneath her fingertips.

When Coralie had moved to Sevenoaks four years ago, she'd had this strange feeling, like she was waiting for something to happen. The first time she'd picked Monroe up on Cam 7, in the north-east section of the Parkland, a year later, she'd thought: *this is it. This is what I've been waiting for.* It was the *connection* she'd wanted. That's why she'd gone back, night after night, until she saw her again. Why she began leaving out treats, and playthings, and eventually – months later – revealing herself. Forming a bond.

200

At first she'd tip out the contents of the bucket and stand back, but as their bond had deepened, she'd enjoyed watching Monroe play and had made the set-up trickier. Leaving the handle upright, or placing a cover over it and watching her upend the bucket herself. Sometimes she brought a cardboard box: cats love boxes. *Big cats are just like small cats*, she'd smiled to herself, watching the cat climb in.

Monroe stepped nearer still, the clearing her catwalk as she sauntered closer. Her crepuscular fur gleamed, the dusting of dim light revealing the merest hint of burnished gold. In bright light her coat appeared jet black, but in the dappled light of the woodland Coralie could discern the curved rosettes of her markings, the ubiquitous leopard print so beloved of her contemporaries. Their cheap imitations could never capture the richness, the intricacy, of the real thing.

She reached her arm out, fingers pearly pale in the dark. Carefully the cat walked alongside her, sleek fur glancing her skin, as though it were embracing her. Coralie closed her eyes.

She pitied the people who thought wild cats couldn't exist here. Pitied the limits of their understanding, the narrowness of their worlds. That they could ignore the many sightings, the reports of livestock predation, the *evidence* from university professors who studied pit marks and saliva samples. Because it was easier to ignore it than admit the truth. *We are all wild things.* How stifled their half-lives were. Her daughters were the same. They'd rather sit inside, slowly dying – for all the wild things are slowly dying – eyes fixed on a screen. Only Elwood seemed to understand. Only Elwood could live in the moment like she did, connected to the natural world in all its vibrancy. Poor Elwood. If only things were different. She would bring him here. How his luminous eyes would alight in delight.

As the cat purred the deep vibrations wrapped around Coralie, took her back to Cresswell Place, to the house she grew up in, to the opulent carpets and the gold side tables, her fingers deep in comforting fur or draped around Cleopatra's neck. She agreed with her grandmother: big cats shouldn't be kept as pets, caged like a domestic animal. No wonder they struck out sometimes.

She'd never blamed Duchess for what happened to Cleopatra. She certainly didn't blame herself. She blamed her mother (*So predictable*, her mother purred in her ear). But, though she was loathe to admit it, she understood it better now. Her philandering father was rarely at home. When he was, her mother was pitiful, dressed up to the nines, touching and pressing herself against him, desperate for any small return in affection: a hand grazing her lower back, perhaps, or a sniff of the expensive perfume encircling her neck. It was no surprise her mother poured all her energies, all her frustrations, all her need for love, into her cats. Now Coralie had the best of both worlds. Her own cat, but in the wild. It *chose* her.

She remembered the first time she'd reached out and touched Monroe, here in the forest. The fear of rejection, or worse: a strike. A claw. Death. But growing up around big cats had diminished that fear. She knew how gentle these animals could be, if they were treated with kindness. Nurtured. Loved. And yes, where necessary, controlled.

Coralie hadn't played with dolls or teddies as a child; Coralie had played with cats. Big cats. And it had been over two decades since she'd been close to one again. Touched one again. As a child, she'd thought to touch a big cat, to stroke it, to hold it, the feeling she felt, was love. But now, an adult, she understood: it was power. The sensations that sent shivers up and down her body: it was so close to sex. It was animal. She had tasted power at Cresswell Place, but it had been wrested from her and now it was back. This was how she'd grown up. And not just big cats either: with parrots and geckos and, at one point, a monkey, although she had treasured the cats the most.

She rarely allowed herself to think of Cleopatra. Cleopatra was always her mother's favourite. Beautiful Cleopatra. And she'd been Coralie's favourite too. But Coralie wouldn't wallow in her loss, how much she wished she could touch, or hold, her again. What's done is done. The past is where it should be. Left behind.

The day after Cleopatra was killed, Coralie had returned to the nursery, surprised to find only the faintest outlines in the carpets and upholstery betraying the horrors of the day before. The staff must have been scrubbing all night. The house was quiet, all the animals removed. A single tear had rolled down her cheek as her nanny, Leonora, placed a hand on her shoulder.

She had been surprised when her mother entered, more surprised still when she crossed the room in a cloud of her familiar scent to gently cup her chin, raising Coralie's face to meet her gaze. For a split second Coralie remembered thinking, *maybe it was worth it, poor Cleopatra's fate*, before the painful swipe was delivered. But Coralie, unlike Leonora beside her, who had to look away, didn't flinch as her mother slapped her face, hard. She smiled, later, when her reflection still bore the imprint of her mother's hand, warning-red against her creamy skin. She knew even then that the violence of it wasn't really for her. It was all for them. Her parents. They had ignored her, neglected her, turned their backs on her, and now she was all that was left. Who would console them now?

Coralie missed the pets too, in the small window of time before she was sent away. She missed Cleopatra, her failsafe playmate. It was Leonora who had smuggled a photo of them together into her suitcase when she was sent away to school. She was the only one who seemed to understand that it was an accident. And perhaps she felt guilty, somehow, that she hadn't been able to stop it, couldn't protect Coralie from witnessing the traumatic scene.

The rational part of Coralie knew this wasn't her cat. Knew it wasn't even one of her cubs. She never knew where her family's cats had gone after that awful day. Had they been destroyed? Released into the wild? But she felt so connected to Monroe. As though she could right the wrongs of the past.

Recent events had made her wonder whether there was more than one big cat living nearby. That was an exhilarating prospect. She was investigating. Recording everything. That's why she'd been checking faeces. Assessing bones. That's why she'd left the stinking fallow deer carcass she'd found in the clearing outside in the scorching sun. She needed to bake the bones, literally, to be able to assess them for pit marks. For the tell-tale triangle imprint of carnassial teeth cusps. Kofi had nearly caught her out, when he came across the carcass in the Parkland that morning. She hadn't expected anyone else to be about that early, but luckily she'd seen him, had time to hide it and later return it to her freezer before he got back from his bike ride. Still, Fwuffy being eaten was a shock. She'd worried briefly that things were getting out of control, before she reminded herself of the facts. *She* was in control.

'Do you have a friend in the woods?' she purred. She knew instinctively that her cat, Monroe, wouldn't have been behind the dead domestic cats. It was too crass a move. Was there another cat, beyond Monroe? It was possible. Anything felt possible now. It had been a big risk, leaving the fawn carcass under Adam's car back in May. It was an impulsive decision when she'd come across it that morning: a fresh kill, barely eaten; the cat must've got disturbed. For a few months at that stage, she'd been dousing Adam in an aftershave proven in studies to attract cats, insisting he wore it because it *drove her wild! (Swoon!)* and spraying all his clothes with it, along with the occasional slick of sardine oil on his trainers, when she got away with it under the guise of feeding Socks. The rush when he started complaining he felt like he was being followed! Even now, as she sat in her clearing, Monroe's tail – a question mark upturned to the sky – tickling her arm, a broad smile spread over her face at the recollection.

When she slipped the carcass under his car early that morning she'd not really expected anything to come of it. She was fortunate that, in early May, the air was still cool enough to keep the smell at bay. Mostly, anyway; it reeked by the time she had retrieved it in the middle of the night, rats scrambling off the bloated mass and regrouping as she dumped it in the parkland. It was fit only for the most desperate of scavengers by then, certainly not for Monroe. Not that she minded them – rats and foxes and buzzards and the like – in fact, she admired their tenacity. It was them she rooted for whenever a stranded fledgling appeared on her lawn. Like that one back in May. Feeble little thing, it stood no chance. She was spurred on by the cut and thrust of the wild. Who would win? That day – the supper party – she had won. She had tempted a wild cat into suburbia. She was certain no one else had achieved it before.

She didn't allow herself a minute of doubt, or guilt. Yes, she'd brought the cat closer to their homes. She'd brought the cat to the Briar Heart Estate. But knowing it would never hurt anyone. Unless, of course, it had reason to do so.

Her hand stroked Monroe's head. Monroe swooped nearer, snuggled further against her palm. She knelt to be closer, their faces beside each other, touching, the deep purrs delving into her ears until it was all she could hear. Her cunt twitched. Her nipples ached. This was as close to sex as you could get. She stayed as long as she could bear it.

'It's almost time,' she said, when she finally stood to leave. She gazed adoringly at the animal. It was always like this: she never wanted to go.

Only Socks knew Coralie's plan. Like she'd always said: cats were more reliable than people.

JULY

The Mystery of the Sevenoaks Panther

Anjit, Number 20: [Pauses.] You know we don't like to gossip.

Joy, Number 20: [Sighs.] Anjit . . .

Anjit: [To his wife.] What? It might be relevant. And it's nothing to do with Coralie! [To the camera.] She won't hear a word against Coralie. [Shakes his head.] Anyway, on this occasion Coralie was nowhere to be seen. This was all about the Dorsetts and the Brooks . . . it was like a Shakespearean tragedy or something, or . . .'

Joy: Get on with it, Anjit! [Rearranges her hands in her lap. Tuts. Looks at camera. Rolls eyes.] This is what happened: You remember that morning Elwood had an outburst in the street, ranting and raving? Well.

Anjit: [Leans in. Cuts Joy off.] It turned out that Henry Brooks was recording the whole thing. Which, you know, I don't like to talk ill of a *child*, but it was really quite unkind. [Lowers voice.] '*Little dipshit!*' Blake was hollering, and Twig had her arms up trying to calm her down, but it was no use. We're not used to that sort of language around here. [Gives a knowing look.] Matt and

Emma Brooks just stood there in total shock. What could they say? Henry had sent the video round the whole school by lunchtime and by night it had gone viral.

Chloe, Number 16: Do you remember it? Cat-boy?

Megan, Number 16: 'She's a cat whisperer!' became that summer's meme. Mortifying.

Chloe: [Shudders.] And then there was the barbecue.

Megan: [Groans.] Oh, Chlo, not the barbecue. [Covers her face with her hands.]

Chloe: I think that's when the beef, or feud, whatever you want to call it, really started. Emma had installed some cameras around the outside of her house the month before. Dad was convinced she was using them to spy on people. 'She's always looking shifty!' he'd say. I think being a property lawyer had put that sort of thing on his radar. [Shrugs]. But that evening, we were in the garden, having a barbecue. Dad was laughing about what had happened, when this drone appears. Hovering above us.

Megan: Dad started freaking out! Do you remember? [Alters tone, thrusts chest out and pulls arms rigid by her side.] 'Recording others without consent, whether by a smart doorbell, or by drone, is a direct violation of the Data Protection Act and the CCTV Code of Practice.'

Chloe: [Dissolves into peels of giggles.] He was just shouting it, first in the back garden, up at the drone, and then he went out the front. Mum was saying, 'Tim, you don't know it's them!' and he was shouting, 'Yes I do!'

Megan: Honestly, that summer, the whole town went mad!

34

Twig

'We should move,' Twig declared to Blake, raising her head from her iPad where she was reading the *Guardian*. She turned the screen to Blake: the viral videos of Elwood and Coralie had pushed the Sevenoaks Panther into mainstream news coverage. That wasn't her primary motivation, of course: she needed distance from Matt Brooks and his family. But it was a useful cover. She hadn't wanted another scene in the street yesterday, but Blake was right: Henry Brooks *was* a dipshit. Not only had he made that video, but he'd used 'A Boy Made of Stars' as its soundtrack. Twig had to witness the song's surge in popularity knowing it was the source of her son's humiliation. *Elwood's possible half-brother,* she thought bitterly. Why hadn't she done a paternity test? To know for sure whether Elwood was Matt's or Kev's? (*He was neither,* she reminded herself, as she always did. *He was Blake's.*)

'How are we going to afford to move?' Blake's tone suggested she was humouring her.

'We'll sell the flat.' Twig was still stinging from the 'Twig show' accusation and felt more guarded with Blake, although the events since had meant that, on the surface, at least, their argument had been forgotten. The fact that neither of them had mentioned the revival of 'A Boy Made of Stars, in the wake of Henry's video, was proof it had not.

211

'You know we can't sell the flat.'

'Someone will buy it.' If they could move somewhere else, somewhere they could re-group, the four of them, and start again. Maybe they could still fix things.

'At a knockdown price. No way. Once the management company agrees to pay the costs for the cladding, we can sell.'

'That could take years in litigation! Meanwhile we're stuck here, stagnating.'

Blake looked at her levelly but said nothing.

'We'll rent,' Twig continued. 'Somewhere cheaper. By the sea. We'll go back to Bali!'

'And you'll be satisfied with the ongoing monitoring of Skylar's *cancer* in Bali, will you?' The way Blake said it set out her stall: she had humoured her enough. She could no longer be fucked with this conversation.

'Margate. We'll move to Margate. We have friends in Margate. *Artist* friends.'

'Our *artist* friends have pushed the prices up in Margate,' Blake responded drily.

'We'll move up North. Manchester. Or—'

'If we move anywhere, it will be back to the US.' Blake removed her black-rimmed glasses and rubbed her hands over her eyes. She'd been in the garage studio working until late last night.

'It's not "back" for me or the kids,' Twig snapped. Twig knew, if they had the health insurance to cover it, Blake would want them in the US already.

'I'm sorry,' she said to Blake's stony face, 'if I'm not ready to go over there on some bonding mission, breaking bread with people who have been so unkind to you.' A clear reference to Blake's parents.

'Well, I am, Twig,' she replied. 'And it's my family and it's my choice. And—' she sighed and looked skywards, her voice losing the hard-casing it wore so often recently – 'I would really like to spend some time with my mom. I didn't have that growing up, and I would really like to make the most of that opportunity now. Is that so bad?'

Twig bit her tongue.

'Where has this come from?' Blake asked. 'You're not seriously suggesting we move our family away from a place where we're settled, where we're fortunate to live with your dad . . .' Twig knew her measured tone was for Bob's benefit if he was in earshot, though she could see him behind Blake, out in the garden, a plastic glove on one hand and a small shovel in the other '. . . close to some of the best hospitals for cancer treatment in the world, all *because of a cat?*'

She said it in such a slow, deliberate, mocking way Twig wanted to reach over the table and grab hold of the strings of her cropped hoodie and yell, *I want to do it to save us. You don't know the danger we're in!* The danger was so close now she could feel it rising like sea water, close to the surface. She drummed her fingers on the table, nervous energy tingling through her.

'It's not just the cat. All this stuff with Elwood and Henry. I feel so . . . *trapped* here.'

She wanted Blake to wrap her arms around her as she'd always done and tell her things would work out, that they would find a way to fix things together. 'Elwood will be fine. This kind of thing is all part of growing up.' Twig couldn't help but note her therapy-esque style of delivery and wished Blake sought her counsel as much as she did her therapist's. 'The cat thing is nonsense. Clickbait.' Blake abhorred the gutter press, social media, anything she considered low brow. Behind her Twig saw her dad shaking his head and returning towards the house. He bent down out of sight then reappeared with a dustpan and brush. 'Even if there was one . . . you get wild cats in California. It's not a big deal.'

'I know.' Twig felt oddly reassured, having seen Elwood's excerpts from Coralie's notebook. The more she thought about it, the more it was clearly all made up. Coralie had stoked Elwood's imagination, using him to feel good about herself. Her captive audience. She probably knew he'd been peeking at her notebook even. What was her elaborate effort in attention-seeking in aid of? To elevate her standing in the community further? To put herself right at the centre of things, as usual? Most likely. Coralie King made her feel sick. But she was essentially harmless. A tragic narcissist with too much time on her hands. She hadn't mentioned any of this to Blake. Couldn't face Blake scoffing at her that of course it was all made up.

'It's not that, it's . . .'

She would never be able to tell Blake the truth. Blake could never know. Blake would leave her. She would realize that everything they'd built – their family, their world – was a lie. And that would be Blake's right. 'It's . . . everything,' she concluded feebly.

'I get it.' Blake sighed, and Twig thought, *do you?* with a ferociousness she wasn't expecting. She wished she'd been able to stay in the music industry, kept a small pocket of her life she could hold on to and earn money from. Where would she be now, if she had? Whatever happened between them, Blake could survive it; Twig wasn't sure she would.

Tears were filling her eyes now, her nerves rattling in her chest, her breath coming in short, sharp bursts.

She stopped abruptly as her father entered the kitchen. Two small pink circles immediately coloured his cheeks. Open displays of emotion didn't come easily to either of them. 'Right,' he said, reaching for the kettle. 'Right.' He withdrew three mugs from the cupboard and filled them with the sweet, hot, milky tea he loved and neither Twig nor Blake had the heart to tell him they couldn't stand.

'I've not been able to help you out as much as I'd have liked with Skylar,' he said stiffly, setting the mugs down on the table.

'No, Dad, you've done more than enough,' Twig said, and it was true. Not only having them move in but also giving them the rest of his savings, what was left after paying for her mother's care. Her parents' financial situation was a far cry from when Twig was growing up. They'd been one of the first houses on the estate to add a conservatory and a swimming pool, both of which sat empty and forlorn.

'I want you two to have the house,' he continued, not making eye contact. 'Some security behind you when this is all over.' The last few years had left an imprint on him. He had shrunk inwards, his eyes smaller, the skin on his face looser, as if his body were contracting.

'That's *so kind*,' Blake began, but Bob was quick to talk over her: 'No, I mean it. Wait there.'

Flustered, he left the room. Blake gave Twig a warning look that said *we're not staying here forever* and Twig widened her eyes in challenge, her temper flaring at the ease with which Blake had deflected her father's generous gesture.

Bob returned with a small stack of papers and slid them over the table. 'I had these drawn up last week. I'd only be leaving it to you anyway. I'm doing it sooner, that's all. You can put down roots. Spend some time as a family without the worry of where you're going to live hanging over you.' His eyes began to glisten, and Twig's did too. 'All I ask is a bed here when I come to visit.'

'You're leaving?' Twig jerked in surprise, ignoring Blake's level stare.

'Not yet.' He patted her on her forearm and stood. 'Not until Skylar's better, when you're back from New York and everything's settled. I'm going to take our trip. The one me and your mother planned.' The trip her parents had frequently discussed and never got to take.

'We'll look after the garden,' Twig sniffed, aware of Blake's pointed glare behind her father's retreating back: *hold up, we've not discussed this.*

Bob nodded, returning to the dustpan he'd discarded by the back door.

'That bloody cat!' he muttered, emptying the dustpan into the bin. Twig was smiling at the return of the atmosphere to normal but jolted at the sight of not cat poo, like usual, but a large feathered mass being slid into the bin. 'I'll have to have another word with Susan at Number 7. It's her Tetley, I'm sure of it.'

'What's that?' Blake baulked.

'A goose!' Bob exclaimed. 'Must've wandered in from the Parkland. Stupid thing. Half eaten! Just a bit of a wing and feathers left.'

'And you're putting it in the bin?' Blake squirmed.

'Would a domestic cat seriously be able to eat *a goose?*' Twig enquired, but no one seemed to notice.

'What do you want me to do with it? Perform a burial service? I'd be at it all day. Do you know how many birds are killed by cats each year?'

Blake pointed at the contract and shot her dagger looks that suggested, *we'll talk about this later* as she headed back into the garage.

Twig zoned out – *there's ten million cats in the UK alone, if they kill twenty birds each a year, and that's a conservative estimate* – one thing becoming clear. If they couldn't move, if they had a *home* here – a home of their own – then the Brooks would have to go.

And if Blake didn't like it . . . maybe she would need to go too.

Perhaps Twig would survive after all.

35

Coralie

Coralie emitted a sigh of pleasure at the conclusion of another successful information meeting. She was holding them weekly now, a sort of clinic, as if she were an MP, where people arrived with their 'evidence', blurry photographs or dried-out animal faeces, and she would talk them through her identification process, invariably concluding that whatever it was, it was not feline.

There was no way now to keep up with the local 'sightings'. No way of knowing what was real or not. The local paper's website had a rolling news bar with updates and every few days a story appeared in the national press. Reporters had been in the Parkland and Knole Park, asking passers-by how they felt about the Sevenoaks Panther. Instinct told Coralie that nearly all the sightings were either made up or misguided, but she had to be cautious nonetheless. That's where these information sessions came in handy, providing an ear to the ground on what was really happening. It had struck her that the mood in the room wasn't one of overriding fear, though that was obviously there, there was also curiosity.

'Bye then,' she called as the hall emptied. 'Yes! See you at Sports Day!'

It was laughable, these well-to-do Sevenoaks types who thought they were civilized, who spent their sedate lives in their sterile houses, blind to the world around them, getting so het up about a wild cat. How safe they felt in their suburban bubble, and yet the wild unknown was mere footsteps away. As if cats – elegant, regal, superior in every way – would give *them* more than a second's thought. How easily these people would toss a discarded apple core into a bush, or tip crumbs from their artisan cinnamon buns off their jumpers on to the street, without a moment's pause to consider what vermin, or predator, they might attract. *We are all wild things*, she wanted to shout. *Some of us can see it, but most people can't.* Little Elwood, he could see it. She felt a stab of melancholy at the absence of her sidekick; cruel but necessary. She hadn't seen him since the ugly scene outside her house.

A young woman with a pushchair wearing leopard-print shorts and a black vest hung back. 'Would you mind if I took a photo?' she asked nervously, as one might when approaching a celebrity.

'Of course.' Coralie smiled broadly.

After the commotion between the Dorsetts and the Brooks in the street, Coralie had finally done the unthinkable and joined all the social media platforms she derided to monitor the situation. Instantly, and without needing to do anything, she'd gained thousands of followers. The modern world was baffling. There'd been a steady stream of teens taking 'selfies' in front of the 'Puddleford Parkland' sign recently too, sometimes splicing her into their footage (she had no idea how). Fortunately, they never ventured further in.

She'd passed Matt Brooks earlier, who returned her buoyant greeting with a sober hello. She used to enjoy the odd flirt with Matt – she'd noticed him watching her on occasion – but too much had been said in the street; the ease that had existed between the inhabitants of Briar Close had disintegrated. Coralie doubted they'd ever gather in her garden again for supper parties. She didn't regret calling Henry out as a bully, even if it had soured her relationship with Emma and Matt. Coralie had a strong sense of justice. She simply couldn't let it go unsaid. And hopefully they'd act on it. Help Elwood, since he was no longer in her protection. Her heart spasmed involuntarily and she rubbed at her chest.

The situation with Twig was more complicated. She had the benefit for Skylar ready to go. The party planners had it all booked and paid for. How would it look if she cancelled now? And how could she execute her plan without it?

She mused on her predicament as she acquiesced to another selfie, waving off the stragglers.

She was picking up the discarded leaflets she'd had printed with helpful 'dos and don'ts' from the floor, a little photo of herself in the corner, thinking how much more effective it might have been if she'd simply made a video and posted it online when she paused: she could do that, couldn't she? She could use her new platform to make the public see that cats don't pose a threat to humans. And maybe, it would be how it was in the room today? Curiosity overriding fear. Her brain leapt ahead. If she gained enough interest . . . Could she lead the campaign to grant wild cats protected status in the United Kingdom?

As she left, still enveloped in her victorious daydream, Pat Duggan sidled up to her. She felt a jolt of alarm before she registered the fear on his face. 'You haven't told anyone, have you? About what I saw.'

'No. I promised you I wouldn't.'

'Good.' He exhaled gruffly, a hot puff of air landing on her neck.

'There's been more.' He stared into her eyes. 'I found a sheep up a tree. Rasped clean. And last night when I went into the field, all the horses were huddled together in the middle. As if they'd been herded.'

The description of the eerie scene made her shudder.

'You sure you've got a handle on this? You think this will be enough?' He gestured at the crumpled leaflets she'd collected.

She huffed irritably. He wanted her to fix this without putting himself, or his reputation, on the line. *Typical man.*

'You know my view. I don't mind losing a few sheep, because they also take the fox, and the badger and some rabbit. But there's all these sightings now. It feels like it's, I dunno, getting out of control.' He smoothed his hair away from his sweaty forehead. 'I don't want hunters turning up on my land.'

His cheeks flushed as he played with the cap in his hands and Coralie understood instantly. He didn't want the cat to be hunted. Well, neither did she.

'The language they're using in the press. *The Beast of Sevenoaks*,' he scoffed.

'There haven't been any credible sightings in weeks, besides yours,' she lied. 'As long as no one gets hurt, it will be fine. It needs to be left alone.' Coralie knew the limits of cats. She knew they could be trained, controlled, kept as pets, in zoos. But she also knew you couldn't fight nature. If you provoked them . . . if you goaded them, or tried to attack them, they could kill. It was a fine line, but she knew where it fell and how to manipulate it. 'The hysteria will pass.'

Adam was waiting for her on the street outside in his Range Rover, doors locked. He jumped as she rapped on the window, slid his phone away into the driver's door. She felt the spectre of his conspirator keenly, his little slut, as she slipped into the car. 'A Boy Made of Stars' played on the radio. She turned the volume up to chase away her thoughts.

Coralie barely kept up with popular culture, but even she'd noticed that Pineapple Punk were all over the media. It was that summer's success story, the song now tied not only to Skylar but to the Sevenoaks Panther, and to *her*, the cat whisperer, thanks to Henry's video playing it in the background. Each item was generating more interest in the other, like perpetual motion. They were all bound together in it.

She'd seen Twig gushing and bleating about how humbling her late bloom of success was online. It didn't surprise her that Twig was milking her moment for all she was worth. It kept Coralie's unease about Elwood at bay: they'd all got something out of it.

The Mystery of the Sevenoaks Panther

Freja, chair of Puddleford PTA: Of course I felt bad. What mother wouldn't? No one knew how bad things had gotten for Elwood until Sports Day. I told Zach afterwards to make sure Elwood was included in things. It was clear he was being bullied. Who by? Henry Brooks, obviously.

Emma Brooks: Oh, come on. [Looks skywards.] It was an accident.

36

Twig

Twig stared at her phone, stunned. 'A Boy Made of Stars' was number one on every major streamer.

'Number one,' she whispered.

Twig – Pineapple Punk – had never had a number one before, and yet here it was, arriving with a whimper, decades after she'd dreamed it possible, about seven years since she'd first uploaded this song and it fell flatly into a streaming abyss without making so much as a ripple. And now it was number one. Her solo track.

Had this happened decades ago, the money would be rolling in. But the music landscape had changed. How long would it be at number one – hours? Days? She'd make pennies from this. The real money came from the spotlight and the opportunities that accompanied it, but fame came at a cost. For Twig, the cost would almost certainly be her marriage. Blake wouldn't be happy for her. Wouldn't be proud. Their relationship already felt precarious. Twig felt certain that eclipsing Blake at this juncture would be the end. *Would it be worth it?*

She couldn't forget, either, that the song's reboot had come at the cost of her son's happiness, but neither could she ignore that its success was having an impact on the fund. That too was climbing. It was close enough now that she truly believed they would have enough money to get Skylar to America, but it was bittersweet.

How could she convince Blake it was the right thing? That they needed to take this leap of faith whatever the odds? Skylar could have her vaccine, they could return to *their home* and they could start living again. For the first time in years, Twig felt optimism surge through her veins. Maybe, things were going to be okay. Instead of sneaking off to the treehouse tonight, for a beer, or a cigarette, she would broach it with Blake.

Arriving at Sports Day that afternoon in a red vest top (Elwood and Skylar's house colour) and her black denim shorts, there was a scrum for her attention.

'You're number one!' a mum from Skylar's class in a yellow floral tea-dress trilled.

She was aware of Blake cringing beside her, shoulders hunched, swatting away the wasps which seemed to have multiplied overnight. They were barely speaking, Blake having delivered her 'great idea' to Twig on the walk here: 'Let's sell your parents' house! I've been looking at real estate prices round here and they're crazy! We could . . .' Twig had simply walked off, her ears ringing in disbelief.

'Congratulations!' another mum, in a green shirt dress, said, squeezing her in for a hug, though Twig was not a hugger.

The excitement was a welcome break in the tension, the communal anxiety growing each day about the wild cat. The annual inter-house event – egg-and-spoon races, sack-jumping and the like – always brought out a competitive edge in the parents, but today there was a giddy feeling in the air, like a *finally! Something good is happening!*

'We've smuggled in some contraband!' Agatha, one of Emma's Admin buddies, in an elegant blue wrap dress, said, lifting the neck of a champagne bottle from her large tote, although it was barely past noon. She felt Blake's glare as she feigned disinterest.

Coralie and Emma materialized separately, and the three of them circulated near each other awkwardly, their previous easy familiarity gone. She hadn't expected to see Coralie at the school

223

but then had a vague recollection of an email regarding a presentation for the governors at Sports Day. It grated on her: why couldn't Coralie enmesh herself with her own daughters' school? Why was she here, at all, in Sevenoaks? Couldn't she piss off back to London? She hoped Elwood, who had been quiet and sullen since the incident in the street, wouldn't notice her. On the surface, she was on better terms with Emma, who had apologized profusely for Henry's behaviour and confiscated his phone, but she couldn't help but wish the Brooks would just disappear completely too.

'Pineapple Punk should perform at the benefit!' Agatha pressed, and it was clear from the chorus of agreement that this idea had already been mooted.

Coralie met her eyes self-consciously, and Twig felt a pulse of irritation: Coralie had nigh on insisted on holding this benefit for Skylar, and now Twig was dependent on her, beholden to her, even though Coralie had hurt her son, inflating Elwood with grandiose ideas of a wild cat, revelling in his excitement, and tossing him aside when he took it too seriously. If it were for anything other than the health of one of her children, she'd tell Coralie where to stick her benefit. But it was the final push to get them to America. She didn't have the time, money or space to pull it off herself. Besides she couldn't deny there was a certain cachet that came with an event being held at the Kings'. Especially now, thanks to Coralie's minor celebrity status. So far, she seemed to have ignored her newly acquired fame, but Twig wondered for how much longer. If one thing was becoming clear, it was that Coralie King loved attention.

'We could do,' Twig said non-committally, gauging Coralie's and Blake's reactions, wary of them both.

Across the small crowd she saw Adam standing apart from the others. She did a double-take at his appearance. Most people were tanned and plump from having little more energy than to sit in the sun, but he looked haunted, his face carved with shadows. *Jesus.* They locked eyes. He'd never replied to her messages asking if he'd scored any weed so she'd taken the hint and stopped contacting him. But even now she felt a magnetic pull to him, and yet, and yet . . . they'd never acted upon it. Adam had been a loyal and faithful husband.

'I'm happy with that,' said Coralie tentatively, snapping Twig's attention back. Twig looked between Adam and Coralie. Could she be trusted?

'I'm sure we could borrow the stage they use for Folking?' Freja, a mum in Elwood's class, offered. Her brother ran a music event each summer at one of the local farms, and Freja helped with the organizing.

Twig looked at Coralie, who shrugged and smiled softly in a way that said, *it's still there if you want it.* Twig blinked, caught off guard. So, it was still happening. She would have to push her concerns around Coralie to one side, for Skylar's sake, try to forget, for one night only, how Coralie had treated her son. She swallowed fiercely. She could only hope that when Elwood was older and he looked back on all this, perhaps if he was a father himself one day, he would understand her decision.

'Sure.' Twig nodded. What choice did she have? She looked in Blake's direction anxiously, aware she hadn't yet said yes.

'You could up the cost of the benefit tickets. Coralie, what's the maximum capacity of your garden?' Freja said, snapping into business mode.

Coralie frowned. 'I'm happy to help, but I don't want my whole garden trashed with hundreds of extra people.'

'What about an online ballot for people to enter? You only need to have five extra tickets but people pay a hundred pounds to enter the ballot?'

'A hundred pounds?' Twig asked, uneasily. That sounded like a lot. Her heart sank as Blake moved away, ostensibly to get a better view of the sports field.

'You're right,' Freja said, misreading her tone. 'Two hundred and fifty?'

The children filed out from the classrooms, skin smeared in

high-factor sun lotion, clutching bottles of water, the Parkland perimeter visible through the wire fence behind them.

As more children emerged from the school, like ants from a nest, the atmosphere returned to the stress of recent weeks. Even though Twig was certain the Sevenoaks Panther was largely a concoction of Coralie's ego, she couldn't help but search the dense woodland backdrop for a sudden flash of movement, a flick of a tail. The pages of Coralie's notebook flittered in her mind. *It couldn't be true*, she told herself firmly. *There was no panther.* Attention-seeking was one thing; putting them all in danger was quite another.

The children began lining up in their house colours, facing the onlookers like a firing squad. Skylar bounced out, pumped, hopping from foot to foot. Elwood trooped out slowly, at a distance to the other children, the last in his class, a teaching assistant scurrying at his tail, hurrying him along. Her heart pinged.

The panther was forgotten when the races commenced in a flurry of hockey sticks and hoola hoops. Sullen fathers in suits rarely sighted at the school gates screamed encouragement at their children. Mums in their children's house colours whooped at a win and politely clapped for the last finishers.

The atmosphere had cooled by the time the children stopped for an ice-pop break, teachers corralling them into tiny pockets of shade. The atmosphere in the crowd shifted again: everyone enjoyed the spectacle of the parents' race, which always took place at this juncture. The competing parents emerged from the sidelines, sneaking glances at each other, their gait carefully relaxed as they walked toward the starting line, their tense bodies telling a different story. Twig bent a foot to her bum, stretching in her frayed denim shorts. She won this race every year; she didn't even bother wearing running trainers.

There was a new face participating this year: Emma. Earlier she'd been sporting an unflattering blue smock dress, Henry and Daisy's house colour, but she removed it now and peeled away from the crowd, her athletic transformation on full display in a vest and cycling shorts. Twig clocked a few jaws drop from other parents, and from Coralie, who wore an admiring *good for her* look.

Coralie stood out among the sea of primary colours in a flowing white dress nipped in at the waist with a wide tan belt. *Did it hurt or help?* Twig wondered, always being at the school, cheering on the children while her own daughters were elsewhere. She felt an odd mix of sympathy and crawling unease.

Twig had a bounce in her step on the starting line. *She was so close. An end to this nightmare was in sight, just like the finishing line ahead of her.*

She glanced at Emma, who shot her a wink just as Mr Ambrose started the race with his fake pistol.

What the fuck? Emma was immediately streaks ahead, halfway to finishing when Twig was still finding her stride and the others were barely off the starting line. Twig worked her arms and legs, really going for it, but it was no use. She couldn't get a gain on Emma, and she panted exasperatedly, Emma's neon-pink cycling shorts fixed in her eyeline. *What. The. Fuck?* Everyone was cheering, even Blake, as Emma shot across the finish line and leapt into the air, shaking her fist.

'Woah!' Twig said magnanimously, finally reaching her and slapping her on the back. 'You got *fast*!'

Emma grinned delightedly, barely out of breath, as Twig doubled over and the others finished. Glancing up, Twig noticed Emma shooting little glances in Adam's direction. But Adam looked as he had all day: like he wasn't really there. And moments later Matt appeared, hoisting Emma up on his shoulders, the pair of them laughing. '*That's my girl!*' he shouted as Emma squealed and gripped the sides of his head as though she might fall. Twig's smile didn't reach her eyes. She had underestimated Emma Brooks.

It was approaching one, the sun high in the sky when the children resumed their positions for the final event: the relay races. There was a growing sense they had to wrap this up; between the heat and the wild cat, the parents wanted their children back inside. The younger classes went first, and Skylar, who was lean and sporty like Twig, won her leg, despite her treatment. Fierce pride blazed across Twig's chest.

When it was Elwood's turn, Twig felt the usual ripple of apprehension. Having a child like Elwood had made her realize how tough school could be if you weren't good at sport. She said a silent prayer as he waited, his skinny body zinging, all agitation and nerves as he twisted his hands and lifted up on to his toes. He fumbled with the baton, but soon he was off, his limbs flying at awkward angles.

'Come on, Ellie!' one of the girls in his class screamed.

'Pretend there's a big cat chasing you!' another hollered, and the rest of the class, and a few parents, fell about laughing.

Twig willed him on with everything she had. *You can do it, Elwood*, she urged. He didn't need to win, just not to fail, that was the thing. To hold his own.

Someone struck up the chorus from 'A Boy Made of Stars' but delivered it in a flat, childish 'la la la' version, and others joined in. It had never occurred to Twig that her song might be used to tease him, but she suspected from the way his neck shrank downwards that this was what had been happening. She'd had no idea. Why hadn't he told her? She frowned as the tune took hold and more people joined in, parents too, not realizing the effect it was having on Elwood. It wasn't encouraging him, or cheering him on, it was like glue binding his muscles.

He continued to run, inelegantly pumping his arms as he fell further behind, and the energy from the other children in his house who had been supporting him seemed to wilt. The boy in the lane beside him, who'd had a late start, overtook him effortlessly, completed his leg and handed the baton to Henry. Henry began running towards Elwood, a big grin on his wide, smug face. As he passed Elwood he leaned towards him, barging him with the full force of his weight. Cheers erupted from his teammates as Elwood flew forward, landing face down on the playground, legs sprawled.

Silence fell when he failed to move, failed to scramble up and continue to run, as expected. Elwood always carried on. Almost as though he hadn't noticed whichever slight had been bestowed upon him. She told herself it was resilience. For the first time, as she watched him, she wondered if it was something else.

A beat passed. And then another. Still, he didn't move.

'Elwood!' she called, running on to the playground. She could hear Matt in angry rebuke shouting, '*Henry!*'

Elwood shifted his face to the side as she approached, his cheek to the asphalt. There was a trickle of blood from his nose, a graze on his sky-facing cheek. A single tear. But worse than any of that, she could tell immediately: all his fight was gone. Her little space-man's spirit had finally been crushed. He'd had enough. Tears sprung in her own eyes.

'Come on, buddy. Get up.' Her voice wavered, the crowd around them shifting, buzzing, restless for a resolution. 'Elwood?'

'What the fuck's that kid's problem?' Blake whispered angrily, appearing by her side, an angry jerk of the head towards Henry, who was being berated by Matt out of earshot. But Twig could tell her anger disguised what Twig was also feeling. Guilt. *We're fucking this up.* Before Twig could stop her, Blake marched over to where Henry stood with his head down, Matt towering over him.

'That was not cool, man.'

'Yes, thank you, Blake.' Matt's voice was raised. 'I'm dealing with it.'

'Not very well,' she responded. Twig could hear the edge of anger spilling over Blake's words. 'You wanna get a handle on your son there.'

And Twig could see the challenge rising in Matt as he angled away from Henry and brought himself up to full height to face Blake.

'You want to get a handle on *yours?*' he said, and there was a provocation there, implicit in his tone, and Twig hoped that Blake wouldn't pick up on it. That the dig was aimed squarely at her. She reached down and scooped her hands under Elwood's armpits, cajoling him up – *come on, baby, please* – as she trained her eyes away from the scene with Matt and Blake. She heard the crunch of Blake's trainers on tarmac as she made to return to them and then the swivel as she went back to Matt, her temper flaring.

'Just leave it,' Twig called, to no avail.

'What do you mean by that?'

From the corner of her eye, Twig saw the headteacher, Mr Ambrose, approaching them both.

'Seriously,' Blake said, streaming forward, chest to chest with Matt. 'You meant something. What did you mean?' She flicked her head to Twig, and Twig looked at Elwood, afraid of what the look on her face might reveal. 'Do you have a problem with Elwood having two mothers?'

'No,' Matt said squarely. 'I don't have a problem with that at all.'

Tension encircled them.

'Well, you clearly have a problem with *something*.' She scowled.

Emma was standing over Matt's shoulder, her gaze skipping between Blake and Twig before stopping on Twig. Coralie was watching them all.

Sweat gathered under Twig's chin, her armpits damp, her hair clinging to the nape of her neck. A muscle in her eyelid twitched rapidly.

Blake swivelled to Twig then too. All eyes were on her as she held Elwood's head against her chest, his chest against her stomach, both their hearts beating furiously. She closed her eyes. She'd set all this in motion and now she couldn't stop it.

Blake was asking her a question, but she couldn't respond. All she could hear was the blood pumping in her ears.

'This place is fucked up,' Blake pronounced, and you could practically hear the rush from the other parents wanting to cover their children's ears with their hands as Mr Ambrose held an arm out to Blake, indicating she leave. 'Don't bother, I'm outta here.'

Emma stared at Twig with a look on her face as though she

wanted to say something. They stood there frozen as the crowd seemed to fall away.

'Speak to Blake' was all Emma said, and she disappeared before Twig could say another word.

37

Emma

They returned home from Sports Day trailing a glum Henry, an irate Matt and an annoyed Daisy (she'd wanted to go to the common afterwards with her friends, but for once Emma couldn't face appeasing her). Fighting her instinct to put her glitterball and favourite playlist on and enlist Daisy to dance around the kitchen to cheer themselves up, she bolted out to the garden and crouched over her phone, ostensibly scrolling social media but really listening to Twig and Blake shouting next door.

'What the fuck is Matt Brooks' problem?'

She'd never understood why Matt was a full-name kind of guy, but she'd observed it many times. For some reason just 'Matt' wouldn't do.

'Is he a fucking homophobe?' Beside Emma, a little brown bird was eating a trail of ants. Her skin crawled. She didn't like ants. Had already squished a few underfoot inside the house. She strained to hear Twig's response, but if she spoke, Emma didn't hear.

'Is there more to this? I've had this weird feeling about him since he came over that night and you said it was nothing?'

Me too, Blake. Me too. She closed her eyes. *It could be nothing. You've worried about this for years, but it could be nothing.* So why was the voice she tried to suppress shouting louder than ever? She'd known all along, hadn't she, what she'd eventually hear?

'Is there something you're not telling me? Do I need to go over there and ask him myself?'

'Fine.' She heard Twig swallow. 'Fine. I—' Emma cut the audio.

When she went inside later, Matt was at the kitchen table. His laptop was open before him, a spreadsheet of names. The back door was open, the breeze coming in waves like a cool drink. The ivy, which had already taken possession of the outside of the house, was trying to creep in through the doorframe, as if they wouldn't notice its stealth.

She reached for an ice-cold bottle of Sauvignon Blanc, sloshing the liquid into a glass. She almost felt too hot to begin the conversation, like it would just be easier to starfish on her bed, on top of the sheets, and wait for the heatwave to pass. But she couldn't. Deep in her gut she knew something was wrong. And not just with them: the carefully constructed ecosystem of their neighbourhood was collapsing, and she feared the fallout would be devastating.

How much longer could she pretend nothing had happened? She readied herself, even as her fingers trembled, the wine oscillating in her glass.

'What's the thing, the – what's going on with you and Blake? Why all the tension?' she finally asked.

'I don't know.' He tutted, frowning at his spreadsheet. The light in the room had dimmed and tiny, winged insects, so frail you doubted they would last the night, appeared in clusters. He swatted them away. 'She's always had a chip on her shoulder. She's got an anger-management problem, if you ask me. Suggesting I'm a homophobe!' he exclaimed. 'I could get in trouble with the Scouts for that. *Baseless. Baseless accusations.*'

A moth thunked against his screen. She shivered in recollection of the carpet-moth larvae wriggling under her bed at the beginning of the summer. It felt like a lifetime ago. She enjoyed the warmer weather because with all the doors and windows flung open wide, and the big garden, she didn't feel as trapped inside the house, but the downside was the house felt more 'alive', spiders appearing from under the sofa, ants in every crevice, silverfish snaking over the bathroom floors. In May, when they put their plans in, she'd felt so close to having it all. To being the success her parents thought she was. Now she felt on the edge of something: freefall into an interminable abyss.

'What are we going to do about Henry?' Matt asked softly.

'I don't know.'

'He pushed Elwood over. Knocked into him on purpose.'

'I don't think he meant for him to fall over.'

Matt cocked his head, pouty lips pursed, as if to say, *come on, Emma.*

'He didn't,' she insisted. 'He misjudged it. Did you see the look on his face afterwards? You could tell he felt awful about it.'

Emma looked down into her glass, marvelled at how easily they'd gone off track. But maybe it was better this way. Daisy was as controlling as ever, and Henry was clearly acting up. He shouldn't have pushed Elwood, but 'bully' was such a strong word. Was the stress of the last few months infecting their children? The irony, when her focus had been on building them their forever home, the house of their dreams. What would it do to her children to unsettle them further now? Maybe her instincts were right: maybe she should have got home and insisted on a kitchen disco?

She gestured at his computer. 'I think you should cancel Cub camp. I doubt anyone's going to send their kids, anyway. I heard some of the parents talking about it at Sports Day.'

'I will not,' he said simply. 'Everyone signed up in May. They've paid. It's all sorted.'

'Who's going to want their kids sleeping outside?'

'Henry and Daisy will be sleeping outside. There'll be around a hundred of us! Two full troops and leaders. It will be fine.'

She knew there was little point in arguing with him, and maybe he was right. She turned the stem of her glass in her fingers, wet circles blooming on the tabletop.

Matt resumed calculating the required volumes of baked beans and sausages for two nights 'away at camp' (although in reality they would be a five-minute drive from home and ten minutes from the big Tesco). The scout hut was at the top of the Parkland, a short distance from the school.

She hovered. What would happen if she outright confronted Matt about Twig? She was sure he'd tell her the truth. She'd never asked him. It was such a simple question, but the ramifications would be the opposite: complex and overwhelming. If she didn't know, if he didn't admit it, she could keep the Disney version of her life: the one where everything went right and she lived happily ever after. She was an optimist, after all.

'Are you okay?' He raised his head from the screen. There was a weariness there; the anticipation of a confrontation neither of them wanted to have. Her brain performed its usual somersault when the truth came too close: She could hide a little bit longer, maybe not for ever, but for as long as she could bear it. Hadn't he been a good husband since? Supported her over her, frankly, deranged, at times, behaviour? Even if, deep down, she knew that behaviour was her chasing away the truth.

'If there was anything you wanted to tell me. About Twig. If anything happened . . .' She couldn't look at him, but she could sense his eyes widening, heard his sharp intake of breath. She swallowed. Imagined Blake and Twig and the horrible scenes that must be unfolding next door. 'I would prefer not to know.'

When she raised her head, tears were glistening in the rims of his eyes. He didn't look relieved as he nodded, he looked bereft. She couldn't hold his gaze. She looked down again, turned the glass in her hands. It was true, at least: she really didn't want to know.

She retrieved the bottle of wine from the fridge and drifted from the kitchen to the garden. At the far end, where the garden rose higher before sloping down towards the house (a common Sevenoaks feature; it would cost a fortune to have it dug out and flattened), a hammock was strung between two oak trees. She inelegantly tipped herself in, holding her wine glass, and the bottle, aloft. She gulped the cool liquid down readily, one glass and then another. She wanted the world to swim out of focus.

She was almost in line with Coralie's greenhouse. Her eyes traced the arched panes of glass, its ornate colours just discernible over the top of her fence from her elevated position. The light was on and she wondered what lay within. She squinted, the lights blurring in her vision. Coralie had tried to catch Emma's eye when she was on the starting line for the parents' race, but Emma had coolly shot her a side-eyed look as she'd turned away.

She stared at the greenhouse. *What are you up to in there? And what's happened to Adam?* He was a shadow of himself at Sports Day. That was the first time she'd seen him leave the house in ages. A tiny part of her had wondered if she might see a flicker of appreciation on his face when she won the parents' race, but he'd basically blanked her. She felt embarrassed by how she'd misread the situation between them. She was, she realized, quite a pathetic creature. She sunk further into the hammock, closed her eyes. She wanted to drift away, but an image popped in her head from the drone footage she'd taken to annoy Tim: Coralie returning from the Parkland with a bucket.

She hadn't thought much of it at the time but now she realized how strange it was. What had she been doing with the bucket? The Parkland was basically a no-go zone these days, outside of the school-run patrol hours. Even those who did venture in, like the odd teenager trying to get footage for TikTok, or a reporter, did so from the main pathway via the public access on Thistle Road. But Coralie continued as she always had. Traversing the Parkland, along the now abandoned track which lined their back gardens, fulfilling her 'conservation work' duties. *What was in the bucket?*

She didn't know if it was the wine, or the woozy-making heat, or the desperation to shift her attention elsewhere, but the idea came to her in a flash: she would break into Coralie's greenhouse! She giggled, alone in the dark, snorting wine. She clutched the bridge of her nose and cleared her throat, stopping when she heard the door to Coralie's greenhouse opening. She scootched up in the hammock, peering over the rickety fence which mirrored the ground's descent.

Coralie emerged, her flowing dress illuminated by the light of the greenhouse. She disappeared into the middle dark of the garden and reappeared like a ghost as the external sensor light flicked on as she approached her house. Emma noticed a glint of silver around her neck. The chain which Elwood had claimed held a key and whistle. You never saw what hung on it.

Seizing the opportunity, Emma flung herself out of the hammock. In seconds she was through the back gate, her heart hammering as she was briefly alone in the Parkland before entering Coralie's garden. Coralie had complained before that there was no bathroom in the greenhouse. She'd probably gone inside to use the loo. Emma had only minutes to do what she needed: find that notebook Elwood had mentioned.

She stepped inside. It was softly lit by lamps, creating pools of light which left the rest of the room in shadow. It was much bigger than Emma had expected, shelves lined with curiosities and small prints of flowers and herbs. On a galvanized-steel table stood a large terrarium filled with delicate pink-veined plants: a world within a world. Vintage photographs were hung along the back wall, black-and-whites of elegant ladies and gentlemen with exotic pets.

Every surface of the floor was covered in investigative paraphernalia: bits of skull and bone, photos of what she now knew to be 'scat' ('poo' to everyone else), papers, books, brushes, those little white gloves Coralie wore. A green notebook lay prone on the table. Emma was hidden by the door, but if she ventured further in, she'd be illuminated; would Coralie be able to see her floating head and torso from the house? She daren't risk it. She dropped to the floor, crawling commando-style over to the desk. As she reached for the notebook a flash of movement by the door made her heart stop. She exhaled shakily, hand to her chest as she realized it was Socks, the little traitor, swaggering in, belly up, tail high.

Her relief was fleeting; she could hear Coralie calling something out to Adam, the heavy swoosh as she closed her large sliding doors. Emma could feel her approach the greenhouse, sensed her coming closer. There was no way to exit without Coralie seeing her. Her heart pounded in her chest as she crawled into the small room at the back, hidden in darkness, and leaned back against the wall, still on the floor. Socks came over and surveyed her curiously, eyeball to eyeball. She silently shooed him away and, when he didn't move, carefully closed the door, shunting him out, just as she heard Coralie reach the greenhouse. It was almost pitch black, but for some red lights blinking from two white units. A fridge and a chest freezer? *Why would she have them out here? Why not install a bathroom instead?*

With the door closed the temperature quickly rose, summoning a revolting stench of fish. As her eyes adjusted Emma could make out the rim of Coralie's bucket. She peered in, covering her nose with her arm; silver-veined fish scales glinted from its depths. She shrunk backwards, trying not to gag, and began to panic.

How was she going to get out? What if Coralie locked her in and she was stuck here all night? She'd left her phone inside. *What was she going to do?*

'Socks! My darling boy! You won't believe the day's developments! I saw that nasty reporter, Sofia Olsen, skulking around the Parkland sign earlier. I only swung by in case there were any TikTokkers to wave at, and there she was, asking silly questions. Yes, you're right: definitely a dog person. It got me thinking though, that and the video of Elwood getting so much coverage . . . Here you go, darling, a little treat.' Emma's eyes narrowed in the darkness. 'You know I *hate* attention, but maybe I should start posting my own videos . . . Take control of things. Might stop people constantly asking me questions. What do you think? Do I have a face for camera?' she trilled as Emma, hidden, rolled her eyes.

As Emma's eyes adjusted further she noticed dark stains on the floor around the freezer, stretching to where she was sitting. She gingerly touched one with her finger. It was thick and sticky. She sniffed at the dark stain: discerned a metallic tang. *Blood?*

She shuddered, her thoughts interrupted by the sound of furniture being dragged, of items being rearranged. 'Would this make a good backdrop? Hmm, it's not the best light, but maybe we could do a little practice run? You know what, I'm going to pop in the house, put on a spot of make-up.'

Emma exhaled in relief, poised to get out of there the moment she heard Coralie leave. She realized that all the times she'd thought she'd heard Coralie wittering on to Adam, him silently listening, she was speaking to Socks. The recordings were so boring Emma had stopped listening. Now she realized how *creepy* they were. Looking down at the blood again, a thought occurred to her: Coralie might be a bit mad, a bit eccentric, but could she also be dangerous?

38

Twig

Twig pressed her hands against the sink, needing the solidity of the smooth enamel beneath her palms, something permanent to remind herself she existed. Bob played with the children in the garden outside, shooting nervous looks towards the house. Blake had stormed all the way back here from school, Twig and the kids close on her heels, and Bob, sensing something was up, had ushered the children into the garden.

'Do you hate me?' Twig asked.

Blake was by the kitchen table, her head thrown back, her hands covering her face. She sighed.

Through the door to the garage, Blake's computer sounded with messaging alerts: *Ping! Ping! Ping!*

'I should have told you straight away.' Twig pushed for a response.

Blake raked her hands over her face. 'Yes. Or just maybe before we moved here?' Sarcasm edged her words. 'That might have been slightly less humiliating than living next door to the man you cheated on me with.'

'We were so caught up with Skylar's treatment and funding the vaccine by then, and we—' *Ping! Ping! Ping!* Her voice crumpled.

'Does he know?' She jerked a thumb in the direction of the Brooks' house.

'I think so. I don't know. We haven't spoken about it.'

Ping! Ping! Ping!

'Can you turn that off?' Twig demanded. 'Put it on silent or something?'

'No,' Blake said simply. 'No. I can't do that.'

Twig looked at her askance. There was more. Something else was moving beneath the surface of this conversation, but she couldn't place it yet.

Ping! Ping! Ping!

'Fine,' Twig huffed. 'If you won't turn it off, I will.' She charged to the garage, reeling as a wave of heat hit her despite the collection of fans Blake had set up in there. She was aware of Blake's chair being pushed back abruptly, her hurrying to her feet and following her. It pressed Twig to move more quickly, although she didn't understand why. She leaned over the desk, grabbing at the mouse, searching in the corner of the screen for the volume control. She couldn't miss the chat box in the middle of the screen.

Susie: Did you tell her, baby?

How did she take it?

I know it will be tough right now, but in time it will all work out . . .

Reams and reams of therapy-esque messages which were somehow, simultaneously, not therapy-esque at all.

'But Susie's your therapist?' She stared questioningly at Blake as she sunk into a chair, feeling dazed by the heat, not comprehending. 'Isn't she?'

She realized with a start that Blake was crying. Finally. The response Twig had wanted. But not like this.

'She was.' She sniffed. 'She hasn't been for a while.'

Reality filled the gaps in Twig's understanding. All the hours Blake spent in here, all the late nights on the phone to her therapist or her mum . . . 'Do you even speak to your mum?'

Blake nodded. 'Sometimes.'

'Huh.' Twig said. She felt winded. The oppressive air in the garage wasn't enough to oxygenate her lungs. Tiny stars flickered around the edge of her vision. 'You've been having an affair?'

Blake tipped her head to one side. 'It's emotional. There's nothing physical, obviously. Although . . .' She glanced at her phone, and Twig's stomach flipped over.

'When did it start?'

'Last summer.' Of course. When Twig was resisting Adam, Blake was locked in here sexting her therapist. She barked out a laugh to herself.

'You were a mess last summer.' Blake defended herself. 'The drugs. And the drinking. I know you stopped after that, but God, Twig. I was so worried. And Skylar was sick, and I was learning more and more about the vaccine, and you wouldn't listen and . . .'

'All this time, and I could have been eating burgers.' Twig laughed, a hysterical edge to her voice.

'Things got real intense real quick. As soon as we realized there were feelings we ended our therapeutic relationship.'

'But then you started an actual relationship?' Twig closed her eyes as her head swam. She thought of Emma at Sports Day. Emma had known, but how? Had the signs been there for everyone to see but Twig? So consumed with her own guilt she couldn't see what Blake was also up to?

'*What a dick*,' she admonished. 'I'm talking to myself, don't worry,' she said to Blake acerbically, a palm in the air.

In her hand, her phone lit up with a notification: she had reached her fundraising target. She wanted to weep. What did it matter now?

All she could think was how *absurd* everything was. Her situation with Matt, and her marriage to Blake, and the way her heart still squeezed when she thought of Adam. And, all along, Blake and her therapist. That Blake would choose to spend her days in here – and honestly, it was so hot you wouldn't expect *a dog* to spend time in here! – and Twig hadn't twigged. She barked out another laugh.

'An emotional affair.' She sobered, realization dawning. 'That's the worst. That means it's really over.' Blake pulled out a low stool and sat in front of her, placing her hands on Twig's knees.

'But we both knew that already, right?' She stared into Twig's eyes and the years between them fell away. She was all the versions of Blake which Twig had known at once: the cocky performer, the laid-back beach bum, the diligent parent and, most recently, the parent who wasn't coping. The parent who locked themselves away, who couldn't make a decision about the vaccine, because it was easier that way.

'When did we last make love, Twig?'

'How can I, in my parents' house?' She squirmed at Blake's directness.

'It started before.'

'I was grieving. I've been grieving ever since.' She choked back a sob.

'I know,' Blake said kindly. 'Me too. We've both been grieving the life we thought we'd have, instead of the one we've got. But we pulled apart, when we could've pulled together.' She cupped Twig's cheek tenderly, smoothed away a tear. 'Listen, the vaccine . . .'

Twig closed her eyes. It was all too much to bear. The release of adrenaline now that she'd finally told the truth about Matt, the reality of Blake's relationship with Susie, the deflation at having worked so hard to raise the money for the vaccine only for Blake to refuse it.

'I've been wrong about that Twig. You're right. There are no guarantees, but we should give it a shot.'

Twig frowned, blinking back tears as Blake gently raised her face.

'I talked it all out with my mom. She said if it were me . . .' Her voice broke. Blake had spent most her life believing her mother didn't love her. '. . . she'd want me to have it. I think I knew it was the right thing, but I've been afraid to get my hopes up. To try for one more thing. It was easier to find all the reasons why we shouldn't do it than dare to dream we might be able to raise the money. I should've been more supportive. I should've helped. I'm sorry.' She had a hand either side of Twig's face. They were both crying.

Twig exhaled, bowed her face to Blake's, their sweaty foreheads touching, all energy spent. She sent a silent *thank you* to Blake's mum, and to her own mum for good measure. She was sure that, somehow, she had had a hand in this. 'We got there in the end.'

The ballot raised almost £400,000. Not just from the entries (all 1,238 of them), but from additional donations too. Some discreet, but most from other performers Twig used to be friendly with crawling out of the woodwork, or artists Blake worked with jumping on the bandwagon via heartfelt (read, insincere) social media posts after she reached out to them.

Twig got so many requests in the days that followed for interviews and radio appearances she had written a blanket message on all her social media profiles thanking people for their time but explaining she needed to focus on her children: getting ready for Skylar's treatment and keeping Elwood safe and happy. She'd let him down and she was determined to fix it.

Blake and Twig had agreed that Twig would travel with Skylar to New York and Blake would stay home with Elwood. When Twig returned, they'd figure out a plan to co-parent. Blake had slept in Skylar's room since. Twig felt a dull ache whenever she thought of it, the stresses that lay ahead, the heartbreak when they ultimately divided their family, but deep down she knew it was the right thing to do.

When she'd received the final tally from the ballot, she'd laid down on the floor of her childhood bedroom and cried. It was over. It was done. The most important task of her life. Even better, they were able to donate the extra money that had come in to the charity to ensure another child in Skylar's position could do the same.

There were three things left to do: perform at the benefit, go to America, and come home and start living.

The Mystery of the Sevenoaks Panther

Online video of Coralie King recorded on 12 July and distributed via social media

Coralie King: Hi, it seems there's more of you watching me than I anticipated. [Smiles shyly at the camera.]

I wanted to make something clear: I do not believe a big cat is stalking the suburbs. [Smiles.] There is no 'Sevenoaks Panther'. Seriously, guys, call off the search! [Laughs.]

However, I do believe that wild cats are present in Britain in small numbers. No doubt one or two have occasionally passed through Sevenoaks and the surrounding areas. And, guys, aren't we lucky, [Beams and raises palms upwards.] to have these beautiful creatures naturalizing in the United Kingdom?

That's why I am calling on the government to give cats recognized status. And if you agree, sign my petition to get this discussed in the House of Commons! We've had a huge number of signatures, but we still need more. Let's save the cats, people! [Grins.]

39

Coralie

Keep your friends close, and your enemies closer. That was the thought running through Coralie's mind as she waited on the Brooks' doorstep, a rhubarb flan in her hands. As Emma opened the front door, her suspicious look countered with a neutral smile, Coralie wouldn't have been surprised if the same thought was flitting through her neighbour's head.

'Emma' – Coralie proffered the pie – 'I wanted to explain. About the other week.'

'Okay . . .' Emma's tone was cautious as she accepted the gift.

Coralie dropped her voice. 'It's Adam.' She glanced around as though worried she might be overheard.

'Would you like to come in?' Emma asked.

'Oh no, no, that's very kind. I don't want to bother you.' The truth was Coralie was extremely sensitive to her environment and she couldn't bear the gloominess of Briar Heart House, even with the jolly name update.

'Adam is . . . well. I alluded to it before . . .' Coralie gazed back towards her own house with a contemplative look. 'He just sits inside all day. Smoking and drinking. He's stopped working. He's imagining things. Crazy things. Cats following him! And with my public profile, well, the pressure of it. Sometimes I feel it all getting on top of me, you know?' She fluttered a hand around her throat.

'And I think I took it out on you, and Henry and Twig, that day,' She nibbled on her lip for effect. 'Everything just got too much.'

Emma looked at her for a long moment and Coralie wondered if she might be a tougher nut to crack than she'd assumed.

'What about Elwood? What did he do wrong?'

Coralie leaned heavily against the doorframe. 'Oh, I'm glad you asked. I've been wanting to get it off my chest. I feel terrible. But Elwood was coming over so much – just turning up! He'd woken me that morning, crept up on me while I was sleeping.' She widened her eyes in horror. 'And I was fearful for him, to be honest. If he saw something he ought not. Adam in one of his moods. Adam . . .' She shuddered and trailed off. 'He was getting jealous of the time we were spending together. I saw the look in his eyes sometimes when I mentioned Elwood. I had to stop it. But we had *such* a bond. I had to sever it. Despite the pain it brought me. To keep him safe. You understand.'

That was the truth, wasn't it? She remembered how Adam had snapped at Elwood when he first saw the cat in the front garden. How often he'd suggested that Coralie put the same energy she reserved for Elwood into her girls, even though they were hardly here. It was an excuse. He was jealous of him! Of a little boy. *She could see it all so clearly now.* She swallowed, 'Can we let bygones be bygones?' she implored Emma sweetly.

When dusk fell and Adam was tucked up in bed with a sedative, she went to the small shed behind her greenhouse and retrieved her bike, filling the basket with items from her fridge and freezer and covering them with one of Adam's T-shirts. She had the sensation of being watched, the fine hairs on her arms standing on end. She glanced up towards Elwood's bedroom window but found it empty. The evening had a wild, midsummer, off-kilter feel to it. Earlier, Emma had blasted one of her musical soundtracks for an hour, causing the earth to tremble. God, she was a moron. But Coralie needed everyone on side. She didn't want to invoke anyone's ire when she was so close to her plans coming to fruition.

Hooking her leg over the seat, she shook the unsettling feeling off. She cycled through the woods, her hair lifting with the gentle rise and hum of the Parkland, the scent of Adam's aftershave wafting in the light breeze she created. It was warm enough that a fine mist disseminated through the bottom of the basket as the items within thawed. She pedalled faster.

She arrived at the clearing and discarded her bike. She walked behind Cam 7, where she'd first seen Monroe, to the small metal box hidden in the undergrowth just beyond the clearing. It was in the top quarter of the Parkland, not too far, really, from the main road through Puddleford, albeit dense woodland divided them. Coralie had been surprised it was this cam that had first picked up Monroe, it being the nearest to 'civilization', but what she'd said about cats using train tracks and being lazy was true, and it was the nearest to those, too.

She unlocked and removed the padlock from the metal box, retrieving the cup she'd clipped to her belt and a metal bulldog clip, humming 'A Boy Made of Stars'. The song kept popping up, reminding her how much Twig had gained from the wild-cat rumours. Not just Twig; Emma too. She hadn't thought to ask what was the latest with her planning application. Coralie had entirely lost track, and no doubt others had too. Honestly, the pair of them should be thanking her. If they only knew.

Since Coralie had started engaging on social media her time was even more squeezed. Although inconvenient, it was proving successful. Her campaign was gaining traction. Photos of wild cats in the UK previously dismissed were being discussed and analysed; footage of a Welsh MP raising the matter in the Senedd, the Welsh Parliament, from a few years ago was trending. *Close Encounters*, a podcast recalling big-cat sightings, had exploded, millions of downloads being listened to across the country, the impact of her work – her redemption – rebounding coast to coast. Coralie at the centre of it all. *The epicentre.*

She breathed out and collected herself, because such community-mindedness left little time for training and, as the benefit approached, she wanted to be training every day. She couldn't take any chances.

She no longer needed to tempt Monroe out of the Parkland. She knew it was possible now. More than that, it was easy. Since then, she'd taken pains to ensure Monroe had everything she needed, to deter her from venturing too close to the estate again, and of course had stopped actively encouraging her and laying bait. It seemed to be working. There were no credible recent reports, although of course there were lots of fanciful ones, their sporadic nature helpful in keeping people out of the Parkland. *If people knew what she'd been doing . . .*

She'd like to say that her childhood nanny, Leonora, had been everything her mother, Violet, wasn't, but in truth they were similar: emotionally distant and hard-edged. But Leonora was paid to care for her, so she did. She baked her madeleine biscuits and let her decorate them, walked her to Harrods to peruse the pet section rather than the toys. And she told her stories. One, in particular, had been Coralie's favourite. 'A Vendetta'. It was about a widow who swore a vendetta against her son's killer. She prayed for a male relative to avenge her son's death, but there was no one. Like Coralie, she had no one. She was a little old lady on the coast in Italy trying to come up with a plan. Exactly how Coralie had felt on the long afternoons when Adam would disappear 'for a run' and come back jacked up refusing to tell her where he'd been, or who he'd been with. All the old lady had was her resourcefulness. That was all she needed: she starved her son's dog, trained it to tear out a throat for a sausage. That was how she took her revenge. How Coralie loved that story. Asking Leonora to add in more details: *What did the hole in his neck look like? Did his blood squirt out like from a hose?*

Coralie's training of the cat was less punitive. She couldn't tie it up and starve it for days at a time (*she wasn't a monster!*), but she did use food. She nurtured the cat. Loved it. Formed a bond with it. And then, eventually, she began to train it. Little tricks, like she did with Socks, for slivers of fish and chunks of meat. As a child, she'd trained her cats with her fairy wand. These days she used a target stick, a black rod with a red ball on the end. She started with the basics: She'd hold the stick and, when Monroe tapped it with her nose, she'd blow her whistle and give her a treat. Monroe mastered it quickly, clever girl. Coralie doused T-shirts in different scents and when it selected the 'right' one – Adam's aftershave – it was the same: whistle and treat. When she cycled, the T-shirt, attached to the back of her bike, and the cat chased the right scent, it was rewarded. Whistle and treat.

When Monroe made a mistake, chased after the wrong scent, or didn't wait for the signal, Coralie withdrew coldly, leaving her there in the clearing. Monroe understood. And at the benefit, when Coralie finally got the truth from Adam, Monroe would be rewarded. Whistle and treat.

Once everything was in place, she took out her flask of tea and a round of cheese-and-pickle sandwiches, and she waited for Monroe.

The Mystery of the
Sevenoaks Panther

Tim, Number 16: [Outraged.] Let me tell you, Emma Brooks' actions that day single-handedly wiped hundreds of thousands of pounds' worth of value off the houses on the Briar Heart Estate. And especially from Briar Close!

Megan, Number 16: [Grimacing awkwardly]: I never told my dad, but that was the day my first post went viral. The views were *insane*! [Grins goofily.]

40

Emma

Emma felt her nerves rising as the kettle boiled. On the counter-top sat an envelope, its contents stuffed haphazardly back inside: an application Tim had put together to have her house officially listed with Historic England. Hot, angry tears peppered her eyes.

Although it was what she'd insisted on, ignoring the truth was becoming harder and harder. The mood was unbearably tense at home. It was Matt, rather than Emma, who was attempting to jolly them all along, cooking fajitas (their favourite dinner) last night and letting the children have fizzy drinks, speaking loudly over Emma's Ultimate Disney Power Ballads playlist while they all exchanged looks in her direction and Emma pretended not to see. She was trying so hard to ignore the crowded thoughts that had taken residency in her mind and *would not go*. She could feel him watching her unravel. And maybe, if she were being honest, a tiny part of her enjoyed that too. Knowing that he felt bad without having to confront it.

She carried the kettle outside, water hissing and escaping in steam and splashes. She was too late: the ants that had been crawling up the side of the house minutes ago now covered its surface and had already begun peeling away, columns of them twisting into the sky and towards the open windows above. She ran back inside, ditched the kettle haphazardly and tore upstairs to close all the windows, her skin crawling at the thought of their invasion.

She sank down on her bed, detecting a waft of the synthetic-lavender moth spray she treated the carpet with each week, which at least served to cover up the pervading smell of damp. She looked around her room: at the moth-eaten carpet, the stained walls, the mould gathering around the window frames, small black beetles for company. It was so hot outside that the room already felt uncomfortably warm, its odours more pronounced. She pictured Tim swaggering around Briar Close feeling pleased with himself. She couldn't bear it.

She pulled out her phone and looked up the listing process. Historic England would review Tim's application. If they found it warranted further investigation, they could carry out a full assessment. That would take months and months and months. The Planning Applications Committee was in August. There is no way it would approve their plans with objections from neighbours and the parish council *and* a Historic England assessment underway. And if Tim's application was successful, if her house were officially listed, they wouldn't be able to do anything to it, ever, without Listed Building Consent.

It was over, wasn't it? Her dreams of a castle, of being a success, were over. She couldn't bear it. *But it wasn't over yet*, she told herself through gritted teeth. *She was an optimist!* She found herself in the car, in the DIY store, loading up her trolley in the paint aisle. She felt the action of *doing* counterbalance the overwhelming feelings of helplessness. She felt, briefly, momentarily, deliciously, in control.

Back at the house, her music crashed through the speakers. She was in a baggy faded maternity T-shirt, pale blue, with Simba's sweet face on it, her old running shorts, her hair scraped off her face, a roller brush in one hand and a large tray of paint at her feet. She felt giddy, excited. Until Matt entered the kitchen in his suit, briefcase in hand, and, with a glance in her direction which seemed to confirm something, flicked off the music.

'You're back early,' she said brightly.

'Emma, I need to speak to you before the kids get back from school.' He was shaking, trembling from his shoulders down through his arms. He took a deep breath, as though to steady himself, but it didn't seem to help.

'I am a weak and stupid man.' Every word seemed an effort, punctuated with a ferocious disappointment in himself, as he unveiled the parts of himself he had worked so hard to hide. 'But I want to do better.'

She didn't nod. She didn't move. She didn't do anything.

Emma could still remember the moment she'd met Twig, on the lawn outside Bob's house, shortly after the Dorsetts had moved in.

'How's Sevenoaks then?' Twig had said in mock joviality to Matt. 'What did I miss?'

'Oh, you know,' he'd replied, head bent as he scuffed at a loose tile on the driveway with his shoe. This was not the Matt she knew. 'Same old, same old.'

'How long have you been away?' Emma had enquired politely, to draw attention away from the strange behaviour of her husband.

'We moved to Bali shortly before my mum was diagnosed, so about nine, ten years . . .' Twig had stopped abruptly, her face flushing, and looked at Blake and Bob, who were carrying shopping in from the car, Skylar trailing behind them. Emma still remembered the strange, pervading silence. Suddenly Elwood had flown out of the house, arms flapping like a bird.

'Mummy! Mummy!' he'd shouted. 'Come and see my experiment!'

'Hello there, young man,' Matt had said, seemingly grateful for the interruption. 'Pleased to meet you.' He'd stuck out a hand and Elwood had smiled, shaking it vigorously.

'You must be about the same age as Henry,' Emma had said, propelling her son forwards, her brain not yet catching up with the leaden feeling in her stomach.

'I'm eight,' they'd both said. 'I'm in Year Four.' They'd spoken in unison, like twins.

Emma just knew. She looked between Twig and Blake, two women, the question clear on her face.

'Elwood's father is a friend of ours,' Twig supplied. 'Kev. A friend in Bali. We Skype when we can.'

Matt had nodded briskly, his countenance changed. 'Well, good to meet you, Elwood,' he'd blustered. 'You should join our Cub troop, once you've settled in. We're the Jutland Scouts. We meet once a week at the scout hut at the top of the Parkland. Near the cricket pitch.'

Elwood had nodded vigorously, tugging on his mother's arm. 'I've made the Mento explode!' he cackled gleefully.

'I'd better come and see,' Twig said, adding to Matt and Emma in mock horror: 'And check out the state of the kitchen!'

Emma had remained standing, transfixed, as Matt and Twig said their goodbyes and hurried back to their respective houses. *Elwood's* father . . . Why hadn't she said '*the children's* father?'

She'd walked slowly back home and stood in the porch, staring at the rows of shoes and trainers and wellies. At the evidence of a life she wasn't sure still existed. It was too much for her to contemplate. To compute. She'd shelved the idea immediately. It was preposterous. Far-fetched. Her husband couldn't have fathered another child. Other people's husbands did things like that. Not hers. No. She remembered the moment exactly. She'd strode into the kitchen, flicked on her glitterball and her favourite playlist. 'What shall we have for tea?' she'd said brightly.

Emma replayed the whole scene as Matt stood before her and, in the same way she'd known then what had happened, she knew now what he was about to say. And she still wasn't ready to hear it. She would never be ready to hear it. But she no longer had a choice.

41

Twig

Twig could hear a commotion outside. Voices raised. A harried 'what do you think you're doing?' She craned her body out of the window. Did a double-take at the scene. Emma was out the front of her house, huge tins of paint around her feet, two trays, filled with a vivid hot pink. She was steadfastly ignoring the heckles; Twig could tell even from here that she was fighting back hot tears. A raft of sudden notifications blinked on her phone: 'SHE'S PAINTING THE WHOLE FLAMING THING PINK!' someone raged. As Twig scrolled, she heard more people arriving, chastising Emma.

Twig rushed down to the garage, ignoring Blake's inquisitive look as she rummaged around, lifting lids – and quickly discarding – boxes, until she found what she was looking for. She paused momentarily at the sight of her skateboard, part hidden behind a box: a reminder of a different life. But she didn't feel the need to dwell. She smiled at Blake, who was wearing headphones and talking animatedly, and ducked out of the garage.

She skipped quickly over to Emma's but stopped abruptly when Emma spotted her, the look in her eyes conveying the moment Twig had been dreading: *I know.*

Some of the assembled group gave her a cursory glance. Emma looked away, resumed rolling the hot pink over the surface of her home.

Twig took a step closer. Faltered. She continued until she was in line with Emma's profile. Could see her shoulders hunched up to her ears, her eyes crunched together, blinking furiously as she pressed the roller against the brick, bending back down to load on more paint. Twig took a final step. As close as she dared. Emma turned sharply and looked down, clearly noting the paintbrush in Twig's hand, and met her eyes questioningly.

'I'm sorry,' Twig said, every cell in her body meaning it. She didn't want to expand any further with a crowd watching. Emma nodded, biting her lip, holding back furious tears.

An electric orange dragonfly appeared, buzzed and darted between them before vanishing.

'I've called the council!' someone shouted.

Twig turned. 'Fuck off, Tim, and mind your own business, would you?' She heard others audibly gasp.

'Twig!' her dad admonished. She hadn't seen him arrive.

'I'm sorry, Dad, but this is bullying. If Emma wants to paint the front of her house, then she can. If she wants to turn it into a "Barbie dream house"' – she lifted words from one of their neighbours' complaints in the portal – 'then she can. Life's too short for all this *nonsense*.' Her voice wobbled. Not because she felt so impassioned about Emma's right to paint her house whatever colour she liked (although she did), but from the guilt she felt towards Emma overspilling. She knew now, if she'd met Emma before that fateful night, it would never have happened. But then Elwood would have never existed. She couldn't live in a world of regret. She had to accept what she had done, be honest, move forward.

'She can't, actually!' Tim piped up. 'Especially not to a *listed* property.'

'It's not *been* listed yet,' Twig snapped.

'Fuck 'em,' she whispered viciously, turning back to Emma. 'Just fuck 'em all.'

Emma shot her a grateful look and exhaled shakily, nodding.

Twig bent down, loading up her brush with the hot-pink paint.

257

Emma watched, sucked in her cheeks, and Twig still thought she might tell her to leave, but instead she said, 'I think you should use a roller.'

They worked industriously, side by side in hushed silence. At some point Agatha appeared with her husband, Kofi, brandishing a ladder and a large carrier bag with more brushes and rollers.

'Oh, for God's sake,' Twig heard her dad mutter, approaching them.

'*Dad,*' she began.

He lifted a spare brush from the grass and gesticulated with it, a glint in his eye. 'It's not even on that side. Eh, Tim? Come and give us a hand!'

Twig looked at him and smiled as he dunked his brush in the paint and set about helping while Tim turned on his heel and stormed away. His twin daughters and wife looked agonized as they followed him, one still filming as they walked home.

The sun was still in the sky when they finished, and all the children were back from school, playing Tag on the lawn. Blake had collected them and led them through the Parkland like the Pied Piper. She ordered pizza, letting Elwood choose pepperoni, something he had long requested and been denied, and laid out blankets and cartons of juice. She seemed looser, more herself than she had in years. Matt bustled around tidying up, a strange, nervous energy about him.

The front of Briar Heart House was now a vibrant hot pink. Sun had leached the rest of Briar Close of colour; only the very tips of Coralie's roses still retained their red hue. Grass had turned to straw, crunching underfoot. Weeds thrived, tangled around bamboo that had appeared overnight, thick stems staking their claim to the land. And Briar Heart House sat in the midst of it all. They toasted quietly – Prosecco in Disney mugs – before its glowing surface.

'You know,' Emma said wistfully, 'this is the first time we've had people over.'

258

42

Coralie

'Gargh!' Coralie blinked, disbelieving, as the comments clocked up below her latest post:

> *How can she say that these animals pose no threat to people whatsoever? She's telling us we have large predators living in the British countryside which are capable of killing people! They are carnivores!*

> *I don't think we should be 'tagging' the cats. I think we should be capturing them and putting them in a zoo where they belong!*

> *Let's shoot the cats, people! She is fit, though, for a MILF.*

Who did these idiots think they were? Questioning her authority! *Fucking dog people!* She looked down at her leopard-print dress, a recent purchase, and sighed. Heard her mother's breathy voice in her ear: *Give them what they want.* Hand shaking, she secured her phone in her new tripod and began recording, her voice trembling: 'Re: the comments on my previous post, *with respect*, all studies of wild leopards and pumas in their native lands, such as North America, show that if they're not stressed, they don't seek out humans and coexist quite happily. You're far more likely to be killed by a pet dog than a wild cat!

'We should ask ourselves, why do we have a problem with cats? Britain has accepted wild boars and badgers . . . why have cats been banished from mainstream society like outlaws?

'Remember, report any sightings to Coralie@TheCatWhisperer. com! Let's save the cats, people!' [Smiles tightly.]

She could see the comments rising, accompanied by love hearts and fire symbols and laughing emojis, before she'd even finished speaking:

Outlaws! That's cute. She's cute.

What about in India, then?

Has anyone seen the cat lady's pussy?

She threw her phone across the room in a rage.

Her campaign was *flourishing*. She'd pointed out in a radio debate just that morning that if cats were officially recognized (and tagged) they wouldn't have had the problems of this summer: the multitude of sightings and opportunists who wanted a piece of the action. And the listeners who phoned in had been supportive, for the most part. Sharing their own experiences. The host, too, was interested, engaged, asked intelligent, thoughtful questions. Something which once felt impossible – wild cats being recognized in Britain – felt within reach. Of course, she was getting ahead of herself, but she was only a few thousand shy of the signatures she needed to have the issue discussed in the House of Commons, and hadn't Leonora always said when Coralie was growing up that she had the wiliness of a politician?

'Who are these cretins?' she railed at Socks as vulgar comments regarding 'saving her pussy' bombarded the screen. 'Oh, I'm sorry, baby. Mummy shouldn't shout.'

She flopped into her grandmother's squishy chair. Socks immediately leapt on to her lap. She stared out at the lavender bushes, finally on the cusp of blooming, drumming her fingers on the armrest. Rosemary beetles (*Chrysolina americana*) clung to the stalks, their metallic-green shells cut into fractions by sharp purple lines which caught the light like umbrella spokes. If only Adam had shown a bit more interest in her pussy, rather than his slut's, maybe they wouldn't be in this situation now.

'Have I ever told you how Adam and I met, Socks? Our romantic love story? On Battersea Bridge, after I stopped and asked him directions and, what would you know, but we were going to the same place? Such serendipity! So destined! Everyone adores a love story, don't they?'

She ran a finger along the soft gold bridge of his nose. The sun was setting outside, the sky a livid pink, like a fresh scar.

'But did I ever tell you how I *really* met Adam? Oh, you'll love this one, Socks!

'I tracked him! Spotted him one day, striding over the bridge. It *was* love at first sight. At least on my part. I couldn't take my eyes off him. But we were going in different directions. He was just a face in the crowd, each of us caught in a swell of people.

'But you know me, I couldn't forget him! So I walked the same route, at the same time, from my flat in Chelsea over to Battersea Park, every day for a month, until I was rewarded with another sight of him. I followed him home that day, which was perfect because it was much easier to track him when I had a starting point.

'I logged everything in one of my notebooks. I had one dedicated just to him. That's when I knew it was true love. All the curious little patterns in his behaviour. Making connections. Fitting together a life. A lonely-*ish* life. He was adopted, you know? Very churchy people. All fire and brimstone. He fell into the wrong crowd at school. They disowned him pretty sharply. But luckily, he was through all that by the time I met him, had almost finished his arboriculture studies.

'There were some girls. One girl in particular. I've told you about her.' Her voice dropped, sullenly. 'I can still picture her fire-red hair. But I could tell he *needed* me, like I needed him, and so eventually I struck up the courage to approach him, casually bumping into him on the bridge to ask for directions. He looked as though he'd never noticed me before, even though by then I'd been trailing him for months. That was the problem with Adam. He never saw what was right in front of him.

'And then the very next day, after our fates had collided, he was back on a date with the redhead!

'Well, what were the chances that I would bump into them and be there too? I know, right!

'Here you go, darling boy. Only the best for you . . .

'Of course, he apologized profusely. Said he'd gone to call it off with her. I gave him the benefit of the doubt. What can I say? You know I always see the best in people.'

She leaned on her elbow, put her thumb in her mouth and bit down hard until she could taste blood. So much effort for one average man. She hoped it had been worth it.

The Mystery of the
Sevenoaks Panther

Sofia Olsen, reporter: The same photos came up in my research: the famous one, of Coralie with her mother, walking a panther along Knightsbridge, a handful that had been released as part of the coverage of the Cleopatra Legacy Ball, and an old one from *Time* magazine, the Campbells in their elaborate drawing room at Cresswell Place surrounded by their animals.

At one point, the Campbells were infamous for practically having a zoo at home – their pets were celebrities themselves! – and then, overnight: nothing. Yet they still hold an annual ball to raise money for endangered animals. Almost like they feel bad about something . . .

And that got me thinking: did anyone ever find out what really happened to Cleopatra?

43

Twig

It had been a conversation running in their house all week: should Elwood and Skylar go to Cub camp?

'But, Mummy,' Skylar sighed, twisting Twig's hair, damp from a water fight, around her fingers. 'Wouldn't it be nice for me and Elwood to be normal like the other children?'

With a hosepipe ban in full swing and their paddling pool water dirty and forlorn, Twig had finally caved and taken the children to the pool at St Michael's with their friends. She saw a small red-faced boy exit the pool with snot streaming from his nose and a full-to-bursting swim nappy and wished she hadn't.

'You are normal, honey,' she said, rubbing Skylar's hands with antibacterial gel. Her heart twanged for all her children had missed out on the last couple of years, but wasn't that chapter of their lives drawing to a close? This time next month, Skylar would have had the vaccine. They'd lived in the danger zone for so long and that cloud was finally shifting.

She tucked her hair behind her ears and lifted it off the back of her neck. The heat today was stifling. She had found them a shady spot beneath a tree, but sweat still dripped off her. Elwood was sitting serenely on a branch just above them reading a book about ants, his interest having been piqued by the recent flying-ant day (or 'nuptial flights', as he kept correcting her). 'What do you think, honey?' she called up.

He didn't answer, but she saw the flick of his lashes in her direction and a small frown dust his smooth forehead; he was weighing it up.

A tiny thought she'd been struggling to squash emerged again: perhaps facilitating Matt and Elwood spending time together was the *right* thing to do? At some point they would need to do a paternity test, but it felt too soon, and everything too raw, to consider now. When you looked, the similarities were there between Matt and Elwood: the shape and set of their eyes alike, albeit in different colours – something in their *form* – in their long, almost gangly legs, in their narrow hips. In the way they moved. In the way they *disagreed*. Both always so sure of themselves. Twig had remembered with a twinge how Matt had also struggled with sports, something else which had made it harder for him to assimilate when he'd started school here. Perhaps it was like the wild cat though. Perhaps if you go looking for evidence, you will find it?

Would it be better, or worse, for Matt to be his father rather than Kev? She imagined Matt would like to be more involved, and she wasn't sure how she felt about that. She'd noticed already that he was making an effort with Elwood, and had instructed Henry to, too. She knew that as much as he pretended to be an arsehole, Matt was a good guy, buried beneath layers of insecurity. He'd take care of Elwood at camp, and maybe in general it would be good for Elwood to have him in his life? The arrangement with Kev was always understood to be a practical one: he'd never intended to be a father to the children and instead angled for 'cool uncle status' on the rare occasions he saw them. So, Kev wouldn't be deprived of anything. And he was still Skylar's biological father.

'You get to do air-rifle shooting and fishing and—' Skylar pressed.

Above them Elwood cocked an ear in her direction.

'Campfires and s'mores and ghost stories!' Skylar's enthusiasm was infectious.

Elwood tucked the book into the back of his shorts and clambered down the tree.

Around them children were dropping like flies, splayed out on swimming towels, beaten by the heat. Those that hadn't were engaged in fervid games of Marco Polo, in the pool, or Man Hunt, on the lawn.

The heat was testing them all. There was no respite, day or night. Although the local cat fever was abating, people were still nervy and on guard, socializing in large, noisy groups, avoiding quieter wooded areas where they might find some respite from the heat. Wasps sought them out in swarms, rendering every ice lolly or picnic outside fraught. There was no end in sight. Forecasters were saying they were in store for at least another fortnight of hot weather.

Elwood had, thankfully, stopped talking about the cat, although on occasion Twig still spotted him gazing over at Coralie's greenhouse wistfully. It felt like she had her son back, albeit a quieter, more subdued version.

Blake thought they should go. *'Did I ever not camp because I was worried about a bear attacking our tent? In an area where there were actual bears? No.'* And Twig didn't take her blunt delivery personally. That was just Blake. The problem was the niggle buzzing in her ear: she was sure it was all fabrication, a platform for Coralie to preside over them all, but there was the tiniest chance that Elwood's transcriptions from Coralie's notebook were true, that there *was* a big cat living nearby.

'What are we going to do otherwise?' Blake had asked. 'Have the kids at the party? Your dad wouldn't want to miss seeing you on stage again.' This was also true. Uptake for the benefit had exceeded expectations, built a fury of anticipation across the community. Everybody wanted to say they were there to see Pineapple Punk reunite. All other childcare options had been exhausted.

Elwood had always loved being outside, scampering about the woods. Was it fair for him – and Skylar – to miss out on camp because of her anxieties, and didn't the benefits – him having fun; developing friendships with like-minded peers; spending time with Matt, and even maybe Henry – outweigh her fears?

A paw flitted into her subconscious, claws bared, but she batted the image away.

44

Emma

Emma was scanning through the children's kit list for camp, marvelling that even when your husband was Akela you still had to do your kids' packing. Of course, actually packing for them was frowned upon. They were meant to do it themselves to earn their Camping Badge, so you could either leave them to it, nervously watching through your fingers as they brought three pairs of thermal pyjamas but no pants, or get it ready, and then scruff up the last few items to make it look like they'd done it themselves. Emma was going for the latter option.

'What will you do this weekend while we're away?' Matt appeared at the door with tea in her favourite Disney mug, the one they'd bonded over at work. It had kept getting pushed to the back of the cupboard, just out of her grasp. It had driven her bonkers, until Matt had reached over her to retrieve it one morning, whispering, 'I put it up here to keep it out of Colin's reach; he uses it when you're not around.' It was only then that she realized it was Matt Brook's *Star Wars* mug that was always nestled beside hers. Most of the executives at work ignored lowly minions like Emma, but Matt had noticed her. After that she didn't mind straining to clasp it, sometimes finding a small chocolate or a wrapped biscuit hidden inside. She'd always been faintly embarrassed by their staid meet-cute but now she recognized the quiet simplicity in it. She smiled at the memory as she placed the mug on Henry's bedside table.

'I'm not sure.' She rolled Henry's swim shorts into his towel. 'I don't think I'll go to the benefit.'

She didn't hate Twig. That realization had surprised her. It helped that Emma didn't envy Twig her life; she felt sympathy for her more than anything. But it still stung, Twig sleeping with her husband, even though it was before Twig knew her, even though they had already slept together as teenagers. It was the intimacy of it, the shared secret in the years since. She felt acutely embarrassed. The pathetic creature she feared she was. The frumpy mum she'd heard others call her. She hadn't told anyone else yet, not even Agatha. Deep down Emma *had* known something was amiss. She wondered if that also helped; it wasn't the shock it might have been.

Matt nodded. 'That's understandable.' She didn't know what would become of her and Matt. He'd explained that at the time he'd slept with Twig he hadn't been coping with IVF or his father's ill health but felt he couldn't tell her; she had had enough to worry about. He had to be strong. And he had failed. She knew it had taken a lot for him to say that. She didn't know if she could ever truly forgive him, but she was thinking about it. 'Why don't you go to see your parents?'

'I wondered about that, but I thought you might want me around? In case there's any problems at camp?' Why did she feel an instinct to stay close to home? Was it because her family felt fragile and precious? Was it because she didn't want to pretend with her parents that everything was okay? She realized she wouldn't be able to do that. She needed to be straight with them. *Life wasn't always a fairy-tale. Sometimes life sucked.* 'You know, you're right. I will go.'

Besides, a break from the house would do her good. Emma had largely made peace with whatever the result would be following the decision of the Planning Applications Committee but felt nervous, nonetheless, as the date nudged closer. After a long wait it was little over a week away. It was gratifying, however, that Tim's spurious application to have the house listed had been dismissed by Historic England. There would be no protracted assessment. At least they would be able to move on, one way or another, whatever the Planning Applications Committee decreed.

The doorbell chimed extravagantly. Emma had removed her smart doorbell. It wasn't, as they say, bringing her joy. Unfortunately, it meant the elaborate bell she'd hated when they first moved in was back in place.

'I do *so love* Westminster Quarters.' Coralie smiled as Emma opened the door. Emma hadn't seen Coralie for the past week, unless social media counted. She waited for her to acknowledge the new pink facade of the house, but she walked in as though she hadn't noticed.

'So glad you're home. I'm in such a pickle,' Coralie trilled, wafting past Emma in a cheesecloth-and-tan-leather ensemble, pencil behind her ear. She smelled kind of bad, musty. 'Is Matt home?' Her eyes scurried around until they landed hungrily on Matt. 'Oh, there you are! My darling Matt Brooks, only you can save me!'

Excuse me? Emma had observed the ostentatious almost-flirting Coralie employed with Matt and a number of the other Puddleford men previously, but it had been good-natured, like a collective acknowledgement of her magnetism, and they all felt in on the joke, but this was ridiculous. Emma felt an unexpected prickle of jealousy as she trailed Coralie into the kitchen.

Matt returned Coralie's greeting with a polite 'How can I help?'

'It's Fraser,' Coralie said, with her familiar moue, lips pursed in distaste. 'He's dropped the girls on me this weekend at the last minute. They're on their way now. Apparently, he and Elvira just *have to* get away. No doubt trouble in paradise. And you know how I *love* to see the girls, but this is the one evening when it's not ideal to have them around, because of the benefit.'

Emma watched her curiously. She was thinner, with a sheen on her cheeks that suggested grime rather than good health. Was this the result of caring for Adam? Emma had forgotten all about him in the stress of the last few weeks. Hadn't seen him leave the house at all. Or was it stress at organizing the benefit? But this was Coralie's skill set. She loved to throw a party. And wasn't it always ideal to have your children around, especially if you hardly saw them? The benefit was 'adults only', but that was Coralie's rule, which the rest of them gratefully followed as it meant they could let their hair down, but she could bend her own rules, couldn't she?

'I've worked *so hard* to get everything ready. I could really do without any interruptions,' she continued.

'*Interruptions?* Your darling daughters that you boast about so much?' Emma burst out, unable to help herself. How many times had they had to listen to the number of sporting medals and spelling certificates her daughters had accrued?

Coralie stopped speaking and slowly twisted her head to face Emma, a cruel smile playing on her lips. *The mask slips.* Emma felt something shift, a little of her old self coming back to her, an underlying defiance that was uniquely her, some inherent Emma-ness that wasn't pathetic at all. She wasn't ashamed of who she was. She met Coralie's malevolent stare with a steely glare of her own.

Coralie snapped her head back to Matt, her voice dripping sweetly: 'I just wondered if there was any chance they could join you camping this weekend? Iris is a Beaver and Bea's a Scout, as you know. They say the membership badge means you can join a troop anywhere in the world, don't they? Do they still say that? Oh, good.'

Emma could see Matt mentally recalculating baked beans and sausages and risk assessments. She suspected he wouldn't mind them joining, ordinarily would love it, in fact, the benevolent leader that he was, but this year, with the stress of everything, it was one more thing to factor in.

'Can't you get a babysitter?' Emma asked. 'They can stay inside the house?'

'Oh, I've tried!' Coralie waved her arms for emphasis. 'Everyone's fully booked. It's a nightmare. I wouldn't ask unless I was desperate.' She touched a hand to Matt's forearm. Emma frowned. Coralie's children were twelve and six; couldn't she put them to bed, or set them up with a movie and pop in to check on them periodically? She was only going to be in the back garden.

'And it will be wonderful for them to catch up with their "Kent fam".' She delivered 'Kent fam' in the manner of a cringey parent to their awkward teen. She was all over the place, teeth bared as she smiled between her sentences.

There was something off with her, Emma thought as Matt was agreeing and emailing Coralie a copy of the kit list, Coralie gripping his forearms with dirty fingernails and repeating her thanks. She pictured the drone footage again. Coralie with her bucket. Emma had been waylaid by her marriage imploding, hadn't had time to consider what it all meant. 'Why do you take a bucket into the Parkland?' she blurted.

Coralie spun on her heel. 'Excuse me?'

'I've seen you. With a bucket. I was curious.'

Coralie's eyes narrowed. Emma could see she was weighing her up, wondering *how* much she'd seen and probably recalling Tim's accusations that she'd been flying a drone over the neighbourhood. 'For my conservation work, Emma,' she retorted snippily, tilting her chin upwards. 'Just because I've been busy with my campaign doesn't mean I'd neglect my other responsibilities. Who else is going to save the badgers?'

Emma's fingers were already tapping as Coralie glided ethereally down their path. As she departed, Coralie seemed to evoke a fury of wind: trees shook, windchimes clanged, playhouse doors slammed. Emma shivered. *The cat whisperer.*

Coralie's story checked out. The RSPCA even recommended helping badgers in hot weather. Feeding them things like dry dog food and cheese and peanuts. No mention of fish, but another site said badgers were omnivores. So, they *could* eat anything . . . Emma tapped her fingers on the counter. She still felt something was amiss . . . What was going on this summer? She'd hoped the season's drama was behind her, so why did she have this disturbing sense of horror unfolding anew?

The Mystery of the Sevenoaks Panther

Pat Duggan, Duggan's Farm: Why did I agree to take part in all this? [Gesticulates around the empty room with a faded navy baseball cap clutched in his hand.] Because I lost everything. *Everything.* And I'm an old fool, I suppose. [Voice cracks.]

[Whispers:] I still hope that some good can come of it all . . . [Stares off glassy-eyed.]

45

Coralie

'Have you ever drunk in a pale lilac dawn, air crisp as it coats your throat? Listened to every crunch of leaf and heavy breath as your fate comes closer?' She sighed. 'If only you and I could have a proper conversation, Socks. I'm so close now. *So close.*'

She'd never wished more that she had a human friend. Confiding in Socks was a relief, but even she knew he couldn't talk back. Not in words, anyway. She smiled at the way he'd paced alongside her as she'd relayed her plan for Adam.

Outside, the lavender bushes finally hummed with bees and white butterflies, the sound rising through the open window. It had said on the radio this morning that the temperature would reach 41 degrees today. It felt close to that already.

She pressed her thumb on the blender. The thick, grisly meat spluttered and juddered in the glass jug. She added more water. She was starting to get the consistency right.

'I'm sorry, Socks, these aren't for you,' she cooed. 'Oh, pudding. You're not jealous of my other cat, are you? It's not a good trait.' She pouted. 'Here, you can have a little lick. What do you think? More kidney?' She rooted around in the freezer. 'Ooh yes! Liver! Yum yum.'

When the smoothie was ready she set to work chopping the watermelons in half, scooping out their stomachs. It was sweaty work, and she appreciated it. The energy was becoming harder to shift. She felt it everywhere: sitting on her chest, in her fingertips, deep inside her pulsing cunt. She felt so *alive*. It was hard to explain. Like every moment in her miserable life had brought her to this conclusion.

She poured the mixture into the watermelons. Carefully put them in the freezer. A splash slopped over the side of one, and Socks was quick to lick it off the floor.

'Good boy,' she praised. 'Cleaning up for Mummy! What do you think? A refreshing blend of meat and offal?'

There was some smoothie left. She poured it into ice-lolly moulds and reusable cups and put those in the freezer too.

'Who wouldn't enjoy a nice blood lolly on a day like today, hey?'

Earlier, while Adam was still asleep, she'd gone out to the Parkland with her hose, as far as she could extend it from her greenhouse, flouting the hosepipe ban, spraying the earth to cool it. Then she'd filled buckets with icy water, heaved them up through the forest to the clearing. The heat had driven away even the most ardent 'Puddleford Parkland' sign tourists, but on the odd occasion she'd been spotted near the paths this week with her buckets she'd called out that she was 'off to save the badgers!' Emma had given her the idea. That had become a meme now too. She was getting the hang of social media, and what struck her as most odd about it was how everything happened online. There was so much fuss about the Sevenoaks Panther, and yet there was rarely anyone else ever actually here.

Later, when the watermelons were ready, she'd bring them into the Parkland and roll them into the clearing. Watch Monroe split one open with her powerful jaws, her tongue rolling out and curling as she lapped up the mixture. She'd tried a few different types of melon, but watermelon was her clear favourite. Coralie grinned with satisfaction.

This was conservation work. Goodness knows how Monroe would have survived this summer without her. There was scant water. The stream in the Parkland was barely visible, its vulnerable bed exposed.

Earlier this week the question of whether wild cats were naturalizing in the UK was finally raised in the House of Commons, her online petition having garnered enough votes. Granted, it was a brief exchange with a lot of heckling on either side, but *nonetheless*, a suggestion was made to set up a Select Committee to discuss it! She'd been eagerly checking her email since, fully expecting to be asked to give evidence. She imagined the look on her father's face (himself unceremoniously expelled from the House of Lords) were it to be televised. *Justice, sweet justice.*

She would save the wild cats; forever be associated with their accepted naturalization in the UK. *They would remember her name*, she thought, anticipation prickling like an aphrodisiac.

Sex was power.

Power was sex.

We are all wild things.

The thoughts swirled around her head until she became giddy with them. She was changing the world. And she'd get the truth from Adam to boot. The whole truth. She needed to hear him say it himself. For him to confess his affair. So she could tell *everyone*. So she could leave him with nothing. Take everything. And no one would judge her for Adam getting what he deserved.

She felt on the edge of something, almost a kind of madness. Lifting her up, propelling her forwards. She could do this. She could have it all.

She was a good person. Her parents had got it all wrong. They'd got everything wrong.

The Mystery of the
Sevenoaks Panther

Lady Violet Campbell: We all felt Cleopatra's loss tremendously. Words can't describe the pain. They still can't. It took me a *very long time* to . . . [Sniffs.] . . . Put myself back together again. I'm sorry . . . could you excuse me.

Coralie: No one believed me that it was an accident. No one believed that it was *me* I wanted Duchess to hurt, not Cleopatra. *Me.* Just so I could get some attention from them. All I ever wanted was their love. But it backfired hugely. I was sent away to school. I was rarely home for the holidays. When I was, they would go away, leaving me with the housekeeper. I didn't see my parents for the next ten years. Then I saw my mother on the King's Road one day. She walked straight past me, as though I were a ghost.

Lady Violet: Honestly, I couldn't bear to look at her. And neither could Frederick. I still can't. I'm only doing this to set the record straight. I know what she's like. She'll lie. She'll say we neglected her. Left her alone all the time with the animals. But the animals weren't the problem. We could trust them. Coralie was the problem.

Coralie: I'd always wanted a sister. It had been fun growing up around the animals, playing with them, but they couldn't talk back. It wasn't quite the same. And back then I still had this silly idea that humans might be something I could connect with. Might even be fun.

Lady Violet: 'A *cat*? Cleopatra wasn't a *cat*. She was my daughter. *Coralie killed her sister.* Goaded the cat into hurting her. And then blamed everybody else.

46

Twig

It was a balmy summer's evening, the air scented with honeysuckle and woodsmoke as the black-uniformed caterers threw luscious king prawns and juicy lamb cutlets on the barbecue, a pig turning on a spit beside them, gleaming metal trays of spicy margaritas being delivered by wait-staff through the crowd. The night of the benefit had finally arrived.

Twig's eyes met Adam's across the other side of the lawn and her heart pumped harder. His eyes flickered with gold, reflected from the elegant torches Coralie had had staked around the periphery of her garden, separating the greenhouse at the bottom from the rest of the party. Twig had queried the safety of this, the lawns having been stripped of any moisture for weeks now, but anticipation for tonight's event had reached fever pitch and Coralie had insisted they close off access to the Parkland to avoid any interlopers and this was the most aesthetically pleasing way to do it. Twig stared back at Adam, locked in the moment. She wished she knew where he'd been these last few months. As her life had grown bigger, he seemed to have disappeared. She thought of his fingertips pressing heat into her skin, catching alight, a trail of fire as he passed her a joint, or circled her wrist, marvelling at its delicacy. They'd never gone further, never pursued their flirtation – *connection* – whatever it was; so why did she feel a swell of guilt as she looked at him now, drawn and thin?

Freja's brother's band, the warm-up act, strummed soft Scandinavian rock as the party-goers arrived, taking in the scene: the stage, the cocktail bar, the parents they usually saw at the school gates dressed in their finery; shimmering cocktail dresses and tailored chinos with dazzling tropical shirts. Coralie King knew how to throw a party. Everything glowed: the fire, the bulbs strung through the trees, the drinks, the guests.

Just as Twig had resolved to speak to Adam, a hand fell on her arm, breaking the spell.

'All ready for your performance?' Coralie smiled, her golden hair falling like honey in the fading, shimmering light. She wore a metallic silk dress with ballooned sleeves tapering at the cuffs. She may have hosted this event for Skylar in name, but it was clear this was her party.

They'd done a soundcheck earlier and it had been Twig's first time on a stage in decades. It was a much smaller stage than in her twenties, coarser too, rudimentary, but the feel of the boards beneath her feet, the vibrations of the base through her chest, it was like coming home. Even Blake seemed to be enjoying herself, behind Twig on the keyboard.

Twig nodded. She didn't trust Coralie, but in that moment she was grateful to her. She knew already that she would never forget this evening.

Afterwards she would draw a line under the last few years. She would enjoy tonight, fly to America and begin her family life again when she returned. Her, Elwood and Skylar. That was all she truly needed. She would *choose to live*. It was an ache, a desire so deep it threatened to consume her, but she knew what to do with it instead: to channel it into her performance.

'I'm ready.'

47

Coralie

Finally, everything had come together. She'd started the day with panicked messages from Matt. Emma had been up all night, with Henry and Daisy vomiting. Norovirus doing the rounds again. Emma was due to go to her parents' for the weekend, so Matt had been close to cancelling Cub camp, but fortunately Emma had agreed to stay to look after them. Not even Coralie would go ahead with her plan tonight if the party was swarming with children. It had been her suggestion to hold the benefit the same night as the Cub camp. She wanted to know all the local children were safely ensconced far away from her greenhouse, either at camp or with a babysitter. It was a strictly adults-only party.

Twig was on stage, all muscle and sinew in her sequin get-up, a vision of petroleum plastics and synthetic resin which would one day pollute the earth, if it hadn't started to already. Twig picked up her mic, chatting to Blake, who looked uneasy. Nervous, perhaps.

Nerves were rarely a problem for Coralie. It was a case of mind over matter. She traced a finger around the chain adorning her neck.

It wasn't easy to train a wild cat. It had taken months, years, of quiet dedication, to get to this point. Not just anyone could do this. Her childhood had helped, growing up alongside them. Her zoology knowledge. Her experience, tracking them as a child with her grandmother, and ever since. But more than any of that, it was *her*. Coralie. It was her unique gift. She *was* a cat whisperer. She was special. And that was Adam's first mistake. He'd stopped realizing she was special. But soon he would be reminded.

She glanced up at the stage, eagerly giving Twig a thumbs-up. *Thanks for the cover*, she thought silently. She wouldn't be able to do this anywhere else, or on any other night. Her garden was too quiet. There couldn't be any children nearby. It had to be here. It had to be like this. She found Adam in the crowd, exactly where she'd left him. It was time.

48

Twig

Twig moved her shoulders and shook out her hands, alive with the inimitable energy that comes when you stand on a stage and stare out at a sea of people, their eyes flickering with anticipation. The sky was slowly darkening, the flames and fairy lights dotted around imbuing the crowd with a note of magic. She opened with 'A Boy Made of Stars', the opening bars silencing the crowd.

Tiny details registered: Blake smiling, for the first time in what felt like forever, as she moved across the stage; the creak of one of the boards each time she stepped over it; the beautiful mixologist flicking a silver cocktail shaker in the air, its surface catching the light, as she lined up rows of margheritas. She noticed some of the crowd crying as the gentle melody weaved through the warm summer air like fireflies, not just the usual suspects either, but a dad or two she was surprised at and barely knew, occasionally seeing them in a fleeting rush at a school event before they disappeared in the direction of the train station.

The song built its own momentum, gathered pace . . . She shared a moment with her dad, in the middle of the crowd, as always, cheering her on. She raised her fist in the air as he held his to his heart . . . Soon she was enveloped again in the music.

There was nothing like it. No feeling on this earth that could come close. She stood on the stage, her sequin crop top and shorts catching all the light in the garden and throwing it back, as she hyped up the middle-aged ravers. And she didn't feel embarrassed, or sad, or old, as she often did these days. They were all there for her and Blake. Like they could personally heal Skylar and their little family with their chants and good will. And in a way, they had.

She'd grown up here, and yet this was the first time she'd truly felt a part of the community. It was like looking down and realizing your feet had sprouted roots; she felt part of the structure and the fabric of Puddleford. She glanced towards Briar Heart House, less imposing in the twilight, since it had been painted pink. Change was coming. She could feel it.

She leapt in the air, and she sang.

49

Coralie

Coralie led Adam through the row of fire separating her greenhouse from the rest of the garden.

'Where are we going?' he asked sullenly, but she *shushed* him and he followed obediently. She allowed herself a smile of satisfaction: like she'd told Elwood, you could train anything if you set your mind to it.

He trailed her into the greenhouse. 'A Boy Made of Stars' penetrated the thin glass. *What a racket!* She'd been right to execute her plan during the first song. As she'd anticipated, the noise, coupled with the heat, was making Monroe restless. She was still on the floor, where Coralie had left her with a little water earlier, but she was no longer stretched out contentedly. Her head was raised regally, eyes alert. She was thirsty and hungry. Coralie locked the door as Adam's eyes adjusted to the dim light. 'What's all this?' he asked nervously. She lamented the days when sneaking off from a party together and locking the door would have a different subtext entirely. He hadn't yet seen the cat.

'Aren't I allowed to want my husband all to myself?' She was aiming for coquettish, but the result was petulant: she was unexpectedly nervous after all. *You've got him exactly where you want him. Don't blow it now.* The fact is, she had Adam entirely to herself these days.

The cat let out a low growl and Adam froze.

'What the—' His voice died in his throat at a second, more insistent growl. To Coralie, who knew every sound this animal made, knew when she was content, or frustrated, or agitated, the sound was little more than a purr. Monroe knew she was there; knew that her reward would come in the end. Whistle and treat.

Adam's eyes were wide with terror, his face bleached of colour. He was staring at Coralie, blinking hard, as though if he concentrated enough the cat might disappear. As if it might be a mirage, or an imagining from his worst nightmare. He was staring at her as if to say, *can you see that?* And she just nodded, one eyebrow raised. *I can see it, Adam, but can you?*

'The door's locked.' She held up the key before sliding it into her bra. 'There's only one way out of this.'

They formed a loose triangle, he in the middle of the room, Coralie by the door and Monroe in the other corner, licking her paws. He backed up, not seeing the bucket of raw chicken legs by his feet. As his heel knocked it, Monroe's head jerked up eagerly. She looked at Coralie, but Coralie kept her training stick pointing down.

'Stay,' she commanded. Coralie reached down to a large bucket beneath her apothecary desk, scooping strips of liver and slivers of steak into a smaller bucket, which she dangled over her wrist like a bracelet.

Adam, clearly afraid to move his feet, leaned his torso back, his hands finding the worktop behind him. She moved towards him, drawing Monroe to her side with the stick. She blew her whistle and threw her a strip of steak. Her pink tongue snaked out hungrily as Adam made a gagging sound.

Finally, she had Adam exactly where she wanted him: pinned back against the low wooden worktop of her greenhouse, Coralie and her cat, her beautiful cat, before him.

Adam wet himself immediately. It was pitiable.

'C— C— C—' He couldn't speak.

She thought of that girl long ago, red hair aflame, her long legs. She almost danced between them like a nymph. Adam's first affair.

Maybe she should never have forgiven him. Then they wouldn't be here now. She wouldn't have had to go to such extreme lengths. Although, it had been fun.

Monroe was gently shifting her gaze, between Coralie and the bucket, waiting for a signal or command. The longer they drew this out, the more impatient the cat would become. So, it was in Adam's interests to conclude this quickly. It was enough that she had the cat. She didn't need her to perform tricks or do anything else. She just had to be here.

'This is how it's going to go. You tell me the truth. I need to know you're not bullshitting me. All I ask is the truth, and I'll send her away.' She placed a hand to the cat's head, Cybele to her lion, and it purred contentedly.

Adam let out a whimpering sound and fell to his knees with a thud. The cat turned its head enquiringly, looked up at Coralie.

'I wouldn't make any sudden movements if I were you.' She smiled.

He began to cry silently.

'Did you have an affair last summer?' She kept her tone casual, almost businesslike, but she felt her stomach clenching, bracing herself to hear him finally admit the truth.

He shook his head. She blinked.

'Adam. Let's try again.' Clearly, he'd misunderstood this evening's assignment. She glanced at Monroe, and back to Adam. He made a tragic, whimpering sound.

A horrible memory flashed in her mind: Cleopatra on the floor, making a similar noise seconds before all hell broke loose.

'Adam.' She swallowed, collecting herself. 'Did you have an affair last summer?'

His whole body was trembling. He shook his head.

'*Speak*,' she growled.

'No,' he managed.

She had been prepared for his confession. To find out who he was having an affair with; which faceless woman he had met and fucked in the forest. What she wasn't ready for was his denial.

That he would be prepared to lie for this woman even as she threatened him with his life.

'No?'

'No,' he confirmed. More forcefully this time.

'Where did you go? What were you doing?'

Adam looked too afraid to speak. His eyes were fixed on her in terror. She saw his head jerking to keep focus, to avoid looking at the cat.

'Adam,' she prompted, twisting her hand to reveal the training stick. Monroe was watching for her cue, growing restless.

'I was with Twig.'

'Twig?' Her lips twitched into a moue of distaste. *Stay calm, Coralie.* She had to use her calm voice with the cat, her trainer voice. Intrinsically, she knew maintaining this was important. 'Twig, with the *wife* and the sick child, who's been far too busy to have an affair?'

He nodded.

She couldn't help it; she let out a strangled cry. A wild, animal sound. She didn't see Monroe flinch. 'You've been having an affair with Twig?'

'No. Not an affair. I told you, I've never—'

'Never?' She cocked an eyebrow.

'We weren't dating then. I met you the day before.' It was true that, at that point, Coralie had invested more time in him than he had in her.

'Well, what then?' Her voice pitched and the cat shifted up on to its front legs. 'If not an affair, then what?' She was struggling to control the tone of her voice, powerless to stop.

'We were at the skate ramps. She taught me to skate.' *What?* She almost laughed. *What nonsense is this? Did he take her for a fool? A moron? Did he not see who she was? With her cat by her side? What she was capable of?* Her eyes gleamed with menace.

He crossed his arms over his chest feebly.

'You're lying.' She took a step closer, her training stick by her side. Monroe followed.

Whistle and treat.

'It's true,' he gasped, his body shaking as he tried to shrink further and further back.

They took another step. For a second, she believed him. *Was he telling the truth?* If he was . . . if she'd got things wrong . . . No. It wasn't possible. He was gaslighting her again.

She remembered a detail: 'Why the second phone?'

Whistle and treat. One more step and there'd be less than a metre between them. Adam, Coralie and the cat.

'We . . . held little parties.' His voice was barely a whisper, suffocating within his throat. 'We sold drugs.'

Her eyes widened in shock.

'Drugs?' *Stay calm.* 'We?'

Other facts slid into place, things she'd barely registered before. She gasped. 'You're the people who were selling drugs in the Parkland? It wasn't teenagers at all. It was you and Twig? Who would buy drugs from you in Puddleford Parkland?' she shrieked, disbelieving. And then it came to her. 'The skaters? *The fucking skaters?*' Her voice was escalating over the music. Beside her, Monroe's eyes were sharp, focused. She began to pace, small steps up and down beside Coralie. *Good girl. That would scare him.*

'Not to the skaters. They're, like, fifteen. No, to . . .' He dropped his head and closed his eyes, like it was all over for him now. The cat was here, the cat was real, and finally he was about to tell Coralie what he'd got himself into. His reckoning. A sigh shuddered from him. '. . . some of the parents from the school,' he mumbled.

'Speak up, Adam,' she hissed. '*Who?* Do I *know* them?'

'I don't know. Kofi, Agatha's husband? Freja, who runs the PTA? A couple of others.'

Freja? The woman who had rushed to buy Coralie ice and lemons this morning?

'Where did you get these *drugs* from?'

'Blake.' He hung his head. 'It wasn't on a big scale. Just people we trusted.'

Coralie waved his words away, flustered. She didn't need these details. She needed to get to the bit where he confessed that she was right. That he'd betrayed her. Had had an affair. 'And then what happened? Why did you stop?'

'Kofi had a fucking heart attack, didn't he?'

'What about the kid? The one that went to hospital?'

'We panicked, rushing to get Kofi to hospital – luckily he was in his Lycra and had his bike with him, so everyone just assumed he'd overexerted himself. But we dropped a small bag with a couple of pills in. A skater found them. You know the rest . . . he went to hospital too.' Coralie opened her mouth to interject, but Adam rushed on, his words garbled. 'But it wasn't an overdose, or a bad trip, or anything like the rumours said. It was dehydration. He was fine. But the police got involved. All they had were descriptions from a couple of the skaters who'd seen us there before. We just . . . stopped going. Kept our heads down. That was it.'

He was speaking so fast she could barely process it all. She staggered backwards. Didn't notice her heel catching on a small patch of Monroe's fur. The cat yelped and Adam scrambled up on to the counter, pushing books and jars aside. There was a series of crashes as they fell to the floor.

He'd sold drugs. . . thrown 'parties'. . . because of him a teenager, a child, had been hurt. Was that worse than having an affair? Maybe? But then, why did she feel so deflated?

'Why?' she shouted. 'Why would you be so stupid?'

Monroe's purrs had tipped into something different. It was a warning signal, but Coralie was feeling reckless. Her dress was sticking to her skin, damp with humidity in the greenhouse. She'd come too far to leave without the answers she needed. There was no going back.

'I said, *why*? What trinkets were you planning to buy? Who did you hope to take out for dinner?'

A steely look clouded his eyes then. He had the air of a man who had had enough. 'Because you were right about one thing. I wanted to leave you. And I needed money.'

Outside, the music rose in a crescendo, a heady mix of bass, drums, chants and claps, heels cracking on boards, rattling the glass of the greenhouse. Inside, Coralie matched its pitch, roaring with anger. She stamped her foot, cast aside her small bucket, threw her training stick at the wall. But it wasn't enough to appease the rage roiling within her. Her eyes fell on her glass terrarium. She lifted it high over her head and smashed it on to the floor. Splinters of glass flew at the cat. Monroe drew back from her. In her peripheral vision, Coralie saw her tense, primed, on her haunches, snarling. *Good girl.*

Adam let out a whimper, his eyes groping around in desperation. He reached to the shelf beside him, holding a glass jar high over his own head to defend himself, his elbows quivering by his ears.

Coralie turned, her back to Monroe as she looked for something else to throw, another weapon, but she kept an eye on Adam. She was so fixed on him, so busy revelling in his fear, that she didn't see the danger herself.

It was only as Monroe flew at her that she remembered the golden rule: *never turn your back on a cat.*

50

Twig

Twig felt as though her soul had wriggled free and she was soaring over the crowd.

By the time they reached the finale of 'Fleeting Heart', their breakthrough song and still their biggest hit, the heat was high, the crowd was high, and goddammit, Twig was high.

She jumped into the air, legs kicking, arms punching. Blake had cranked the bass up louder and louder, appeasing the crowd, who were jumping up and down, hollering for more.

A flock of birds soared high overhead as the sun was going down and, right there, that was the moment. *That was the fucking moment!*

She gripped the mic as she raised both hands; it felt like the sky was splitting with claps and whoops and cheers. The ground thundered, the stage shook. The roar of the crowd shimmered, like glass breaking, the high-pitched shrieks so intense they could have been mistaken for guttural cries of pain.

In the heat, the crowd had grown wild, and it was all for her. Suddenly Blake was by her side, arms around her despite it all. 'I'm sorry,' they whispered to each other, sweat meeting as they pressed their cheeks together, hands clasped around the other's head. The noise of the crowd thundered in their ears. Finally they let go, smiling as they separated, fingers entwined as they bowed to the crowd.

Twig dropped her head to her chest. She was done.

51

Emma

Emma removed her ear buds, her mouth slack with shock. She had ceased her surveillance escapades, but Coralie's visit the day before had been enough to convince her to undertake one last operation. Now she wished she hadn't. She couldn't reconcile what she had just heard with the happy sounds emanating from Coralie's garden next door. *What the . . .*

She flew to Henry's room. He was in bed watching a YouTube video about an ant colony which Elwood had sweetly recommended when he'd heard Henry was missing camp. 'This is actually pretty cool,' Henry said as she entered. 'They're putting a live cricket in the tank!'

Her hand fluttered over the doorknob. She'd come to get Henry's drone, but it was already too dark outside; she wouldn't be able to see anything.

She nodded at Henry distractedly, but he didn't notice, his eyes already back on the screen as the cricket was devoured by a swarm of ants.

Outside his room, she faltered. What could she possibly do? If what she'd heard was true . . . She could call the police, but would they even believe her? And if they did, they wouldn't get there in time.

She gulped, scurried downstairs, opened a bottle of wine and flicked on her favourite playlist.

What if she pretended she'd never heard it at all?

52

Coralie

Coralie was knocked sideways by the force of the cat pinning her to the ground. Its claws grazed over her porcelain skin, rivulets of blood immediately springing up on her cheek. She screamed, an animal sound that rasped in her throat.

Get off the floor! she thought to herself. *Get off the floor! Once a cat has you pinned to the ground, that's it. You're fucked.*

Monroe raised her paw, ready to swipe again, when Adam lunged for the bucket of meat, whistling and flinging roughly chopped chicken parts to the other side of the greenhouse. The cat tossed its head, distracted by each throw, before finally leaping over and licking the meat up with its thick pink tongue. Adam recoiled, eyes fixed on the cat, nudging the bucket as he crawled over, then stopped to kneel, putting himself and the bucket between Coralie and the cat.

'Adam!' she cried, but her shrieks mingled, lost within the frenetic cheering for Twig and Adam's grunt of frustration as he exhausted the supply of meat.

'*Fuck's sake,*' he muttered urgently. He raised the empty bucket as if to throw it at the cat but thought better of it, tossing it behind them. There was a loud crash, followed by another. A pane of the delicate glass in the greenhouse shattered. Coralie blinked, discombobulated, reality beginning to splinter.

Adam looked around frantically for more bait, his eyes alighting on the bucket of liver under the desk, but Monroe was right beside it. Too close for him to reach.

Monroe opened her huge jaws and roared, the force so strong that more glass split in the frames, cracking like ice. Seizing the opportunity, Adam shifted back into a crab crawl, using his leg to hook the handle of the bucket of liver from under the apothecary desk. His taut arms and legs quaked with tension, sweat slipping down the back of his neck. Finally he had it, drawing it towards them until it was close enough to reach. He sprung to his feet and grabbed it. Eyes darting, he ran to where the glass had shattered and flung the rest of the meat out of the window, flattening himself against the back wall.

The cat sprung up on to its haunches, its sharp teeth exposed, its inhale audible. The scent of Adam's aftershave, potent as it mingled with the heat and sweat radiating from him, invaded the small space, overpowering. Monroe inhaled again, deeper this time, her neck elongated, her head high, a greedy look in her eyes as she held her position. *What had she done?*

'*Monroe*,' she whispered. '*No. Please . . .*'

Time seemed to stop.

The cat surveyed Adam with a long, hungry look and then leapt past him, out of the window.

'Jesus Christ!' Adam slumped to the floor as Coralie murmured, 'Good girl,' sinking back, a hand to her cheek, warm blood trailing over her fingers.

Adam had saved her. Put himself between her and the cat. It was the single most romantic moment of her life.

'*Good girl?*' he repeated incredulously. '*Good girl?* We were both just nearly killed by a fucking big cat!' His eyes bulged unattractively.

'She wouldn't have killed us.' That *couldn't* be true. 'She was agitated. The heat. The noise. She's not used to being inside.' Coralie was relieved she'd set up a torch perimeter to protect her guests.

Adam was watching her carefully. 'What *the fuck* have you been doing?'

Coralie said nothing. Watched the truth slowly dawn in Adam's eyes. He clambered to his feet, struggling for breath, somewhere between relief at being alive and a panic attack.

'You put everyone we know in danger? Your *daughters?*'

'Of course I didn't,' she snapped. 'Everything I said is true. There is no danger.' She truly believed that. Her sister, Cleopatra, would never have died if she, Coralie, hadn't riled up Duchess. And in turn that would never have happened if her parents hadn't neglected her. 'If humans leave cats alone, there's no risk.'

'But you didn't leave the cats alone, Coralie, did you?' His voice was leonine, with the bite of a growl.

She looked away, petulant. 'I needed to know what was going on. I knew you were planning to leave me. You've been keeping secrets from me.'

'Don't play the victim!' he thundered. 'This is all just you in your fantasy land, as usual. Needing to be sweet, kind Coralie,' He put on a cutesy voice and her blood broiled beneath her skin. 'But you're *horrible*. To me. To the girls. We creep around you, walking on eggshells, never knowing when you're going to lose it. So yes! I was trying to leave you. And I *needed* the money.'

'You don't *need* any money. *I* give you everything you need. How many times do I have to say it?' She thought they'd got over that. It had been so long since he'd brought it up.

'I want my own money. My own choices. My own freedom. To go where I want. To work for who *I* want.'

'You make it sound like you're a prisoner!' she snarled, daring him to contradict her. 'Leave if you want to!'

'I have nothing,' he spat. 'Everything is in your name.'

'Because I can't trust you! And thank God, because I was right, wasn't I?'

'I've *never* given you a reason not to trust me.'

'No, except for the times you threw little drugs parties with Twig.'

His face twitched.

She asked the question she feared the most: 'Do you love her?'

He looked down at his soiled trousers. Pinched his forehead between his fingers and thumb, his jaw clenched. 'Nothing ever happened between us.'

It was as if Adam had taken a scalpel and scored pain directly into her heart tissue, dividing it into parts.

'You should go.' She shrugged, businesslike. 'I'll tell the girls you said goodbye.'

He laughed softly. 'Fraser won't let the girls come here if I'm not around.'

She reeled backwards. 'I knew you were in cahoots with Fraser! Just like my parents! He's behind all this, I suppose? Your bid for freedom! What's he said to you?' Her voice rose, almost sing-song. 'He's using you, Adam!'

Adam dragged his hands down his face with a look which said, *I'm done.* He gestured around the greenhouse, at the broken glass, the bits of plants, the raw meat and blood smeared over the floor. 'Do you think this is normal, sleeping out here in the garden? Your only friends being cats?'

By God, he sounded like her mother.

'I sleep here because I'm afraid of you,' she said robotically. He knew she didn't mean it. Knew instead that was the line she would churn out if required.

'You don't really sleep here, do you? I bet you prowl around the Parkland at night, obsessing over that cat, fussing with your nightcams. It's weird, you know that, right? Being obsessed like this is weird.'

'I'm a zoologist!'

'Look at all this shit.' He pointed at her jars and books, the shelves crammed with objects and knowledge.

'I was doing it for you, remember? The investigation.'

He shook his head from side to side. 'You don't do anything for other people, Coralie. You do things to make yourself feel good. I've never met anyone as broken and twisted and nasty as you.'

He looked her square in the eyes as he said it. 'What will people say when they know the truth?'

'No one will believe you.'

'Fraser will. The girls will. I'll make sure they don't get sucked in by you and chewed up and spat out, like Elwood. Poor kid.' He was breathing heavily, hands on his hips. 'You should get that looked at.' He gestured at her face. Blood was still dripping down her neck, blooming like deadly roses on the thin fabric of her dress. 'Good luck explaining that, by the way.'

He was speaking rapid-fire, collecting himself. He thought it was over. He thought he'd won. That they were even. He'd held illicit drugs parties with Twig, but she'd terrorized him with a melanistic leopard. Like anyone would believe that.

He was shaking his head in disbelief and, for a second, he still looked handsome. He still looked like a man she might want to impress. Back before all this began.

'I needed to know, Adam,' she said in a more conciliatory tone, her eyes tender.

'You're *insane*.' He jabbed a finger at her.

She raised one eyebrow. 'Funny, because I think that's generally what people say about you. I hope the doctor made a nice little note about your wild theories and hallucinations when you spoke to him. It's always helpful to have a record.'

He leapt at her then, as fierce as the cat, gripping the fabric around her neck, the thin silk tearing in his hands.

'You're right,' she whispered savagely, nose to nose. 'I did it. I tamed the cat. I brought it to our home. You were an experiment to me. Too stupid to notice. The aftershave. The sardine oil.' She affected a dumb-jock-in-a-high-school-movie voice: '*Oh, Coralie, I think I saw a cat.*' She dug a finger into his chest. 'And I didn't just tame the cat,' she said with disgust. 'I tamed you.'

Adam didn't scare her. She knew he would never hurt her physically. God knows she'd tried to get him to retaliate and do something in the past. But still she willed him to do it now. Willed him the same way she had willed Duchess to hurt her all those years ago, and she didn't think to see beyond that, to remember how that turned out. 'And it was pretty fucking easy.'

His hands moved from her dress, slipped over the blood-streaked skin of her neck, gripping tighter, and for the first time since she was a child, Duchess leaping over her to maul Cleopatra, her claws slicing her arm, Coralie King feared for her life.

A movement behind him, outside, caught her eye. She felt a rush of dizziness as Adam squeezed tighter, but instead of backing down, she batted harder: 'No one will believe you. Not even Fraser. Not when they know you've been dealing drugs. That it was your fault a child got hurt.'

Through the ornate stained-glass section of the greenhouse, between yellow flowers and green leaves, she could see Twig, all pink hair and iridescent sparkles, running towards them. Did she feel a tug around her neck? Later, she would be convinced she had. She glanced back at Adam, their faces inches apart, and bared her teeth in a grin as his grip loosened.

'Got ya,' she whispered, just as Twig entered and Adam spat violently in her face.

'Adam!' Twig shouted. 'What the fuck? Get off her!' Her head moved to take in the trashed room, the gash on Coralie's face, the blood dripping down to her collarbone, and to Adam, physically unscathed and unharmed, his eyes raging, his hands springing back from Coralie's neck. But without catching her breath, she yelled, 'Coralie, you've got to come. The panther! It's at the scout hut!'

53

Twig

They ran up the lawn towards the house, phones ringing and beeping all around them.

'The panther is at the scout hut! The panther is at the scout hut!'

Cars were backed up down the street, blocking theirs in. Everyone was at the party. Minutes ago, that hadn't mattered, but now they were stuck.

She contemplated running, all the way up the hill, but it would take at least twenty minutes. The cars that could extricate themselves began to move, speeding off towards the main road.

'I need to come with you,' she said to a random man, getting into his car. There was no need to ask where he was going. They were all heading in the same direction.

Why had she agreed to let them go to camp? What had she been thinking?

The closer they got to the scout hut, the more the traffic slowed. Drivers began abandoning their vehicles on the main road, parking haphazardly in the street, or not parking at all, lights still on as they bolted from their vehicles. Behind them Twig could hear the blare of the emergency services, struggling to forge a path through. Twig got out and began to run. She winced in pain as she trod on something sharp. Remembered she wasn't wearing any shoes.

A lone Scout leader Twig didn't recognize stood by the entrance to the car park, waving traffic on, shouting, 'We need to keep this clear for the police!' Twig, and the other parents on foot, ran past him.

The scout hut itself looked deserted. The open field behind was populated with army-green tents, uniformly pitched and vacated, like an abandoned town. The parents began to pick quietly through the eerie scene, pulling back canvas to peek inside, staring at each other in confusion and fear. *Where was everybody?*

An owl hooted, a movie jump-scare, and Twig was managing a shaky exhale in relief when another noise reverberated through the field of empty tents: a low, loud roar. Twig locked eyes with the mum to her left, who she recognized from gymnastics drop-offs in a different life. *Holy shit.*

She didn't wait another second. She'd spent the last decade trying to hide from any threat, but now she ran forcefully towards it, her blood pumping, her instinct saying only: *find your children.*

She stopped at the edge of the woods bordering this side of the Parkland. Silence reigned once more, and she didn't know which way to enter. Where to go? Were the Cubs in the woods?

'*Psst!*' A noise caught her attention. She saw a single slit of yellow light from the back door of the scout hut which hadn't been there moments before, and a hand beckoning her and the other parents over. She crept inside, the room shrouded in shadows and darkness, waning light falling in oblongs and triangles over the faces of the children, who were huddled together on the floor.

'Mummy!' Skylar emerged from the group on all fours and rug-by-tackled Twig's calves. And then: 'You're bleeding.' She pointed at Twig's cut feet.

'Oh, thank God,' Twig breathed, a hand on Skylar's budding nest of hair as she searched for Elwood, but before she had the benefit of a full exhale, one of the other Cub leaders grabbed her – a woman she knew as 'Rikki-Tikki' – and whispered in a heart-stopping tone: 'Twig, Elwood's still outside. He thought he saw the panther. He ran after it into the woods.'

All the blood drained from Twig's face. Elwood was out there. 'Where's Matt?'

'I don't know. I think he might have followed him.'

'Keep hold of Skylar. Don't let her go.' In seconds she was back outside, scanning the tree line, straddling the divide between mowed lawn and untamed woodland; suburbia and the wild; safe and savage.

Coralie appeared to her left, a flash of silk and sturdy walking boots, and then she was gone, disappeared within the trees. Twig turned back to the scout hut to see if anyone else had noticed, but it was still shrouded in darkness. Without missing a beat, Twig was on her tail, darting through the woods.

She stumbled over an empty beer bottle, one of many discarded near a campfire from long ago. Beneath it, the grass had grown long, dried to straw. A field of kindling waiting for a light.

Coralie marched with purpose, as though she knew where she was going. Twig made to call after her and thought better of it: if there were a cat in the woods, better not to startle it or alert it to their presence. She felt safer somehow, knowing Coralie was there, as though she was storming to the rescue. *Could she be trusted though? Was now the time to find out? But what choice did Twig have?*

Eventually Coralie slowed and Twig slid into a space beside her, framed by two slender silver birches. Coralie turned to face her, a finger to her lips indicating that Twig be quiet. Twig startled again at the blood streaking down her face. Up close, the gash to her cheek looked worse than before, as though it were opening in the heat. Her face asked the question, eyebrows and lips pursed and knotted. Coralie mouthed, '*Adam.*'

Twig swallowed. *Is this what his depression had made him?* Did the Adam she knew no longer exist? She didn't want to believe it.

There was no time to reflect. Coralie walked on through the forest. She tried to stop Twig following her, flapping her hand towards the ground in a 'stay there' motion, but Twig was propelled by a thousand winds, by the DNA of her own mother, and all the mothers who'd come before her, embedded in her cells.

Nothing could stop her from saving her boy.

54

Coralie

Four sets of eyes were trained on her as she entered the clearing: Elwood, Twig, Matt and Monroe. She knew this is where they'd be: within range of Cam 7, where it all began.

Monroe was in the middle of the clearing, illuminated by the remnants of twilight. Her eyes were locked on Elwood and Matt, who were across the clearing from where Coralie stood, with Twig cowering behind her. Monroe swung her head at Coralie's approach. Matt was stooped behind Elwood, his hands looped as far over the boy's chest as was possible, like a shield. She could hear Matt's shallow breaths from where she and Twig stood.

Matt fixed her and Twig with an imploring, desperate look: *what do I do?*

Coralie had to make a decision. *Should she break her cover? Risk everything to save them all?*

'Elwood.' She paused, Monroe giving her a look as if to say, *don't come another step closer.* 'Elwood. Move slowly towards me.' She was very careful to keep her voice calm. Her trainer voice. That's where things had gone wrong earlier, losing control in the face of her bottomless, molten rage towards Adam. A lifetime of tiny knife cuts sprung open at once.

Elwood took a tiny step to his left, in her direction, but Monroe immediately snapped her head back to where Elwood and Matt were standing, adjusting her stance like in a mirror.

'Okay, wait,' Coralie instructed. Behind her, Twig emitted a strangled cry.

Elwood was a better apprentice than her, for he never failed to keep his eyes trained on the cat. In fact, Coralie realized, he had an arm raised towards it, his palm facing Monroe, as she would have right now, were she not fearful of exposure.

'Elwood. What are you doing?' She used the same light tone.

'I'm training it. Like you. This is what you do with Socks.'

'Well, there's a difference, Elwood.' Her voice was sharply tipped, like the dry straw underfoot. 'Between a domestic cat and a big cat.'

Should she break her cover? The thought niggled desperately like a full, urgent bladder, her own arms limp by her side, impotent. *What should she do? What should she do?*

Matt's eyes were boring into her. Monroe's upper lip curled, light glinting off the saliva coating her yellow teeth as she bared them and audibly inhaled, assessing Elwood and Matt, as she had Adam: *friends or foes?*

Coralie's thoughts were beginning to fracture, scurrying like rats. The control she had worked so hard to conjure was weakening, power seeping from her grasp. She needed to fix this without giving away her part in it. Her life would be over if everyone knew how she had interrogated Adam.

Monroe roared. A deathly, feral call. Terror wound round the clearing, its coils binding them all, and Coralie could resist her instincts no longer. She raised her left arm, fingers silver in the moonlight, threads of her gossamer-thin sleeves falling like ribbons from her pale skin, revealing the lumpen, scarred flesh beneath. She heard Twig's sharp inhale of breath, anticipated her reaction: *monster.*

Monster she may be, but this was her woodland, her cat, and it was her alone who could spare them all from being clawed to death. She splayed her fingers, her hand rigid, her palm towards Monroe.

Monroe recognized the movement. Slowly, with careful

deliberation, she turned her powerful body away from Elwood and Matt, and towards her and Twig.

Twig gasped, and Coralie, on reflex, elbowed her, hard, with her right arm, her left arm still raised. *Shut up, you stupid bitch. I need to think. I need to think.*

But there was no time. Monroe eased back on to her haunches in one fluid moment. Poised to launch. Coralie became very conscious of the sticky blood congealed on her skin – her mind flicked to the blood lollies – she imagined Monroe consuming her face in one enormous gulp.

She would have to break her cover; it was the only way to survive. With her free hand she groped around her neck for her whistle, but the chain which held it and her little desk key wasn't there. She thrust her right hand into her bag, eyes fixed on Monroe, who was returning her gaze with a ferocious intensity. She discarded useless objects, identifying them by touch: a pencil, a small brush, her blood-smeared penknife. Keep that. She might need that again later. Finally, she clasped a small stout metal container, pulled from her freezer on a whim as she left. *If this didn't work . . .* She held it in front of her and Monroe immediately tensed in recognition, her tongue lolling out of her jaw. She was thirsty. *Poor baby girl.*

'Stay,' she said, her palm still up. 'Stay.' She shot a look at Matt, a tiny flick of her head, her intention clear: *I'll make a distraction, and you take Elwood and run.* Matt nodded, releasing his arms from Elwood's chest and straightening up. Every motion was small, executed with painstaking slowness; even chumpy Matt sensing, in the face of danger, that he mustn't alarm the cat.

He clamped his hands on to Elwood's shoulders proprietorially. Something flashed in Coralie's mind. Some sort of half-recognition. Her senses were on fire, electric, charged by the heat and the tension in the air. She had sensed something was amiss between them all but had been unable to place it – connect the dots between Matt Brooks and Elwood – until now. *Of course*, she thought. *Of course. Good old Twig.*

305

She passed the small flask into her raised left hand, clasping it as Monroe's steely gaze followed it. She moved her right arm behind her, palm facing down in an indication to Twig to stay. Too many sudden movements could be a disaster, and it was Elwood she wanted to save. In fact, she was half tempted to feed Twig to Monroe herself.

'I'm going to leave this over here.' She spoke gently to Monroe.

She breathed out shakily, her hand trembling.

You can rescue this. You can save the boy. Elwood. You can save Elwood. Stay focused.

Swallowing, she proceeded forward, eyes still on Monroe. The cat's moss-green eyes were fixed on Coralie, tracking every moment.

She unscrewed the lid with painstaking precision. The silence picked out the grind of steel as it released.

'It's water,' she explained softly, for the others' benefit, hoping they wouldn't discern its reddish tint in the moonlight. Monroe's head jerked towards her. She didn't flinch. This is what she wanted, what she knew. How to control a cat.

Cat whisperer!

Monroe chuffed; a short, loud burst of air through her nostrils. She heard a sound behind her; Twig's legs buckling and her hands grasping at the silver birches. Coralie moved a step closer.

Cat whisperer!

This is how she would keep them all safe.

'I'm going to leave it on the ground down here.' She bent down to roll the flask towards Monroe and stood, again raising her left hand. 'Stay.' She commanded. 'Stay.' Her eyes still locked on emerald green.

'Beautiful girl. Sweet, gentle girl,' she whispered, her lips tracing the words, so quietly that no one else could hear.

It happened in a second. The cat bent its head down to the container and Coralie flung her right arm out, indicating to Matt and Elwood to run. Matt jerked Elwood backwards, against his will, protesting that he couldn't leave – '*Mummy!*' he screamed.

'*Coralie!*' – but Matt hoisted him over his shoulder and bolted from the clearing.

The yelps and shouts caught Monroe's attention. Frustrated by the size of the container, the cat flicked it away with a paw and growled. Coralie felt the vibrations travel up through her whole body, felt her hair lift with the force. Monroe rose to face Coralie and began rhythmically moving towards her, thick, robust legs swinging from side to side. The ultimate bombshell.

Twig screamed, but Coralie maintained her composure. Understood what she had to do. Each time, she was learning and adapting. That was nature. She'd changed the rules. She'd nurtured the cat, given it a safe space, but then lured it to the benefit. She was certain Monroe had returned to the clearing because she felt protected here. *She's afraid.*

Only Coralie, and her voice, could calm her.

'I'm sorry, my sweet girl.'

The call shifted something, restored some of the balance. The cat hung her head in submission, as if to say, *finally.*

Coralie kept her arm extended and, step by step, Twig making strangled sounds behind her, she and Monroe moved towards the centre of the clearing. At last, with half a metre between them, Monroe yielded to her touch. Tears sprung in Coralie's eyes. She dropped to her knees and wrapped her body over Monroe's, whispering fervent apologies.

'My sweet, sweet girl. I'm so sorry, my sweet darling girl.'

Her tears were falling already; Coralie knew this had to be goodbye. She had shone a spotlight on the cats, with the best intentions, but she'd gone too far. By morning the area would be swarming with police, cat fanatics and, worst of all, hunters. The thought shot a rocket of fear into her chest.

'*My darling girl. My sweet, sweet girl.*' It was how her mother used to speak to her own cats. How Coralie had always longed to be addressed, but never was. She ran a hand over the animal's sleek fur, the melody of her voice and the deep vibrations of Monroe's belly-purrs drifting through the still-warm air. The moon had cracked open above, the light casting silver shadows through the spindly trees.

She put a hand on either side of Monroe's jaw. Felt her whiskers brush against her skin.

'You must go, my beautiful girl. Follow the train tracks, follow the rivers. Find someplace to hide. Do you understand? *Monroe, please understand.*' She felt as though she were speaking human to human, sister to sister. She was beyond reason. She felt more a part of this wild, raw earth than she ever had.

The cat stared back at her solemnly for a beat, then extended to its full height. A queen. Coralie stayed kneeling, her hands still clasped around Monroe's neck, twisted into her fur. 'I'm so sorry, my sweet girl,' she whispered for the final time.

She glanced over her shoulder as she stood. Twig's pale eyes were fixed in terror. She followed them to the moonlit woodland floor, where the blood lolly was melting and oozing from the toppled container, ruby-red liquid sinking into the bleached grass.

'I'll keep your secrets, Twig, if you keep mine.'

She turned back to Monroe, raised her arm and pointed into the distance, the summons for Monroe to leave. But Coralie never saw her go. At that moment, the silence in the clearing was broken once more, by insistent shouts, hands cupped over mouths, desperate words being shrieked into the woods: *FIRE! FIRE! FIRE!*

55

Emma

Emma stared from her upstairs landing window as flames licked the Parkland. She'd never been so relieved to have vomiting children, home and safe, but where was Matt?

She'd messaged Agatha; the Cubs were safely in Puddleford School's hall, being checked over before they could be released to their parents, who were gathered outside in tear-stained clumps, the booze long burned off by adrenaline. Adam was there (*Adam was safe*, Emma thought with relief when she saw the message). Blake too. But no one had seen Matt, Twig or Coralie.

She toggled across local news and social media, struggling to take anything in. There were banners declaring *BREAKING NEWS! WILDFIRES TEAR THROUGH PUDDLEFORD PARKLAND!* And *SEVENOAKS ABLAZE!* Posts requesting information or speculating on what was going on. One leapt out at her: *'Anyone else heard a big cat was involved tonight? Spooking the Cubs, who started the fire as they ran away?'* Her legs felt weak, her bones and muscles fluting in on themselves like quicksand.

There was a montage of footage from the benefit, up to Twig's rendition of 'Fleeting Heart', as though time in Puddleford had stopped at that moment.

Despite the posts and retweets and comments, she couldn't see any actual footage from camp; phones were strictly forbidden.

No footage could mean none of the speculation was true: it was simply rumours. The Cubs had been evacuated because of the wildfires, nothing more.

She tried Matt's phone for what felt like the hundredth time. Nothing.

She called Agatha, exploding with a 'What happened?' as soon as she answered. In the background she could sense restless panic, shifting like waves, interspersed with sirens.

'No one knows.' Agatha's voice was high-pitched, her speech choppy and fast. 'There's so many crazy—'

'Has anyone seen Matt?' Emma interrupted, desperate to know.

She held the phone away from her ear as Agatha shouted: 'Anyone seen Matt Brooks?'

Emma thought of her children tucked up safely in their beds. She had drawn their curtains and ordered them to sleep off the last of their stomach bugs. They had no idea of the nightmare their friends, and father, were going through. *Thank goodness they didn't go to camp! But where was Matt?*

Emma imagined a sea of people either ignoring Agatha, or shaking their heads blankly, for seconds later she said, 'I'm sorry, babes. Hopefully he's on his way home?'

'Probably. Yes.' Emma strained to hear his key in the lock as though she could magic him there, but she knew he'd never abandon his Cubs. That, for all his faults, he would be waiting at the school until the last child in his care had been safely dispatched back to their parents if he could. She swallowed a sob as her phone slipped from her hand to the floor.

Her eyes were caught by the twitching fire beyond the window. The flames intermingled with her reflection, as though it were her hair, her face, going up in flames. Beyond her back garden, the Parkland *burned*. Red streaks of flame and trails of black smoke twisting into the air. Could Matt be trapped out there somewhere? Alone in the forest? She couldn't bear to think of it. She would *do* anything, *forgive* anything, for him to walk through the door right now.

The fire seemed to be advancing closer to their homes. She was wondering whether they would need to evacuate when the knock on the door came. Outside, with the children tucked into her sides, sirens wailed, firefighters moving like foot soldiers, preparing to enter the Parkland.

A thundering chopping began overhead. She craned her neck, watching the helicopter hovering, its searchlight picking through the Parkland. Who were they looking for? Was it a person, or a cat?

56

Twig

Twig had already begun edging away from Coralie, walking backwards through the wood, feet bare, cut and bleeding, eyes – and ears – disbelieving. Her breath was ragged, hands groping behind her as she felt for spaces within the trees.

I'll keep your secrets, Twig, if you keep mine.

What did Coralie know? About Matt? About selling drugs with Adam last summer?

Seconds later the shouts began: *FIRE! FIRE! FIRE!* The sound already being suffocated by a violent roar, wind and flame and the forest floor – *miles* of kindling – meeting and combusting, crackling and snapping, energy building with a ferocious pace.

Never turn your back on a cat, Coralie had said, but what about on a fire? She turned on instinct, her body already sensing the flames licking the trees behind her, dry leaves and thin branches being speedily consumed, the thick trunks holding out, resisting, but for how long?

The heat was beginning to build. She looked for a gap in the flames, an arm held over her mouth and nose, her torn sequined clothing providing little respite. *How quickly would this fabric burn?* Her forehead began to tingle, like the beginnings of sunburn.

'*Mummy! Mummy!*' Was that Elwood's voice or was she imagining it?

She tried to run to her right, where she could see a gap in the fire further up, her face contorting in confusion and pain when her feet protested and didn't comply; she hobbled instead, as fast as she could, her eyes fixated on the gap, growing thinner and thinner as the heat built to her left, the temperature climbing.

It was Matt on the outskirts of the Parkland. Matt with his hands cupped, shouting ,'*FIRE! FIRE! FIRE!*'

'Twig!' He shouted when he saw her, nigh on collapsing as she emerged from the trees back on to the field, hacking and coughing. 'Come on.' He gripped her hand and dragged her around the outer perimeter of the field. Through the smoke, she could discern the field of tents ablaze. They passed the scout hut, its door swung wide open like a yawn, empty.

Twig had never *heard* a fire before. Had no idea of its violence, like a monster gnashing its teeth. She thought of the huge expanse of the Parkland. Over two thousand acres of land. Houses, pets, farms, cattle, cats. Big wild cats. She believed in them now. What would be left when this was over?

'What happened?' Twig asked Matt. They were in the scout hut car park, fire engines and ambulances swarming. Someone – *a paramedic? A policeman?* – had assured her that Blake was among the parents waiting at Puddleford School. Twig and Matt had been asked to wait to give a statement about what they had seen. They huddled under silver blankets and sipped water they couldn't recall being given.

'Elwood started the fire,' Matt whispered. 'I tried to stop him. I didn't realize what he was doing. We ran back from the woods. I was doubled over, getting my breath back, wondering what to do – who to leave him with so I could run back to you—'

'You didn't have to do that,' Twig managed, her teeth chattering.

'I did.' He stared at her. 'But Elwood . . . he must've picked up a stick. He ran over to the campfire, and then back to the woods, waving it. He was shouting – "*Mummy! Coralie! I have to save them!*" It was surreal, this little boy, holding a giant matchstick and . . . I wish I'd realized what he was doing, if only I could've stopped him . . . He was shouting "*Cats don't like fire!*" and then, "*This is how they train them in the circus!*" He was just – babbling. I didn't connect. I chased after him and grabbed him, but I was too late. He'd flung the fire into the woods. The whole thing went up.'

His face still wore a look of astonishment, fixed there, as though it might never change. 'I should've listened to Baloo. He said we were mad to have a campfire, but I'd followed all the protocols: drawn a circle around it, dampened the ground. It should have been safe. It *would* have been safe . . . If Elwood hadn't had his binoculars, hadn't spotted the cat in the first place . . . Luckily I was right by him when he ran off into the woods, following it. Who knows what would've happened if I hadn't seen him go.' His voice cracked, mirroring his bleeding lips. He pressed the back of his hand against them to stem the blood.

'You can't say anything,' Twig managed to get out, all her efforts going towards trying to control her jaw. 'About Coralie. About what you saw.' She was dimly aware she was in shock; that this couldn't last for ever. She noticed her feet had been cleaned up and bandaged but couldn't remember it happening.

'Well, thank God she was there.' His voice was awed. 'She saved us.'

'She doesn't want anyone to know about the cat. That it exists.' Twig shivered, groping for the most plausible explanation to deter Matt from telling everyone the truth. *I'll keep your secrets, Twig* . . . 'I guess, in case it's hunted.'

'Okay.' He nodded as though they were having an ordinary conversation.

They sat shoulder to shoulder, waiting for someone to tell them what to do, which seemed to neatly sum up Twig's experience of adulthood.

'I bought Jutland House because I thought I'd see you.'

Twig looked away, pain squeezing her chest.

'Not every day – when you were back for holidays. I'd heard you'd had a baby. Around the time I had. I always wondered . . .'

His voice drifted. 'I thought I'd see him when you visited Bob. From the window. I never thought you'd move back here. You always said you couldn't wait to leave.'

'We were just kids,' she reminded him. 'I've grown up a bit since then.'

'But we weren't kids, *then*, were we?' She knew he was referring to that night.

'No,' she agreed. 'We weren't kids then. How are things with Emma?'

'I think she might leave me,' he said simply. 'But it's all I deserve.'

She took his hand and held it in hers companionably. 'I hope you can work things out.'

'It's funny, after what happened between you and me . . .' He looked down at their clasped hands. '. . . I couldn't imagine loving anyone else. But the minute I met her, I knew. I love her, I really do. I was *such* an idiot.'

'Me too,' she sighed. 'Me too.' And then: 'I'm sorry I didn't tell you sooner about Elwood.'

He looked at her for a long moment, without malice, then he put his free hand on top of hers. 'Thank you. I appreciate that.' He squeezed her hand, and she couldn't help thinking he sounded like an American leadership manual even now. 'I hope it's okay to say this, but . . . I really hope he's mine.'

'I do too.' She squeezed his hand back.

'I've been keeping him at arm's length. He probably thinks I'm a right old dickwad.' The resurgence of an oft-repeated insult from when they were teenagers made Twig smile. 'But it was too painful to wonder. To not know. I'm going to make it up to him. Whether I'm his father or not.'

They sat quietly, sipping their water.

'I hope we can go soon.' Tears burned her eyelids like acid, stinging from the smoke. 'Where's Coralie?'

Matt shrugged, his eyes still lost to the middle distance. 'I mentioned her girls to the police; Adam's waiting outside the school for them. I should call Emma. I left my phone in the scout hut.'

Hers would still be by the stage in Coralie's garden, she remembered.

Adam. What had been going on with Coralie when she burst in earlier? She knew what she'd seen – Adam with his hands around Coralie's throat, spitting on her – but she couldn't connect the sight to the Adam she knew. Nothing tonight made sense.

How well do you ever know somebody else, or their relationship, even when you live next door? When you're busy hiding secrets of your own?

She stared into the dark woodland, smouldering amber, black and gold, looking for a flicker of silk, but Coralie never emerged.

57

Coralie

Helicopter rotors churned overhead. She knew armed police would be closing in on the Parkland as soon as the blaze was under control. But Coralie knew the Parkland better than anyone. She followed the river on hands and knees, the earth still sunken and dry but damp enough to resist the fire. She had to get home to destroy the evidence.

The area bordering the back gardens of Briar Close was as yet untouched by fire. Nonetheless, there was an eerie silence, no gentle rustles through the undergrowth, no owls hooting in the trees. *Nature always knows first.* She passed through her back gate, the torches still separating the back end of the garden from the rest, which now lay abandoned, the cocktail bar, stage and dance floor deserted, like a scene from an apocalypse movie.

There was no time to retrieve her cameras, camouflaged in the woodland, but they were unlikely to survive the rampaging fire in any event. If they did, no one would know they were hers. She'd say they were the stolen ones. She assumed Adam would have gone for the girls. He was good like that. Still, she didn't have much time. She emptied her freezer and fridge, heaving out the fallow carcass she'd laboured over and tipping out the contents of the carefully stacked Tupperware boxes – livers, kidneys, intestines – into a black bin liner. Her heart twanged to see all of it wasted, but it was too big a risk to keep them.

She felt again for the chain she wore round her neck, the little key and whistle. Remembered it was gone. She crawled on the floor, shards of glass cutting into her knees as she clawed through the remains of her terrarium. Finally, she saw a glint of metal from beneath her heavy apothecary desk. The key, the whistle resting nearby. She grabbed at the key and thrust it into the lock, a clock ticking in her ears. *Come on, come on.* She hastily flung out the drawer and gawped. It was empty.

Adam. Fucking Adam. He must have snapped off her necklace when he had his hands round her neck. Stolen her notebook as she was on her way to save them all! Putting herself in danger! Perhaps that was his intention: not to strangle her, but to expose her.

She'd deny it if she had to. Deny the notebook was hers. Tell them he'd forged her handwriting and blackmailed her with it. *Yes!*

She gathered the bin liner in her right hand, as heavy as if it contained a human body rather than an amalgam of animal ones, and dragged it out of the greenhouse. She seized one of the flaming torches, wrenching it from its holder and gripping it in her left hand. She felt like an avenging angel, her silk dress ragged and flaring around her, heat rising in the distance beyond, her hair flailing around her shoulders.

She would win this battle, whatever it took. She would win this war. Good luck, Adam.

She dragged the bag into the Parkland as far as she dared, hearing the fire approaching. She upended it, forming a grisly pyre, and left it to the fate of predator or flame.

Then she calmly stalked the residential streets, taking the long, quiet way, rounding back on herself, meandering like a river, all the way up to the top of the hill to the school. She walked regally, head high, arms scarred and exposed through the tatters of her dress, blood blooming through the thin material at her knees like stomata, her face disfigured and ugly, sticky with blood as she walked with her palms open, to find her beautiful girls.

*

That was the photo circulating online the next morning. She stared at it uncompassionately on her way home from the hospital in a taxi, her face now cleaned and bandaged.

There was no big scene on her return. No showdown with Adam.

'That's a pretty big dressing for a graze,' he observed, scanning her face.

He was screwed, and he knew it. If he said anything, if he showed anyone her notebook, she'd tell them about the drugs and she'd deny everything else. There would be no one to back him up, since she'd secured Twig's secrecy. She didn't know if Twig understood the full consequences of her stupidity. Probably not, but Coralie would make sure she grasped it soon: you can't fly to America with a drug charge against you.

She didn't even mention the notebook, in case he was recording her. She simply nodded towards the door, and he left. The girls – the little renegades – stayed tucked away upstairs. She'd deal with them later. *All she'd done for them, and they couldn't even be bothered to look pleased to see her last night! Selfish, just like Fraser!* Instead, she walked straight down to the back of the garden and opened the gate.

Her gasp caught in her throat like a choke. As far as she could see, the earth was scorched black, charred and soft, like volcanic ash. She had seen footage of firefighters along the perimeter of the estate, battling againstthe inferno, stopping it before it reached their gardens, but she couldn't help but wish they'd focused their efforts on saving the Parkland instead.

She strode on, the ground still warm, heat radiating through her boots as it smouldered in parts. The funeral pyre of animal remains was gone, reduced to dust.

Coralie's heart ached for all that had been lost: the habitats, the nature, from lichen to leaves, woodpeckers to woodlice. The Parkland she knew and loved so dearly had been destroyed. And it was all Adam's fault. Adam and his accomplice . . . Twig. They had set all this in motion.

319

She made her way back to her garden. Blake had materialized and was dismantling the stage and sound system from the party last night. The last evidence that mere hours ago her garden had been filled with people enjoying themselves, having fun.

She smiled weakly at Blake, trooping on despite her physical and emotional wounds. 'At least we raised the money for Skylar,' Coralie said, deploying her brave-victim smile.

'Uh huh.' Blake didn't meet her eyes. The air was spiked. What had Twig said to her about last night? Coralie felt her outer shell harden.

She hadn't planned to tell Blake; she'd liked the idea of Twig's secret belonging to her, a bartering chip, but her anger with Twig ran deeper than she'd realized. There was no stopping it. Adam had loved her. Maybe still did. And to Twig, no doubt, Adam was just one in a long list of conquests.

She dropped the comment casually as she passed: 'Twig sold drugs with Adam.'

Her golden hair flicked as she turned her head over her shoulder, a detonating bomb in the direction of Blake's open mouth: 'Your drugs, apparently. *Kingpin*. And a child got hurt. Sloppy little empire you're running. I know a tourist like Twig wouldn't be allowed into the US with a charge for selling drugs against her, but tell me, does the same rule apply for an American citizen? Could you be barred from going home? Very sad,' she purred, arching an eyebrow, fixing Blake with one long, last look. Then she sauntered away, her hips swinging from side to side as she left.

Her intention was clear: if Twig wouldn't keep quiet on her own account, she'd make damn sure she did for Blake and her family.

55

Emma

'*Wildfires tore through the Puddleford Parkland last night, destroying over two thousand acres of land,*' Emma read aloud to Matt. He'd finally arrived home in the early hours, dazed and wrapped in a metallic blanket, escorted by the police. He remained shell-shocked, his face blank and ashen.

'*The fires appeared to start at the annual Jutland 5th Cub Scout camp. Local residents have been quick to criticize the event leaders for having a campfire, given the recent heatwave. The troop's leader, Matthew Brooks, apologized but emphasized last night that he had taken all necessary precautions to prevent a wildfire.*'

Emma expected Matt to shake his head in consternation at that, but he merely sipped his sugary tea. Every now and then he jumped, hot builder's slopping on to his lap, which he didn't seem to feel.

'*As the wildfires spread, rumours abounded online that a wild cat had entered the Cub camp and the fire began in the ensuing hysteria. Sevenoaks and its surrounding areas have been plagued with sightings of the 'Sevenoaks Panther' in recent months. However, we have been unable to confirm a sighting of a big cat with any witnesses.*

In a further twist, Coralie King, local 'cat whisperer', was initially thought missing during the fire but appeared outside

Puddleford School around midnight, in a state of distress. It has since been reported that her injuries were sustained during a domestic incident, rather than owing to the fires.

More as we have it.'

She clicked on to the video accompanying the piece, Coralie disfigured and ethereal, like something from a horror movie, as she approached, crying and calling for her girls. The shock on Adam's face as she approached him, his eyes wide and unblinking, the awkward, undefinable energy flowing between them. The two girls, slowly trooping outside, stiffly being embraced by their mother, recoiling as they took in her face.

Emma would never doubt a victim of domestic violence, but with what she knew about Coralie, what she had seen, she couldn't help but wonder whether she was victim, or perpetrator? She was struck by the well of fear in Bea's eyes and couldn't help thinking that perhaps there was a more sinister reason why Coralie's girls lived with their father.

'Wow!' she exclaimed. 'What a drama.' Her relief was palpable: Matt was safely home. Adam was there too, outside in their garden, chainsmoking cigarettes on the rickety old bench, shivering in a T-shirt despite the balmy weather. Emma had spotted him from a window earlier, knees to his chin on the pavement, and had invited him in. Matt had eyed him warily, but Adam had gone straight outside, where he had been ever since, his back rigid, his body angled away from the direction of his own house.

There was a time when Emma would have been desperate to know everything, would have been glued to her earbuds listening in as Adam exited the Kings', but now, she felt content in her bubble. Grateful, even, for Briar Heart House. Her pink fortress.

No one had said they couldn't go out, but no one wanted to. They were voluntarily trapped inside their homes, the heat overpowering, the prospect of a potential wild cat on the prowl overwhelming. She shuddered again, grateful that Henry and Daisy had been at home (though Henry, feeling better after his bout of sickness and pumped up with the bravado of a ten-year-old boy, claimed he *wished* he'd been there, at which point Matt had snapped at him to grow up). It had been half a day and they already had cabin fever.

'What do you think happened to Coralie?' Emma realized she wasn't asking about yesterday, she was asking full stop, and she had a feeling Matt, when he answered, was doing the same.

He pulled the blanket he was wearing tighter over his shoulders, shrinking his neck within its folds. His hand shook gently as he raised the scalding tea to his lips once more. He stared in the direction of the Kings' house. 'I have no idea,' he said faintly.

Later that afternoon Emma was enjoying a cold glass of wine alone, Matt having retreated upstairs for a nap, when she heard a car pull up outside the Kings'. She peered through her curtains, closed to block out the unrelenting sun, and saw Coralie's girls, with their watchful eyes, leaving with their father. He always looked so uptight when she glimpsed him waiting in the car, but he had his arms clasped around them, fervently kissing their heads. He glanced up and locked eyes with Emma. She gasped and closed the gap in the curtain. Seconds later there was a knock at the door.

'Is Adam here?' Fraser's tone was impatient, agitated, which matched Coralie's descriptions of him, but there was a warmth to his features she hadn't expected. He raked a hand through his hair. 'The girls thought they saw him coming over here earlier. They're worried about him.'

'He's in the garden.' She nodded. 'He's not saying much. Shall I let him know you're here?'

Fraser hesitated, his eyes shooting back to his car, where he'd left the girls, their big eyes still fixed wide.

'I'd better get them home, but please – tell him to call me.' 'Ask him to call me, please?' The imploring way he spoke lent his face a certain nobility. He was *handsome*, she thought as she raised a hand to wave the girls off, and he seemed *nice. Normal.* She wondered what had really happened between him and Coralie to lead to their divorce.

She closed the door as the car peeled away. Socks trooped into the hall, tail raised, as though wanting a piece of the action. Thank goodness she'd locked him inside last night too.

This was a town where mere months ago children had streaked through the sunlit paths of the Parkland, pets had moved freely inside and out, and the Kings were the darlings of the neighbourhood. Conversation in town was no longer 11+ tutors and catchment areas, or which local building currently needed renovating. It was the wild cat. The wildfires. The wild scene outside the school between Coralie and Adam. Sevenoaks' golden couple had been swiped off their perch and the whispers had already started: *Weren't the big cat sightings this summer a little too convenient for 'the cat whisperer's' campaign? Hadn't it all started with her husband? Had she made the whole thing up?* Wildness had encroached upon their carefully ordered lives, their manicured suburban vision, and it felt like normality would never be restored.

She returned to her spot in the kitchen. Something else occurred to Emma, and she allowed herself a small wry smile as she visualized herself running, a flag held aloft. She raised her glass in salute, toasting herself, and drained the rest of her wine. The other thing no one was talking about was her planning application.

AUGUST

The Mystery of the Sevenoaks Panther

Megan, Number 16: I mean, PLOT TWIST.

Chloe, Number 16: Right? When the news dropped about Coralie King. The Tiger Princess. [Whistles.]

Megan: We didn't leave the house all day. Partly we couldn't, everyone was freaking out, but also: rolling news.

59

Coralie

THE TIGER PRINCESS.
REPORTER: SOFIA OLSEN

What would you get if you took Joe Exotic, raised him in a Chelsea townhouse, and armed him with a high IQ, a zoological degree and a trust fund? The answer, it appears, would be Coralie King, a Sevenoaks mother of two, rumoured to be behind the mysterious case of the Sevenoaks Panther. Daughter of disgraced financier Frederick Campbell and socialite Lady Violet Campbell, and ex-wife of the eco-entrepreneur Fraser Prendergast, Mrs King (née Campbell) has been an outspoken advocate for big cats in the United Kingdom, calling for the government to recognize that they are naturalizing here and to take steps to protect them. However, Mrs King's history with big cats is a little more complicated.

Below the first paragraph of the article was the photo of her as a child which she'd pinned up by her bed at school: one arm wrapped around Duchess and the other draped over her little sister; and the photo she had up in her greenhouse: her mother strolling along Knightsbridge taking Jasper for a walk, her baby bump just visible, Coralie following glumly behind her.

The Campbell family have a traumatic history with big cats. Their younger daughter, Cleopatra, was, until now, believed to have died from an undisclosed medical condition. However, the Times has learned that she was in fact mauled to death by a snow leopard (Duchess, pictured above) at the family home, Cresswell Place, at the age of three. 'After that we didn't keep any more wild animals. Including Coralie,' Lady Violet is reported to have said privately to friends.

There have been a number of alleged sightings of big cats in Sevenoaks this summer. Critics of Mrs King claim that rather than protecting big cats, she has been putting them in danger by bringing them to the public's attention.

It is believed the Mystery of the Sevenoaks Panther will be explored in a documentary of the same name.

Coralie's heart started and faltered, like a fledgling.

Who had disclosed the truth about Cleopatra? There were only a handful of people who knew the full story: Coralie, her parents and Leonora. There were the other staff who had worked through the night to restore the nursery, and the policeman her father had in his pocket, but they had all been paid handsomely to keep quiet.

Leonora, then? But Coralie had felt the acuteness of Leonora's guilt at the time. She was certain it wouldn't be her. Besides, if she came forward she could easily be discredited . . . Filling Coralie's head with stories of bloodthirsty retribution from such a young, impressionable age. *Shame on her!*

If her parents had entered the fray, that was another matter entirely. Her mother didn't have any true 'friends'; she viewed all other women, including Coralie, as competition. She would never have confided the depths of her family's shame to anyone. *Would she?* Coralie hoped this wasn't another one of her parents' misguided attempts at redemption, like her father confessing to the hole in the pension pot, or renaming the ball to become the Cleopatra Legacy Ball. They'd told Fraser it was all in aid of a relationship with the girls, their sudden desire for honesty, but Coralie didn't believe that for a second. It was all to get at her.

She scanned the garden through the broken glass of the green-house. Everything that was vibrant was now hard and dead. Her alliums, once lustrous spheres of purple, were reduced to violent spikes, a crop of medieval weapons. The brown ground glowed orange in the late-afternoon sun, swarms of wasps, their tight marigold bodies and gossamer wings, the only sign of life.

She tried to stop it, but her mind kept flicking to Fraser. Fraser and all those other women that had ended her marriage. Her parents had covered it up, even paying Fraser off . . .as if he'd have secured that *Forbes* piece on his 'stratospheric rise' otherwise. It was so frustrating; if they'd only spoken to her first, and given her a chance to explain, rather than presenting it all as a fait accompli. They'd just struck that ridiculous deal whereby she could only see her girls if she were supervised. She rolled her eyes. Before she met Adam the girls always had to have their nanny with them when they visited. But Fraser liked Adam (as Coralie suspected he would when she began tracking him; part of her project to find a suitable mate), and so, without knowing, Adam became part of the Campbell family house of cards.

Adam was wise to it towards the end. At some point Fraser had clearly got loose-lipped. No doubt he would have offered to speak to her parents, offered to secure a healthy sum for Adam too. But Adam had stuck it out, hadn't he? Too proud. Adam wouldn't have wanted a pay-out from Fraser or the Campbells. He was always banging on about forging his own path after being abandoned. Adam's parents flickered in her subconscious too; she batted them away. It killed him when she bought him all the Treescapes equipment and the Range Rover. Every gift a reminder of how impotent he was. *Oh, Adam.* She sighed heavily.

She folded the newspaper over, tucked it under her grandmother's chair. She should rip it into a million pieces, throw it away, but even in the depths of her despair part of her liked seeing her name in print. Thought it could be something she might want to return to later, once she'd shifted the narrative in her favour.

She was contemplating another dinner of cheese and biscuits when she heard it: Monroe's low roar emanating from the Parkland. She rose, gasping, clutched her hands to her chest and closed her eyes. It was agony not to go to her, but she knew she had to resist. There were so many eyes on her now, she couldn't put Monroe in danger.

'I'm sorry, baby girl, I'm sorry,' she whispered, her eyes misting with tears for all that had been taken from her, her brain recalibrating, running through all the ways she might take her revenge. After all, she was resilient. She was a survivor.

60

Emma

Three days after the fire, Matt finally spoke. Emma had been patiently waiting to discover what had really happened in the Parkland. She knew Matt would tell her the truth when he was ready, and her faith hadn't been misplaced.

Adam was still staying with them and, like Matt, acting oddly, his usual laid-back demeanour rendered frantic as he set to work on the overgrown garden at Briar Heart House: trimming, mowing, sculpting. He did all this with his top off. Emma was starting to see a future again for her and Matt, the events of the last week having put things in perspective, but she was no saint: she couldn't resist the odd ogle, although it wasn't as satisfying as one might think. She tried to reassure Adam he didn't owe them anything, but he carried on with the garden landscaping regardless.

He and Matt had taken to spending the evenings staring out at the Parkland together, a bottle of Scotch between them, even though Matt had never been a big drinker. Every now and then Matt would lurch, or double-take, at the slightest noise, while Adam repeatedly rubbed his eyes as though to clear them. Neither spoke.

Two men at her disposal, and it was a nightmare.

Finally, on the third night, after Adam had mournfully sloped off to bed, Matt took a deep breath and turned to face her. 'Emma,

I need to tell you something, but I warn you; you're not going to believe it.' Emma swallowed. She knew she would.

Emma's open-mouthed shock belied the guilt tearing through her as Matt recounted what had transpired in the clearing. *Could she have stopped it?*

No, she reassured herself. *No way.*

'We haven't even cleared up from Cub camp yet.' Matt sighed, wearily. 'It might be my last action as leader.' The public was calling for an inquiry into how the wildfires started. Who was responsible for such mass destruction? Someone must be blamed, strung up, publicly flagellated.

'Let's go and do it tomorrow then.' She squeezed his hand. 'Forwards, not backwards, remember?'

He gazed up at her with a hopeful smile and placed his hand over hers.

The next morning the four of them piled into the car, the idea of walking up through the Parkland out of the question.

'Can Elwood come?' Henry asked as they were about to reverse off the drive. 'I want to talk to him about another ant video I watched.'

Emma pressed her foot on the break, exchanging a look with Matt.

'Great idea,' Matt said.

'Skylar, too, if she fancies it. We can put the seats down in the back,' Emma called as Henry ran across the lawn to Twig's.

Inside the scout hut the flag was still raised; it had been lifted to signal the beginning of camp and should have been lowered at its successful conclusion. Of course, that hadn't happened.

'We'd better do it properly,' Matt said formally, in his leader's uniform, back straight, his hand raised in a salute. 'Go ahead, Henry.'

Henry, also in uniform, dutifully assumed the correct position opposite his father; Elwood, in a tie-dye T-shirt with a hastily added scarf and woggle, and Skylar and Daisy, in Black Panther

333

and Elsa costumes respectively, held their hands up in salute behind him. Matt unknotted the thick rope of the flag, holding it out for Henry to reel in. He suddenly dropped it, as though electrocuted. Or as though the rope were moving of its own accord, Matt whipping his hands back in terror. His eyes widened, his hand flew to his chest.

'Are you okay, Dad?' Daisy asked, but Matt was immobile, staring at the rope, curled at his feet like a snake. Or a leopard's tail.

'Dad's gone mad,' Henry observed. The four children shrugged, collecting up the discarded plates and mugs. Outside, the ground was charred, the tents reduced to piles of poles and scraps of black fabric. Guilt tugged at Emma again at the sight. She reminded herself firmly: *there was nothing she could have done.* She bit her lip, hands on the steering wheel, as their eclectic ensemble clambered back into the car.

The image of the charred remains of Cub camp replayed in her mind that evening as Emma stared out of her kitchen window. The heat was still oppressive. All the doors and windows were flung open to the garden, in the hope that the cooling evening air to bring some respite. Matt and Adam were sitting at the kitchen table behind her in silence.

'Maybe we should have a celebratory glass of wine?' Not a single person had attended the Planning Applications Committee the day before to contest their plans. In the furore, neither of them had noticed the date quietly slip past, but their architect had confirmed with them this morning that their plans had been approved.

Matt shrugged, his face blank, his new expression – autopilot – back on, and had just turned to leave the room when they heard it. A low, deep growl coming from the Parkland, echoing over the garden and reaching the house.

Emma saw Matt and Adam share a quick, desperate look before they both tore around, closing all the doors and windows, locking all of them in.

61

Twig

Twig's heart had skipped a beat when a message arrived from Emma: *Can you come over?*

In the silent gaps as she wondered what to do, she was sure she heard a belly-growl, deep from the Parkland, an unmistakable sound that shot through her nerves and placed her back in the clearing that night. She shook her head to dislodge it. She was having a traumatic response.

There was a strange crackle of energy in the air as she walked next door. Oppressive. Frustrated. It was muggy outside, with thunderstorms predicted later on in the week. The ground needed it. They all needed it.

She exited through her back garden, taking the Parkland path to Emma's to avoid the reporters who had started to gather on Briar Close, hoping for a glimpse of Coralie. Everyone was desperate for an angle, a story, a means to uncover the truth. *What had really happened at Cub camp? What was the real story behind Adam and Coralie?* She paused, a movement in the bushes catching her eye. She smiled, walked on: Twig Dorsett had faced a big cat head on and she had survived. She wasn't going to let fear hold her back from anything any more.

There were no show tunes audible at the Brooks', no glitter-ball turning in the kitchen. Everything seemed muted, strained, as Emma, Matt, Adam and Twig sat round the dining table with pints of iced water. Emma stood up suddenly, pulling on Matt's elbow. 'We've got a few things to be getting on with.' She gestured ambiguously, leading him out the room.

Socks coiled around Twig's leg. She scooped him up to her lap, stroking his soft fur. Adam shot a contemptuous look in the cat's direction, his eyes red and watery, cheeks flushed, his hair curling with sweat.

'Are you okay?' A hopeless question. He clearly wasn't.

He traced his finger up and down the glass's wet surface, making trails in the condensation. 'Coralie's telling people I hurt her.' His voice cracked.

Twig said nothing. Remembered his hands around Coralie's neck, the way his spit flew, the aggression written on his face as he did it.

'What you saw . . . it wasn't how it looked. No one will believe me if I tell them what she did.'

Adam didn't know what Twig had seen in the clearing. No one did, other than Blake, Matt and Emma. They'd all agreed not to disclose it in an effort to protect themselves. To protect Elwood from the inevitable media circus that would ensue, to ensure they could get Skylar to America and Blake back home to Susie and her mum. But Twig wanted to protect Matt, too, who was suffering his own fall from grace as his judgement – and future leadership of the Cub Scouts – was being called into question. He had been king of the jungle, but – she thought of his haunted look as he'd sat at the table moments before – you wouldn't know it now.

She took in Adam's sallow complexion, the way his body seemed to perpetually tremble, his arms wrapped across his thin torso. Her skin crawled as she thought of all the time Elwood had spent alone with Coralie. Earlier that afternoon he'd been sprawled on their couch, feet up, a self-satisfied smile on his face. 'People wait their whole lives to see a wild cat,' he'd said. 'And I've seen one twice. I could go on *Close Encounters* now. But I won't. Real cat people don't talk.' He'd tapped a finger to the side of his nose. Twig had felt a deep unease, certain he was echoing something Coralie had said.

What was Coralie King capable of? *Anything*. 'Try me.'

Twig felt a pang of guilt that her actions with Adam the previous summer had led to the grisly scene she'd run into in the greenhouse. When she thought of that time now, she thought of sun-dappled afternoons, the heavy scent of weed, smoke twisting and refracting above them as she and Adam lay in a scoop of the skate-ramps. They hadn't sold huge quantities, but it was good stuff. Blake always had good stuff, brought back from whatever music event she'd been involved in. Even though she rarely took drugs, she was often given them for free, and like everything with Blake, she didn't want to seem uncool, or not part of the scene. She'd throw it away and Twig would dig the little plastic bags out of the bin.

It was easy money. The parents Twig and Adam sold to were so grateful to be tapped into a low-risk, high-quality supply,;they would've paid anything. Adam took a cut – he always did the actual transactions – and keenly too, which made sense now: he never had any money. All those times he'd shown up without his wallet, and Twig had paid for his drinks. She'd thought it was his rich entitlement, but she saw the reality of it now. He couldn't even buy himself a cup of coffee. Coralie had made sure of it.

For Twig, the extra money had meant she could treat herself to the expensive moisturizer she used to like before Skylar got sick. She bought Elwood his iPad, to help with his homework, and Skylar the Black Panther claws she wanted. It meant she didn't have to ask Blake for money. But Blake had noticed the drugs had gone missing one time and worried that one of the children had fished them out the bin thinking they were sweets. Twig had had to 'confess', pretended she'd hoovered the whole lot up herself and promised to go 'dry'. No drugs, no booze. That bit was easy. She rarely drank. It was only the weed she missed. She couldn't tell

Blake she'd sold those drugs. Made Blake, unknowingly, part of the supply chain. After Kofi and the kid were hospitalized, they'd flown under the radar. They'd stopped hanging out at the skate ramps. They'd got away with it. At least until now. Who knew what Coralie would do with the information.

The older Twig got, the more she felt like her charmed childhood, as perfect as it was, hadn't prepared her for the challenges of real life. When the going got tough, Twig did really stupid things. And when they got tougher, she did more stupid things. The truth was, she'd been a bit of a brat. But she was ready to change.

'Coralie said I had to keep quiet,' she said, resigned, as she concluded telling Adam what had transpired in the clearing the night of the fire. 'About what I saw.'

Adam nodded, the thin line of his mouth rupturing.

'I'm sorry I can't help.' She squeezed his hands. Finding them cold, she ran her hands over his arms as though to warm him up. He huddled them closer to his body, pinning his hands between his thighs.

'It's okay. I get it. I understand.' Red lines snaked over his eyeballs like the contours of a map.

'What will you do?' she asked, rising to retrieve a blanket that had been slung over the sofa and draping it around him.

'I don't know.' He shrugged helplessly. He was rootless, Twig realized. How lucky she was, in contrast. 'I don't have anything. She made it impossible for me to work. I lost all my clients. She took everything from me.'

He broke down, his body wracked with sobs. She wrapped her arms around him. The bulk of him, his musky scent, a balm for her too. 'You've still got me,' she whispered. 'We'll figure this out.' And she meant it, because she needed a friend too. She held him until his tears subsided.

'Give me your bank details. I'm going to transfer you some money.' She pulled her phone from her pocket.

'No, Twig. You need that money.'

'It's fine. We've got enough. This is mine. Royalties.' She smiled wryly. All the times she'd dreamed of a cash injection of royalties in the past. 'Please. Where's your phone? Text me your details.'

He shook his head. 'I don't have one. Coralie cancelled my contract. And I don't have a bank account. She said I should close it when we got the joint account.'

'Fuck this.' Twig scowled. 'Set up an account. Today. I'll get you a burner.' And despite, or perhaps because of everything, they shared a smile.

62

Emma

Emma was waiting outside for Twig when she left.

'What do you think?' she asked anxiously. 'He's not in a good way, is he?'

Twig shuddered in affirmation. 'What a mess.'

'I haven't seen Coralie. Have you?' As far as Emma could tell, Coralie hadn't left her house at all.

'No,' Twig said briskly. 'I don't plan to.'

'Are you okay?' Emma asked gently.

Twig bounced on her toes, restless, eyes blinking, face flickering. 'Just focused on America now. Want to put it all behind us.'

'Well, it will soon be over and you can start afresh. A healthy, happy new start for you all. And . . .' Emma stopped, ran through what she was about to say to check its veracity. *Yes, that's what they'd do* '. . . I think we'll do the same. A fresh start.' Tentative, but optimistic.

As Twig made to leave via the Parkland, she stared at Coralie's house, a whip of emotions passing over her pretty features, her pink hair and green eyes electric.

Emma was about to say goodbye when Twig said softly, 'Someone needs to take a stand against Coralie King.' But it had a wistful edge to it, as though that person wouldn't be her.

She turned and, on impulse, Emma struck out her hand,

surprising them both as she caught Twig's arm and closed the gap between them.

'Let's do it,' she urged. 'Let's do it together.'

62

Coralie

She wasn't surprised to see Adam at the door. She was only surprised it had taken so long. She'd been looking forward to him begging her to take him back, had already settled on the conditions: Twig was out, obviously. And he'd need to earn back her trust. And start cooking again. He'd really let things slide towards the end there. He hadn't made the flatbreads she loved for months. It was Adam who made all the pies and flans and vegan meringues she wowed her neighbours with. Like having a personal chef. Plus, she'd need some help with her new social media accounts. Perhaps there was a course he could do? Learn some basic photography and design skills.

'Adam,' she said with a closed smile. *Welcome back.*

'Hi,' he said nervously, eyes darting around.

This should be good. She wouldn't make him beg on his knees on the doorstep, although it would be quite satisfying for the neighbours to see. She hoped Twig was watching.

'Well?'

He swallowed, looking around uncomfortably. Then he lifted his head and straightened his back, as though psyching himself up.

It wasn't easy admitting you were wrong, was it?

'I'd like my passport, please,' he said politely, as though ordering in a restaurant.

'I'm sorry?'

'My passport. I need my passport to open a bank account.'

She glared at him, caught off guard.

'I would like my passport, please,' he repeated, a little louder this time. 'I need my passport to open a bank account.'

'Keep your voice down,' she hissed. 'Come inside.'

'No, thank you.' He was practically bellowing. 'I would like my passport, please. I need my passport to open a bank account.'

'Do you want everyone knowing our business?' Furtively, she glanced around. Twig was out front, fiddling with a car tyre, which seemed incongruous. She gave Coralie an empty smile and a half-wave. Emma was on her lawn, a twee pink scarf knotted over her hair as she pruned the rose bush on the boundary of their front gardens. She, too, met Coralie with a fake-seeming smile and a wave. Coralie felt cornered at her own front door. Further along the road she could see Valerie with her shopper. Tim with his twin girls, opening the boot and dropping the ramp. All the windows at Anjit and Joy's were thrown open, while a supermarket delivery van was pulling up outside Susan's. Any moment, she would be at her front door hearing their conversation too.

Adam took a deep breath and barked, loud enough for the whole estate to hear: 'I would like my passport, please. I need my passport to open a bank account.'

'Fine!' she snapped. She closed the door and let out an angry 'rargh!', not caring who heard.

She stormed up to her room, retrieving Adam's passport from her safe, kicking a large vase over, wishing it was his head, while he waited below. She'd only hit him once or twice, when he'd pushed her to it, but it had been surprisingly stress-relieving. She glanced out of the window. Saw him looking at Twig and her lifting her gaze from the tyre and giving him a thumbs-up.

Adam would never have stood up to her alone, she realized. Twig, and hopeless, deluded Emma, must have put him up to it. Rage billowed out of her like the breeze streaming through the windows and lifting the curtains, carrying the first strains of autumn. She flew down the stairs, threw the passport at Adam and tore over the lawn, grabbing Twig's hair from behind, wrapping it around her fist and dragging her to the floor.

63

Twig

Twig looked up at the blue-and-white sky, dazed, a hand to her burning scalp. She craned her neck; Emma, as fierce as Coralie, was dragging Coralie off Twig, pulling her backwards, gripping her shoulders with her gardening gloves.

'Oh. No. You. Don't,' Emma grunted with effort, but Coralie's rage was channelling a fierce strength.

Twig rolled over. Emma and Coralie were wrestling on the floor, Emma – muscles flexed and taut – gaining the upper hand. She had Coralie pinned to the ground. The exertion had dislodged the pink Minnie Mouse scarf she'd fashioned into a hairband. It hung loosely round her neck. Coralie tried to reach for it to drag Emma down to her, but in a fluid movement Emma tore it off with one hand, jettisoning it, and doing the same with her muddy gloves. Cameras were clicking, their neighbours spilling out of their houses, creating a hubbub of voices, shouts of 'what's going on!'. A car screeched to a halt, doors slamming.

'Mum?' a wobbly voice called, fear evident in its high-pitched tone.

At the noise, both women stopped wrestling and slid off one another. They stood, smoothing down their clothes, Emma in floral cycling shorts and a baggy Simba T-shirt, Coralie in one of her long, white, flowing dresses, now stained brown. Coralie pressed around the edges of the bandage covering her cheek; it flapped open above her left eye, briefly revealing bloody stitches and a gruesome purple bruise.

Coralie's girls stood with their father, his face mimicking the thunderstorm brewing above them. He held them back. Adam was beside them, and Iris turned to him for a hug, her huge eyes full. Coralie turned away from them with a haughty, disinterested look, as if she was having too much fun, too much sport, to stop on their account.

Twig sprung to her feet, panting, the three women facing each other, eyes flashing.

'Very forgiving, aren't you, Emma?' Coralie sneered quietly in Twig's direction. 'Or are you not up to speed on your domestic situation?'

Twig recoiled, grateful their children were all in summer camp today and not witness to this ugly scene.

'That's between me and Twig.' Emma's voice was authoritative and calm, in contrast to her mussed-up hair and askew clothing. She looked up as a crash of thunder ripped through the sky, the storm that had been threatening for days finally on its cusp. 'It's over, Coralie.'

'I decide when it's over,' Coralie spat. 'It will be over when I call the police.'

Emma took a step closer. Above them, dark grey clouds, full to bursting, like tears threatening to spill, scudded together, covering the sky. The earth darkened beneath them.

Twig followed suit, dropping her voice as she drew nearer. 'You can go to the police, Coralie. I'll tell them what I did. I'll make sure they know it was nothing to do with Blake. She can take Skylar to America if I'm arrested.' They had talked it all through. Twig had lived in the shadow of fear for too long. She couldn't live with Coralie having a hold over her. She would take her punishment if that's what it took to move on.

'Give Adam his share of the house,' Emma urged. 'His truck and his half of everything else.'

'I'm not giving him a payout!' Coralie jeered, laughing. 'That's what guilty people do.'

'It's not a payout. It's basic family law. It's what he's entitled to.'

Coralie sneered at her. 'He won't divorce me.'

'He's already instructed a solicitor,' Twig said.

Coralie lunged for her again, but Emma stepped between them. 'Think of your girls,' she growled through gritted teeth, and Coralie stilled, tension visibly rippling through her rigid frame. She was immobile, but her body was pulsing, veins bulging from her neck.

'What do I get out of all this?'

'We won't tell anyone.' Emma paused, then added meaningfully, 'About *Monroe*.'

64

Coralie

Coralie glanced between them, panting, oscillating between rage and disbelief. She'd thought she had Twig Dorsett in her debt. Where she deserved to be. And she had held out hope that if Twig had been stupid enough to confide in that deluded *idiot* Emma, or anyone else, what she had witnessed – Coralie's evident relationship with the cat – that she wouldn't be believed. Clearly she had.

She looked back over to the growing crowd, as her anger decorticated, like bark peeled from a tree, a sense of embarrassment, of exposure, blooming raw on her skin. Valerie's eyes were agog, her pupils huge behind her jam-jar glasses. Later Coralie would explain how they'd driven her to it. It was all a plot! To take the house from under her, so Adam and his mistress could shack up there together, no doubt.

And her girls . . . her beautiful girls . . . Iris was pressed into Adam and Bea into Fraser. *Why couldn't they love her unconditionally the same way?* But then, they had seen this all before, hadn't they? And still they came back. Just as she had with her own parents. They would always come back. She was still their mother.

There was another crash of thunder, as if the sky were being ripped apart. Finally, it split, like flesh torn in two, heavy rain spilling like blood, splashing the dry earth.

Coralie felt it seep through her clothes, dampening her skin.

She felt herself baptised. *Perhaps the deal was worth it? She could keep Monroe safe, have a clean break from Adam and his lies, a rebirth of sorts?*

'Fine,' she said. 'Fine. You have your deal.'

Coralie approached the crowd, covering her bandage, which was dissembling as the rain pummelled down. She stretched out her free arm to her daughters. 'Well? Come along inside, you must be getting soaked.' She smiled, a rictus smile, her stitches pulling beneath her bandages.

The girls looked up at their father. He nodded. 'Just for a few minutes.'

'I assume this isn't a social call?' she asked, once they were inside. The girls had run straight up to their rooms, no doubt to collect some more of their books and toys.

Fraser eyed her coolly. 'The girls have come to say goodbye. I explained you needed a change of scene. I've secured you a research position abroad.'

'Abroad?' She curled her lip, pressing a towel against her face to keep her sutures dry.

'New Zealand.'

She looked beyond him, outside. The rain was easing off, photographers beginning to reassemble, some calling her name. 'I'm happy here.'

'You need to lie low until all this blows over.' His face was kind. She wondered what trick he was playing. 'It's not good for the girls. They're being teased at school.' Confusion painted her face. 'It's all online, Coralie. People are calling you a liar, saying you and Adam made up the Sevenoaks Panther. Started the fires, even. I've seen environmental extremists threaten to come here and burn this place down too. Your address is online.'

Fear gripped her. 'What if I don't want to go?'

'It would be terrible timing if, on top of all this . . .' He waved a hand towards the door, 'the truth about Campbell Enterprises came out.'

'Are you threatening me?' She shook out the hand towel with a snap.

'No. I'm saying there's a reporter sniffing around, asking questions about why our marriage ended, and these things have a habit of getting out.'

She lifted her chin. 'I would explain what happened. I was only saying what those girls would have said, if they hadn't been afraid to speak out.'

'You had no proof.'

She arched an eyebrow. Shrugged nonchalantly. 'I knew you were having an affair. It was the only way to flush it out.'

'You made anonymous – bogus – claims of sexual harassment against me because you were jealous of my work colleagues. I almost lost everything. And your father too.' Coralie had met Fraser at one of the legacy balls. He had been her father's head of innovation.

'Except you didn't,' she scoffed. 'He paid you off. Like everyone else.'

'I spoke to Adam's parents.' He said quietly. 'His birth parents.'

She froze. 'How?' she croaked, before straightening herself. She should have predicted they might crawl back out of the woodwork. 'What did they say?'

'That you hired a private investigator to track them down and paid them to stay away.'

She turned her lips inward, squashing them together while she marshalled her thoughts. New Zealand wasn't all bad. She'd always wanted to see penguins in the wild and had never seen a kiwi bird. 'It wasn't like that. It was to protect his heart. I didn't trust them.'

'Of course. But with you and Adam in the news . . .'

'They might try to spin it.' She nodded in agreement. 'Manipulate it to make *me* look bad. Yes, I can see where you're going with this.' Of course, all this was further evidence of Fraser's guilty actions in the past: why else would he be helping her? But Coralie was a fair person, magnanimous.

Impulsively, she reached for his hands and squeezed them. 'Well, thanks for the job offer. I'll certainly consider it.'

65

Twig

'Why don't you just throw her to the lions?' Blake asked Adam, feet up, throwing peanuts back and catching them in her mouth. 'Why's her ex setting her up abroad?'

Adam was looking more like himself these days, with a dusting of tan and his lean, rather than too-thin frame, restored. He was staying with the Brooks' until his money came through from Coralie. In the meantime, after bringing the Brooks' garden back to life, he had built a seating area at the far end, beneath a pergola, just like he and Coralie had had next door, where they were gathered now. Twig clocked Emma's sigh of satisfaction as she returned from the house clutching an ice bucket, surveying the garden scene.

Matt pulled a face as Emma set down the bucket and he reached for the wine. 'He's thinking of their daughters, I suppose.' The air around them hummed with the static sounds of summer: crickets in long grass, bees in banks of lavender, lawn mowers, planes flying overhead. As if the last few months hadn't left the residents of Briar Close irrevocably changed.

'It's a kindness. She'd never cope if she knew the truth about herself.' Adam raked a hand through his hair nervously, as he had been doing all day.

Blake clicked her fingers and pointed them at Adam. 'Susie said a similar thing, actually.'

'And it is better for the girls. Some of the coverage online is vicious,' Twig said. The fight in the street had prompted a slew of opinion pieces on the residents of Briar Close. Conspiracy theories and memes and TikTokers assessing everything from their role in the Cub camp fiasco and the wildfires to their style and accessories. The reporters were gone, but the appetite for the story remained voracious.

'But she's dangerous,' Matt grumbled, topping up all their glasses.

'I have a feeling she won't be able to hurt anyone where she's going . . .' Adam said, wincing. 'And her parents have taken back control of the trust. She won't have the same financial independence she's always had.'

A shriek of laughter carried over from the hammock, where Skylar and Daisy were attempting to push Elwood and Henry as though they were in a swing. Twig noted the smile exchanged between Emma and Matt as they watched. Twig was pleased that an investigation had shown that Matt had followed all necessary procedures at Cub camp and wouldn't be punished for Elwood's actions, although he had decided to step down anyway, to bring his focus closer to home. She glanced back over to Elwood and Henry, who each had a test tube filled with cotton wool protruding from their pockets, in the hope they might find a queen ant to start their ant farm in the terrarium Matt was helping them build. Brothers, as the paternity test had confirmed. They were going to tell them when Twig and Skylar were back from America.

'What time are you off tomorrow?' Emma asked Twig, reaching for a bowl of crisps.

'Six. We're all packed.' No more stuffy cars with malfunctioning air conditioning for them; Twig's old record label – thrilled with the recent success of Pineapple Punk – were arranging their transfers.

Adam was peeling the label from his bottle of beer.

'How you feeling, buddy?' Twig rubbed his back. Sometimes when she touched him, she still felt that same static shock of electricity. A current between them. But the only way she could view it was as a spark of friendship. Who was Twig when she wasn't defined by being in a relationship? She was looking forward to finding out.

'Nervous.' He swallowed.

'We'll all be waiting out here if you need us,' Emma soothed, and Twig had the feeling she often did these days that Emma had taken on the role of a doting aunty to Adam, clucking and fussing around him. Not that he seemed to mind. He was even thinking of buying a flat nearby to them all. He'd told Twig recently that they felt like the – dysfunctional – family he'd never had. And here he was on the cusp of meeting his birth family. Twig's eyes glistened.

The doorbell rang and Adam jerked to his feet. All eyes and eager smiles were on him, his nerves palpable as he placed down his undrunk beer. 'Guess I'd better go and meet my mum.'

'Go get 'em, tiger.' Twig grinned.

66

Coralie

The nurse gently peeled the padded bandage away as Coralie watched in a mirror. She gasped at the sight. The scar was slashed across her cheek, the jagged stitching pulling at her eye, causing a droop. Her beautiful face. She began to cry, but that too felt strange, her eyeballs dry, as though lacking in moisture.

'The skin will loosen over time,' the nurse said warmly, dropping the blood-stained bandage into a bin, but all Coralie could think was how it would look as she aged, as wrinkles crowded her skin. *It will be worth it*, she promised herself. *I'll make it worth it.*

Coralie could sense the tide had turned against her. Whenever the wildfires were mentioned online, her name came up. When the wild cat was mentioned, her name came up. She had risen from the quagmire of suburban life, to save them all, but now her name was entwined with disaster and couldn't be untangled. She had been the darling of the community and now she was its nemesis. She had been mercilessly trolled online and had had to close all her accounts. Any hopes of speaking at a Select Committee were over. Her campaign was dead. She missed Monroe. She missed Socks, since Emma, like the rest of the town, was still keeping her pet inside. She still had her online calls with her girls, but they had become even more distant. Fraser was right: she had to get away.

She'd packed up the house while she waiting until her stitches could be removed, and had the glass repaired in her greenhouse. The other residents of the street had started to go outside again; the self-imposed lockdown was ending. People were questioning now whether there was ever a big cat at all. A good thing, she supposed. Many of the households had shut up and jetted off for the summer, as was usually the case. The town was growing quieter, her world smaller.

She spent the evenings alone in her greenhouse, ears primed, listening for the sounds of life returning to the Parkland. She strained for the call of a bird, or the susurration of leaves, but the most she heard was the tinkle of glasses and cutlery as the Brooks hosted guests beneath their pergola next door. She never left food out any more. She couldn't risk Monroe, or any other cat, being spotted.

She spent her last night at home in her greenhouse, her suitcases ready by her front door. The air around was silent as she drifted off to sleep in her grandmother's chair. When she heard it, she didn't know if it was real or a dream: Monroe's belly-purr, making the glass of the greenhouse vibrate.

She felt it, deep in her gut: Monroe waiting for her outside in the Parkland. Tears streamed down her face as she resisted going outside to pet her. To reassure her she was still there. It wasn't safe for Monroe here any more.

She glanced up at Twig's place. Saw Elwood at the window, his binoculars pressed against the glass. He'd heard it too. She felt a sudden bloom of hope blaze across her chest.

She walked outside, illuminated by the outdoor lights. The air had perceptibly cooled, the gardens of Briar Close quiet as the earth resettled, preparing for nature's next great shift. She looked up at Elwood's window, a hand in a half-wave. In the shadows she heard it: a wild cat's tail hitting the ground heavily, its body flattening as it slunk into the undergrowth and away.

Elwood lowered his binoculars and met her gaze. She smiled. He turned away.

The Mystery of the Sevenoaks Panther

Freja, chair of Puddleford PTA: Twig Dorsett knows what happened that night, but she's not telling.

Twig Dorsett: My eyes were on Elwood the whole time. I couldn't make out what was going on through all the smoke and noise.

Emma Brooks: I was at home with my children the whole evening. Food poisoning. I've never been so grateful for it coming out both ends.

Agatha, Puddleford parent: Elwood shouted that he'd spotted a wild cat and rushed into the forest, Akela – Matt Brooks – in hot pursuit, while the other leaders rushed the rest of the Cubs inside as a precaution. That's what I heard.

Dino 'Baloo' Richards, assistant Cub Scout leader: Did I see Coralie King approach a wild cat? I don't know, man. It was chaotic. The fire was stinging my eyes. The kids had been in bed for a while, so we'd been hitting the beers.

Matt Brooks: That is categorically not true. No leaders were drinking at camp.

Mei, teaching assistant at Puddleford School: It was clear Adam was tanked up. He'd soiled himself. Drunk and violent. What a stand-up guy.

Matt Brooks: Did I see the Sevenoaks Panther? No.

Mei: Her parents neglected her and then her husband abused her. It's a terrible, but entirely expected trajectory. Coralie King deserves our sympathy.

Lady Violet Campbell: I haven't met this young man – Adam – but I believe him.

Samantha Cade-Harris, criminal barrister: Funny. She also believes her husband's a good guy too.

Adam King: I knew what she was up to the second I saw those bandages. 'It didn't look like that. When the cat got you,' I said to her. 'You cut your face, didn't you? Made it look worse?' But all she did was smile. As much as she could by then, anyway.

Valerie, Number 14: He was *revelling* in the injuries he'd inflicted on her. Can you fathom it?' I don't know what they did to her. That poor woman.

Chloe, Number 16: I'm Team Coralie, for sure. She's badass.

Megan, Number 16: [Rolls eyes.] Look, when you're at home a lot [gestures at her wheelchair], you notice things. She isolated Adam from his friends and family. Convinced him a wild cat was stalking him. *He's* the victim here, not her.

Chloe: [Scoffs.] Come on, does anyone believe this story about a wild cat? Did anyone see it other than Adam King? Yeah, okay, he's hot for an old guy. But is he, like, also deluded?

Megan: How many followers do I have now? Almost a mill. Yeah, the collab's coming out this summer. [Grins.] *Twin Things*. We're modelling it together. Yes, this is a Donald Duck handbag. What can I say? Emma Brooks was the style icon we never saw coming!

One Year Later

Emma switched off the television and reached for her glass of wine. *The Mystery of the Sevenoaks Panther* docuseries had finally dropped and was already trending: number one in the UK and the US. 'She's just making him out to be a monster. It's not right.'

'I know.' Matt sighed, settling his arm around her shoulders as she nestled back.

A ripple of laughter emerged from upstairs. They both glanced towards the source of the noise. Elwood and Skylar were having a sleepover with Henry and Daisy, a frequent occurrence these days between the 'riblings,' as they called themselves ('random-siblings'), since Twig and Blake had divorced. Blake was now splitting her time between the UK and the US, and Twig was busy these days, her last two tracks – 'Ghost Run Mum' and 'On a Thousand Winds' – having also gone straight to number one. Everything seemed to have settled. Even Daisy was more relaxed, no longer insisting on helping Emma get dressed.

'At least they included that they couldn't prosecute him for GBH,' Emma consoled herself.

'Hm, but you know how it sounds? Like there's a lack of evidence, rather than that he didn't do it.' Matt stroked his thumb along the back of her neck.

'Yes, but that medical expert said her injuries couldn't have been sustained by him scratching her.' She dipped her head closer towards him.

'True, but Coralie says he used some of the shattered glass. You saw the photo of her greenhouse. It looked like he'd totally smashed the place up. He could've used anything. I'm not saying he did,' he added quickly to her furrowed brows. 'I believe him. I'm just saying what the average person will think.'

'I know.' She groaned. 'I bet this conversation is being had up and down the country.' She glanced down at her phone, humming with notifications, and turned it over.

'I wonder how Coralie's getting on? She looked so different.' Which was a diplomatic way to put it. It seemed researching sandflies on remote, windswept New Zealand beaches didn't lend itself to glamour.

Emma didn't care for Coralie, although it was sad to see her house sit empty. She couldn't help but remember the evenings they'd spent there, the happy times they'd shared with the children tearing round the garden, before this all started.

'I wonder if Adam watched it?' she mused. He had relaunched Treescapes, which was thriving.

'I doubt it,' Matt replied. 'He's probably out on a date.' Adam was back to fighting off women, despite the rumours about him hurting Coralie. The accepted local view seemed to have landed on them being as bad as each other, but the documentary would no doubt stir everything up again.

Emma sighed. She wished the rest of the world could know that Adam King was a hero, without her having to reveal herself. Far from hurting Coralie, he had even been trying to *save* her that night at the benefit. Despite everything she'd done. But what no one knew was that Emma had saved them both.

Even though she had removed her smart doorbell and most of her other listening devices weeks before the benefit, there was one which Emma couldn't bring herself to disable: a tiny device she'd affixed to the back of Socks' new collar. She'd bought a few of the surveillance products the website had recommended, but none had stuck as well as that one. Plus, she'd resolved to keep an eye on Coralie, although in truth she'd grown bored of listening to her talking to Socks, dividing their neighbours into dog and cat people. Nonetheless, she didn't cancel the automatic downloads of the recordings to her cloud account.

After Coralie had asked Matt if the girls could go to camp, Emma had spent that afternoon trawling through hours of recordings of Coralie talking to Socks, until she found what she was looking for: Coralie detailing her plan. It sounded *ridiculous*. Unbelievable! Even so, Emma had sprung into action, creeping down to Coralie's greenhouse the next morning while Coralie was distracted with preparations for the party and setting up one of her more reliable listening devices by the window of Coralie's greenhouse, just in case.

Fortunately, she'd also resolved to keep the kids at home; a generous dusting of Coralie's home-made lavender and baking soda carpet-moth eliminator over their ice cream the night before (with extra sprinkles!) had been enough to give them a tummy ache. She still felt bad about that, but she had been desperate. She wasn't thinking straight! Who would want their kids out camping with a wild cat on the prowl, however fantastical it sounded? And she hadn't been wrong.

During the benefit, she'd listened in on Coralie's greenhouse from Henry's bedroom, which had the best vantage point of the party. When she'd heard Coralie's insane plan actually come to fruition – heard the unmistakable *roar* of a wild cat in her ear over the din of the music – her first instinct was to put on her show tunes and pretend she hadn't heard anything at all. But that only lasted a few minutes. She crept out her usual way to the Parkland, scuttling behind the kid's playhouse and along the path to Coralie's greenhouse. She managed to scare off the panther, launching rocks at the windows and smashing the glass. In the furore, neither Adam nor Coralie had realized. Adam told her later he didn't know if it was the bucket he'd thrown, or the loud music, he was just grateful it had happened. She felt terrible when she discovered the panther had escaped up to the scout hut, but that hadn't crossed her mind. What Coralie had said about wild cats was true. They *didn't* like to go near people. They were elusive and secretive. She had no idea Coralie had trained the cat so close to the scout hut, nor that a child would glimpse it and tear after it. Mind you, she didn't know another child besides Elwood who would. If she'd had any clue that might happen she'd have made more of an effort to poison Matt, too. Shut down the whole camp. The whole plan. She did sprinkle his ice cream when she did the kids', but he had the constitution of an ox. And he'd never have believed the truth of what Coralie was planning if she'd told him. She knew Matt: he'd still have gone ahead with camp.

Once Coralie and Adam had bolted from the greenhouse, she slipped inside, threw the rocks back out and, seeing the desk key on the floor, finally got her hands on Coralie's secret notebook. She had every intention of giving it to Adam as evidence of Coralie's subterfuge. That, along with the recordings, would be a record of her abuse. But then she read the notebook. Saw the little '*e.b.s*'s in the margins next to all the things that Emma had done, like the bones and roadkill thrown into Tim's back yard. Somehow, Coralie had been on to her. She assumed not everyone would laugh at her big-cat antics the way Matt had done and didn't love the idea of that going public. She'd be a source of neighbourhood ridicule once again. Or worse. Could she be convicted of harassment over her behaviour towards Tim? And the recordings didn't cast her in a great light, regardless of her intentions. Weren't they evidence that she had been illegally spying on the other residents? Could she be prosecuted for that, or for withholding evidence, since she hadn't surrendered the notebook or the recordings to the police immediately? It was all so confusing! Plus, even if she produced them they would be contested by conspiracy theorists. *There was little point*, she reasoned. Instead Emma and Twig had confronted Coralie together, secured Adam's future. *He didn't need the notebook or the recordings!*

So, Emma believed Adam. Only Emma – and Socks – knew the

whole story. She was still mulling it over as she took Matt's hand, the pair of them giggling, and led him to their palatial master suite on the third floor, a wall of glass framing the Parkland beyond, green buds hinting at its future: it would sing again, verdant and luscious, its secrets kept safe within its branches. She pictured Coralie's green leather notebook, buried at the top of her pale pink, bespoke fitted wardrobes, as her feet sunk into the plush leopard-print carpet in her dressing area and smiled. She finally had it all.

Acknowledgements

[to come – leave 3 pp]

Kit Conway lives in Kent with her husband and three sons. Prior to writing she worked as a corporate lawyer in London. *Cat Fight*, her debut book club suspense novel, will be published by Transworld (UK) and Atria (US) in Summer 2025. You can find her on Instagram and TikTok @kitconwayauthor.